Fallen Heroes

"We killed him…we killed him, but he came back…he said he would…his face...his face was different, but his eyes…it was him…it was him…we tried to stop… but … he kept coming, oh God he kept..."

"Who?" yelled Dean. "You trying to tell me one man did all this?"

"It's no good," said Beauford. "He's dead."

Dean laid Gonzalez's body on the floor and stood up. "I don't buy it, one man took out fifteen heavily armed professional killers? No way, Gonzalez must have been tripping on his own product. It's got to be a hit team sent by one of the other cartels - Benet or Hymoto perhaps."

"I don't think so," Beauford said quietly.

"With all due respect, Captain, I've been working this case for years, these men may have been scum, but believe me, one guy, no matter how…"

"Before you spout off any more of your 'DEA knows more than us regular cops' bullshit, maybe you should take a look at this."

He handed him a folded and bloodstained piece of paper. "I found it inside Gonzalez's shirt."

Dean opened the paper and began reading the contents aloud. "Despair for I walk among you, and I am the right hand of vengeance."

"I don't buy it, one man couldn't do all this," said Dean.

Beauford looked around as the crime scene investigators began the grisly work of processing the scene. "If you want my advice, start stocking up on empty body bags and making space in the morgue, I get the feeling this guy is just getting started."

To Bob, hope you enjoy!

[signature]

Fallen Heroes

Barry Nugent

ISBN 978-1-84753-852-9

My thanks go out to the following people who have helped to shape and craft Fallen Heroes.

To those friends who provided the inspiration for some of the characters used within this book. Dave, for reading the huge and unwieldy first draft and telling me it would make a fantastic twenty-four part TV series. Vicki, for her proofreading and editing skills and allowing me to hassle her with new plot lines over many a cup of tea. Jo and Marianne, whose contributions were not only invaluable and timely, but had a greater effect on this book than either of them know. Junbobkim, for bringing Napoleon Stone to life with his amazing cover art.

And my partner, Sue, for her unwavering support and for always seeing the light at the end of the tunnel even when I could not.

Fallen Heroes by Barry Nugent

This book is dedicated to the memory of Icilda Nugent, who would always ask her youngest son before he left the house. "You off to save the world again?"

I'm still trying, Mum.

Chapter One

Out of suffering have emerged the strongest souls; the most massive characters are seared with scars.

Edwin Hubbell Chapin

Jason stood in the middle of the street, his mind struggling to accept a simple truth: this was not the world he remembered. It was as if Mother Nature, enraged by the senseless abuse of her creation, had unleashed her wrath upon the Earth she once cherished.

There was no wind, no sound, even the air Jason breathed seemed stale, somehow tainted by this place. If this was not Hell, it came a close second. Surrounding him on all sides, buildings torn from their foundations lay in ruins. Those left standing were little more than blackened, burnt-out husks of concrete, blighting the skyline.

The street was littered with vehicles that once had been an extension of their owner's pride and desire for freedom, but now they were a rusting epitaph to their fall from grace. The shocking image of a world driven to its knees was only surpassed by the scale of human destruction. Everywhere Jason looked there were skeletons, their bones bleached by a sun blind to the reality that no one was left alive to appreciate its warmth. Shreds of clothing still clung to some of the bodies, giving a few of them, at least, a semblance of identity.

As Jason tried to discern any meaning from the horror surrounding him, something brushed against his leg. He leapt back, almost falling over his own feet, as several piles of bones rose up in front of him. Common sense told him to run, but he was overcome with the morbid desire to keep watching. A jawbone snapped into place with a sickening crack. Veins began to emerge out of the bones themselves, followed by intestines, then organs. Skin crawled across the bodies, even as the muscles and tendons formed underneath. Clothing was the last thing to materialise, like everything else, as if from thin air.

Jason now faced five men, their faces smooth, devoid of any features; the effect was terrifying. Their upper bodies were protected by chain mail, over which was draped a grey tunic that extended to their knees. Like the chain mail beneath it, the tunic was split at the front. Each man wore a sword strapped to their side, and a large, bright orange emblem of a bird, similar to an eagle, embroidered on the fronts of their tunics. The bird's wings were unfurled, and grasped in its claws was a flaming sword. There was something about the emblem that confused

1

Jason, it was as if he knew exactly what the emblem represented, yet at the same time, he was convinced he had never set eyes on it before now.

Where the hell am I? he thought.

I would think the where was obvious. You are dreaming; you are also in danger.

Jason did not know whether he was hearing his conscience, was going mad or if someone was communicating with his mind. None of the prospects thrilled him.

"Who are you?"

The men did not answer, but Jason began to hear a low-pitched humming. He opened his mouth to speak, but instead doubled over as the sound flooded his senses, overwhelming him. His view of the knights became blurred, appearing to shift in and out of focus.

Concentrate, boy, fight them! They must not enter.

"Enter what?"

Jason was fast accepting the idea that perhaps the disembodied voice was not his own.

Too late.

Jason screamed as every thought, every emotion or memory from nineteen years of life was torn from his subconscious and held up for scrutiny. He slammed his hands against his ears and sank to his knees, begging them to stop. Alongside the intense pain was the anger that someone was stealing the one thing in his life that he had control over. Even though the images that flashed through his mind's eye were a blur, he still felt the pain, the loss, the happiness that the memories evoked. He tried to hold back the tears, but the onslaught of emotions was too great even for the wall of cynicism he protected himself with.

At last, a calmness settled over Jason's mind, easing the pain until it was little more than a dull ache, leaving him with the sensation of waking from a deep sleep. The emotional pain, however, was not so easily soothed. His memories had been violated, leaving him raw, his vulnerability exposed; a side to him that he struggled to keep hidden all his life.

He has what we seek. This time, the voice inside his mind was not one, but many. Jason found it impossible to tell if any of the voices belonged to the man who had tried to help him earlier.

The sleeper shall awake.

Jason had heard enough, his curiosity was swept aside by the thought of what they might do next.

If you run, we will find you... wherever you go, we will find you.

Jason turned and ran across the uneven pavement with no idea where he was heading. The direction was unimportant, at least for now; the only thing that mattered was putting as much distance between him and his faceless interrogators as was humanly possible.

Stay, stay and help us, Jason.

Jason tried to shut out the voices as he ran, terrified they might enter his mind again. He cried out as something struck him from behind, pitching him to the ground and into darkness.

"Jason!"

"Jason, snap out of it!"

Jason's eyes snapped open. The view greeting him was no longer of a desolate world, but the sight was no less daunting. He was sat on the second row from the back of a large lecture theatre. At least fifty pairs of eyes were watching him as the embarrassing realisation set in. The voice had been right; his entire experience was nothing more than a daydream gone bad.

A short, stocky man, his arms folded, stood at the front of the lecture theatre beside a table on which sat an overhead projector. He seemed oblivious to the patches of sweat that stained his white shirt. Jason, however, was not oblivious to the angry scowl on the man's face, even from this far back in the room.

"Mr. Chen, if you wanted this much attention, you should have joined the circus."

Jason fixed his brown eyes on the floor, allowing his thick mass of black hair to fall over his face, hoping the gesture would somehow lessen the rising humiliation.

"Damage control," coughed Quincy, a skinny blond-haired teenager, who was sitting to Jason's left.

Jason tried to regain some sense of composure. The dream had been so vivid, the horrors witnessed there so real. He glanced back at the exit, half expecting the faceless knights to come bursting through the doors. Perhaps the lecture room, the lecturer with a serious sweat issue were just another part of the dream. One look around the room shattered that idea. His imagination was not varied enough to construct so many subtle emotions to convey the same point: he had made a complete fool of himself.

Half of the class were trying not to laugh; a few others were either smirking or chuckling quietly. The rest, unable to contain the emotion, were laughing themselves hoarse. Jason needed to take control of the situation or he would still be living this down three months from now. The nightmare had been terrifying, there was no question of that, but he was awake now and there was nothing to fear except the destruction of his reputation, which had never been that great in the first place.

"Sorry, Professor, I must have nodded off."

Jason wondered if everyone else thought his words were as lame as they sounded. Quincy leaned towards him.

"Told you not to reheat that curry last night," he said in a hushed tone. "But would you listen?"

Jason shot his best friend and roommate a 'not now' look. Quincy fell silent, instead opting for unleashing his charms on an attractive Asian girl sitting three seats to his left.

Jason knew the next few minutes were crucial to his short-term academic and personal survival. Professor Ivanov was notorious for humiliating a chosen student in front of their peers. Jason had often heard Ivanov sharing his deluded belief that his methods aided the learning process. Jason wondered if the inquisition had gone about their work with a similar mindset to Ivanov.

"Perhaps you would like to summarise the report I asked everyone to prepare for today."

So much for treading carefully, Jason concluded, sighing to himself.

"I trust you have the report with you, Mr. Chen?"

No, Mr. Sweaty, it's up your ass. If the report had been lodged in Ivanov's rectum, at least, thought Jason, it would be here and not sitting half-finished beside his games console.

"Dreaming again, Mr. Chen?" Ivanov's grating voice conjured images of violence in Jason's mind, all directed at his lecturer. "I wonder if your parents realise how seriously you're taking the education they're paying for?"

Like they cared. Jason had barely spoken to his adoptive parents, the Carsons, since starting university over eighteen months ago. To be fair, the lack of communication was more his fault than theirs. He was supposed to be striking out on his own, but all that the token phone conversations with them did was remind him that he was still tied to them, even if that tie was only a financial one.

"We're waiting, Jason."

Jason ignored the patronising inflection Ivanov always added when using his first name; he was trying to provoke a reaction. He got to his feet, steeling himself against his inevitable fate. Ivanov was beckoning him down with a wide grin: this was not going to end well.

If you run, we will find you.

Jason froze, his head snapped round. There was nothing.

"It was just a bad dream," he said to himself, continuing down towards the front.

Wherever you go, we will find you.

Just a bad dream.

4

Fallen Heroes

Classified United Nations Research Centre, Tokyo.

Ben Ashodi masked any fears behind the black balaclava he wore. His body language displayed a confidence that verged on arrogance.

He hung, upside-down, beneath the helicopter. The only thing keeping him from an abrupt and messy appointment with the roof below was the trapeze-like hoist that his legs were strapped to. Like his job was not difficult enough, without some smart ass deciding it would be a good idea to cover the roof with pressure sensitive tiles, wired into the building's alarm system.

"The cameras are blind," a female voice sounded inside the transmitter fitted in his right ear. "You sure you want to do this?"

"Just keep this thing steady."

Ben gripped the small dial attached to his belt and turned it clockwise. The apparatus responded by lowering him towards the roof. He kept his eyes fixed on the target, a large metal grille, stopping the hoist once he was close enough to touch it.

He changed the setting on his goggles from night-vision to infrared, and stared through the grille. An electronic spider's web of infrared beams criss-crossed the ventilation shaft. He knew that if any of the beams were broken, a toxin capable of rendering an intruder unconscious within seconds would be released.

He took a small object resembling a ballpoint pen from a pouch strapped to his belt. He twisted the lower half of the object, activating a laser the thickness of a human hair, which began slicing through the grille bars. It took less than four minutes for Ben to remove three of the bars, attach them to a second cable and winch them up to the helicopter.

Ben was astounded but not surprised by the blind faith placed in the security measures. The grille was constructed of a prototype alloy developed within the centre itself, and thought to be 'virtually indestructible'. That kind of sloppy assumption screamed 'accident waiting to happen'.

He pulled a grappling hook and a coil of heavy-duty nylon rope over his head.

"Security status?" he said, whilst attaching the grappling hook to one of the remaining bars.

"Oh, you still need me then?"

Ben sighed. Steph always picked the strangest times to re-evaluate her position in their criminal partnership.

"Listen, love, if you don't tell me what I want to know, I'll make sure you get what you deserve when this is all over."

"Promises, promises," said Steph. "You've got a good forty minutes before the security team hit that area; no one's come through on the radio so I guess our cover's still holding."

Their plan, as always, had been simple. Posing as one of the helicopter tours that offered a spectacular aerial view of Tokyo at night, they were able to reach the centre without raising suspicions. Ben was confident Steph's Japanese was more than a match for any impromptu radio chatter. Once he was dropped safely on the roof, Steph would continue on as if still giving the tour, and return to pick him up once the job was done.

"Right, deactivate the infrared grid on my mark," said Ben.

"I'm still not happy about this."

Ben remembered the last time he had seen Steph unhappy. It was six months ago. She had broken her ex-boyfriend's arm in three places after he had made the mistake of stealing from her.

"We've been through this, it's a simple job, an hour max."

"Famous last words," said Steph. "Give me a few minutes to get set up."

Ben was left listening to static, while Steph went about her work. Her abrupt tone told him she was angry with him. He did not take it personally: Steph was ex-military, which in his mind meant she was not happy unless she was worrying about every single facet of the jobs they undertook.

"Ready," Steph said at last.

Ben lowered himself through the grille, stopping the hoist several inches above the first row of beams. He gripped the rope with his left hand and cleared his mind of distraction.

"Be careful."

"Aren't I always?" he said, ignoring the concern in Steph's voice. "Three, Two, One, Mark."

Everything happened at once. Ben switched his view back to night vision as the beams vanished. He dropped the rope into the shaft, detached himself from the winch, and descended into the darkness as overhead, he heard the helicopter peel away. The adrenaline surged through him as he plunged down the shaft: this was what he lived for, the thrill of entry. He gripped the cable, pulling it behind his waist, bringing him to a jarring halt as the ground fast approached.

He unclipped himself from the rope, landing silently on the base of the shaft, his senses alert. Ahead, another shaft stretched off into the darkness. At least the first part of the mission had gone without a hitch. Remembering the time schedule, Ben began crawling north. His progress was slow, his movements hampered by the cramped conditions. The shaft was a lot narrower than he had estimated; he took it as a bad omen.

He saw himself as a perfectionist when it came to his work, and the thought of miscalculating something so trivial was annoying.

Ben stopped at the end of the shaft, which opened out into a T-junction, and recalled his memories of the facility's layout. He needed to veer right, which would lead to another grille and down into a maintenance room. He set off again and was halfway to the grille when he thought he heard sounds in the corridor beneath him. Ben flattened himself against the base of the shaft, slowed his breathing, and waited. Placing his palm against the base of the shaft allowed the circuitry built into his glove to amplify the sounds below and feed them through to his earpiece. He picked up two male voices locked in a heated exchange heading in his direction. He was grateful that the conversation was in English as his knowledge of Japanese was functional, at best.

Keep walking, just keep walking, Ben repeated the mantra, hoping the patron saint of professional thieves was listening and in a generous mood. The voices were now beneath him and were not moving.

"… that gizmo's bloody useless, hasn't worked right all night," said one voice with a heavy Irish accent, "much like its owner."

"Will you give it a rest, Kelly?" said a second voice, this time American. "And stop moving about. You're messing up the signal."

"I'm telling you, this is a bloody waste of time."

"And I'm telling you, with the adjustments I made, this thing is twice as effective."

The conversation paused and Ben heard someone pull back the slide mechanism on an automatic handgun. It was a sound he had heard too many times before to mistake; it meant the first round had been loaded into the chamber. He felt his back and chest becoming clammy with sweat.

"That signal was moving too slowly to be someone walking or running. That leaves one place."

Ben berated himself for assuming the security here would be different from any other country he had worked in; underpaid, overworked, and possessed with little enthusiasm for their jobs. The men were not Japanese, but the country's reputation for demanding the best from its employees, whatever their nationality, was second to none.

Another miscalculation, and this time a potentially fatal one.

"For Christ's sake, Clancy, that signal spiked for a second; it could have been anything."

"Maybe, but it wouldn't hurt to fire a couple of rounds up there."

The feeling of annoyance crept into Ben's stomach as he listened to the conversation below. He preferred to react to a situation rather than the wait and see approach he was being forced to adopt here. Weeks of planning were on the verge of ruin at the hands of an overzealous

7

security guard. The only option was to stay put, stay quiet, and hope his luck held. There were times when being a thief plain sucked.

"Are you insane? We're on camera!" said the voice Ben now associated with the guard named Kelly. "If you want every guard down here asking questions, then you go right ahead."

Ben heard a click and hoped it was the sound of the gun's hammer being put back into place.

"I thought so," said Kelly. "Now come on, we've got to meet up with the others."

Ben relaxed slightly as the footsteps moved away, but the conversation still unnerved him. Whoever the two men were, his instincts told him they were not security guards: they were also not alone.

He and Steph had been watching the centre for weeks, and neither of them had noticed anything out of the ordinary. Had these men been sent here to trap him? There was more than one government willing to pay to see his head take pride of place in a trophy cabinet. The whole thing was beginning to smell of a setup. The smart thing to do was to get the hell out while he still could, but pride threw out the sensible option of escape. He had never failed a client during his eight-year career. It was bad for business, and in the cutthroat profession of grand larceny, it was the risk takers who got the biggest scores.

Deciding to err on the side of caution, Ben waited another minute then moved forward until he reached the grille.

He then set his cutting tool to work on the bars. This time, the task went quicker as the bars were constructed from ordinary steel. He smiled to himself. *You can even find cheapskates in the UN.* He lowered himself into the darkened room and waited until he was convinced the room was free from any 'hidden' security devices bar the compromised CCTV camera in the right-hand corner. He moved up to the door, took out a small electric screwdriver, and quickly removed the silver panel fitted next to it, revealing the circuitry beneath. It took him less than ninety seconds to override the door's locking mechanism.

"Damn, I'm good."

Turning off his night-vision, he opened the door and moved into a dimly lit corridor.

Ben knew, from this point on, the Japanese work ethic was his greatest enemy. Although his path should be free of security, the research centre employees were impossible to predict. During his stakeout of the centre, he had seen staff working well into the night, before heading off to the nearest Izakya for a few well-earned drinks. Ben was surprised that with the non-stop array of tempting distractions offered by Tokyo's nightlife, anyone made it into work at all.

He set off, keeping low and moving through the corridors, pausing at every corner to check for guards or research staff. At last, he came to a large pair of oak doors and, as expected, the locking mechanism had already been disabled. If a trap were going to be sprung, then this would be the perfect opportunity.

Ben imagined himself staring down the wrong end of twenty automatic rifles upon entering the room. He braced himself for whatever awaited him and walked into a large executive boardroom.

In the centre of the room, an oval-shaped table attempted to consume all sense of space. The fine art decorating the walls and the ornate chairs surrounding the table's edge were at odds with the minimalist, sterile environment he had just traversed. Obviously upper management liked to reserve some creature comforts for themselves and their guests.

Ben gave a low whistle at the panoramic view offered by the large windows lining the wall opposite. It portrayed a deafening, neon-encrusted metropolis of skyscrapers, restaurants, bars and hi-tech shopping centres. He had visited Tokyo several times before, but had never seen a better example of the city's many modern and westernised threads so eloquently entwined within a cultural and historical landscape of temples, shrines and museums. The sight was breathtaking and demanded a few appreciative seconds in respect of its beauty.

Ben turned his eyes from the window to the figure hugging what little shadow there was at the far end of the room. He guessed the person was male, with a slender frame and stooped appearance, betraying a distinct lack of physical exercise.

Ben noted the two-piece, dark blue suit the stranger wore as he approached him; it was tailored and made for the individual, the expensive kind. Given his receding grey hair and weathered skin, Ben figured the man had just seen the other side of fifty. The man's nervous and bloodshot gaze never seemed to focus on one spot; it was clear that something or someone had him scared. Ben suddenly wished he had asked a few more questions before accepting this job. His own rules, however, would not allow it. Once a client was accepted (which was a lot harder than it sounded) and payment agreed, his client's motives were no longer a concern. However, one look into his contact's frightened eyes told Ben that perhaps it was time to rethink that strategy.

"I should have crawled back up that bloody shaft when I had the chance," he told himself.

Chapter Two

Steve Lucas ran, cursing his bad luck and diet choices with each step. He had been living and working in Japan for little over a year, and was still struggling to cope with its 'work till you drop' lifestyle. His mistake was in deciding that, after fourteen hours of staring at the fifty-six security screens, he was due a break. Heading upstairs to his locker, he had grabbed the two roast beef and mayonnaise sandwiches that were stuffed into the Bento, which his wife Emi had reluctantly prepared for his lunch. Steve would not be swayed by Emi's attempts to get him to take a healthier meal of rice, fish and vegetables. Over the months, it became a habit he referred to as his 'little piece of home'.

Steve was on his second mouthful when the message came through on his radio ordering him back to his station. He dropped the sandwich and started back. If he was lucky, he could expect a fine equal to a month's salary, at worst, a visit to the 'Hello Work' branch in Iidabashi, Japan's equivalent to the job centre.

Steve rounded the last corner and found two security guards stood by his station. He felt the blood drain from his cheeks. Over the months, he had got to know the faces of the different security teams, especially those who were foreigners, like himself. He had never set eyes on these two before. They were wearing the uniforms of the security team, which meant they outranked him, so he had no choice but to follow their lead.

One of them, a tall, broad-shouldered, barrel-chested man, strode towards him. His short brown hair was framed with flecks of grey that he seemed too young to have.

"Sorry...I...was...just..."

"Save the excuses," the man spoke with a menacing tone that unnerved Steve even more. "Play back the security recordings for the last ten minutes."

Steve risked a questioning glance at the wiry, ginger-haired man, who was leaning against the wall, arms folded. He felt his anxiety rise when the man smiled back.

"If I were you, I'd do as he says," said the man. "Clancy doesn't like repeating an order."

Steve took his seat and began operating the playback controls for the security cameras. He kept an eye on the timer on the small display in front of him as the footage on the screens rewound. He paused the recording when it hit ten minutes then began replaying it.

10

"There!" yelled Clancy, after a few minutes of watching. "Kelly, look at the time index!"

"Looks like I'll be buying you that drink after all."

"What?" asked Steve, his curiosity overcoming his unease. "I don't see anything."

"Exactly," said Clancy.

Steve noticed Clancy move to block his view of Kelly.

"When the cameras were recording this footage, we were standing right here."

Clancy pointed to a screen showing the image of an empty corridor.

"What's it mean?" Steve was becoming worried about what Kelly was up to behind Clancy.

"It means that if you hadn't deserted your post, you might have seen someone switching signals on you." Clancy gestured to the wall of screens. "Congratulations, you fell for the oldest trick in the book."

Realising his mistake, Steve moved for a row of buttons on the security console, his dreams of a pay rise and a long career crumbling before his eyes.

Clancy grabbed Steve's wrist inches from the console.

"What are you doing? I have to activate the alarms and initiate a lockdown."

"Not your problem." Clancy released Steve and stepped to the left. "Not anymore."

Steve's eyes widened in horror when he saw the gun Kelly was now aiming at his chest.

"No, please," Steve started to rise from his chair, his thoughts turning to Emi. "Please God, No!"

Steve's pleas were cut short by three silenced gunshots, which punched through his chest. Death was instantaneous. He slumped back in the chair, the momentum wheeling him away from the blood-splattered console. The chair came to rest at the feet of ten armed men, dressed in black combat fatigues, who had just entered the security station.

"Bravo team," said Clancy, not wasting a second glance on Steve's corpse. "I want those charges in place and set to detonate in twenty minutes. If you encounter any resistance, shoot on sight, no witnesses."

With a nod to Clancy, Kelly led the main bulk of the team out of the room, heading for the elevators. Only Clancy and three others remained.

"You've read our target's profile," said Clancy. "This man is not to be taken lightly."

One of the men stepped forward.

"With respect, sir, he's already outnumbered four to..."

Clancy backhanded the man before he could finish. The man fell back against the console, a reddish bruise already forming on the left side of his face.

Clancy hoisted him up by the lapels of his uniform, the man's legs dangling several inches above the floor.

"I don't remember giving you permission to speak."

"Sorry sir." The man made no attempt to meet Clancy's angry glare.

"Better."

Clancy shoved him back with the others. He knelt down and opened a briefcase one of the others had placed at his feet. He took out four metal batons with rubber grips, and handed them to the others, ensuring he held one back for himself. He then led the men out of the security station. Clancy wondered what the elusive thief would be like. One thing he knew for sure, the thief who the press and the authorities had dubbed 'The Hand' was about to be given a rude awakening.

"So, what do I call you...? The Hand, will that do?"

The Hand. Hearing the name was like nails down a chalkboard to Ben. He had talked himself into adopting the alias after the press first used it five years before. He hated the name but figured a bit of notoriety never hurt anyone, even a thief. He just wished they could have chosen a cooler name for him.

Ben unzipped one of the pockets of his bodysuit, pulled out a tiny black velvet pouch and placed it on the table.

The businessman took a drag on his cigarette. "Not a fan of small talk I see."

Ben slid the pouch across the desk and into the businessman's outstretched and unsteady right hand. He decided not to mention his earlier close encounter: he would not risk his nervous friend pulling out on him at the last moment.

"Pemrose, I don't have time for this. Either you have something for me or this meeting's over."

"Neither of us has time for this."

Ben watched as Pemrose picked up the pouch, opened it and emptied the contents onto his palm. He gazed in undisguised wonder as Pemrose ran his fingers over the small mound of perfectly cut diamonds sitting snugly in the palm of his hand. Now that he was here, Ben began to understand Steph's concerns: something was inherently wrong with this situation. He was a thief, and yet here he was handing out diamonds. The fact that the stones had been supplied by someone else did not ease his discomfort; they were thieves, not a delivery service. Why pay him to break into a heavily guarded facility to perform an exchange they could have easily made anywhere?

12

Ben studied Pemrose's face as he poured the diamonds back into the pouch as if they were made of glass. There were several days' worth of stubble and he doubted Pemrose had changed his expensive clothes in that time. He wondered what circumstances could have transformed a representative of the United Nations into a piece of human flotsam.

"Now your turn," said Ben, holding out his hand.

Pemrose rolled up his shirt to reveal something taped to his stomach. He tore off the adhesive tape to reveal a transparent case housing a computer disk. Ben caught the disk as it was thrown to him, and he saw how Pemrose's haunted expression was now fixed on the disk as if he had just surrendered his only child.

"That's it," Pemrose said quietly. "My chance for redemption."

Ben moved to reply, but was distracted by what he thought was a flash from the building opposite. He adjusted his headset to magnify his view, but whatever he might have seen was lost in a maze of neon. I must be losing it, he concluded.

"I hope your employer knows what he has there."

"Not my problem," said Ben.

Once he had taken on a job, his client's motives were no longer a concern. After all, when someone placed an order with a mail order catalogue, they were never asked why they wanted that particular item. Ben saw the service he and Steph provided in much the same light.

Just as Ben was about to leave, he caught a glimpse of a red dot resting on Pemrose's chest.

"Move!" shouted Ben.

The warning came too late. The huge windows shattered from an explosion of automatic weapons' fire. Pemrose took four rounds in the chest, screamed and fell back onto the plush thick pile carpet. Ben threw himself under the table, the hail of bullets threatening to remove his head. He swore as a bullet struck his left leg, but there was no time to focus on the pain; the urge to stay alive overrode everything else. Gunfire tore into the desk, peppering the air with splinters, sections of the table, and pieces of upholstery from the chairs. The shooting stopped as quickly as it had begun and the room was silent, save for the sounds of the city and the fresh air now whistling through the broken windows.

Ben cursed his mistake. He should have realised it was a laser sight he had seen earlier. Letting his guard down had nearly cost him his life. This was without a doubt his worst job ever. He gently probed his leg, trying his best to ignore the waves of pain. Luck, it seemed, was still with him. The bullet had grazed the skin, but nothing more.

Keeping low, he moved to where Pemrose lay face down. Ben turned him over and felt for a pulse, but it was too late. He closed

Pemrose's eyes just as he heard the unwelcome sound of approaching footsteps.

"Oh for Christ's sake, give me a break."

He hoisted Pemrose's corpse onto the boardroom table before moving back to the corner, right of the entrance. He raised his arms up and behind, whilst slightly flexing his wrist muscles. Beneath his sleeves, a device strapped to each forearm fired a small piton and a high tensile cable into the ceiling.

"Retract."

Responding to his voice, the devices began to reel in the cables, lifting Ben off the floor and up into the corner. He wedged his legs into the sides of the corner and waited. His injured leg made its feelings clear, with a sudden twinge of pain.

Three men entered the room; the beams from their flashlights coming to rest on Pemrose's corpse. As they neared the body, Ben swung his legs out in front of him and detached himself from the cables. He ploughed into the man closest to the door, robbing him of consciousness as his head smacked against the table. Tumbling into an easily executed roll, Ben was halfway to his feet as the other men turned.

"What the...?"

Ben never gave the man the chance to finish his sentence. He delivered a powerful sidekick to the man's right leg, feeling the bone snap under the weight of the blow. As the man toppled forward, Ben drove his left knee into his face, lifting him off his feet and backwards onto Pemrose's body. Working now from instinct, Ben ducked under a baton swung at his head by the remaining attacker. He countered with a right hook only to find it deflected with ease. Ben sensed the fight was getting away from him even as the attacker smashed a palm into his sternum. Too dazed from the strike, Ben was unable to stop himself from being grabbed and thrown onto the boardroom table. His suit absorbed some of the blow, but his chest still felt as if someone had just dropped a house on it.

The man moved towards the table. Ben saw him drop the baton and draw a handgun. He threw himself at the man as he brought the weapon to bear. A shot was fired, but went wide. Ben slammed into the man's midriff, pushing him back against the wall. He threw two quick jabs into the attacker's stomach before wrenching the gun from his grip and jamming it under his chin.

"Who?"

The man was silent.

Ben buried his knee in his attacker's groin. The man collapsed in a fit of coughing, only to be dragged to his feet. Ben shoved the gun into the man's mouth and pulled back the hammer.

14

"I want you to think long and hard about what you're going to say in the next ten seconds."

The man swallowed hard, but gave no indication he was going to co-operate. Ben hoped his bluff was not about to be called, he could never shoot anyone. Give someone a good kicking, fine, no problem, but actually killing someone? That was not his style.

Without warning, Ben felt a jolt of electricity shoot through his lower back. The agony lasted only seconds, but it was followed by fatigue and paralysis in his limbs. The gun fell, his legs buckled and he crashed to the floor. A boot cracked against his chin, no doubt a gift from the man he had just threatened.

"Bastard never got anything out of me, Clancy."

"Except my name."

Ben then saw a large man, who he guessed was Clancy, appear from his left, grab the unarmed man, plunge a knife into his spine then remove the blade and slice open the man's jugular. The last thing Ben saw before the blackness clouded his vision was Clancy coming towards him, the bloody knife still clenched in his right hand.

Ben came back from the realms of unconsciousness to the sound of muffled voices. He opened his eyes; his vision was distorted but soon began to clear. He was still paralysed, but he held back the fear that came with the realisation. Fear would not help him get out of this alive. His goggles and balaclava were gone, but his earpiece was still in place. He was unable to tell what else was missing due to his lack of movement. Whoever these people were, they were not taking any chances with him, paralysed or not.

Ben watched as the corpse of the attacker, murdered before his eyes, was dragged from the room by two others. He then caught sight of Clancy, who was carefully lifting a small glass cylinder off the boardroom table. The cylinder was roughly the same dimensions as a beer can, and within its transparent casing was a complex mechanism of wires and circuitry. At the top of the cylinder was a small timer, currently reading fifteen minutes.

Ben was having trouble finding a bright side to the situation as Clancy came towards him carrying the cylinder. His headgear was gone, taking with it his anonymity, and the man he had come to meet was dead; this was not his finest hour. Clancy stopped a few feet from Ben and placed the cylinder on the floor. Ben tried to lift his head, but it was no good. He experienced the same lack of movement in his vocal chords when attempting speech.

"If you're trying to move, forget it," said Clancy, crouching down in front of him; Ben could now see he was holding the disk in his hand. "Your muscles won't respond for at least another hour."

Ben stared at the metal baton strapped to Clancy's belt.

"They have a fancy scientific name, but I prefer to call them pain-givers," said Clancy.

Ben hoped he was not about get a further example of the pain-giver in action.

"If it makes you feel better, you got by me and took out three of my men. You almost live up to your rep."

Clancy pointed at the cylinder. "That, as you may have guessed, is a bomb. Fifteen minutes after it's armed, it will detonate along with the other bombs planted throughout the centre." Clancy moved next to Ben's ear. "And you, my friend, will be blamed for all of it."

Clancy got to his feet, stuffed the disk into one of his pockets and walked away, pausing by the door. "I suppose you'd like to know who's putting up the cash for your head?" He took out a tiny black rectangular-shaped device.

"Guess we can't have everything," said Clancy, pressing a button on the device. "Can we?"

Ben watched the timer begin to count backwards. He did not see Clancy leave, locking the door behind him, or hear the sound of heavy boots thudding hastily away from the room. His eyes were shut, allowing his mind to close in on itself. He focused on his muscles, every fibre, every tiny contraction or movement they were capable of, willing them to reactivate. Seven minutes and twenty-five seconds later, he could move his right arm, not the best of starts for an escape.

He looked at the timer; he was not going to make it. Even if he could reach the bomb, it was a safe bet it would to go off if tampered with. He racked his brain, hoping inspiration would lead him to a miraculous last minute escape. He heard his mind whispering its conclusions back at him over and over again.

You screwed up, Ben.

It was Karma. The Universe had finally got round to punishing his cockiness. Ben's profitable eight-year career had not been without incident. He had been in a few close scrapes, even shot at a few times, but he always found a way out. This time was different; he was cornered like an amateur, without a plan.

You're going to die, Ben.

Not like this I'm not, he told himself. He kept at it for another two minutes trying to move any part of his body. When he was rewarded with any kind of sensation, he homed in on that body part. The process was working but it was taking too long. He felt well enough to move after another minute: not much, but he had to hope it would be enough. He gradually tilted his head so as not to disturb the device, and looked down his body.

There were no signs of injury other than the earlier graze to his leg. On the minus side, all his equipment was gone. He looked at the timer: there were less than three minutes left. Ben wondered why the bad guys always set up these elaborate death traps, instead of the infinitely more practical bullet through the brain, which seemed much more like this Clancy's style. He mentally calculated the time it would take him to get to the door and override the locking mechanism. He figured at a push, it would take him twenty-five seconds to unlock the door, but he would never reach the elevator before the bombs went off.

Ben pressed down on the face of his watch, turning it anti-clockwise to send out an emergency signal to Steph, hoping she had been listening in and was on the ball. He staggered to his feet, exhausted: there was no time to worry about setting the bomb off. He marshalled what strength he had into a desperate race against the final seconds of the timer. He reached the window's edge and threw himself through the shattered window, his body propelled forward by the blast. The searing heat from the explosion threatened to engulf him at any moment. Ben's final thoughts were of satisfaction, at least he was checking out on his feet. He saw something coming into view through the smoke, something that told him his appointment with the grim reaper was cancelled for now. He seized the cable with both hands, giving a silent, exhausted thanks to Steph, who was already activating the mechanism to winch him in.

Ben clambered into the helicopter, closing the hatch behind him as it rose upwards, veered off to the left and away from the building as the remaining bombs detonated. The air outside the cockpit was filled with flaming debris and smoke, as the research centre went up like a giant firework, spewing flames and rubble out into the night sky. The helicopter buckled under the force of the blast. Warning lights and sounds began making their presence known throughout the cockpit.

Ben, instead of scrambling for the nearest parachute, pulled off his boots and lifted his injured leg up onto the instrument panel. He opened a nearby flask of orange juice, taking several well-earned gulps before leaning back into his chair. He was not concerned by Steph's struggle to keep the helicopter in the air. She was far too stubborn and too good a pilot to let them die. His faith was vindicated as the helicopter levelled out and hovered high above the blast site. Ben stared out over the destruction the bombs had left in their wake, his thoughts turning to those within the research centre whose lives had been taken by the explosion, and the innocent bystanders killed or injured. Why, he thought, why all this just to get him? There had to be more to it. Something else was going on, and whatever it was, Pemrose had been in it up to his neck and now he was dead.

"What the hell happened in there?"

Ben was too tired to offer any argument, and spent the next few minutes relating everything that had taken place inside the research centre.

When he was finished, Steph pulled a cigar from the top pocket of her flight suit. The cigars were specially imported and were the only brand she smoked; Ben hated every last imported one of them. Usually, he would be making his feelings clear with a few well-timed remarks, but sarcasm was the last thing on his mind. All he wanted to do now was sleep.

"Someone went to a lot of trouble to make sure you, Pemrose and that disk wouldn't make it out of there in one piece."

Ben held out his empty hand, a few inches from Steph's face. He flicked his hand back and then shot it forward, only this time, a small gold disk was sitting snugly between his thumb and forefinger.

"You mean this disk?" he said, sagging back into his seat. "You switched them?"

"I wasn't going to let a couple of jokers with machine guns mess up weeks of planning."

Ben failed to mention that he had done a pretty good job on that front all by himself.

"So, what next?" asked Steph.

"Lay low until we know what's on this disk."

"And use it to find out who's behind all this?"

Ben nodded as he found himself, once more, drawn to the smouldering wreckage, his mood turning sombre. He was thankful that he could not hear the screams of the dying or injured. There would be time enough for that in his nightmares.

He leaned his head back, closed his eyes and willed the onset of sleep. "A lot of people died tonight that didn't have to. I want to know why."

18

Chapter Three

Humans will never learn; with each generation, their need for mastery over each other grows, as does the desire to control Mother Nature. They ache to break her spirit, and harness her essence as if it were their birthright. They surround themselves with objects they believe will make their insignificant lives rich and productive. I almost pity them; all these objects have done is dull their senses and erode their imagination. Instead of strengthening their will to strive forward, it pulls them back, making them lazy and content, thus making my task all the easier to accomplish.

Perhaps if they understood the fleetingness of life, they would waste less of it trying to prove their superiority, and instead, simply live.

I sit and watch the house, as I am perched on the highest branches of an oak tree. I wonder what the people inside are doing, what they are thinking. I wonder if they know they are moments away from death, and what would they do with that knowledge.

I drop to the ground, taking care to make no sound. In front of me is a security fence; on the other side, two armed men stand guard at the entrance to the house. I could enter the house unnoticed if I wished, but I will not deprive these men of the joy I bring them. How could I deny them the exquisite sensation of watching the lifeblood flow from their bodies? To feel it congeal in their throats, seeking to release their souls to the eternal void; I shall not disappoint them. Vaulting into the air, I somersault over the fence with room to spare. As I land, one of the guards glances in my direction and for a moment, I think this time will be different. The guard, believing he saw nothing, returns to the conversation with his colleague. I move across the soft and warm grass. They do not see me until I am a few feet away. As they behold my beautiful countenance, I see the light of fear in their eyes. They hide their fear well, good, very good. They are stunned only for a moment before reaching for their weapons, they are fast and their reactions are almost instant. I am faster and I strike without thought or concern. When I am done, they lay before me, their faces a twisted and blood-soaked parody of bravery. I watch as their blood flows into the earth, and feel nothing but contempt. I know now that the traitors within the house will be no match for me, otherwise they would not need protection. They too will die except, unlike these men, they already know the reason and the cause of their deaths. *Where is the challenge?* I ask

19

myself as I enter the darkened house and make my way to the bedroom. My hand tightens around the door. I enter and gaze upon the single female I find there. She lies asleep on the bed, unaware of the delights I bring her. As I approach, the woman's eyes flicker and open. Her piercing screams fill the house as I set about my task. It is then I hear something behind me. The husband bursts into the room firing in all directions, hoping a stray bullet will save his life: he is wrong. I wait until his ammunition is spent and then it is my turn. He hears my whispered laughter in his ears as I sever his hand. He had used his wife as the bait to try to trap me; such treachery should and will be rewarded.

When I am done, I leave their remains where they lay and leave the house as silently as I entered. In the distance, I can hear police sirens; they do not concern me. The night will always be my ally: it protects me, clothes me within its dark embrace. Now I must return to those who have summoned me forth, but deep down I yearn for the one thing that has eluded me these many years: a challenge.

Clancy was relieved to escape the media frenzy that was gathering pace following the destruction of the research centre. All of the major Japanese television networks were now covering the disaster. So far, the authorities were saying they believed the explosion was the result of an industrial accident. Clancy had seen this kind of thing before: someone did not want the real truth revealed, at least for now. An attack on a United Nations facility would no doubt reflect badly on the Japanese government.

The collateral damage from the explosion had been higher than anticipated. Clancy put that down to the incompetence of the bargain basement mercenaries he was forced to work with. However, the primary objectives, despite the high body count, had been achieved, and that would have to be enough.

Following the usual protocol for this kind of operation, they split into teams of two, each pair tasked with making their own way out of Japan.

Clancy and Kelly took the Shinkansen from Tokyo station to the coastal city of Atami. There were a large number of tourists on the train, which helped to ensure their need for anonymity. Clancy soon realised there was little to be concerned about; the occupants of the crowded train were too busy sending texts on their mobiles, sleeping, or reading to notice anything out of the ordinary. Clancy did not like the fact that their escape route was planned and financed by their employers. He had tried to argue the matter, but the stipulation had been a deal breaker. His concern was that the route could merely be a means of herding them into a trap, and yet he still accepted the arrangement. Betrayal was a way of life for people like him.

Once they reached Atami, they boarded a ferry bound for Izu Oshima, one of the islands south of Tokyo. The sea appeared to be in a forgiving mood, and was content to remain calm as the ferry set sail. The sky was cloudless, the air warm and refreshingly clean.

In the distance, rising up from the centre of the island, Clancy could see a volcano. Surrounded by the forest, it stood like a solemn guardian of rock, steam and molten lava scrutinizing all who passed under its shadow.

During the trip, Clancy overheard one of the tour guides explaining to his group, twenty or more senior citizens, how Mt. Mihara's last eruption in 1986 resulted in the evacuation of the entire island. It was at that point that Kelly voiced his fervent wish that the volcano keep its big, lava-filled mouth shut while they were on the island.

After the ferry docked, they hired a car and, following the route mapped out by their employers, drove to the airport without incident. The airport was small, isolated, and suited their needs perfectly.

A private jet was fuelled and waiting on the airport's single runway; in less than twenty minutes, they were in the air.

Both men took turns in sleeping, whilst the other made frequent checks on the cabin crew. Some might label their actions as paranoia: but to Clancy, there was nothing paranoid about wanting to stay alive.

The flight was uneventful, though long. The plane finally touched down at Urbe airport just outside Rome. A car was waiting for them as they left the main terminal. Clancy got in the front, beside the driver, with Kelly taking the back seat. They set off towards the centre of Rome. The silence of the trip was broken by sporadic Italian outbursts from the driver as he weaved in and out of the busy traffic. A Vespa that narrowly avoided ploughing into the side of the car twenty minutes into the journey earned the bulk of the driver's fury.

Clancy had ignored the driver's attempts to make conversation with him. He saw no point talking to a man he was poised to kill at the first hint of betrayal. A conversation, however trivial, would evoke images of family, friends, thoughts that could lead to empathy, and encourage hesitation. Clancy had witnessed first hand, on and off the battlefield, the fatal results of hesitation.

The car pulled up outside one of the many large complexes that formed the Esposizione Universale di Roma, the heart of Rome's financial distinct. As they got out, they were greeted by a nervous dark-haired man in a grey pin-striped suit, who led them to a small, windowless office situated on the building's third floor. The room was sparse: only containing a desk, two armchairs, a table, and on it a laptop.

"All this way and they couldn't even lay on some food," said Kelly.

"Bloody cheapskates."

Clancy ignored the observation, being hungry was a permanent state of mind for Kelly. Right now, they were about to enter the most dangerous phase of the mission: getting paid.

"Do you have the disk, Mr. Wallencheck?"

Clancy looked around. Besides the two of them, the room was empty; the voice had seemed to come from nowhere. He stood up, walked over to the right corner of the room and stared into the smoke alarm attached to the ceiling. Inside the housing of the alarm, he saw a tiny speaker. He guessed if he searched further, he would find a surveillance camera.

"Well, well," said Kelly, joining him. "Someone's been enjoying the show."

"The disk, Mr. Wallencheck, do you have it?"

"Right here," said Clancy. He took out the case containing the disk and patted it paternally.

The laptop's power light came on, the operating system booted up and seconds later, the laptop's disc drive door slid open.

"Insert the disk."

Clancy opened the case, removed the disk and inserted it into the disk drive. After a while, the screen went black and was followed by the words:

Better luck next time, guys.

"Bastard pulled a switch on us," said Kelly, burying his knife into the table.

"Well, Mr. Wallencheck?" said the voice.

"He's good."

"That is not an answer."

"Ok, try this one. If The Hand's alive, we can pick up his trail. If not, then the disk is scrap along with the rest of the centre. Either way, you win."

"If he learns what's on that disk…"

"Don't waste your time threatening us," said Clancy. "Me and my men, and I mean my men, not those amateurs you stuck me with, can get your disk back, but it's going to cost you double."

"You failed to recover the disk, allowed the thief to escape and you expect more money?"

"My team don't come cheap, besides I was more than happy to put a bullet in The Hand," said Clancy. "But no, you wanted to pull all this, 'Make his death look like an accident' crap."

The voice did not answer, leaving Clancy wondering if he had pushed too hard.

"A fair point, Mr. Wallencheck, double it is," said the voice at last.

"Assemble your team and we will be in contact."

"And The Hand?"

"Kill him, kill him in whatever way you see fit."

"That's the best decision you've made since hiring us."

Chapter Four

Nelson had first seen her during a trip to Le Forum des Halles, Paris' huge underground shopping complex. She possessed the most captivating smile he had ever seen, as well as a slim body, nicely showcased in a tight-fitting white blouse and black skirt.

Nelson had woven a path through the crowd and followed her into a small boutique, hoping his behaviour was not crossing into stalker territory. As she was finishing her shopping, Nelson grabbed the cheapest ornament, a small crystal unicorn, and positioned himself behind her at the checkout queue. He made a disposable comment about her shopping in an attempt to start a conversation. To his surprise, she responded well and after discovering her name was Michelle, he decided to press his advantage. Somewhere during the conversation, Nelson found himself invited to lunch at a nearby restaurant. Although he was more used to being the one to make the first move, for someone with curves like Michelle, he was more than happy to let her take charge, for now.

An hour later, they were sharing a decadent seafood platter of oysters, clams, crab, lobster, and prawns, which Michelle had heartily endorsed.

As they talked, Michelle revealed she was an Art buyer from Stockholm, in Paris for a few days to acquire some new pieces for her client. When she reversed the question of employment, Nelson explained that he worked in Marketing and was here to help the launch of a new product. A lie, of course, but a well told one, he thought.

After lunch, Nelson walked Michelle back to her car. He knew if he did not step up the pace, he was going to end up spending the weekend alone. As he held open her car door, he mentioned that he was free this evening and would she consider having dinner with him? The move was made under the guise of learning more about the art exhibition. Michelle readily agreed and the pair exchanged numbers. Nelson did not know anything, or care about art. He did care about women, or rather, what they could do for or to him. Nelson considered himself an expert on the members of the fairer sex; not that there was much to know, they were a pretty easy species to work out. Nelson could not understand why other men had so many problems with them. Sure, even he suffered a modest share of failure, however, when stacked up against his successes, there was no comparison.

It was easy for Nelson to call Michelle a few hours later and change their dinner date to a more intimate affair in his bedroom suite. Soon after her arrival, Nelson was confident they would never make it to the second course.

With Michelle now laid beside him, Nelson could not help feeling a little cheated by the whole situation. He had spent much more time and effort in women far more obtainable than Michelle. Regret over the ease of seduction, however, was more than compensated for by the marathon bout of lovemaking that followed. Michelle was transformed from the slightly reserved art buyer to a sexual carnivore, devouring every carnal pleasure on offer. Nelson was hard pushed to remember the last time he was so sexually challenged. If he was honest with himself, he was actually glad when Michelle had finally fallen asleep, allowing him some well earned recuperation time.

Nelson could feel Michelle's breath on his skin, invoking memories of pleasure, tinged with the promise of more to come.

"Hey there," he said, biting her ear. "You still with me?"

Michelle groaned, stifling a yawn. She slid her hand across his chest, her fingers pausing over his right nipple. Nelson moved her hand away and rolled onto his side.

"Haven't you had enough?" he said, glancing at his watch on the bedside table.

Michelle began biting Nelson's wrist, moving up his arm; upon reaching his neck, she concentrated her attack.

"Look, I'm already late; I really need to get going."

Michelle lifted the sheet draped across Nelson's waist. "Really?"

"Really," he said, giving her a quick kiss.

Administering himself with an extreme dose of will power, Nelson slid out of Michelle's surprisingly firm grip, and rose from the bed. Still half-asleep, he staggered into the bathroom, the only thing on his mind was a cold shower.

Nelson knew he should have left for the embassy an hour ago, not the best impression to make as head of the security detail. Still, it was the third day of the conference and so far, the event had been incident-free.

There had been the usual nutcases and extremists talking big and making threats before the conference, but nothing pointing to any kind of terrorist action.

The seed of an idea formed in Nelson's mind as the first blasts of cold water struck his body. Rogers, his second-in-command, was a competent operative, and more importantly, he owed Nelson a favour, one that Nelson would go to great pains to stress could only be repaid by covering for him.

Nelson leapt from the shower invigorated by the prospect of another round of bedroom Olympics. He snatched a towel from the rail, threw it around his still wet lower half, and ran into the bedroom to give Michelle the good news. He froze when he saw the silencer that Michelle was screwing onto the 9mm pistol she was holding. It took Nelson a second to realise it was his own gun in her hands.

"Game over," said Michelle, pulling the trigger.

The bullet struck Nelson's forehead and shattered; a bright red liquid exploding across his forehead, leaving a stain that resembled a surreal expressionist painting.

"You're dead, Trainee."

Turning, Nelson faced a tall, broad-shouldered man stood in the doorway, silhouetted by the corridor light. The man's hair was cut short, almost to the scalp, and he wore a grey two-piece suit, which seemed to struggle to contain his muscular frame.

Nelson had no problem discerning the anger in the man's stern gaze and tight-lipped frown, even in the half-light from the bedside lamp. The man turned on the room's main light as he walked in and closed the door behind him. Recognising the intruder, Nelson immediately snapped to attention, the suddenness of the movement causing his towel to slide to the floor.

"I guess I screwed up, sir," he said, making no attempt to retrieve his towel.

"You were killed by your own weapon, what do you think?" said the man, his voice calm and measured; but still, thought Nelson, he was able to convey his disappointment.

Nelson aimed a fierce scowl at Michelle, who returned the look with a grin.

"Bitch!"

Now it was Michelle's turn to scowl. She aimed the gun at Nelson again; this time, however, her aim was much lower. "Careful, Trainee, I can still put live rounds in this thing."

"Enough," said the newcomer.

Nelson's throat went dry and he was gripped with a need to be anywhere but here. He knew from experience that Luther Washington was not known for his compassion.

It was Luther's job, like the many other field instructors, to weed out those not suitable to join the unique task force Nelson had spent the last two years training to earn a place within. The Tactical, Operational, Response and Control Headquarters, or TORCH, was a specialist unit created to take on operations sanctioned by the United Nations across the globe. The operations themselves took many forms, but mainly involved the investigation of crimes against the UN, as well as providing security for the high-ranking UN officials and diplomats.

"Ok, Trainee," said Luther, folding his arms. "How about you give me an analysis of the situation?"

Nelson wondered as he stared at his superior's massive upper torso how he managed to find clothes that fit. He became aware of Luther's eyes locked on his own, waiting for him to speak.

"Michelle was working for one of the factions threatening the conference."

Nelson paused to give his superior a chance to intercede with any comments, but Luther said nothing; he just stood there waiting. This was not going well.

"She was obviously aware of my movements and ..."

"Why you?"

The question caught Nelson off guard, disrupting his well-ordered answer, but he guessed that was the intention. He had seen Luther use the same approach with other trainees. It was Luther's belief that an operative working for TORCH should be able to analyse, understand and learn from every action they made.

Nelson found the method frustrating. He did not need anyone, not even a veritable legend like Luther, telling him how many ways he had screwed up.

"Michelle must have known I would have documents on me regarding the security arrangements for the conference."

"There were at least ten other trainees who possessed the same information. So I ask again, why you?"

Nelson swallowed hard.

"I was the easiest target, sir."

"Exactly. You're a loudmouth who likes to think he's a hit with the ladies. She exploited that fact."

"I try my best, sir," Nelson smiled back.

"You think this is funny?"

Nelson fell silent.

"Better. I would think by now even you would realise the usefulness of these live exercises."

"I do, sir!"

"Do you?" Luther leaned in closer. "If this had been real, room service would be wiping your brains off the wall by now."

Nelson fought against the need to defend his actions; it was difficult to make a case about professionalism when standing naked in front of one's training instructor.

"We've had this conversation a dozen times, and a dozen times you make the same mistakes," said Luther. "If you want out of the selection process, then you just keep going, son."

"No, sir; I don't want out."

What kind of stupid question was that? Nelson felt a sudden bitterness towards Washington. For the past two years, he had experienced first hand TORCH's training and selection process. It was a process known for its intensity throughout the law enforcement community. Every mental and physical aspect of a potential operative was put under the spotlight. He or she would be pushed beyond their own perceived levels of endurance, and then pushed again and again.

The statistics surrounding the process were equally as frightening. Over seventy percent of the trainees never finished their training; out of the survivors, less than ten percent were selected to join TORCH. Nelson had no intention of being one of those failures. He had given up too much for this chance.

"On assignment, we act as one unit," said Luther "yet you didn't inform your team members about Michelle. Why?"

"I thought it was a chance meeting, sir, so I didn't see the point in mentioning it."

"You didn't see the point?" said Luther. "Rule fifty, paragraph three, section five…"

"Any unauthorized assignation during an operation must be first cleared with command, and the unknown person or persons subject to a level four background check," finished Nelson.

If Luther was impressed with Nelson, he was not showing it.

"Damn shame you can't follow the rules as well as you quote them. If you had, you would have discovered that Michelle was formerly Anna Rushmore, who spent eight months in a Dutch prison convicted of a minor drug offence. During that time, she shared her cell with Yvette Escobar, who is?"

"A known member of New Dawn, one of the terrorist factions who had made repeated threats against the conference," said Nelson, recalling his briefing notes before the training exercise was launched a week ago.

"Fantasy is often more attractive than reality."

Great, thought Nelson. Now Luther was going to start getting all metaphorical on him.

"I'm sorry, sir."

"This cavalier attitude towards the rules your fellow trainees have no problem following stops now!"

"But, sir, if I may…"

"You may not."

Nelson checked his anger, unable to believe the hypocrisy of his superior. Luther's own record for rule breaking during his time at MI6 was no secret. An incident sparked by Luther led to him leaving MI6 and gaining his appointment to TORCH. "You've got two days leave before your next live exercise," said Luther, tossing Nelson's clothes to him. "I suggest you use that time to sort out your attitude, or you better start circling the job ads."

Tucking his clothes under his arm, Nelson moved to leave, then stopped.

"I won't let you down, sir."

"Wrong answer, son, you should be more concerned with how you let yourself down," came Luther's harsh response.

Burying his anger and frustration at being treated like a freshman in college, Nelson dressed in record time. He was by the door when something occurred to him.

"This is my room," he said in a whisper.

"And your point being?"

"None, sir," said Nelson, wondering where the hell he was supposed to go at this time of the morning, with no shoes, and covered in red paint. He gave Michelle a final angry look before half jogging from the room, his bare feet making a dull thudding sound on the wooden floor panelling in the passageway.

Luther closed the door and faced Michelle, who now wore a crumpled white blouse and little else. He still felt uncomfortable with operatives ending up in bed together as part of a training exercise. He knew no amount of classroom training could prepare a trainee for their life in TORCH as much as the live exercises did, but it still left a sordid taste in his mouth. Perhaps the real reason for his unease was the half-naked woman playing the part of Michelle. Not only was Eve Appleton one of the most capable undercover operatives he had ever worked with, she was also a good friend. Seeing her like this was like catching someone in bed with his sister, if he had one.

"Ok, Eve," he said. "Let's hear it."

"What?"

"You're giving me that look."

"I didn't realise I had a look."

"Trust me, you do," said Luther, taking a seat on the edge of the bed.

"You're pushing him harder than the other trainees, and I think I know the reason," said Eve.

"Every time that boy draws breath, he puts lives at risk, especially his own."

Eve nodded but did not reply.

"He needs to learn the importance of teamwork and playing by the rules."

"Because you used to be so good at towing the party line, didn't you?"

Eve's words hit Luther like a freight train.

"He's not the man you used to be, Luther. He's just inexperienced, he'll learn."

"At whose expense? If someone had been on my case back then, maybe…"

The words faltered and Luther bowed his head in silence. Eve moved across the bed to give his arm a gentle squeeze.

"What happened wasn't your fault," said Eve. "It's been what, ten, twelve years? You need to let it go."

"I destroyed a man's life; how am I supposed to let that go?"

Luther did not expect an answer. Eve would never understand. The guilt he felt would never pass and never fade. The strange thing was, in some sick way he was grateful for that. Allowing the guilt to eat away at his soul was the only form of penance left to him.

"You're right about Nelson though," he said at last. "He made a mistake, but I didn't need to go psycho on him."

"I wouldn't have gone that far."

"Wouldn't you?"

"Ok, maybe you were a bit Captain Blythe," said Eve, smiling. "I wouldn't worry too much, I'm guessing it will take a lot more to dent that ego."

"I'll have a word with him, if he doesn't put a bullet between my eyes first."

Eve thumped him on the shoulder. "When you do, tell him the next time he calls me bitch, he better be running when he says it."

Looking into Eve's bright cheery face, Luther found it hard to retain his dark mood.

"Did you really have to sleep with him?"

"Mr. self-involved was never going to drop his guard unless he thought he was pulling all the strings," explained Eve. "Besides, I've not been laid in five months and he does have a nice ass."

Luther was never so grateful as when his mobile started to vibrate in his jacket pocket. Trying to wipe the uncomfortable images Eve had just placed in his mind, he pulled his phone out and pressed the button to answer the call.

"Hello," said Luther, catching a glimpse of Eve's shapely legs as she walked into the bathroom, carrying the rest of her clothes.

Remember, she's like your sister.

"Sir, this is the Command Centre. We have Director Chardon on hold for you."

"Just what I need," said Luther under his breath.

"Sorry, sir, I didn't catch that."

"Nothing; put him through."

"Yes, sir, stand by."

Philippe Chardon was the Director of operations, and head of TORCH, answerable only to the Secretary-General of the UN, Jane Morton.

Chardon was a duplicitous man, who did little to assuage Luther's fears that he was far more concerned with advancing his own career than protecting the lives of those in his charge. What annoyed Luther the most was that although he viewed Chardon as little more than an annoying bureaucrat, he was also forced to concede that Chardon was dammed good at his job.

"Washington," said a voice with a heavy French accent. "Is that you?"

"It's me, sir," said Luther, hoping his fake 'I'm eager to please' voice was not too noticeable. "What can I do for you?"

"Consider yourself back in the field, Monsieur; see to it your training duties are handed over to one of your colleagues."

The order caught Luther off guard. All operatives were required, once they reached a certain level of experience, to assist in the training of new operatives. The reason was to ensure the training was always fresh, relevant and constantly evolving.

"Sir, I still have another year before I'm due back on the active roster."

"I just received further intelligence reports from Tokyo, regarding the destruction of the research facility."

Luther knew the facility had been destroyed in an accidental explosion several nights ago. Although the preliminary reports gave no indication of foul play, he still harboured concerns regarding the whole situation.

"The explosion was no accident," continued Chardon. "Fragments from several explosive devices were found in the wreckage."

"Do we know who's responsible?"

The pause from the other end of the line, then a slight cough followed by a relived sigh told Luther that Chardon was indulging in his favourite pastime; smoking.

"Our underworld sources suggest the attack was carried out by The Hand. I take it you've heard of him?"

"A professional thief, and if half the stories are to be believed, a dammed good one. He works for just about anyone who can afford him, which at his prices aren't too many," said Luther. "To be honest, we can't even be sure if he's a man."

"Yes well, this androgynous thief is responsible for the deaths of an entire security team and six lab technicians," said Chardon. "And I've yet to see the civilian death toll."

"Sir, in all the years The Hand's been operating, his jobs have been flawless. It's hard to believe he would suddenly resort to mass murder."

"Fortunately, I have no interest in your pet theories, Monsieur. I expect you to follow orders, you do remember how to do that, don't you, Agent Washington?"

"Of course, sir," said Luther, his hand tightening around the bedpost.

"One more thing. A British lawyer working with the French embassy was murdered tonight, along with his wife and their bodyguards. I promised the ambassador I'd send someone over so that I could pass on a full report, and you're the closest to the crime scene."

Luther knew of at least half a dozen agents who were also in Paris, obviously one case was not enough in Chardon's eyes.

"How were they killed?"

"The poor wretches were cut to pieces," explained Chardon. "There were also some strange markings found at the scene that no on can make any sense of."

Eve came back into the room fully dressed. Luther put a finger to his lips before she could speak. After a few seconds, Luther made a writing motion with his left hand, whilst cradling the phone between his neck and shoulder. Eve scooped a pen and a message pad from the bedside table drawer, then passed them to Luther.

"Ok, sir," said Luther, scribbling furiously. "I'll leave right now, yes, I'll contact you after I've visited the crime scene …goodbye, sir."

"I take it that was our illustrious boss?" said Eve.

Luther did not reply. He was already dialling in another code. It was several seconds before someone answered.

"What?"

"Hi, Kathryn, it's Luther."

Luther's words were met with silence.

"Kathryn?"

"Sorry, I was busy writing your suicide note."

"Bad time?"

"It's bloody three thirty in the morning, of course it's a bad time."

"There was a time when you didn't know the meaning of the word sleep."

"But I do know the meaning of the word dead," Kathryn snapped back wearily. "As in you will be if you don't have the world's best reason for waking me up."

"How fast can you get dressed?"

"How about never?" Kathryn's voice was sounding less weary. "I'm due to speak at the Psychological Institute tomorrow, remember? We had a dinner date afterwards."

"You know I wouldn't call unless…."

"Anytime you want to get to the point, feel free."

"There have been four murders committed at a residence just outside Paris."

Luther knew what was coming even before he had finished.

"Ok, let's stop right there, Sherlock," said Kathryn. "I'm a book worm now, it's nice hours, I get to travel, oh, and no one tries to kill me."

"These crimes sound like they may have been ritually motivated and you did ask me to contact you if anything like this came my way. You're also in Paris so it would be a shame to waste the coincidence."

"I really hate it when you make sense."

"No pressure, I promise, just take a look, tell me what you think and dinner is on me."

"Along with a disgustingly fat cheque for my consultancy fee?"

"Maybe, no promises. Well, shall I have a car pick you up?"

"Have it here in twenty minutes."

The phone went dead.

"Sorry," he whispered down the silent phone line.

He slipped the phone back into his pocket.

"Who was that?" asked Eve.

"An old friend."

"Ok, I get the message. So what did Chardon want this time, besides a kicking?" said Eve grinning. Luther was more than aware of Eve's dislike for Chardon, as was most of TORCH. On more than one occasion, he was called upon to speak up on her behalf to stop her from being transferred, or worse. Luther doubted his opinion carried much weight with Chardon, after all he was not exactly top of his list of favourite people. He guessed it was Eve's prowess as an undercover operative that saved her from incurring Chardon's full wrath.

Luther brought Eve up to date on the destruction of the research facility and The Hand. At no time did he mention the other purpose of Chardon's call. For some reason, there was something unsettling about the murders. He did not know why, though he felt better that at least he would have an expert he trusted on site.

"Eve, I want you to drop whatever you're working on."

"I take it you want me to fly out to Tokyo ASAP?"

Luther nodded. "I need to know everything that happened out there. I haven't got time to get anyone else, so take Nelson with you for backup, and try not to break him."

"You don't agree with Chardon, do you?"

"It doesn't matter what I believe,"

"It does if you expect me to head out on an unsanctioned mission with a trainee," said Eve. "A trainee who probably hates my guts by now, even if I was fantastic in bed."

"Don't worry, it will be sanctioned by the time you get back," promised Luther, ignoring the bed reference. "Besides, Chardon told me to find The Hand at any cost, and that's what I'm doing."

"Fair enough," said Eve. "But it isn't like you to mess around with orders from above, especially after you just gave Nelson a going over for the same thing."

"I know," agreed Luther, seeing the irony, "but I won't sit back and let someone be wrongly accused of mass murder, even if they are a criminal."

"Maybe you haven't changed as much as you think,"

"I hope you're wrong."

Chapter Five

Jason stared at his reflection in the mirror. His dark brown eyes looked bright and alive, but the rings underneath told a different story. Filling the bathroom sink with cold water, he leant forward and began splashing water onto his skin. He welcomed the numbness the freezing water brought to his face, he only wished the same could be done with his memories.

When questioned about his real parents Jason's reply was always the same: nothing, he remembered nothing. How could he? His only contact with them was for barely an hour after his birth. He kept the truth hidden, deep within his mind. He should have been too young to remember his real parents, and yet he did as clearly as if they were looking out of the mirror at him now. He remembered his mother's eyes filled with tears as she spoke words he could not hear. She had placed him gently down on one of the seats inside the hospital foyer, and then they were gone, amidst the sounds of footsteps and shouting as the hospital staff realised what was happening. Jason would sit alone, for years afterwards, trying to decipher his mothers' only words to him. Eventually, he concluded there had never being a secret message, save perhaps one of good bye. Despite abandoning him, his parents saw fit to leave a note explaining that his name was Jason, and to take care of their son. Why had they done it? Why name something you have no intention of keeping? Why should they care if the people that found him fulfilled the last wish of parents who did not care enough about their son to keep him in the first place?

Jason lifted his head, still wet with water and stared again into the mirror. His black hair fell across his eyes in its annoyingly regular fashion. He made another promise to cut his hair shorter. There were certain girls who liked his hair long, and their collective wishes always managed to win out over his occasional frustration.

He reached out and touched the hand of his reflection. There were times when his reflection was the only person in the world who came close to understanding him.

"Who am I?"

"Someone who's got a lot of explaining to do."

Jason turned to see Quincy coming into the bathroom.

"Jesus, mate you look like shit," said Quincy. "More nightmares?"

"Something like that," said Jason, drying his face. It had been three days since his episode in Ivanov's lecture. Since then, the images plagued him every time he closed his eyes. It was as if they were goading him; pushing him towards doing something. He just didn't know what that something was.

"You want to talk about it?"

"No it's fine. Just stress I guess."

Jason saw the look of relief cross his friend's face. Quincy was not a great fan of anything touchy feely.

"I thought you were supposed to be going home today?" asked Quincy.

"You and me both, mate."

Jason pointed to a stack of text books decorating his desk. At least this time he would have a valid reason for not going home.

"Let me guess, Ivanov?"

"Apparently, it's to help me regain the focus I seem to lose on the way to his lectures," said Jason, doing his best impression of Professor Ivanov. "He wants it in by Monday, before Professor Stone gets back."

"But it's Friday night?"

"Somehow, I think he knew that when he set me the essay," said Jason frowning.

"You should have told him where to stick it, mate, this isn't boot camp."

"Well, he gave me a choice; do the essay or fail the module outright."

Jason moved back into the other room and began sorting through the stack of books he had checked out of the library a few hours earlier. Although initially there to start the research for his assignment, he found himself scouring the library's books on Heraldry, in an effort to see if the coat of arms worn by the knights in his nightmare actually existed.

After hours of searching, without success, Jason began to realise that not only was his new hobby affecting his real studies, but it was on the fast track to becoming an obsession. Right now, he needed to keep on Ivanov's good side if he even had one. If his father found out he was failing grades, he would be treated to a two-hour, award wining lecture on 'how not to be a failure' next time he saw him.

"That man gives new meaning to the word prat," said Quincy. "Anyway, seeing that you're stuck here for the weekend, how about you grab your coat. There's a house party with our names on it."

"No can do, mate. Got to get this essay done."

"Fair enough," said Quincy, making for the door. "Make sure you get some sleep though, mate, you'll feel better for it."

"I will."

Quincy smiled and left the room, closing the door behind him. Jason stared at the pile of books.

"Get some sleep," said Jason, laughing to himself.

He settled down at his desk, switched on his laptop and opened the first of his books. "I don't think so."

The thing was, Jason did not mind doing the work; as scary as it sounded, he enjoyed it. When his father had insisted he take Occult Studies as one of his subjects, he thought he was mad. The only reason he had taken it was to keep the man happy, after all, he was the one paying the bills. He soon came to enjoy the subject in spite of Ivanov's presence. Some of this was down to Jason's unexpected fascination with the subject, but also the teaching style of Ivanov's superior, Professor Napoleon Stone. Apart from the boring array of suits he wore, Stone looked like the sort of man you did not mess with. The look was enhanced by the black eyepatch, covering his scarred left eye, and contrasting his brown skin. No one knew how Stone lost the eye, and no one had yet managed to drum up enough courage to ask him. Jason had come close a few times, but then decided against it. All these factors only served to heighten the air of mystery surrounding the frequently absent professor.

When Professor Stone was at the university, he was a quiet and private man, although his sheer presence in a room commanded the respect from those around him. His need for privacy, however, did not detract from his commitment to his students. Jason had been one of many students who, on several occasions, had been tutored by Professor Stone well into the night. Although they weren't exactly on first name terms or heading to the student union for a pint together, Jason considered Professor Stone a friend.

After glancing at the Heraldry books again, Jason decided he would mention the coat of arms and the nightmare to the Professor upon his return.

He'll think you've gone nuts.

"That will make two of us," he said, in answer to his subconscious.

New York.

Ben had gone to great lengths to secure a base of operations that would be hard to discover. Once he had amassed enough money from his various criminal endeavours, he bought a record shop in an area known for its high levels of drug-related crime. The main reason behind the purchase was his discovery that hidden several levels beneath the shop was an abandoned drug lab. The lab's former occupants were killed in a hit orchestrated by their rivals.

With Ben's vision driving the redesign, the lab had been converted into a four-floor state of the art home, workshop, gym and communication centre.

Although there were several other safe houses located in other countries, it was here that Ben felt most at ease. Here, he could enjoy the quiet moments snatched between jobs when he could introduce some semblance of the mundane. For a while, at least, he was able to hold back the chaotic and surreal world of his criminal alter ego.

This time, however, his thoughts were troubled.

There were many things in his life he regretted or wished he could change; he put that down to human nature. Who was not filled with the desire to embrace a life to the full without consequence? But this was different, this time he had played the game and innocent people had lost.

Though he tried to hide it, he knew Steph had seen the look on his face as the research centre went up in flames. Before her dishonourable discharge, something she would not talk about even now, Steph was a member of Naval Intelligence. Although she never went into the specifics of the work, Ben knew she had taken lives. During the journey home, she had tried to absolve the guilt he was feeling. She pointed out that he was not the one who set the explosives, he was not to blame.

Ben saw things differently. He was as responsible as the mercenaries. His presence in the building caused those deaths; there was no escaping that truth. The blood was on his hands, despite all rational explanations to the contrary. Steph had said from the outset that something felt wrong about the job; they were thieves, not a delivery service. As usual, Ben's ego won out over Steph's pragmatism. The only way to appease his conscience was to find those others responsible.

What was worse would be that the news of what happened would eventually reach Raven. It would kill the old man.

Will Raven had saved Ben's life. There was no simpler way to put it. Whenever he thought of the old man, he could not stop himself from smiling, although their first meeting had not exactly been ideal.

There was nothing new in the fact that Ben went into prison claiming his innocence. In his first month, he met over a dozen inmates all claiming the same virtuous title. The irony was he actually was innocent. The arrest, the court case, and the conviction had all been swift and airtight. An array of upstanding witnesses all claimed they had seen someone fitting Ben's description leaving the bank, carrying a gun in one hand, and a mailbag full of cash in the other. The security guard wounded in the robbery served to heighten the prosecution's desire for a swift decision in their favour. Ben's alibi, that he had been out jogging at the time of the robbery, was laughable as proved by the prosecution lawyer, who tore it to shreds. With his alibi in ruins and the evidence stacked against him, Ben's eventual incarceration was a foregone conclusion.

Ben's lawyer visited him in his first week in prison. He assured Ben that he was working on a way to get him out; he just needed to have a little faith. As Ben looked into the eyes of the other prisoners, saw the barbed fences, the armed guard towers and heard those cell doors shut night after night, he realised that faith had no place here.

It had been one month to the day he entered Fulworth Prison when Ben was attacked in the exercise yard. To this day, Ben never discovered the reason behind the attack, other than in prison, the inmates seldom needed a reason to inflict harm on one another. Ben could tell from the way the men swaggered towards him that they were expecting a short fight. Moments later, their wish was granted but not in the way they expected. They lay sprawled on the ground in front of Ben, nursing a broken arm, two cracked ribs and a broken nose between them.

The crowd of inmates that had gathered to watch began jeering and shouting. A few used the opportunity to trade punches with their enemy of the day. A strong hand grabbed Ben's arm, pulling him out of the crowd just as the guards arrived to break things up.

Ben threw the hand off once he was free of the crowd. He faced his helper, an old man, whose dark and leathery brown skin contrasted his thick beard that was more grey than black. His scalp showed the passing of years; faint wisps of hair clung to the sides of his head. Though old - he looked to be in his early sixties - Ben could see the man had kept himself in good shape, and his eyes, though small, showed a fierce alertness.

"Damn, boy," said the man, grinning to reveal a large gap between his two front teeth. "You got some quick hands on you; you a fighter or something?"

The man's deep, rasping voice sounded like he survived on a diet of dirt and gravel.

"No offence, but I don't know you," said Ben, wishing he was back in his cell, where at least it was less exposed.

"Don't they teach manners where you're from, British boy?"

Ben was grateful for the help. The guards took a dim view of inmates scrapping, and he would have wound up in solitary. However, he learnt that in here, nine times of out ten, when someone helped you, it was less about helping you and more about helping themselves.

"Look, old man, I'm not your boy or your son. I just want to get back to my cell."

"The name's Will, and don't think I'm too old to open up a can of prime WA on you."

Will caught the confused look from Ben and laughed. "Whup Ass, son... good old-fashioned, grade A, American Whup Ass."

It was clear the comment was a dig at his British accent. He was getting used to that in here.

"Look, I'm getting old, my fists ain't as quick as they used to be, you get me?"

"No."

"Man, you are going to be hard work. Look, there are a few cons in here who wouldn't shed any tears in my passing, the more violent, the better. I could use an extra pair of eyes watching my back."

"What, you want me to be your bodyguard?"

Will stepped in, and before Ben could mount a defence, he was on the floor and the old man had his hand around Ben's throat. "Do I look like I need a bodyguard, son?"

"No," Ben was able to force out.

"Like I said, I could use an extra pair of eyes to watch my back, that's all." Will released Ben and stepped back. "If you're up for that, you let me know."

With that, Will strolled back into the yard. He was soon lost amongst the other prisoners.

Ben smiled at the memory. It wasn't until later he learnt from his cellmate that not only was Will a trustee, and as such could help make Ben's time a lot easier, but years ago, Will had been known as The Wraith, one of the world's foremost jewel thieves.

He had watched Will's back for pretty much the entire time he was in prison, and the two became great friends. Ben's father had walked out when he was five so it was no surprise that Ben came to see Will in that role. The old thief offered to teach him his trade. At first, Ben turned the offer down flat. He was innocent, he was not going to inflame the situation by training to be a criminal; it would be as bad as giving up. People were working for him on the outside; he would be out before the year was over.

Two years later, the day after another failed appeal, Ben discovered something, something that sent him straight to Will demanding to learn everything he knew. He realised it was a knee-jerk reaction to what he had heard, but it didn't matter. Ben had never regretted that decision as much as he did now.

"Once they label you as a killer," Will would say, "that's all you'll ever be to them, it won't matter if you steal the crown jewels, you'll still be a killer, an animal. Make sure you don't make that mistake, Ben. Keep your jobs clean: no guns, no violence, no problem."

No guns, no violence, no problem. Three phrases that had been the guiding work ethic for Ben's criminal career, and unless he did something, that career would be forever stained with blood.

"You ok?"

Steph was standing by the entrance to the gym. Ben quickly masked his concerns with a wide grin. He was suspended at least twenty feet above a trampoline by a chain, his legs and hands both bound with a thick rope.

"You really are something," said Steph, shaking her head.

"Thanks."

"It wasn't meant to be a compliment."

Steph walked up to the trampoline, clutching a wad of papers in one hand. "Most normal people like to kick back, have a few drinks, read, listen to music but no, what do you do to chill out? You talk me into tying your ass up and playing Houdini for half an hour."

"It's difficult to explain."

"Not really," said Steph. "You're weird, I get it, see, it wasn't that difficult."

"What did you find out?" asked Ben, trying not to show his annoyance.

"I'm not telling you anything whilst you're up there."

Being a recipient of Steph's stubbornness on a daily basis, Ben knew there was little point arguing. He lifted his wrists up to his mouth and set his teeth to work undoing the rope knots. Once his hands were free, he bent forward and freed himself from the restraints on his legs.

He released his grip on the rope and as he fell, he twisted his body causing him to hit the trampoline feet first before being catapulted back into the air. After performing a single somersault, he landed next to Steph, his arms stretched out like a gymnast, awaiting the judges' verdict.

Steph stared at her watch as she handed him a water bottle. "Six minutes, you're getting slow."

Ben took a well-earned drink before reaching for a towel.

"Ok, let's hear it," he said, wiping the sweat from his arms and forehead; the result of the two hours of training he had done before his thirty-minute flirtation with escapology.

Steph pulled out a single sheet from the papers she held. On it were the images of two men.

Ben pointed to one of the images. "That's the chump who tried to kill me."

"I was able to create a good digital composite from the description you gave me. I ran it through all the government, naval and army records I could access. After an hour of file crunching, I struck gold."

Ben leaned back against one of the trampoline's supports, throwing the towel over his shoulder. "Who is he?"

"Major Clancy Wallencheck, head of a special ops unit codenamed Blacklight. They worked black op missions for the United States government. Its members were pulled in from all over the world and

41

given US citizenship."

Ben let out a heavy sigh. "Professional bad asses, just what we need."

"Oh, it gets worse. Wallencheck also received several commendations for bravery."

"A regular GI Joe."

Even as Steph's face contorted into a mask of irritation, Ben realised he had said the wrong thing.

"I respect anyone… anyone who puts on a uniform and is willing to serve their country, you got that?"

"Got it…Sorry."

Ben sighed to himself. He was always managing to put his foot in it with Steph on this rather sore point. Steph had been discharged from the navy under circumstances that were not of her own making, and yet she still believed in the military and fighting for her country. Ben never knew whether to envy her patriotism or pity her naivety.

Born in Nigeria, Ben's parents had brought him to England, aged two, where he grew up. He felt no real ties to either country. He did have a fondness for England, and had several properties there. He had also been back to Nigeria on several occasions; the last being his mother's funeral.

"Around seven years ago, things get hazy," continued Steph. "But from what I could piece together, most of Clancy's team was wiped out during a mission in Cuba. Clancy and a few others, including Jack Kelly, his second-in-command, survived the massacre and then dropped out of sight."

"Decorated soldiers turning mercenary. They must've been seriously pissed with someone. Still doesn't explain what they were doing in Tokyo and who put them onto us."

Steph smiled. "I can't answer the why, but I can pretty much cover the who."

"Let's have it."

"It's seems your hunch was right." She produced a small mini disc recorder and threw it to him. "Recording comes courtesy of our good friend, Elijah."

Elijah Barrington was a dilettante, which was just a fancy way of saying he thought he was better than everyone else. Elijah spent money like it was going out of fashion; his one overriding principle was that with a good suit and a lot of money, you could go as far as you want in life.

Not content with his wealthy lifestyle, Elijah operated a specialised recruitment agency for those whose talents he contracted out for financial gain, regardless of whether by legal means or not.

Will had first put Ben onto Elijah. He had told him to look him up when he got on the outside. According to Will, Elijah could put Ben in contact with the kind of jobs that would really pay out. Ben never trusted Elijah, despite working with him for years. No one earned Ben's trust, not even Steph, at least not fully; you could not earn what was never available in the first place. Ben's trust once in another human being had been his downfall. It was a lesson that he learned well whilst rotting in prison for seven years.

It was after his first job through Elijah that Ben saw to it that Elijah's private and public phone lines were tapped. Over time, the endless discussions regarding business deals became a severe chore, and he stopped listening. Ben felt his guilt grow stronger. If he had paid more attention to Elijah's activities, the needless slaughter in Tokyo might have been averted. He pressed the play button on the recorder.

"You there?" said a deep voice, which he recognized as Elijah's.

"No contact: That was the deal."

"Sound's like Wallencheck," whispered Ben.

"Your employers insisted."

"You've got twenty seconds."

Wallencheck's reply sounded sharp and on edge. Ben could sense, even through the garbled recording, that like himself, Wallencheck was not a trusting man.

"My employers wanted me to inform you that one of their operatives will take care of Pemrose, you just make sure you obtain the disk and The Hand dies in the explosion as agreed."

"Understood."

The next sound was the phone line going dead.

Steph took out her silver-plated lighter. She started to flip it open and shut, in an almost ritualistic manner. Ben knew the significance of her actions. *She's nervous.*

"Well, we're in the shit now," she said, pocketing the lighter.

"Wouldn't be the first time."

"True," admitted Steph. "But you should see the file on Clancy and his boys; it reads like an episode of "The A-Team", but with a higher body count."

If Steph was trying to convince him how bad things were, she was doing a hell of a job. "Any luck with the disk I got from Pemrose?"

"It's like trying to crack the Fort Knox of security protocols. I've never seen such complex levels of encryption; this is way out of my league."

Ben frowned. He had hoped for better news. "We need to know what's on that disk; it could be the key to this whole mess."

"I've already contacted Alex and put him to work on it, but so far nothing," said Steph. "But until he has something we can work with, we should make for the nearest non-extradition country."

"I'm not running," said Ben, his face reflecting his intent.

"Are you…?"

"I'm not insane or crazy, but I'm not running," he repeated, only this time more firmly.

Ben knew the longer he was away from the situation, the more chance Steph might be able to convince him that the blame was not his, that they should put Tokyo down to bad luck, and move on to the next job.

"Why don't you just paint targets on our asses, save them the trouble of aiming?" said Steph.

"You're overreacting. They need to find us first."

"If Elijah's sold us out, then it's a good bet they know where this place is, and if not, it won't take someone with his connections long to find us," Steph pointed out.

Ben met her fierce gaze. Steph was always the practical one in their partnership, but this time he needed to convince her that there would be no changing his mind. "I don't give a shit who's after us, I'm not running."

Steph's shoulders sagged and she gave a sigh of what Ben hoped was resignation.

"Ok Mr. Last Stand, do you even have a plan?"

"We sit tight until Alex can give us something to work with, and then we pay Elijah a not-so-friendly visit."

"Why not go for Elijah now, I could make him tell us what he knows?"

Ben had no doubt about what Steph would do if she got her hands on Elijah; betrayal was not something she looked well upon.

"We need to know just how big a hole we've dug for ourselves first."

"Ok," agreed Steph. "But look, if we're going to do this, then we're going to need backup."

It took a second for Ben to realise what or rather who Steph was referring to. "Don't even think about it," he said, moving off the trampoline support and shaking his head. "We're not bringing that nutter into this."

"I admit he has his ways."

"His ways," said Ben. "The man's a psycho; I don't want him anywhere near us."

"A psycho? And what makes you so different Mr. I-want-to-take-on-professional-killers-single-handed."

"Single-handed," said Ben, looking confused. "I thought you were staying."

"Staying is insane, but not getting in someone who can help us? Now that's just stupid," said Steph. "And we both know you're not that, well, most of the time you're not."

Ben could feel his resolve slipping under Steph's argument, but he was still uncertain about her idea. Bringing in the help she was referring to was like wheeling in a barrel of TNT, strapping it to your ass and waiting for the inevitable big bang.

"Wherever he goes, people die," said Ben, trying one last time to change Steph's mind.

"You say you don't want to run, fine, but if we're going to see this through to the end, then we need the Reverend," said Steph. "Otherwise, I'm gone. I mean it, Ben."

Ben tried not to smile at the ultimatum. It was not overconfidence that told him Steph would never abandon him; leaving a man behind was not in her makeup. However, the fact that she would even suggest it showed the depth of her feelings on the subject.

"Damned if we do, damned if we don't," Ben murmured. "Make contact."

Steph headed for the door. "You won't regret this."

"I already am."

Chapter Six

The good man brings good things out of the good stored up in his heart, and the evil man brings evil things out of the evil stored up in his heart. For out of the overflow of his heart his mouth speaks.

Luke Chapter 6, Verse 45

Six years ago.

It was a freezing January night when Maria Constantine first stumbled into the mission, and Reverend Jonathan Bishop's life, half-frozen and wearing nothing more than her underwear. Jonathan had just finished evening mass and was about to head home when he saw her, sobbing by the church doors. Even through the bloody gash on her forehead and the bruises on her arms and body, her natural beauty had captivated Jonathan. In his time living and working in this neighbourhood, he had seen enough to know the young woman was suffering from a drugs overdose. He rushed her to hospital and stayed with her, praying for her survival through that long night. In spite of her terrible condition, Maria was a fighter, and despite the doctor's claims she wouldn't survive the night, she pulled through. Seeing something in the young, fragile woman and knowing she had nowhere else to go, Jonathan invited her to stay with him until she was fully recovered.

Over the three months she lived in his house, Jonathan grew to admire and respect Maria's quiet inner strength, her compassion towards others. With his help, Maria was able to break free of her drug addiction and start taking control over her life, little by little. She got herself a job as a waitress, it was not much but it allowed her to move out of Jonathan's house and rent a nearby apartment. Jonathan stayed in constant contact with Maria despite repeated requests from his superiors to break off their 'friendship' as, according to them, it was not seemly to be so close to someone like Maria. What did they know? Maria had become an open doorway to a part of himself he never knew existed. Finally, the thing his superiors most feared happened; Jonathan and Maria fell in love. Torn between his commitment to his faith and his feelings for her, Jonathan battled long and hard against the inevitable choice he would be forced to make. In the end, Jonathan was a man, and prone to the same needs and desires as any man, be he saint or sinner. After many weeks of prayer and soul-searching, Jonathan decided to leave the church, but as in everything, wherever he went his faith would go with him. His faith was more than the church, more than his calling as a priest; it was his friend and his companion. Like his God and saviour, his faith never judged, never criticised his actions; it was simply there to give strength, guidance and love when he needed it.

Jonathan was on his way home from Church for the last time. The first thing he saw when he entered his house was Maria pinned against the wall by three men, while the other two men were busy smashing his possessions to bits. He did not even acknowledge Vincent Gonzalez; an infamous and particularly ruthless drug lord, who also happened to be the ex-boyfriend who had tried to kill Maria the night she stumbled into Jonathan's life. With all this going on, the only image Jonathan could see was the face of his father, and in his mind, he heard the words he had spoken the day Jonathan had left to join the priesthood. "Remember, Jonathan," his father had told him. "Anything good in your life - enjoy it, because you never know how long it will last."

The second Jonathan remembered his father's words, a strange madness overcame him. He started to laugh: he didn't know why, perhaps it was the fear, whatever it was, he kept laughing, even as the first blows struck him. He tried to hit back with the only weapon to hand, his fists: even though it went against his beliefs, his instinct for survival would not just let him surrender. His fists did him little good against men whose sole aim in life was to hurt people. All his attempts at defence earned him was a broken right arm, courtesy of a hulking Chinese man and the now blood-stained baseball bat he was holding. Through the beating, he never screamed, never begged, he just lay there and took whatever they had. The concept of mercy was beyond these men. Sooner or later, they would grow bored of his reluctance to die, and finish him with a bullet through his brain or a knife across his throat.

The method of his death was irrelevant to Jonathan; nothing mattered to him now. As he crashed to the floor, his thoughts turned to God and whether this was His way of punishing him for turning his back on the church. Someone's heel cracked against his skull and Jonathan realised that God had nothing to do with this.

That had been an hour ago. All through the beating, Jonathan had occasionally glanced up at his wall clock. It was a gift from his mother when he first opened the mission, now it was the only thing left undamaged in his house, in his life.

Maria, the only woman he ever truly loved, the woman who had cost him his mission and soon, his life, was dead. In one last act of defiance, and again finding the strength Jonathan had seen on their first meeting, he watched her grab a pair of scissors from the bedside table. She plunged the scissors into the chest of the sweaty pig of a man who was still busy trying to get his trousers off to finish what the others had started. She somehow rolled him off her and staggered off the bed. Jonathan cried out as Gonzalez, who had done nothing but watch until now, drew his gun and fired five times into his former girlfriend. Maria slumped to her knees, tears of relief flowing down her cheeks. She looked at Jonathan and mouthed the words 'I love you' before falling face first onto the floor in front of him. The beatings, the taunts, nothing mattered to Jonathan anymore. He was dead now, all they could do now was destroy the shell that was his body.

"Stand him up," ordered Vincent, snatching a can of gasoline from one of his men.

Two men grabbed hold of what was left of Jonathan and hoisted him to his feet. Jonathan remained silent, not even the merest groan or murmur left his ruined mouth.

Vincent walked up to Jonathan and grabbed his broken arm. Jonathan stiffened visibly, but said nothing.

"I'll say this for him, boys," said Vincent, opening the can of petrol handed to him by one of his men. "The priest sure knows how to take a kicking."

Vincent's comment was met with instant howls of laughter from his men, but still Jonathan remained silent.

"Seriously, Jonathan," smiled Vincent. "Can I call you Jonathan? I feel I can seeing that we've shared so much, you and I."

Not a word from the former priest.

"I've known men who have made killing their life, and yet at the end they begged like bitches, but not you, Jonathan, here you stand, not a word, nothing."

Vincent began pouring the petrol over Jonathan; it washed over him, burning into his wounds like acid. When he had finished, Vincent took a step back to admire his handiwork.

"Now come on, Jonathan, admit it, that's gotta hurt," said Vincent, opening a gold-plated case and taking a cigarette from it. "I'll make a deal with you, Jonathan, because you're a tough man and you took care of my Maria. One scream, that's all I want, I get that then I promise you, I'll make sure you die quick, one shot and it's all over. Come on, how about it, Reverend?"

Jonathan lifted his head and stared unblinking at Vincent, his jade-coloured eyes showing the lack of emotion behind them. There was no fear, no anger, just a cold indifference radiating from his stare. He watched Vincent take a lighter out of his pocket. In one flick, the bright flame was dancing in front of Vincent's smiling face as he lit his cigarette.

"Anything to say, Reverend?" he asked, blowing out several smoke rings towards Jonathan.

Jonathan drew himself upright from his stooped position. He looked around at each of the men in the room, and held each of their gazes for several seconds, engraving their images into his mind. Finally, his eyes came to rest on Gonzalez.

When Jonathan began to speak, every word was an immense effort. "You will be punished for your crimes seven times over."

"Thanks for the sermon, Rev," said Vincent flicking the cigarette at Jonathan's feet.

Jonathan welcomed the searing heat from the flames as they engulfed him, it washed away the thoughts of his loss. Maria had been taken from him, but his faith endured. God would find a way to punish them all for their crimes and when that time came, he would be the instrument of God's vengeance.

For he is the minister of God to thee for good. But if thou do that which is evil, be afraid; for he beareth not the sword in vain: for he is the minister of God, a revenger to execute wrath upon him that doeth evil.

Romans Chapter 13, Verse 4

Two Years Later.

Special Agent Dean Smith led the thirty-man team into the large dockside warehouse. The regular police, although there to provide cover, were kept out of harm's way. The last thing he needed was a bunch of flatfoots coming in and spoiling his career bust. At the request of his superior, and in an effort to promote good will between the Drugs Enforcement Agency and the police, he had been ordered to take Captain Paul Beauford along to see how the real professionals earned their pay.

Finally, after a five-year sting operation, Dean was about to nail the lid shut on Vincent Gonzalez. Inside the surrounded warehouse were Gonzalez, his enforcers, and a shipment of drugs with a street value of one hundred million dollars. Dean had taken every precaution, made sure every rule had been followed. Nothing was going to mess this up for him now. There was no way some slimy, deal-making lawyer was going to get Gonzalez off this time.

After trying to communicate with the occupants of the warehouse with loudhailers, and against the advice of Beauford, Dean and his men stormed the warehouse.

"This doesn't make any sense," said Dean, looking around at the sight that now greeted his confused eyes.

Dead bodies were everywhere. The stench of death was so strong that Dean did not need a coroner to tell him they had been dead for some time. Some of the victims had been shot, others stabbed. Dean could tell that whatever had taken place, it had struck fast and without warning, most of the men never getting a shot off. Dean and his men began to search for any wounded and found the barely breathing, blood-soaked body of Gonzalez in one of the upstairs offices. As Dean cradled the dying drug lord, Beauford at his side, he noticed the seven deep stab wounds on his chest and was amazed the man was still alive.

"Gonzalez, who did this to you?" demanded Dean.

Gonzalez was his only link to some of the major players in the drug world. It would have been his dream ticket for life, and now his hopes for a glorious career were fading away right along with Gonzalez.

Dean watched as Vincent opened his eyes and looked up at him, sheer terror in his face. "We killed him…we killed him, but he came back…he said he would…his face…his face was different, but his eyes…it was him…it was him…we tried to stop… but … he kept coming, oh God he kept…"

"Who?" yelled Dean. "You trying to tell me one man did all this?"

"It's no good," said Beauford. "He's dead."

Dean laid Gonzalez's body on the floor and stood up. "I don't buy it, one man took out fifteen heavily armed professional killers? No way, Gonzalez must have been tripping on his own product. It's got to be a hit team sent by one of the other cartels - Benet or Hymoto perhaps."

"I don't think so," Beauford said quietly.

"With all due respect, Captain, I've been working this case for years, these men may have been scum, but believe me, one guy, no matter how…"

"Before you spout off any more of your 'DEA knows more than us regular cops' bullshit, maybe you should take a look at this."

He handed him a folded and blood-stained piece of paper. "I found it inside Gonzalez's shirt."

Dean opened the paper and began reading the contents aloud. "Despair for I walk among you, and I am the right hand of vengeance."

"I don't buy it, one man couldn't do all this," said Dean.

Beauford looked around as the crime scene investigators began the grisly work of processing the scene. "If you want my advice, start stocking up on empty body bags and making space in the morgue, I get the feeling this guy is just getting started."

Miami, present day.

The two guards stood side by side. One watched the monitors relaying pictures from the closed circuit cameras placed throughout the mansion. The second was busy cleaning his gun. As he put the finishing touches on his cleaning job, he noticed a red dot resting under his colleague's Adam's apple. Before he could shout a warning, a steel crossbow bolt punched through his flak jacket, cleanly slicing a path through to his heart. Terror gripped him as blood filled his throat and mouth. With seconds of life left to him, he turned and staggered toward the console, his only thought now to trigger the alarm and gain a small measure of victory against his murderer. A second bolt hammered into his back as he stretched out for the alarm switch. The last thing he saw was his colleague slumped back against the chair, a crossbow bolt lodged deep in his right eye.

Lawrence Benet, head of one of the four largest drug syndicates in Miami, looked around the table at his dinner companions and biggest rivals. He of course knew the men by reputation.

Frankie 'the hatchet' Bartoli, a disgruntled and overweight Italian, sat shovelling the gourmet food into his mouth. Manners maketh the man, mused Benet. Beside Bartoli was Fernando Castillo, a frail man, who, despite his young age, was dying of cancer. The fact that Castillo was predicted to have only a few years left in him did not stop from becoming a powerful force within the drug world, as many of his rivals would attest to, were they still capable of speech. The final man completing the trio was Jin Hymoto, a man of medium height and build, who played the role of a polite Japanese businessman to perfection. However, when it came to ruthlessness, Hymoto won hands down. A relatively new player in Florida, he had made a place for himself in a very short time. Hymoto's outwardly pleasant manner was contrasted by the extreme acts of cruelty he was known to visit upon his enemies.

Hymoto stared straight ahead, nodding and smiling politely at Bartoli when the situation warranted it, all the while his eyes taking in every exit and the guards positioned at each door. Benet's admiration for the man grew.

The men ate their lavish meal in silence, each one lost in their own private thoughts and schemes. Only when dinner was over and the table cleared did the meeting begin.

"I trust you enjoyed the meal, gentlemen?" said Benet, taking a sip from his large glass of brandy.

A huge belch erupted from Bartoli, who was in the middle of wiping the remnants of lobster from his thick black beard.

"I'll take that as a yes from Mr. Bartoli," said Benet, no hint of sarcasm in his words.

Hymoto, who was seated at the other end of the table, rested his elbows on the surface and interlocked his fingers. "The dinner and the brandy were both excellent, and I compliment you on a well-trained kitchen staff. However, we have not allowed ourselves to be brought into this house without our own security merely to discuss your culinary expertise."

Benet pushed back his chair and got to his feet, still keeping hold of his brandy. "Very well, although I have never met any of you face to face before tonight, we each have two things in common." Benet looked around the room to make sure he held everyone's attention before continuing. "One, we all deal in illegal substances. Some of you, like myself, have diversified into other areas, such as gun trafficking, prostitution, and counterfeiting, to name but a few. However, the bulk of our revenue has been from our drug shipments."

"Get to the point, Benet," said Castillo coughing. He raised a handkerchief to his mouth. "Before I die of old age."

"That cancer of yours will eat your heart out long before old age does!" boomed Bartoli, breaking into a bout of raucous laughter.

"Watch yourself, fat man, otherwise I'll let some air out of that gut of yours."

Bartoli's face turned a deep shade of red and he vaulted out of his chair. "Try it, you lousy greaser, see how far you get."

Benet held up his hands for silence. "Gentlemen, if I wanted to enjoy bickering at its best, I would have paid a visit to the local nursery. We are wasting time we do not have."

Bartoli snorted, mouthed something under his breath and took his seat, all the while still scowling at his Mexican counterpart.

"I apologise for my outburst, Señor Benet, please continue."

Benet nodded his thanks to Castillo. "Our second shared interest is the reason we are here tonight. A man who, in the last six months, has cost each of us a fortune in destroyed shipments. A man who appears from nowhere, strikes and then vanishes without a trace. A man not one of us has been able to put a name to save the one he has christened himself with."

"The Reverend," said Hymoto quietly.

The thought of the marathon poker game being held in the barracks did not help Doug's sweep of the perimeter move any faster. He side-stepped the small mound of freshly dug earth and the anti-personnel mine buried beneath it. One of these days, he was going to take a wrong turn and wind up having his body parts sprayed all over the grounds like fertiliser.

In the distance, one of the other guards was waving frantically at him. As he got closer, Doug noticed someone was standing behind the guard. Even in the faint moonlight, he could see the guard's uniform was covered in blood, blood which was pouring from a deep gash across the man's throat.

"Sweet Jes…"

Doug collapsed, screaming, clutching his right leg where the bullet had shattered his knee. There was no sound, the shot fired had been from a silenced weapon.

Doug felt the cold tip of the gun jammed against his temple. "Please…please don't kill me."

"Where are the rest of the mines?"

"I can't…"

A second shot, this time removing the left kneecap. Doug tried to scream, but a gloved hand clamped over his mouth. Seconds later, the hand left his mouth. Doug bit back his pain, having a good idea what would happen if he screamed again. "In my left pocket…map…of mines…"

The gloved hand began rummaging through Doug's pocket. It took out the map that all the guards carried in case they forgot the location of the mines. Doug heard the hammer being pulled back on the gun, the silencer still pressed against his forehead.

"Please don't…please…I just work for them…"

"No one just works for evil," said the soft voice, as its owner pulled the trigger.

"The man's a damn ghost," put in Bartoli, guzzling what was left of his brandy. "No one's even laid eyes on this guy, no one still breathing anyway. Jesus, I wish he was working for me."

"As do we all I'm sure, but that is not an option. This man must be dealt with quickly, otherwise we risk turning one man's obsession into a crusade others will seek to finish should he be killed. And that, I think we can all agree, would be bad for business."

"Some of my men are superstitious, Señor Benet and this Reverend has them scared. They say he cannot be killed, that he is a messenger from God sent to punish us."

"A colourful but ridiculous theory," said Benet, trying not to sound too derogatory.

"Is it?" said Castillo. "Do you know they call him Dios Del Asesino?"

"What the hell does that mean?" asked Bartoli.

"God of Assassins."

If not for the huge sum of money he was being paid, Martinson would have told Benet where to stick his job. They were just going to spend the night patrolling these roofs waiting for this master killer to appear, a killer who probably didn't even exist.

"The Reverend," he said to himself. "My six-year-old could come up with a better name than…"

Martinson's sentence was cut short, along with his breath, as a garrotte was slipped around his neck. He tried to slide his fingers into the garrotte, but it was no good. His back arched as his legs were now left dangling several inches above the floor. His vision blurring, Martinson struggled to free himself but the powerful grip that held him had no intention of relinquishing its hold.

"Who…are…you?" Martinson forced out the question as his vision finally gave out and the darkness closed in.

"I am wrath."

"This is exactly what I'm talking about," said Benet. "This climate of fear breeds carelessness, making it all the easier for this Reverend to go about his work." Benet began to walk around the table. "We must find this lunatic and make an example of him, before he can do any more damage to our finances and our reputations."

"To label this man as insane is a mistake," said Hymoto. "He is skilled, patient and utterly ruthless in his endeavours. To us, he is a costly inconvenience; to him, we are a crusade."

"What's your point, jap?" said Bartoli, refilling his glass for a fourth time.

"My point, Mr. Bartoli, is that given the Reverend's past history, I think he may come here tonight."

Benet laughed at the statement. "Hymoto, believe me, if the Reverend did entertain such a notion, it would be his first and last mistake."

"You seem pretty sure of yourself," said Castillo. "What are you not telling us?"

Benet smiled; it was a smile full of smug self-satisfaction. "I already anticipated an attack by this Reverend tonight, and have taken precautions for such an eventuality. I can assure you, we are perfectly safe."

As Benet finished, a deafening explosion shook the room, plunging it into near-darkness.

"Impossible, someone's disabled the generator," said Benet, taking out his gun.

The other men followed suit, drawing their weapons. Benet pulled out his mobile and pressed the speed dial button. Jack Wild, his head of security was two seconds in answering.

"Sir, we have a problem," said Wild.

"A solvable one, I trust?"

"I've just reached the roof, all of the men are dead."

"What about the patrols?"

"No one's answering their radios."

"Call out the rest of the men," Benet told him. "Surround the house; no one goes in or out."

Silence.

"Wild, did you hear me?"

"Sorry, sir," said Wild finally, his voice sounding strained. "I thought I heard something. It must have been the...no...no...Christ no..."

Benet watched in horror as his head of security crashed through the glass ceiling. Everyone dived for cover to avoid being hit by flying shards of glass. Wild ploughed into the dinner table with a sickening thud, the crossbow bolt jutting from his chest displaying the cause of death. Everyone in the room opened fire at the ceiling, bringing more glass down upon them. They continued firing until they were forced to stop to reload.

"It's him," said Castillo, making the sign of the cross over his chest. "The Reverend, he's here."

"If he was up on the roof, one of us must have got him," said Bartoli.

The round of bullets that caught Bartoli full in the chest told them otherwise. His bullet-ridden body was propelled backwards through the window. As everyone's attention was momentarily distracted by Bartoli's final moments, a man, dressed in a black, two-piece collarless suit, dropped through the shattered ceiling, firing from two 9mm Uzi pistols killing a guard instantly. As he landed, the Reverend span and fired at Hymoto, who anticipating the move, was already leaping for cover. Three more guards ran into the room. The Reverend threw something small at the entranceway. He ran down the length of the table as the device erupted at the feet of the guards, throwing them in all directions. One of the guards flew into Hymoto and they both crashed to the floor. The only words Benet could use to describe the Reverend, who weaved and fired with apparent unconcern at the amount of lead flying in his direction, was controlled chaos. Even as he ran out of ammo, Benet saw no panic in the Reverend; he just pressed a button on the handles of each weapon then threw them at Castillo's feet.

Both guns exploded, showering the Italian with shrapnel. Castillo slumped screaming to the floor, where he lay twitching until the screaming stopped and he was still.

Trapped under the dead guard, Hymoto watched the Reverend go about his work. The man was every bit as awesome as his reputation. He saw him produce a semi-automatic pistol, moments after killing Castillo, and set about finishing off any remaining threats. It was then Hymoto realised something. Looking around the room, he saw the body of Castillo, and he had already seen Bartoli killed, but there was no sign of Benet.

The gunfire ceased and an uncomfortable stillness fell over the room. Hymoto risked a glance from where he was: the room was empty except for dead bodies. He stretched out his hand and retrieved his gun. Slowly, he pulled himself from under the dead guard and got up. He surveyed the carnage around him. In the space of a few of minutes, one man had reduced a heavily-guarded building to a killing field.

"Did you think I had forgotten you?" said a voice from behind Hymoto.

Clutching the gun to his chest, Hymoto took a deep cleansing breath and with it exhaled his fear. This Reverend was a man, after all, and every man, no matter how fearsome, could be killed.

Hymoto span round, firing. The Reverend dived right, rolled and came up firing his crossbow. The bolt smashed into Hymoto's skull, killing him instantly.

Lawrence Benet watched his mansion from the relative safety of his limo. Sitting snugly in the palm of his hands was a detonator. Even with the amount of planning put into this operation, Benet was sure something would go wrong but, fortunately for him, everything had gone exactly as planned. Thanks to the timely and anticipated intervention of the Reverend, his three major rivals had been removed, leaving their organisations ripe for take-over.

When the shooting in the dining room had started, Benet had headed for the hidden passage leading from the dining room to the mansion's grounds. As the only survivor, he would be free to create his own story regarding tonight's events.

"Time to tie up the loose ends," he said, pressing the button on the detonator.

Benet watched with satisfaction as his five-million-dollar mansion exploded into a mass of fire and wind. Flaming debris spewed out in all directions, some of it landing near the limo.

Benet was not pained by the loss of his house. A new property had already been commissioned and would be ready by the end of the year. In the meantime, he had more than enough properties to choose from.

"Rest in pieces, Reverend," said Benet, turning the ignition key.

"His eyes shall see his destruction, and he shall drink of the wrath of the Almighty."

Lawrence looked in his rear view mirror. "Impossible."

"Inevitable," said the Reverend, rising up from the back seat, clutching a serrated blade.

"So close," whispered Benet.

The Reverend drew his knife sharply across Benet's throat, the arterial spray splattering across the windscreen.

Benet slumped forward against the steering wheel, clutching at the wound, the life draining from him.

The Reverend leant back in his seat, placed the knife beside him and closed his eyes. Lifting a small silver crucifix from its place around his neck, he held it tightly as he bowed his head. He prayed Benet and the others would find forgiveness, for they would find none with him.

How long? The Reverend asked himself. How long could he walk this path of retribution he had set for himself? The evil of man was colossal, and he could see no end to it.

He remembered the message he had received from a friend, earlier that same day. Stephanie needed help and she needed him to come at once. Perhaps after he had helped her, he would allow himself a little rest.

Several cries for help from men making their way out of the burning mansion drew his attention. Leaving the blade, he drew his guns and left the car. His rest would have to wait, for now there were more in need of judgment.

Chapter Seven

Luther was not surprised to find the media vultures already circling as he drove up to the main gates. Several television stations were already running live broadcasts from their vans. Cameramen were jostling for the best position to zoom in on the murder house. There were four policemen at the entrance gate, who were being hounded by reporters no doubt trying to gain access to the grounds. Nothing like a good murder to bring out the best in the press, Luther concluded.

Even in death, there was no dignity for the victims, no escape from the media's obsession with relating every gory detail to an audience who thrived on such grisly affairs. Luther did not bother opening the car window as he stopped in front of the gates, giving the media the exact measure of respect he believed they deserved.

A battalion of reporters descended on his car. All the questions, demands and accusations aimed at Luther were lost in a flurry of garbled words and shouting. Luther beeped the car's horn twice while ignoring the fists being pounded against his window. Upon catching sight of the United Nations identity sticker plastered to the windshield, a policeman wasted no time in activating the gate mechanism, whilst his colleagues fought to clear a path for the car through the press. Pulling up alongside the policeman, Luther pressed a button by his gear stick and the window on the driver's side slid downwards. He flashed a grin at the policeman, together with his TORCH security identification.

The dark-haired police officer, obviously eager to please, offered Luther a crisp salute.

"No need for that, Officer," said Luther. "Has Dr. Monroe arrived?"

"Oui, Monsieur," said the young officer cheerily. "As per your orders, she has been given full access to the crime scene."

Only a rookie could look that happy about being here. The joys of ignorance, mused Luther, as he shifted the gear stick into first. He felt sorry for the young officer, because one day that easygoing manner would be replaced with a sarcastic, almost fatalistic view of the job he performed. The price of justice was always hardest on those who fought to uphold it.

"Make sure none of these 'distinguished' members of the press get into the grounds," Luther told the officer. "If they do, you have my permission to shoot on sight."

The policeman seemed unsure how to take the command.

"Just kidding," said Luther, not holding out much hope for the young man's future in law enforcement.

Leaving the officers to deal with the mass of reporters, Luther drove up the path towards the darkened house. In the distance, he saw the camera flashes from the forensic team, and the luminous outline of yellow police tape. There was nothing like visiting a murder scene in the pouring rain at four thirty in the morning to reaffirm one's belief in the human race.

Luther stopped the car and got out. As he ducked under the tape, he caught his first glimpse of Kathryn. She was crouched beside two corpses mutilated beyond recognition. Next to her stood a policeman, who was attempting to shield her from the rain with an umbrella.

Not being waif thin, some would describe Kathryn as bordering on overweight; not that it mattered, she looked good for it in Luther's opinion. She wore a baggy, dark blue, hooded fleece top and jeans, which, like her trainers, were covered in mud and grass. Luther was glad to see her taste in clothing had not changed. When she had worked with Luther at TORCH, she had always opted for a more casual dress code, despite disapproving glances from her superiors.

Luther knew he should say something, but he could tell she was engrossed in her work.

"Are you actually going to say hello or are you just going to carry on staring at my ass?" Kathryn turned away from the corpses, got to her feet and walked over to Luther. She cocked her head to one side. Luther noted the blond and copper highlights that streaked her dark brown hair; they were new. Luther remembered how it usually took her a couple of weeks before she decided she was bored and wanted a change. "Hi, Sir Lancelot, long time," she said, brushing some of her hair to one side, revealing a pair of large and inquisitive brown eyes.

Luther stiffened at the name. "I thought you might have grown out of calling me that."

"What and miss winding you up? Never."

Even though she was a well-respected authority in the fields of Criminal Psychology and Behavioural Studies, Kathryn still liked to get her kicks from pushing people's buttons and watching their reactions.

"Been here long?"

Kathryn shrugged, stuffing her hands into her pockets. "Long enough to know you're late as usual, I wonder if you'll ever understand the concept of timekeeping?"

"Yeah, I'm…"

"I know, you're sorry," said Kathryn. "Don't worry about it. I didn't expect you to have changed that much in three years."

She gave Luther a quick sideways look that he remembered from old. The reunion was over; it was time to go to work. He turned to the officer holding the umbrella, sneaking a quick look at his badge to get a name.

"Sergeant Bonnise, why don't you head off home? We can take it from here."

"Very good, Monsieur," said Bonnise, saluting and then setting off down the path.

Once Bonnise was out of earshot, Luther and Kathryn headed back to the corpses. Luther tried to hide the horror and repulsion at what he saw. He had never been very good at crime scenes. The jagged scar at the base of his skull was a constant reminder of that fact. He had received the wound after his head struck a chair when he fainted during his first autopsy.

"Not a pretty sight," said Kathryn, who was now kneeling beside him. "We need to be quick; the coroners have already taken the bodies from the house."

"What have you got?"

"Forensics will give us a full report once they get back to the lab." Kathryn pointed at the corpses. "These two were found by their backup unit, who were covering the rear of the house at the time of the murders. According to their statements, they radioed for help after hearing screams and gunshots from inside the house. Their superiors contacted the police, whilst they entered the building after finding their mates here cut to pieces. They found John and Mary Carson dead in the upstairs room."

"Time of death on these two?"

"No confirmation on that yet, but the coroner reckons that it might have been a matter of minutes before they were found."

The implications of Kathryn's statement were not lost on Luther. "Minutes?" he said, more to himself than anyone else. "And the backup unit saw no one when they got round to the front of the house."

Kathryn shook her head.

"But that's…"

"Impossible," finished Kathryn. She twisted round and gestured to the gates, where there was still a mass of reporters. "I spoke to the backup team; they say there was no way anyone could have approached the house without being seen or heard."

"Well, someone managed it," said Luther. "Got any history on these two?"

"Both were ex-military," said Kathryn. "Not the sort of guys you just sneak up on."

"What's your impression?"

"That someone approached two highly trained soldiers, face on, across open ground and killed them both before they could get off a shot or call for help."

"Unlikely?"

"Very," said Kathryn, her face, becoming pale and ashen.

"Hey, it's ok," said Luther, placing a hand on her shoulder. "Do you want to take a breather?"

Saying nothing in response to the question, Kathryn set off for the darkened house. Luther gestured to the nearby coroner's assistant that it was ok to move the bodies, before heading up to the entrance himself.

Kathryn stared at the gaping entranceway to the house and the flight of steps leading up to the second floor. She was breathing heavily, desperately trying to suppress the impending panic attack.

You can do this: you can do this.

She repeated the words over and over again in her mind, trying to believe them.

To Kathryn, fear was an entity that could be both felt and seen. Staring into the darkness ahead, she shuddered, sensing the fear around her, clawing at her soul. She sensed its desperation, its need to crawl inside her, casting horrific images of what awaited her. She bit down hard on her bottom lip until she tasted blood on her tongue. A spasm of pain followed, but instead of allowing it to subside, she clung to it, anchoring her mind to the sensation. Pain was good; it gave her focus.

She imagined what it must have felt like to have ripped two human beings apart. To have feasted on their fears as their lives ebbed away. The last time had been three years ago. She was more focused back then, more in control of her emotions, able to channel the horror, to use it. She wished she had never heard the phone. Luther should never have asked her to do this.

"You don't have to do this," said Luther.

Kathryn did not turn her head when she spoke, her eyes staring straight ahead. She gradually raised her hands, examining each of them in turn.

"Their blood washes over me, through me," she spoke softly, but there was a menace behind each word. "No matter. I wear it like a cloak; it warms me as it did them. I remove their foulness from my fingers." Kathryn began to rub her hands together over the spot where, according to the information she had, pieces of what was thought to be human skin were found. She told herself that all she was doing was role-playing the murders, using the information. The knowledge gave her little comfort. The stench of evil was a lot harder to remove once you were stained with it.

She wiped her right hand across her mouth, revealing a thin smile.

"I was right, their blood tastes warm." She ran a finger down the side of her neck. "They lay there saying nothing; they should thank me for what I have done."

"What have you done?"

"I don't know," said Kathryn, sounding more like herself. "But I do know he gutted them like this for a reason."

"He?"

"Whoever did this was male."

"But..."

Kathryn was already moving again, further into the gloomy and silent house. Luther pulled on a pair of latex gloves and took out his flashlight; Kathryn placed her hand over it.

"No light, not yet."

She set off down the hallway, casting her eyes over the framed certificates lining the walls, all of which had been smashed. They were all for John Carson, all a trail of successes, moments of glory frozen in time.

"Fool," Kathryn's voice becoming deeper, more guttural as she slipped back into character. "I do not need to show others my success. I am beyond pride, beyond vanity."

Kathryn wondered how many of the destructive thoughts she had were from the killers she sought to understand, and how many from her own fractured psyche.

"You disgust me. The only gift I can offer you now is oblivion." Kathryn stopped and stared open-mouthed.

Luther came up behind her, this time turning on his flashlight. "My God."

Along the wall, illuminated by the flashlight, were several shapes and symbols scrawled in blood. Kathryn pulled a small digital camera from her pocket and snapped off a few shots.

"Are these symbols occult?" asked Luther.

Kathryn nodded.

"I don't want to speculate until I've consulted my research, but they look familiar. I just can't place where I've seen them before. Once we've been upstairs, I'll come back and take a better look, see if something jogs my memory."

Together, they walked to the foot of the stairs. Kathryn started to walk up to the first floor. She was halfway up when she stopped, turned and stared at the open door.

"You ok?" said Luther, from behind.

"Something doesn't feel right about this place."

"It's not supposed to. Come on, let's get this over with."

Making up his mind not to dwell on his unease, Luther followed Kathryn up to the first floor. Neither of them heard the faint laughter

Fallen Heroes

that faded into the night as the rain outside grew louder.

63

Chapter Eight

I wait.

I watch.

I listen.

They tell me I must be swift, deadly, and act without mercy. So I strike like the fiercest of storms, and then back to the abyss, back to a world of nightmares and oblivion. I know I once walked upon this Earth, but my memories are hidden from me, shrouded in darkness. Who I am, how I came to be, are all mysteries to me. If they knew of my ritual, I would be punished. I do not seek their anger, for without them I am nothing, just another monstrosity. I cannot help myself. After my work is complete, I do not fade, I watch and wait, after all, what good is the game if I cannot see my opponents? It is not long before the police arrive, then those who seek to learn more of my work so that they may tell others of its greatness. I watch them fight and argue. I move freely among them. They peer through the gates, squabbling, like their young. It is now as always I feel the need, the urge to cleanse myself of the filth surrounding me. Humans! Even to whisper the name causes my tongue to blister. It has been hundreds of years since I was one, that much I do remember, but now the thought of my former human existence sickens me. I see their wide eyes and their warm bodies, and I cry out in disgust, but they do not hear me. How easily I could rip the spine from the overweight bald man attempting to bribe the policeman guarding the gates. The joy I would feel as my hands pierced the lungs of the red-faced photographer, who stands inches from my outstretched hand. As I move past him, he is no longer red-faced, his face is pale and he feels cold. He draws his coat tighter. It is not the cold or the rain, it is fear you feel, stark, unforgiving fear: it is me you feel.

There is nothing of worth for me here. Once more, I leap over the fence and run towards the house. The rain feels good; though I have no real substance, save when I strike, it gives me comfort to imagine it pouring down my face and into my open mouth. Although nothing in this world can harm me, it is good sometimes to taste nature's fury.

I crouch some distance from the house and watch the two humans standing by the entrance to the house. I move closer and see a man and woman moving up the stairs. Their fear flies to me like a dying lover seeking a last embrace. The woman senses me, her fierce gaze bores into me. I have seen enough. I will not strike now, I will return and tell those whom I serve what I have seen. I concentrate and shield myself further. Finally, they doubt their eyes and continue up the stairs. If only they understood. There is more to the world than what can be seen and heard. There is me.

"Relax, Kelly," suggested Clancy.

Kelly walked over to the drinks cabinet, which lined the wall of the large hotel suite. He snatched a half-full bottle of gin from one of the shelves.

"It's easy for you to say, chief," said Kelly. He filled his glass with gin, downed the contents and then poured himself another.

"Hey, go easy on that stuff," said a tall, dark skinned man who, like Clancy and the others in the room, was wearing dark blue overalls with the words 'Repair Service ' emblazoned on the back.

"Back off, Hammond," warned Kelly, fixing an angry stare at the man.

Hammond appeared un-phased by the threat. He continued sharpening the combat knife he held with the aid of a small whetstone.

Kelly, pointed his empty glass at Hammond, like an accusing finger.

"Hey, I'm talking to you!"

Hammond drew back some of his shoulder length dreadlocks, revealing an ugly scar running from the tip of his left eyebrow down to his mouth. He laughed and then went back to his knife sharpening.

The other men in the room, who had been engaged in their own preparations turned to watch the drama unfold.

"Come on, Kelly, knock it off, mate," put in a slim, tough-looking, blond-haired man shouldering an M16, he was stood by one of the windows. His cockney accent along with Kelly's Irish and Hammond's deep southern drawl gave the group a definite international flavour.

"Stay out of this, Stony," said Kelly, without bothering to look in the Englishman's direction. "Unless you want a piece of me."

"I wouldn't know what to do with it," Stony replied, before returning to his window vigil.

"Anyone else here have a problem with my drinking?" said Kelly, spreading his arms out to either side.

No one answered.

Kelly walked over to Hammond, who was sitting on a wooden chair that had been reversed, allowing him to rest his large forearms on the chair's back

"Seems like it's just you with a problem."

This time, Hammond stopped what he was doing and looked up at Kelly. Clancy could not read anything from the big man's posture, which was never a good sign. Dammit, like he did not have enough things to worry about.

"Looks to me," said Hammond, staring at the bottle Kelly was holding, "that the only one here with a problem is you."

Kelly dropped the bottle and his right hand instinctively flew to his holster, a second later, the tip of his gun was inches from the bridge of Hammond's nose.

"How about now," Kelly sneered. "You still got a problem?"

"No," said Hammond, his eyes narrowing. "Now we both have one."

Clancy glanced downwards to see the tip of Hammond's combat knife resting against Kelly's groin.

"You so much as breathe; little man and you'll be singing soprano, you hear?"

"And you'll be missing a forehead."

They held their positions, each one appearing to wait for the other to make the first move. Clancy strode across the room to the two men.

Removing his own gun from its holster. Clancy folded his arms, ensuring the gun was clearly visible. He looked at both men before speaking.

"You have three seconds to start acting like professionals before things get real messy in here. It's your call."

It did not even come to Clancy beginning his countdown, before the two men lowered their weapons. Satisfied the situation was resolved, Clancy holstered his gun and snatched the glass out of Kelly's hands, pouring the remaining contents out onto the floor.

"No more booze."

Kelly nodded begrudgingly. Clancy placed the glass back in the cabinet. Where had it all gone so wrong?

At the beginning, their objectives were clear ...payback, pure and simple retribution, now everything was different because they were different.

They had served their country, even if some of them were not native to its soil, obeyed their superiors, and always remained loyal.

In the name of freedom and to protect the United States from her enemies, they had committed atrocities that had dammed them forever and tainted them all.

Every time Clancy's morals caused him to question an order, the only reply he received from those in command was 'the price of freedom is often high'. Clancy was amazed how easily he had been convinced back then. It was nothing more than crap to feed the foot soldiers, the cannon fodder. The suits in Washington did not give a damn about who lived and who died. They never lost a night's sleep worrying about all the innocent deaths they had ordered: no, to them they were statistics, flags on a map, representing places they would never visit.

Clancy and his men bought into the bullshit, the fake flag waving and off they marched to another bloodbath, another massacre.

After years of faithful service and unquestioned loyalty, Clancy and his men discovered the most brutal rule in war: everyone is expendable.

In a single, dispassionate moment, their lives were deemed acceptable losses by those whose only concept of warfare was computer-assisted strategies.

On a mission to assassinate an arms dealer, they arrived to find that said arms dealer had, only hours earlier, secured a deal with the CIA to pass on valuable information on terrorist activity in that area. With the government taking on the role of Judas, Clancy and his team were sold out. Details of the mission were passed to the arms dealer, and an armed security force was on hand to ensure Clancy and his team were given a fitting reception.

It was only thanks to Clancy's leadership that he and his team were able to escape their captors and flee into the jungle. After a bloody game of hide and seek which lasted fourteen days, and claimed the lives of more than half of Clancy's team, the survivors made it back to the States.

They were alive, but now men without a cause. Like the Ronin warriors of legend who wandered the Earth master-less, Clancy and his men embraced a new career. They sold themselves on the mercenary marketplace. Friends, allies, all were now potential targets; no one was spared.

As the years passed, Clancy saw the atrocities they had committed begin to take its toll. Kelly, who had been with him since the beginning, was the most affected. The nightmares, excessive drinking and bouts of unnecessary anger like the one Clancy had just witnessed were all symptoms. Another year, at the most, and Kelly would become a dangerous liability to the team. When the time came, Clancy promised himself he would take care of the situation, permanently. Secretly, he hoped Kelly would stop a bullet before he would have to face that time.

"Wheels is here," said Stony.

Two blasts sounded from a car horn outside.

"Time to move, people," said Clancy. He grabbed his automatic rifle and placed it inside a large duffel bag.

No words passed between the others as they checked their weapons before concealing them and heading out of the room in single file.

Clancy led them out of the hotel and round to a secluded side street, where a grey van was waiting for them. Clancy poked his head through the van's side window, where the youngest member of their unit, Boris, or 'Wheels' as he liked to be called, was waiting. Always eager to please,

Wheels possessed driving skills rivalling any rally driver. His bleached white hair, which gave him his distinctive albino look, was safely tucked away under a navy blue baseball cap. However, the silver nose stud and earrings were not so easy to miss.

"Any problems?"

"No, sir," said Wheels, traces of a German accent showing through his forced American. "Everything was, as Stony would say, a piece of piss."

"Good. Get ready to move out."

Wheels nodded. Clancy walked round to the back of the van. The men were seated inside, checking their weapons and equipment, whilst going over their assigned duties. "Gentlemen, I want no unnecessary civilian causalities, but our employers must have that disk back or we don't get paid. Are we clear?"

"Yes, sir," the men answered back in unison.

"Our target is a dangerous man. He makes a move you don't like, take him down."

"Yes, sir!"

Clancy said nothing more. He slammed the van doors shut and made his way round to the passenger side of the van. Wheels was already starting the engine when Clancy climbed in.

"Let's move."

The van pulled out and set off down the street. Clancy noted the speedometer creeping up and reminded Wheels to keep to the speed limit. They could do without attracting any unnecessary attention before they reached their destination.

Clancy hoped The Hand had enjoyed his stay of execution in Japan, because he was about to discover it was a short-lived reprieve.

Four years of peaceful and uneventful academia. Fours year of swearing never to return to TORCH. Kathryn would not play the game anymore.

She envied those who would never see what she saw, save in their nightmares, shielded from the horrors they found there by the simple act of waking up.

Kathryn's nightmares were inspired by the real terrors of her former work; murder, rape, mutilation, they were not just headlines in the morning paper. Each headline brought with it past images that were burned into her subconscious. The faces of those she could not save. Kathryn saw them all, felt their pain, their frustration. Why? Why them? Each time the answer was different. A different craving that could only be satisfied with blood.

But in spite of the horror and bloodshed, she was still drawn to darkness, to the need to know why.

Fours years ago, she had left TORCH in an attempt to preserve what little of her sanity still remained. She turned to writing and researching the criminal mind in the hope of turning her talent to a different, less dangerous use.

"Here we are," said Luther, wrapping his hand around the door handle.

"Wait. Let me."

Luther stepped aside. Kathryn moved to the door and pushed it open. The bedroom was shrouded in darkness save for the occasional flash of red and blue from the police sirens outside, and the beam from Luther's flashlight.

Kathryn entered, switching on her own torch as she did so. Blood was everywhere. The lavish cashmere carpet, the blue satin sheets, all had been transformed into a crimson mosaic of blood and gore.

Kathryn tried to stem the imagery that was flooding her mind; the torment inflicted upon the sleeping couple. It was hopeless: the savage but beautifully efficient brutality almost overwhelmed her. Time to concentrate. There would be time enough later to deal with the effects of what she had seen tonight.

"They did not go quietly."

"I take it you're referring to those." Luther was pointing at several shell casings strewn about the bedroom floor. The forensic team had already been through the bedroom and noted the position of the shell casings; they had left them unmoved.

Luther crouched down, picked up one of the casings and turned it over in his hand.

"This is special ordnance. Armour piecing."

"What's a lawyer need such serious firepower for?" asked Kathryn.

"Whatever he needed it for, it wasn't enough."

Kathryn stared at the bed. It was here the bodies were discovered, lying spread-eagled on the bed. According to those first on the scene, the Carsons had been ripped open from just below the navel up to the throat. An even more disturbing aspect of the crime was the apparent removal of Carson's internal organs, though she would wait for the autopsy to confirm this.

Walking round the king-sized bed, Kathryn's eyes never left the spot where the bodies had lain. She stopped when she reached the other side. Once there, she continued to stare for a few more seconds, then she looked over at the door and then down at where she was standing. Finally, she lifted her head and locked her eyes with Luther's patient yet questioning gaze.

"He was paying them homage," she said quietly. "He respected them."

"Carson was butchered like cattle. I wouldn't call that respectful, would you?"

The look on Luther's face told Kathryn her colleague was still unconvinced. She went over to him. "Look at the facts, Luther."

"What facts?"

"The guards outside were virtually torn apart, battered beyond recognition, right?"

"So?"

Kathryn knew it was Luther's nature to never accept anything at face value, it was a good trait, but it was also an annoying one.

"He kills two well-trained soldiers in seconds. He's angry, it was too easy, there was no challenge. He goes mad and tears apart what was left of them."

Kathryn gestured to the bed. "And here, in the last place he expects, he finds a challenge and he pays them respect for giving him that gift. Yes, the bodies were mutilated, but their faces were unmarked, their eyes were left open to see their enemy."

Luther rubbed his chin. "I suppose that sort of hangs together."

That must have hurt, thought Kathryn, but she refrained from voicing her opinions.

"Look at the spread of the ammo casings," said Luther, changing the subject. "Looks to me like our lawyer friend was firing blind."

"I know," said Kathryn. She began opening the draws of the dressing table behind her. "It's almost as if…as if."

"What?"

Kathryn knew Luther was not going to like her reply one bit, but then that was pretty much par for the course between the two of them, even after all these years. "As if he knew something was in the room, but somehow couldn't see it."

"Right," scoffed Luther, his voice laced with sarcasm. "You want me to walk into Chardon's office and tell him we're looking for an invisible serial killer."

If it was not for the victims already in her head demanding someone grant them justice, Kathryn would have left there and then. She glared at Luther for a second or two and then calmed herself down before speaking. There was no use flying off the handle at him. Luther had been one of the more tolerant agents she had worked with when it came to her 'leaps of intuition', as she liked to think of them.

"There are a lot of things I'm not even close to understanding about the killer yet." As Kathryn spoke, she lifted a large black organiser from the bottom of the middle drawer of the bedside table. "But I am convinced these murders are ritualistic and have been influenced by the occult."

"And the second thing?"

It took a moment for Kathryn to reply to Luther's question. She was far more concerned with a particular page within the organiser she was holding. "Whatever our friend may be, he's no serial killer."

"How...?"

"Can I be so sure?" said Kathryn, finishing her friend's sentence. "Our friend would be better described as an assassin as opposed to a serial killer. He just enjoys what he does."

Kathryn saw the utter disbelief in Luther's eyes, but pressed on regardless. "Those first on the scene stated the other rooms were ransacked as if the killer were looking for something, why bother if you've just come here to go on a crazed killing spree? Nothing was reported taken from any of the other rooms; besides the Carsons' organs, the killer took no trophies, nothing that would allow him to relive the experience. That doesn't fit a usual profile for the majority of serial killer cases."

"But couldn't the Carsons' organs be considered trophies?"

"True," agreed Kathryn, not lifting her eyes from the book. "But I think once the police have done a thorough examination of the grounds, they'll find what's left of the organs. Our friend didn't need them; the act of removing them was enough to honour his victims."

"What are you saying?"

"I'm saying maybe the Carsons weren't the real target," said Kathryn, tossing the organiser over to Luther. "Take a look at yesterday's page."

There, clearly marked in black felt tip pen under yesterday's date were the words:

Jason home from uni, pick up from station.

"You reckon he came to kill this Jason?"

"I know it's a wild theory."

"You're dammed right it's wild. Let's just assume this nut is some kind of sick cross between a serial killer and a hitman, why couldn't the target have been the Carsons?"

"You dragged me into this mess because you wanted my insight, and I'm telling you this boy is in danger."

Luther and Kathryn shared a look for a moment. Kathryn knew he was trying to decide just how damaged she still was. At last, Luther sighed and took out his mobile. She listened to the brief conversation but was unsure what Luther was trying to find out.

"It seems our Mr. Carson and his wife had an adopted son studying in England," he said, after hanging up.

"Jason, right?"

"Jason Chen," said Luther, closing the organiser. "It looks like..."

Luther became silent. He was just staring into the empty drawer.

"What, what is it?"

"The window," he shouted. "Go!"

Kathryn watched Luther slide across the room at such a speed, it appeared as if he were gliding on a sheet of ice. Reaching the bedside table, Luther lifted the table with both hands and hurled it though one of the bedroom windows before setting off towards it, Kathryn two steps behind him.

Kathryn had no idea what was happening but Luther's flair for spotting danger had saved her life in the past, so she was willing to trust it now. The table crashed headlong through the window and out into the torrential downpour outside. Behind it, both Luther and Kathryn dived through the shattered second-floor window. Time froze and caught its breath. A second later, the first floor of the house exploded in a blazing cataclysm of flames and debris. A silence followed only to be broken by the crackling of the inferno that now raged through the top floors of the house.

From his vantage point inside his patrol car, Sgt Bonnise watched the carnage unfold like a silent melodrama. Police cars and officers were already racing up to the house.

"Too late," said Bonnise, watching the mad exodus towards the house.

Placing the detonator back in the glove compartment, Bonnise flipped open his mobile. He dialled the number he had been given, and waited.

"Is it done?" asked a voice.

"Yes."

"Excellent," said the voice. "Of course, I will ensure that no stone is left unturned. I will do everything to ensure this senseless double murder does not go unpunished."

If it were not for the money now winging its way to his private account, Bonnise might have felt sorry for murdering the two TORCH agents. He dismissed the emotion as a brief lapse in character. In less than five minutes, the laptop beside him would register the transfer was complete, and he would have one hundred thousand ways with which to appease the remainder of his conscience.

Chapter Nine

It had been a warm summer's evening in June over twenty years ago when Philippe Chardon first heard the voices. He was naked. The breeze from the open window in his room enveloped his body, allowing a temporary respite from the oppressive heat. He carefully climbed up onto the chair. He did not want to risk a twisted ankle, not now. He noted the absurdity of the thought as he slipped the noose over his head. Suicide: Philippe wondered why it had taken him so long to come to such a simple solution to his problems.

He tightened the noose until the coarse rope began to affect his breathing, and then he kicked the chair away from him. Instead of the release he so desperately sought, Philippe found himself frozen in mid-air unable to move.

"What's happening?" he called out. "Am I dead?"

A blast of cold air struck him, and in a heartbeat summer was transformed into the deepest winter. It was then he heard the voices. At first, they sounded like a thousand whispers, it was only when he concentrated that he began to distinguish one overriding voice.

Why, Philippe?

A blinding pain shot through Philippe's mind. Images from his past flashed through his mind's eye. His birth, a troubled and friendless childhood. A young man unable to come to terms with his mother's death, or his father's hatred toward him. The pain was now, and once more, Philippe was aware of the voices.

We have seen your pain, Philippe and we share it, but self-destruction is not the answer. We can heal your pain. We will be both mother and father to you, we will show you the true nature of the world.

They were right; suicide was no longer an option. He had touched the heavens, what peace could death offer him now?

"Tell me what I must do?"

Serve.

Sgt. Bonnise tried to gather his thoughts as his car sped away from the crime scene. He remembered staring through his binoculars in disbelief. Agent Washington and Dr Monroe had survived the explosion. They were now surrounded by a swarm of police and paramedics, making the use of the sniper rifle laying on the backseat unfeasible.

Bonnise replayed the events in his mind, trying to understand what went wrong. One of them had opened the drawer containing the diary and set off the sensor he had placed within it. He allowed them a minute or two before he detonated the bomb, to ensure they were both in the room. The notion of them discovering the device in time was ludicrous, and yet, he had seen the proof.

The phone on the seat next to him started to ring; he gingerly reached across and picked it up, knowing all too well who the caller was.

"Hello?"

"I've just received a call. It seems your earlier claims of success were a little bit premature, weren't they?"

"Something went wrong."

"I'll be sure they put that in your obituary."

Bonnise never knew what hit him as the bomb went off. His car was reduced to flaming scrap metal before he drew his next breath.

"Amateur," said Philippe Chardon, rising from his chair.

He made a mental note to ensure the payment to Bonnise's bank account was reclaimed as soon as possible.

"How hard can it be to kill two people? You plant the bomb, they go in and boom," he shouted, hurling his phone against the door.

"Are you alright, Mr. Chardon?" said a muffled female voice from beyond his office door.

"I said no interruptions!" said Philippe, as he banged his fist against the door. "Doesn't anyone understand simple instructions?"

There was no reply, just the clicking sound of a pair of high heels moving swiftly away from the door.

Philippe was furious with himself. He should never have trusted such a critical mission to an incompetent like Bonnise.

Philippe.

The word coursed through Philippe's mind; the agony that followed in its wake pushed him onto his hands and knees. His vision became hazy. The room and its contents shimmered and then blended in a swirling maelstrom of colours and light. The sensation was a short-lived one.

Philippe was no longer in the safety of his penthouse office. He was kneeling in a large chamber, flaming torches were hung along the walls, providing the light.

He kept his head bowed and his eyes fixed on the intricate carvings that decorated the floor. He had been summoned to the sanctuary of his benefactors, who called themselves the Cabal, many times before. He never knew when or how he was brought here, it just happened and the experience unnerved him every time.

Philippe had never met any of the Cabal, save one. Usually, their orders simply filled his mind. He never questioned their commands or motives. To do so would invite death. Besides, the Cabal had changed his life; more than that, they had saved it. Through them came the power to strike back at the world that had spurned him, and for that he would give his life for them if it came to it, he just hoped it never did.

"I am here as summoned," he called out.

Pain unlike anything he had ever experienced surged through Philippe. Unrestrained grief took him and he wept, begging them to stop. The pain continued as Philippe writhed on the floor, his cries for mercy unanswered.

You have disappointed us.

Philippe did not want to die. He was so close to gaining the power he craved. As if hearing the plea, the pain began to lessen.

Both men still live; even as we speak their paths have become interlinked.

"I have no excuse except that the thief and Washington are both resourceful men."

Philippe's attempt at justifying his actions earned him a fresh jolt of pain, sending him into a fierce spasm that left him on the brink of consciousness.

"Wallencheck and his men will not fail against the thief a second time, the disk will be in your hands soon enough," said Philippe, forcing the words through the agony.

Washington knows of the boy's existence. He should never have been assigned to the investigation.

"The orders came from the Security Council. I could not go against them without raising suspicion, but I think I can turn Washington's involvement to our advantage."

Ensure that you do.

"What about the Demon Stalker, what if he learns of the boy?"

Philippe found the strength to resume his kneeling position as the pain subsided.

He will be far too busy to be concerned about the boy.

He is the real danger to us. He must not reach the boy. This voice was different. It belonged to the member of the Cabal Philippe knew. She always liked to make her presence known. He got the feeling her outbursts were not encouraged or liked by the others.

Do not concern yourself, he will never reach Jason.

Philippe was glad to be ignored, considering the painful greeting he had received.

It is not long now to the event. How goes the rest of the plans?

Philippe smiled to himself. At last, he could pass on some good news.

"Everything is progressing well. We will be ready."

They must all die.

"I understand."

Be wary, Philippe. The voices, now little more than an echo, grew fainter. *Fail us again and an eternity of pain awaits you.*

Philippe sensed himself being pushed from the Cabal's presence. Now back in his office, he opened his eyes, doubled over and vomited. Serving the Cabal was not without its side effects or its risks.

Chapter Ten

During his ten-year career at the Enquirer, Bob Kelsey had developed a knack for uncovering great stories with very little information to go on. His wife, Fran, preferred to describe his gift as being 'the right bastard in the wrong place'. That was now past history. Fran's final attempt to rescue their floundering marriage had ended in a blazing row. After hurling their wedding crockery at him, Fran left, swearing never to set foot in their house again. She took their daughter Julie with her. Bob found the nearest bar, twenty minutes after they left, and bought everyone there a round of drinks.

Bob's only regret about his impending divorce was that it had not come fourteen years earlier, before Julie's birth. God, there was a daughter to be proud of. She ate more in a day than most third world countries saw in a year. Bob shivered when he thought of how much he had splashed out on diet sheets, books and exercise videos.

Julie had numerous sessions with 'diet' counsellors, who took great pleasure in taking Bob's money before telling him he did not understand his daughter.

Bob understood just fine: Julie was lazy, foul-mouthed and fat; in fact, she was the spitting image of her mother.

The next day, Bob had come into the office determined to enjoy his first day of bachelorhood. It was then when everything started to go wrong.

At the morning briefing, he was given a news story to chase up. A strange series of murders had been committed in and around Mexico City.

After making some calls, he learned all six victims had been branded on their arms. As yet, no one had managed to decipher the markings.

In each case, the victim's heart was torn from their chest, and their throats slashed. Exotic locale, ritualistic murder; a story which had started out as a time filler now had the potential to be front page material. If he had known where the trail would lead him, he would never have set foot on Mexican soil.

Upon landing at Benito Juarez International Airport, Bob was annoyed to find the hall packed, and was forced to fight his way through the crowd. Within the mass of people, a short man dressed in a white shirt and blue trousers had appeared. Although Bob's Mexican was non-existent, the simple act of the man pointing to a trolley stashed by one of the walls and then Bob's bags made his intention clear. Bob brushed past the man without a word. He had no intention of parting with money in this god-forsaken place unless it was on booze, food or hookers. He shoved his way over to the ticket counter, where he bought a ticket for one of the airport's licensed yellow cabs. The thought of taking the Metro was squashed when he heard about the frequent muggings from one of the mail-room guys who had visited the city several times. Bob had been mugged twice over the last two years, and was not about to earn his third strike. He had then marched from the airport and out into the blazing heat dutifully provided by the Mexican sun. The air was foul and Bob coughed his way to the taxi. He had heard pollution here was sometimes bad, and now he was experiencing it first hand. When the taxi arrived at his hotel in downtown Mexico City, Bob made the driver wait while he dumped his luggage, before being driven to the coroner's office.

Fernando Alvarez was not thrilled to find a member of the American press disturbing his afternoon lunch. Alvarez was a tall and anaemic-looking man with, as Bob discovered, an unswerving dedication to his job. He learnt nothing from Alvarez except that the only two words of English he spoke were 'no comment'.

Next, Bob tried his luck with the curator of one of the city's many museums, who proved more willing to assist. He admitted to being approached by the police and shown photos of the victims but was unable to help. He had told the police he would contact a colleague, who was the one person he knew who might be able to make sense of the markings.

The mysterious colleague, who had arrived in Mexico City just before Bob, was one Professor Napoleon Stone. According to what Bob could dig up on the internet, Stone was somewhat of a legend amongst his scholarly peers. He had published various papers on the occult, and was considered an authority on the subject. Before taking up his post at a university in England, Stone had spent most of his career documenting various cults and their practices.

All Bob's attempts to find and interview Stone came to nothing. He did, however, locate Vincent Marconi, the professor's assistant, a well-built Italian in his late twenties, fresh faced, not a mark or blemish on him, with deep-set brown eyes obscured by a pair of black rimmed spectacles. Marconi's wide smile and easygoing manner made him a difficult person to dislike, which was Kelsey's usual response to anyone he met for the first time.

Vincent was friendly but firm on the non-disclosure of Stone's whereabouts. He was forced to become more co-operative when Bob threatened to go public with Stone's involvement in a multiple murder investigation. Vincent told him that after examining the victims, Stone believed there was no occult connection to the murders. Bob questioned Vincent on the subject of the markings found on the victims. Vincent assured him that as far as Professor Stone was concerned, the markings were just random scribblings with no meaning. Unfortunately for Vincent, one of Bob's talents was knowing when someone was feeding him a line of bullshit.

Realising the 'nice' approach was getting nowhere, Bob decided it was time to revert back to his own unique brand of journalism. Several hours from dawn, two nights later, found him inside the coroner's office. The security, as expected, was a joke; one decrepit night watchman and a couple of rusty window locks. It was still a risk, as Mexican law tended to lean towards the idea of a suspect being guilty until proven innocent. Bob hoped he had enough money to bribe his way out of trouble should he need to.

Once inside the office, Bob forced open a filing cabinet and began rifling through the files. It did not take long to find the information he needed. Taking out a palm-sized image scanner, he scanned the photos of the six corpses, especially the blown up photos of the markings found on the victims.

The next morning, Bob was busy at the desk in his hotel room. As he started to copy the files from his scanner onto his laptop, he flicked a large bug off the keyboard. He smiled at the satisfying 'crunch' his size nine boot made as it sealed the insect's fate.

Despite the less than ideal surroundings, Bob was grateful that the hotel at least had Internet access.

Once the files were uploaded, Bob e-mailed everything to Ed Steinberg, a fellow drinking buddy and the best researcher on the paper. He had asked Ed to find anyone who could translate the markings and get back to him within twenty-four hours.

Ten hours, seventeen minutes and fifteen seconds later, Bob's laptop began bleeping, alerting him to a new message. The e-mail explained how Ed, posing as a fellow occult expert, had contacted a Doctor Keith Harridan, one of the world's foremost authorities in cryptography, especially ancient texts. Harridan had replied to Ed's e-mail with surprise when he was told Professor Stone had not discovered anything of value in the markings. According to Harridan, Stone should have been able to decipher the markings in his sleep. Harridan went on to explain how the markings were a kind of ancient seal or pact; it branded the victim as a servant of a cult known as the Book of Cademus, which had existed several hundred years ago.

Harridan was sketchy on the details of the cult. Originating in eleventh century England, it had been founded by Sir Oliver Cademus, an English knight, upon his return from the first crusade. The reasons behind Sir Oliver's infamy were rumoured to stem from the numerous deaths and strange rituals said to be conducted in the privacy of his castle. Harridan concluded by saying that the cult was destroyed when all its members, including Cademus himself, were put to death when the castle was stormed by soldiers under the orders of King Henry the First.

Bob tried to contain his excitement after reading the email. An ancient cult, long thought destroyed, appeared to be alive and well, butchering its way through the Mexican unwashed. More importantly, a renowned expert in all things occult seemed to be covering up vital information about the murders.

"Professor runs death cult," it had a nice ring to it. But before Bob could spend the revenue from the eventual book and mini-series, he needed proof.

He spent the rest of the day sat in a rental car, parked down the street from the hotel were he had met with Vincent. The day passed uneventfully with no sign of Stone or Vincent. As evening approached, Bob began to get concerned as one of the hotel staff had mentioned the rise of 'express kidnapping' where the victim was carjacked and beaten. As Bob decided whether he should call it a day, he caught sight of Vincent leaving the hotel. The young Italian was wearing an unbuttoned navy coloured jacket, not unlike those worn by the American Cavalry in the old west, a white T-shirt and black combat trousers. A large knife was strapped to his right thigh. A navy bandanna was wrapped around Vincent's head, giving him the appearance of an old style buccaneer.

The wind swept up underneath Vincent's jacket and Bob saw a pair of gun holsters strapped to either side of his chest.

Bob grabbed his camera and snapped off a few shots as Vincent tossed a backpack into the back of his jeep before climbing in. The jeep then pulled away from the hotel, following the road leading out of the town. Bob was about to set off in pursuit when the front and rear passenger doors opened and three figures slid into the vacant seats. Bob did not voice any kind of opposition. The last thing you did was argue when staring down the barrel of a sawn-off shotgun. He did what any sane human being would do when faced with a life-threatening situation: he wet himself.

"Good evening, Señor Kelsey."

The voice came from the seat directly behind him. Bob recognised it at once, the knowledge causing even more discomfort than his urine-soaked shorts.

"Alvarez."

The coroner bent forward, folding his arms on the back of Bob's chair.

"You have involved yourself in things that do not concern you, Señor Kelsey," said Alvarez.

"I'm a member of the press, you can't just…"

"Kill you?" said Alvarez, clicking his fingers.

The last thing Bob saw was the butt of a shotgun coming towards him, then nothing.

"Kelsey! Kelsey! You still with me?"

Vincent's voice brought Bob's thoughts back to the present. The uncomfortable soreness in his arms reminded him of the iron restraints shackling his arms above his head to one of six stone statues, whose grotesque and misshapen bodies fitted perfectly with the rest of the chamber's decor. The statues, along with several marble pillars, formed the main support for the ceiling.

The chamber was vast and old; Bob could scarcely imagine the time it took in its construction, or the blood spilt. He was stood atop a large plateau situated at the far end of the chamber. The plateau itself could only be reached by a flight of stone steps. On the plateau floor was an image made of coloured paving tiles. It was of an odd-looking orange bird; in its claws it was holding a flaming sword. Looking left, Bob saw Vincent chained to a pillar a few feet away. He was unarmed and sporting an ugly bruise on the right side of his face. His left eye was just beginning to show signs of swelling. Bob did not need his journalistic eye to tell him the young man had not been taken easily.

"Where the hell are we?"

"Beneath the ruins of a building destroyed in a terrorist attack two years ago," said Vincent.

"What does this have to do with the Book of Cademus?"

"Who?"

"Please," said Bob, rattling his shackles. "I think it's time to cut the crap."

Vincent seemed to be mulling over what Bob had said. Bob hoped the kid was not as stubborn as he looked.

"A corporation that we know has links to the Book of Cademus tried and failed to buy the building. Two days after their last offer was rejected, the building was destroyed."

"Who's we?"

Vincent said nothing.

Bob did not push the matter further; he had enough for now. If they made it out of here in one piece, there would be time to get the information he needed.

A crowd had gathered inside the temple, and were now knelt on opposite sides of a paved series of carved tiles leading from the far end of the temple up to the steps. What drew them here? Bob wondered.

"They come for power, knowledge, the desire to find a better life, who knows," said Vincent.

The eyes of the crowd were fixed on two pairs of iron manacles that lay waiting on a stone altar at the front of the plateau. A fresh wave of hysteria surged through Bob when he saw the bloodstains covering the altar and the floor surrounding it.

"I wouldn't worry," Vincent told him. "that's not for us."

Bob let out a sigh of relief.

"Our deaths will have a lot less ceremony and a lot more pain."

Bob wished he could reach across and wring the stupid Italian's neck.

"Bet you wish you'd gone to bed instead of trying to following me."

"You knew?"

Vincent nodded. "The plan was to lead you on a wild goose chase, but obviously Alvarez had other plans."

"Indeed I did, Señor Marconi."

Alvarez mounted the stone steps leading to the plateau. He wore a set of white robes, its sleeves adorned with gold and silver ringlets. The image Bob had seen earlier of the bird and the flaming sword was on the front of Alvarez's robes, in thick gold and yellow stitching. A golden sash was wrapped tightly round Alvarez's waist. He was followed by six others, all wearing plain red robes, all with identical markings stitched onto their clothing. Three of them were carrying guns, while the others carried long daggers thrust into their black sashes.

As Alvarez marched toward him, his gloating grin did little to allay Bob's fears. He relaxed when Alvarez moved past him and went over to Vincent. Bob watched him raise his right hand, backhand Vincent and then smile as the blood flowed from the resulting wound on Vincent's lip.

"Where is the Demon Stalker?" said Alvarez.

Vincent said nothing. Alvarez signalled to his men and Vincent's defiance earned him a rain of blows. Bob looked away, unable to watch the beating. The defiant Italian slumped forward, straining against the chains holding him, his face a mask of blood. The robed men seized Vincent's arms and hauled him upright. Vincent somehow managed to regain his composure and shrugged them off, his look of contempt returning.

"So, still a little fight left in you, boy," said Alvarez. "Good, I will enjoy your screams before you tell me what I wish to know."

Alvarez began to head towards the altar.

"You may be disappointed," Vincent called after him.

Alvarez did not turn. Bob watched Alvarez walk to the edge of the stairs. Everywhere Bob looked, there seemed to be men and women kneeling and swaying. Never once did he hear their chants falter. He could almost hear their joy as much as he sensed the fear behind the chants. Their fear of Alvarez, who stood with his hands outstretched, palms facing upwards. The chants from the crowd grew louder, their chorus was now matched by the slow and steady drumbeat provided from several followers at the chamber's rear.

"Kelsey," whispered Vincent. It was obvious he didn't want to alert the robed man who was stood in front of him. "Kelsey, can you hear me?"

"I'm going to die; they're going to rip me open, just like those others."

Bob did not want to die, not like this. Any time after eighty-five was fine, peacefully passing away during the last of a long line of alcohol-induced sleeps.

"Kelsey," said Vincent. "You need to pull it together, otherwise I'll leave you here."

"Ok," said Kelsey, trying to push back his fear. "How about you break our chains in half and we can wave as we walk out of here?"

"I had planned on running."

If there was any sarcasm or humour in his tone, Bob was having trouble hearing it. It was clear to him that Marconi's earlier beating had left him unhinged.

Bob saw a procession entering the main chamber. All noise ceased as they made their way through the silent crowd. In all, Bob counted five hooded, red-robed figures surrounding a young boy dressed in white robes, who was not more than eight years old. Two figures walked several paces in front of the boy, scattering flower petals. Another two marched behind the boy, both carried spears. The last man, who walked beside the boy, carried a silver tray. A white satin sheet was draped over whatever lay on top of the tray.

"They can't have found it," said Vincent, his voice betraying his concern.

"Found what?"

"The right hand of Cademus."

"You trying to tell me there's a hand under that sheet?"

"Not a hand, an ancient ceremonial dagger said to have been used by Sir Oliver himself," explained Vincent. "The old man was right, as usual."

"Who's right?"

"Never mind," said Vincent. "It's game time."

The procession was now at the steps. Bob saw the boy clearly now, or more importantly, the markings on the boy's upper left arm. They were identical to the markings found on the murder victims. Alvarez took his place behind the altar. He signalled to the men with the boy, who judging by the way he moved appeared to be drugged. Four of them, along with the boy, mounted the steps to the altar. Bob's fondness for his own daughter had pretty much expired years ago, but he still would kill anyone who tried to hurt her. Sure, she was annoying, irresponsible and an all round pain in the ass, but she was still his daughter.

"You've got to do something," Bob whispered.

"Just be ready."

All Bob could do was hope Vincent's boasts were not just that, or this would be the shortest escape attempt in history. A sense of loss then filled him. Here he was, playing witness to perhaps the greatest story of his unremarkable career and there was not a damn thing he could do about it.

Carefully, two men took hold of the boy and lifted him onto the altar. They secured his arms and feet inside the restraints. Alvarez wiped a lone tear from the boy's cheek. Oh God, thought Bob. Whatever they had given to the boy to induce a more docile state was wearing off. He began to whimper as he struggled to free himself. Bob began to pull at his own chains, even though he knew escape was hopeless.

"Do not be afraid," Alvarez told the boy. "One moment of pain and you will know the joy that Cademus brings us all."

Alvarez faced the crowd.

"Soon we will skulk in the shadows no longer."

"Cademus is Lord!" the crowd screamed back.

"The sleeper shall awake and we who prepare the way, we who have remained ever faithful shall rule at his side."

"Cademus is Lord!"

Alvarez gestured to one of his men.

"Pedro, bring me the right hand of Cademus."

"This is madness! They're going to kill him!"

"Just stay with me, Kelscy!"

The chants began again as Bob watched the man who he guessed was Pedro approach the hooded figure holding a silver tray.

"You carry the right hand of Cademus?" asked Pedro. There was no reply. The figure stood motionless, keeping his head bowed and his face hidden.

"You carry the right hand of Cademus?" This time, Pedro said the words much louder. Again, no answer. By now, the chanting had ceased and all was quiet again, allowing a tense silence to blanket the chamber. Pedro reached out with shaking hands, and took hold of the sheet and pulled it towards him. The silken sheet glided to the floor, leaving Pedro gaping, open-mouthed at the two automatic pistols resting on the silver tray. The figure, holding the tray, snapped his head back and in doing so, threw off the hood. Of all the images Bob imagined under that hood, a one-eyed, bald-headed black man was not one of them.

"Mi dios!" shrieked Pedro.

"The Demon Stalker," snarled Alvarez.

"Stone?" said Bob, remembering one of the photos he had seen on the Internet. "Napoleon Stone?"

"About time," said Vincent smiling.

Chapter Eleven

Vincent caught sight of Pedro's hand moving for the dagger hidden beneath his sash.

"Mistake," said Napoleon, his expression hardening.

He released the platter, snatched both guns from it as it fell, and fired, point blank, into Pedro's chest. The force of the bullets threw Pedro screaming from the plateau. He landed with the nauseating sound of his spine snapping.

Vincent pulled with all the strength he could muster and the chains began to give. He knew Kelsey would be staring at him, trying to understand how he could break solid steel. He would have to deal with that revelation later.

As Vincent broke free of his shackles, Napoleon threw the guns towards him. Rolling forward, Vincent caught the weapons and fired into the disbelieving man stood in front of him, who slumped to the floor without a sound. Alvarez's bodyguards opened fire. Napoleon dived behind one of the pillars as ricochets and sparks flew off the masonry.

A burst of gunfire from Vincent's twin automatics cut down the first of Alvarez's men while they were reloading. As the others ran for cover, one was caught in the leg by a stray bullet, and slid onto his stomach. The wounded man's gun clattered across the floor; a bullet smashing into his skull as he tried to retrieve it.

The remaining bodyguard came out from his hiding place. He got as far as two feet before a small throwing knife flashed from Napoleon's right hand, piercing the bodyguard's right eye. With all the armed bodyguards removed from the scene, Napoleon threw off the white robes and came out from behind the pillar. Underneath, he wore a white shirt, brown trousers and a dark brown combat vest. A shotgun was strapped to his back, in a black, weatherworn leather holster.

"Kill them!" screamed Alvarez, who was the only person on the plateau not to have sought cover when the shooting began.

Napoleon took two canisters that were fastened to his belt, and tossed them to Vincent, who was stood by the steps, facing down a mob of enraged worshippers.

"Crowd control," said Napoleon.

Vincent tore the rings out of the canisters and rolled them down the steps. The crowd paused then began to back away. Two seconds later, the canisters exploded and the chamber below the plateau began to fill with a thick gas. Panic started to take hold as coughing fits broke out amongst the crowd. Others rubbed painful eyes now streaming with tears. A few began doubling over clutching their stomachs.

Vincent fired a few warning shots over their heads and it was enough to instigate a full-scale exodus. Followers who earlier had sat side by side in fellowship were now trampling over one another to get out.

"So much for the love of Cademus," said Vincent.

Sure he was safe for the moment, Vincent turned to see two men dead at Napoleon's feet, as a third crawled away from the scene. The remaining men had grown more cautious and had encircled the one-eyed professor.

"Take Kelsey and follow the crowd, I'll meet you up top," ordered Napoleon.

"I think…"

"Don't think, Vincent, just do it!"

Vincent ran over to Bob, who seemed to have lost all sense of reason and was mumbling to himself. Vincent blasted the chains holding Bob, before hitting him with a driving uppercut. Hoisting the unconscious Bob over his shoulder Vincent took a deep breath, held it and plunged down the stairs into the gas.

Napoleon stared into the faces of those around him. He noted the men's stances, their greater numbers inflated their confidence, he could use that.

One of the bigger men stepped forward. "You're dead, old man."

Napoleon's right palm smashed into the big man's nose, the bone driving up into the man's brain. The man sank to the floor, twitched for a second or two then lay still.

"Next?"

Not waiting for an answer, Napoleon went on the offensive. He elbowed a man behind him in the face, then drove his left heel back into the man's ribs, feeling several of them shatter under the weight of the strike.

From nowhere, a dagger flashed towards Napoleon's face. Ducking under the blade, he came up, threw two quick punches into his opponent's abdomen and finished him with a right hook. Grabbing another man to his right, Napoleon hurled him over the plateau edge. A sharp pain flared as a dagger was thrust into his side. Napoleon seized the hand holding the dagger and wrenched it upward, snapping it at the wrist. Ignoring the screams from the knifeman, Napoleon dragged the dagger out of his side and hurled it into the throat of a man trying to reach one of the fallen guns. Now only the man who had stabbed him remained. Napoleon pulled the knifeman towards him and met him with a crushing clothesline from his right forearm. The man's legs sailed up into the air, his back striking the stone floor hard. Napoleon knelt down beside him.

"Please don't kill me," the man wheezed, barely able to get the sentence out.

It was the last thing he said before Napoleon broke his neck.

"I'm sure the last six people you butchered said the same thing."

The sound of applause filled the chamber.

"The killing of an unarmed man," said Alvarez, who was stood at the other end of the plateau. "I expected more compassion from the fabled Demon Stalker."

"He got more compassion than his victims' families would have shown him."

"And what about me? Have you come here to kill me as well?"

"I've come to take the boy. What happens after that is up to you."

"You will never understand us, understand the freedom the Book of Cademus grants us."

"Oh I understand," said Napoleon. "I understand that you prey on the fears of others. I understand that you twist their minds until all they see is what you tell them. I understand that your promises of power and freedom are nothing more than lies and deceit."

"We give them hope."

Napoleon pointed to the now-screaming boy strapped to the altar. "Burying a seven-inch blade into a child isn't hopeful, it's murder."

"And you would know all about murder, wouldn't you, Demon Stalker?" said Alvarez. "What makes your cause any more justified in the taking of lives?"

It was a question Napoleon often asked himself; but he always found his answer in the tearful eyes of grateful victims, or those blinded followers forced to see the truth. Alvarez, in a way, was no different. He had been lied to, deceived, but he was also responsible for the murder of innocent people and he would have to answer for those crimes. Napoleon had hoped he could reach Alvarez, but one look into his eyes and he knew he was too far gone to be reached. He would die before he would be turned.

"The Cabal warned me you would come; they granted me the power to become your executioner."

Alvarez screamed. The pillar nearest to Napoleon exploded and he was thrown across the plateau floor. He managed to grab hold of the edge as he slid over it, and dragged himself back onto solid ground. Alvarez was now hovering several feet from the floor. His eyes were now blood red and glowed with a violet hue. Flames had risen from the ground to encircle him like a shield.

Napoleon's right hand moved behind him and he slid the shotgun from its holster. The sound of the weapon being cocked carried through the now empty chamber. Napoleon never tired of hearing the sound; it was the sound of the gauntlet being throwing down.

"I hope you die well, Demon Stalker," boomed the nightmarish creature Alvarez had now become.

Vincent, still carrying Kelsey, made his way back through the tunnels. His only guide was the memory of being forced down to the chamber at gunpoint. Eventually, he came to a rope ladder. He took hold of one of the rungs and started the long climb to daylight. After a while, he felt Kelsey's body jerk, followed by a groan.

"Take it easy, Kelsey, we're almost out."

They were already halfway up the ladder, if Kelsey acted up now, the inevitable fall would not be a pretty one. The remainder of the climb was not easy for Vincent, due to the extra weight provided by Kelsey, combined with his injuries and the effort spent on freeing himself.

Vincent's hand cleared the last rung of the ladder and finally touched solid ground. He dug deep into the earth and hoisted Kelsey up onto the ground. As Vincent climbed out of the pit, the dawn rays kissed his skin, welcoming him out of the darkness. Drawing his guns, he scanned the vicinity, searching for any signs of danger. Surprisingly, he found none. He concluded that Napoleon's sudden appearance, matched by the confusion and hysteria caused by the gas may have given the impression that the intervention was a prelude to a larger raid. The followers of Cademus obviously harboured no desire to tangle with the authorities, and had fled the scene. Vincent hoped some, at least, would return to whatever lives they had known before the Book of Cademus.

Vincent harboured no hatred towards the followers, although it was not always that way. There was a time when he would have thrown live grenades into the crowd instead of gas canisters. Given Napoleon's history, he had more reason to hate cult members than anyone else, but he went to great lengths to protect them. When Vincent would question him about it, Napoleon had said, "I never blame them. They only come to find something better, something greater than they know. It is their leaders who profit from their loyalty. Their followers give them everything and they repay them with pain. Understand this, Vincent, in everything, there is good and evil. Some sects I've investigated have been truly spiritual and enlightened in their pursuits. I have seen others willingly cross the line between good and evil. We are the ones who see they pay the price for crossing that line."

It was those words which guided Vincent's actions, although he found it hard to think of grown men and women as innocents. Anyone who could watch as a helpless infant was butchered and do nothing was anything but innocent.

"Thank God! I'm still alive."

Vincent looked to see Kelsey coming towards him.

"They thought it was funny to bring me here in my own transport," said Vincent, patting the jeep's bonnet.

"That's great; now let's get out of here."

Vincent said nothing. He began rummaging through his sports bag lying on the jeep's back seat. He stuffed some items into a pouch, which he then threw over his shoulder and started back towards the entrance. Bob seized his arm.

"Did you hear what I said?"

Vincent spun round, producing both guns as if from thin air. Bob froze.

"My friend is down there and I'm going back to help him. You so much as breathe the wrong way and I'll put a bullet in you. It's your choice."

It was strange to Vincent that his threat seemed to have little effect on Bob. Even stranger was the mocking smile Bob now wore.

"I know people, Marconi. You're not going to kill me, I'm the victim here…right?"

Vincent fired a single round into Bob's thigh who collapsed, clutching his injured leg and screaming abuse at Vincent.

"I said I'd put a bullet in you," said Vincent, stepping over Bob and starting back towards the ladder. "I don't remember saying anything about killing you."

"You can't leave me like this, I'll die."

"There's a first aid kit in the back of the jeep."

"Marconi, you son of a bitch, don't you leave me! Marconi!"

But Vincent was already descending back into the darkness.

Napoleon threw himself down as another bolt of energy sailed over his head. He felt the searing heat from the blast. It smashed into the far wall, blowing a ten-foot crater in it.

"Too close," he said, looking back at the gaping hole.

Alvarez was not the first supernatural foe Napoleon had faced, but he was by far the strongest.

The screaming coming from the altar told Napoleon that the boy was putting his lungs to good use. The boy needed help and he needed it now. Napoleon ran for the altar as two more energy bolts flew at him. He leapt into the air, somersaulted over the bolts and fired three shotgun blasts into Alvarez's chest. The shells from the shotgun were fitted with armour piercing tips, and coated in silver, perfect ordnance against this sort of supernatural opponent.

Alvarez screamed as the shells exploded against his chest and propelled him backwards, his arms flailing helplessly. Napoleon landed on his feet and sprinted for the altar. He began snapping open the iron shackles holding the boy, who stared up at him wide-eyed.

"Trust me," Napoleon said in Spanish, as he opened the final clasp. He offered his back to the boy, "Put your hands round my neck."

The boy hesitated and then leapt onto Napoleon's back.

"Stone!"

Alvarez had begun to pull himself free from the rubble.

"Time to go."

Napoleon ran for the relative safety of the three stone pillars at the far end of the plateau. He was half way when he was lifted from the floor. The boy dropped from around his neck and continued running toward the pillars. Telekinesis, guessed Napoleon, resisting the urge to drop his gun, as his body rotated to face Alvarez. Three gaping wounds were evident in Alvarez's chest, wounds that were already beginning to heal. Alvarez stared down at his injuries and smiled. "Did you really think you could kill me with that toy?"

Napoleon felt an invisible noose slip around his throat. His head snapped back as the noose began to constrict, starving him of air as it grew tighter.

"Can you feel it, Stone?" Alvarez held out his right hand, which he was closing slowly as if there was something caught between his thumb and forefinger. "Can you feel the shortness of breath? Your heart rate becoming erratic; your lungs burning. That is death, my friend."

Napoleon ignored Alvarez's taunts. He closed his eyes and began to concentrate, focusing on the shotgun still clutched in his right hand. He always believed in hiding his most powerful weapon in plain sight. He fought to bring his shallow breathing under control; there would be no second attempt if he failed.

"What does it feel like, Stone?" laughed Alvarez. "To have someone holding your life in their hands."

With seconds of air left to him, Napoleon channelled all his focused strength and power down his right arm into the shotgun, which acted like a lightning rod, harnessing his own strange abilities. The air rushed back into him as he broke free of Alvarez's grip.

"No one holds my life," he said, raising his shotgun.

Closing his eyes, Napoleon mouthed a single word of power. It had been taught to him many years ago when he had first chosen the path to become what he was now: a stalker of demons and monsters. Streaks of pure white lightning flew from the barrel of the shotgun. It tore into Alvarez, coursing over his body, the resulting howl which came out of his mouth hit Napoleon like a shock wave, hurling him back across the plateau. He smashed against one of the pillars, his back taking the full brunt of the impact. He crashed onto the floor face first, the shotgun sliding out his hand. Alvarez's screams of agony grew, as the lightning encircled his body. The temple floor began to tremble and shudder underneath Napoleon. He dragged himself upright using the pillar as a support. His face was gashed and bleeding heavily. The young boy ran to his side, trying to help him. By now, the whole temple was caught in the midst of what appeared to be a massive earthquake. Fissures began to appear in the floor at Napoleon's feet; giant, spider-like cracks snaked up the temple walls and across its ceiling.

Napoleon grabbed the boy and swung him round onto his back. One of the pillars at the other end of the chamber crashed to the floor, hurling large chunks of masonry across the temple.

Through the chaos, Napoleon saw Vincent running into the chamber and right into the path of a flying section of the pillar twice his size. Vincent drew his guns, with a speed that would put any gunslinger to shame, and fired into the centre of the debris. The armour piercing rounds sliced the chunk of pillar into two sections, both of which tumbled harmlessly past him on either side. Napoleon watched him run for the plateau steps, dodging falling debris from the temple's roof every step of the way. He skidded to a halt by the stairs when he saw Alvarez.

Napoleon hefted his shotgun and pointed it at the section of the ceiling directly above Alvarez, hoping Vincent understood. Vincent nodded, holstering his guns and taking three grenades from his pouch. He pulled the pins on all three, waited for a few seconds before throwing them up into the air over Alvarez's head.

Napoleon did not wait to see where the grenades hit; he was already making a desperate dash for the plateau's edge. He flung himself from the plateau as the grenades detonated above Alvarez, engulfing him in the resulting explosion. A sheet of flames shot out across the plateau, just missing Napoleon and the boy. Tons of rock came crashing down on Alvarez, burying him under a barrage of stone and flame.

Napoleon hit the floor and kept running, the boy still managing to cling to his neck, halfway to where Vincent waited and with the chamber collapsing behind him, a large fissure opened up in front of Napoleon. It ripped along the floor, uprooting sections of rock and patterned paving slabs. The crack widened to at least ten feet. Napoleon managed to stop himself from sliding into the abyss. Instinctively, he jumped back; a second later, a wall of flames rose up from the fissure, then came the familiar laughter.

The boy's grip tightened and Napoleon not only sensed the boy's fear, he shared it.

The two unlikely companions watched a section of flames darken, and from it floated Alvarez. Napoleon could imagine the rage consuming him. His temple was destroyed, his followers scattered; all that was left was vengeance. Napoleon saw several more wounds on Alvarez's chest, as before they were already healing, a lot slower than the last time, but they were healing.

"You cannot kill me, Stone!"

Napoleon's right hand rested on something hidden inside his jacket, tucked into his belt.

The last of Alvarez's chest wounds was beginning to heal itself. *This is it*, thought Napoleon, a plan already formulated, no second chances, and no margin for error.

Dragging out a large spear-like object, Napoleon hurled it at Alvarez. It plunged deep into the last wound, right up to its hilt.

"Fool! No weapon can harm me!"

"I think you'll find this one will."

Alvarez stared at the hilt of the weapon, the fear on his face clear for all to see.

"The right hand of Cademus," he whispered.

Blood began to stream from his eyes, ears and nose. His flesh started to blister and crack, as the heat of the flames, which before had protected him, now turned on their former master.

Napoleon held his shotgun in one hand, and cocked it. He pointed it at the dagger jutting out from Alvarez's chest. "I thought it might come in handy."

All that now remained of Alvarez was a screaming mass of flames; the stench of burning flesh filled the air.

"This is not the end, Stone! You cannot ..."

Alvarez's shouts were silenced by two blasts from Napoleon's shotgun. Alvarez was lifted off his feet and sent tumbling down into the abyss of flames. The threat gone, Napoleon took several steps back and hoped his failing strength was enough to see him through.

"We leave now, Señor?" asked the child.

"We leave now."

Racing towards the edge, Napoleon leapt towards the other side, not realising the floor was collapsing beneath him. His momentum carried him through the flames and over to the other side. He landed on his feet, almost losing his balance as the tremors increased.

Napoleon tore past Vincent, heading for the temple entrance. "Come on!" he yelled back, threading his way through the falling debris, the child being thrown around on his back, struggling to stay on. The thought that none of them would see daylight again grew louder with each step.

"Bastards!" swore Bob, as he dragged himself into the driver's seat of Vincent's jeep. Every movement he made caused a spasm of pain from his gunshot wound. Gently taking hold of his blood-soaked leg, he gradually eased it into the chair.

"Let's see who laughs now."

Bob leant forward, grasping for the ignition key and found he was grasping at thin air.

"Planning on abandoning us, were we?"

Turning round in his seat, Bob saw two figures striding out of the large dust cloud that billowed out from the cavern entrance. Vincent led the way, followed by Napoleon Stone. Perched on Napoleon's shoulders, apparently unaware of how close to death he had been, was the boy.

Upon reaching the jeep, Napoleon placed the boy on the ground and seized Bob by his jacket lapels, lifted him out of the seat and threw him to the ground. Napoleon was about to say something to Kelsey when he began to hear a buzzing sound, like a swarm of bees trapped inside his head.

Do not fight me, Stone. Your mind is strong. Do not make me damage it further.

Napoleon closed his eyes and allowed his mind to float free and calm.

Good, you learn fast, I like that.

I take it this is some kind of telepathy? said Napoleon, forming the words inside his mind.

Perhaps I am merely an echo of your own mind?

My mind doesn't work that way.

Well said, Demon Stalker, your reputation is well founded.

Is there a point you're getting to?

Of course, time is against us and we must act quickly. My name is Joshua Grey and I am here to aid you.

Aid me? Aid me in what?

Your world balances on a knife-edge between salvation and destruction.

Isn't it always? Despite the glib remark, Napoleon listened intently. It was hard to write off someone who was powerful enough to use telepathy to communicate. An image flashed in his mind, a young man, with a face that he instantly recognised.

Jason ...Jason Chen?

You know him then?

He's one of my students. What does he have to do with this?

Everything.

Why?

The why does not concern you. All you need to know is that the boy must be kept safe.

Napoleon did not like what he was hearing. He was not about to follow anyone's orders without good reason, no matter who gave them.

You being here was planned, Demon Stalker. The Cabal wanted you out of the way so they could act. They have already dispatched an Erogian to retrieve the boy. If you do not act now, all will be lost.

How do you know all this?

At that point, Napoleon sensed the voice was fading away.

Remember, Demon Stalker, protect the boy. They must not take him. The voice was now barely a whisper, then nothing. Napoleon felt his mind return to normal and he opened his eyes, just in time to see Kelsey hit the ground. The enormity of what had just transpired sank home to Napoleon.

"He slowed time," he said quietly. "He slowed time."

"What?" Vincent asked.

Ignoring the question, Napoleon looked at the boy and pointed to the back of the jeep. They boy did not need to be told twice and he scrambled into the back seat.

"What now, boss?"

"Take the boy back to the board of trustees and let them give him the choice."

The look on Vincent's face told Napoleon he was far from happy with what was being asked of him.

"I take it you have a problem with my orders, Vincent?"

Vincent frowned. "Yeah, I've got a problem." He pointed at the boy. "He's too young to understand the choice."

Napoleon was unconcerned by Vincent's protest. "Join Icarus or have your memory of these events wiped seems pretty clear to me."

"You can't just take him away from everything he knows, what about his family, friends; they could be looking for him."

Napoleon glanced at the boy. He did not seem to understand what they were arguing about, he was just glad to be alive.

"He'll adjust, Vincent, he'll have to…you did."

"To hell with you, Napoleon. I was different and you know it. I was nineteen and I believed from day one this was what I wanted. This boy deserves a chance at life…he…"

Vincent's speech was cut short by Napoleon's right fist smashing against his jaw. Vincent fell against the bonnet, immediately his left hand shot inside the folds of his jacket, seizing the handle of his gun.

"If that gun moves another inch, I'll have to kill you."

Vincent glared furiously at Stone, who stood unmoving, weaponless. Although Vincent's own gun was halfway out of its holster, Napoleon knew one fact that was as unchangeable as the seasons; if Vincent moved another inch, he would be dead before his gun cleared

95

the holster. Vincent had not been doing this for as long as he had, so did not see the bigger picture, at least not yet. The boy had been through too much to just return to a normal life. With the Icarus Foundation, there was safety and a purpose. The look of anger diminished on Vincent's face as he slid his guns back into their holsters and pushed himself up off the bonnet.

"Napoleon…I…"

"Apology accepted."

"What about me?" asked Bob.

Napoleon leaned into the jeep, smiled at the boy and ruffled his hair before picking up a canteen of water. He threw it onto Kelsey's stomach and pointed at the expanse of the desert to the south of where they stood.

"There's a service station two miles that way."

"What?"

"My advice. Get out of Mexico, keep moving, don't contact anyone you know, not your paper, your family, no one, and especially don't go to the police."

"But…but," said Kelsey standing. "You took out Alvarez and his followers."

"What we took out was a chapter of the Book of Cademus," said Napoleon. "There are many more hidden out there, and after today, they'll all be looking for you."

"How the hell do you know all this?"

"If I told you, you wouldn't believe me, besides if they catch up with you, I don't want you telling them anything more than you already know."

"I know your names," said Bob, his tone desperate. "If you don't take me with you, I'll tell them who you are."

Napoleon bent down and grabbed Bob's injured leg. He screamed for several seconds before Napoleon released him.

"I don't take well to being threatened, Mr. Kelsey. I hope we understand each other."

"You said the boy's going to see these trustees, can't I go there? I'd be safe there."

"It's not about being safe, it's about being prepared for a life you didn't ask or wish for," said Napoleon. "You wouldn't last five minutes, and someone like you wouldn't want his memory wiped, would you?"

Bob did not answer.

"I thought so," said Napoleon, walking to the jeep, and without looking back, he climbed in. Vincent was already there, starting the engine.

Kelsey started crawling towards the jeep. "Please," he pleaded.

"Don't leave me like this, you must help me."

After a few moments, a revolver flew back over the jeep, landing next to Bob. The next he knew, he was bursting into a fit of coughing, his lungs full of a combination of carbon monoxide, gravel and sand. The tears came easily as he watched the jeep pull away from him, leaving him alone with the revolver.

"You sure there was no other way," said Vincent, the words chosen with care. "I mean, leaving him like that."

"There are those who'll fight and those who'll run, Kelsey was definitely a runner. He'd have sold us out first chance he got."

"I know you're right, but it's just that..."

"It doesn't feel right. It sticks in your throat, doesn't it?" asked Napoleon.

Vincent nodded.

"And so it should."

"I get the feeling there's something you didn't tell me back there."

"There was," admitted Napoleon, shifting in his chair to check the boy was ok. Satisfied, he continued. He told Vincent everything regarding his encounter with Joshua Grey. Vincent listened closely, saying nothing. When Napoleon had finished, he let out a heavy sigh.

"Well? Think I'm insane?"

"On a daily basis, but if you say someone tapped into your mind and delivered some kind of doomsday warning, then that's what happened. Now, what do we do about it?"

"Take the boy back to the Foundation," said Napoleon. "I'm headed to the university; if Grey's right, then Jason may not have much time."

"They won't like you taking off to England, especially after what happened with Alvarez. This whole 'Book of Cademus is after one of your students' feels like a trap."

"Agreed."

Napoleon placed a reassuring hand on his young friend's shoulders.

"I need you to check through the archives when you get back, I need everything on the Book of Cademus and anything you can find on this Joshua Grey."

"You think there's a connection?"

"Not sure, but he definitely wasn't telling me the full story."

Napoleon took a roll of film from his pocket and placed it in Vincent's palm. "These are photos I took of the inscriptions etched onto the right hand of Cademus, see what you make of them when you get back, I don't want to risk taking them with me."

"Got it. Anything else?"

Napoleon fixed his gaze on the horizon. "The next time you try to pull a gun on me, I will kill you."

"How many times are we going to go over this? I'm fine, understand? Christ, do I need to use sign language?"

Kathryn propped herself up on the stretcher, using the arm that was not bandaged.

"A broken leg, a fractured forearm and possible concussion is anything but fine, madam, I'm surprised you're still conscious," said one of the ambulancemen.

"She's far too stubborn to let a small thing like excruciating pain get in the way of letting you guys cart her off," said Luther, who was standing at the foot of the stretcher, trying his best not to laugh.

"You think this is funny? I've been with you for less than a bloody hour and I'm already in an ambulance. Thanks, Luther, no really thank you; this is exactly what I wanted from my first trip to Paris."

"If you've finished, do you think we might get back to the small matter of someone trying to kill us?"

Kathryn's features softened and she gave him a faint smile. "Sorry, I suppose I should be thanking you for saving my life." She turned to the ambulancemen. "Guys, can you give us a minute please?"

One of the men gave her a quizzical look.

"Five minutes," said Kathryn. "Then we can go and if you're really lucky, I'll let you put the sirens on, won't that be nice?"

Begrudgingly, the two ambulancemen moved out of earshot.

"You know, it would be easier to just tell them you have a phobia of hospitals," said Luther.

Kathryn winced and shifted position. Luther realised her anger was more about taking her mind off the pain she was in.

"Who said I had a phobia? I just get a little apprehensive sometimes, that's all."

Luther remembered the last time Kathryn got apprehensive about being in hospital. She ended up punching one of the nurses, who later filed a restraining order against her.

"No one knew I was coming until the last minute, except you," said Kathryn. "So I'm guessing the bomb was addressed to you. I was just the bonus prize."

"Agreed," said Luther. "Someone gave us enough time to get inside, get to where he needed us to be, then boom. But the real question isn't who, but why?"

"My real question is how did you know there was a bomb in there?"

"Just lucky, I guess," said Luther.

Kathryn did not look like she was going to leave it at that, but before she could speak again, Luther's mobile began to ring. After listening to the caller for a few minutes, he hung up and turned back to Kathryn.

"I think I can answer 'the who' question," he told her. "Seems our Sergeant Bonnise had an accident on his way home."

"You're having me on?"

"His car's a smouldering wreck not far from here; they made a positive ID at the scene."

"Pretty big leap. That crash could have been caused by anything."

"True, but let's look at the evidence: someone tries to kill us."

Kathryn coughed; Luther noted the intent behind the action.

"Sorry, someone tried to kill me, someone who would have had to have planted a bomb within an active crime scene."

"Someone who had access to the crime scene in the first place. Someone like Bonnise."

"Whoever Bonnise was working for decided to take him out of the equation before anyone could put the pieces together. I bet there's a tidy little paper trail already set up, leading right to Bonnise's door, case closed."

"Any ideas?"

"Not really. There are a lot of people out there who wouldn't mind seeing me in a body bag."

"I'm saying nothing."

Luther went to reply then opted to change the subject instead.

"I've arranged to have your laptop picked up from your hotel. It will be waiting for you once you reach the hospital."

"If you hadn't noticed, I'm seriously injured," said Kathryn. "I should be resting, not off doing your dirty work...I assume that's what you're asking me to do."

Luther noticed the ambulancemen returning and leaned in closer. "Listen, Kathryn, you said you may have some insight into those symbols we found, and right now, that's about the only clue we have to go on."

"What about the son, Jason?"

"I'm heading for England as soon as I leave here. I get the feeling that if someone doesn't get to this Jason kid soon, we may never get a second chance. After that, I plan on finding the people who set up tonight's little surprise and make sure I thank them properly."

By this time, the ambulancemen had returned. Kathryn and Luther shared a look that said their conversation was on hold for now. The possibility of Bonnise's involvement meant that anyone at the crime scene could have been working with him.

"Ready to go?" asked the ambulanceman.

"Load me in and let's go, I haven't got all night," she said.

Luther squeezed Kathryn's hand gently before he stepped back. He was sure he saw one of the men mouth a silent 'at last' to his comrade as they lifted her stretcher into the ambulance.

Luther raised his right hand to his ear and made a phone sign.

Kathryn nodded and smiled. Luther watched the smile disappear as the ambulance doors closed. He wondered how much of the concern was aimed at him, and how much about her trip to the hospital; probably about fifty-fifty, he concluded.

The sirens sounded and Luther stood quietly watching as the ambulance set off. Even though he knew her help would prove invaluable to his investigation, Luther wished he had never made the phone call dragging her back into all this. In a sick way, he was glad she was injured, otherwise she would have insisted in coming with him to see Jason. Considering the fate of the boy's adoptive parents, being confined to a hospital bed was the best and safest thing for her now.

"Sorry, Love," he whispered. "Sorry I got you into to this mess."

The guilt returned, not over involving her in this, but rather the earlier lie he had told about the bomb's discovery. Although it was not so much of a lie, but more of an omission, as he was still trying to understand what had happened.

He remembered being in the bedroom and opening the diary Kathryn had passed him.

GET OUT!

The voice had screamed through his mind, and Luther's reflex for self-preservation had overridden any rationalising about where the warning had come from. The biggest shock had come a little later as he lay on the wet grass, staring up at the flames from the house. He gagged at the smell of burnt flesh from his arm. It was agony when he tried to move the damaged limb. Luther was unsure of the extent of his other injuries; he was in too much pain to be sure of anything. He slowly moved his head to one side. In the distance, he saw a man. Other than the fact he wore a two-piece suit, Luther was too far away to make out any distinguishing features. The man bowed towards Luther before turning. Luther tried to call out, but instead, he felt his body go rigid for a second, then there was nothing. The pain was gone. He sat up and lifted what remained of his sleeve. The skin beneath was smooth and unblemished.

Time is against you, save the boy.

Even as he had tried to figure what had just happened, Luther heard a groan. Beside him, he saw Kathryn was beginning to stir. He looked back to where the man had stood, but he had gone.

Chapter Twelve

"J! It's Quincy. Open the door, man!"

Quincy was oblivious to the amount of noise. The hallway behind him was packed with bleary-eyed students, most of whom were dressed for bed. They all shared a look of disgust and a common goal to return to bed or whatever nighttime pursuits they were engaging in as quickly as possible. To the casual passerby, it appeared that the cause of the mass exodus into the hallway was Quincy's incessant banging, which was now bordering on panic. The sudden high-pitched scream from the other side of the door, however, told a different story.

"What the hell's going on?" a deep voice boomed out from the far end of the corridor.

Quincy recognised the voice as belonging to Garth Pullman, a good friend and more importantly, the captain of the rugby team.

"Garth, mate! Over here, something's up with J!"

Seemingly unaware of the wall of people in front of him, Garth ploughed his way through them as fast as he could. Not pausing to exchange pleasantries with Quincy, he shoulder barged the door. The door was no match for Garth, and it caved in on itself. What Quincy saw when he entered the room, he would never forget. Levitating above the bed, writhing and screaming was Jason.

"They're dead!" shrieked Jason. "They're dead!"

"Jesus Christ," said Garth.

Quincy did not look in Garth's direction, his gaze was fixed on the blood pouring down the bedroom walls. As he stared, the blood faded away. "I don't think so, mate," he said quietly.

Why am I risking my career on a hunch? Luther was minutes away from the university Jason Chen studied at, against the direct orders of Chardon, who had contacted him minutes after the TORCH jet was airborne.

He glanced at the hastily scribbled down directions fastened to the steering wheel with tape, which he got from a twenty-four hour garage, along with two microwave egg and sausage rolls, the remnants of which were sitting on the passenger seat.

Chardon's orders could not have been clearer. He was to return to headquarters for debriefing and reassignment. Luther explained Kathryn's belief that Jason Chen was in danger. He remembered suppressing his anger as Chardon described Kathryn as an unstable former agent who should never have been brought into the investigation in the first place. Chardon warned Luther that he was overstepping the bounds of his authority, and the resources of the agency were not there to indulge his whims. Luther thought it best not to mention that there were two agents conducting an investigation he should have been handling alone. Bending the rules was one thing, but this was trampling them underfoot. This was the first time since joining TORCH he had disobeyed a direct order, despite having a flair for it when he worked for MI6. Sometimes, he wondered how he managed to keep that job for as long as he did. It was his zeal and dedication to queen and country, and all the other tired clichés that landed him in more trouble than he could have ever planned for. He believed back then that no one was above the law.

God, he thought as he pulled onto the school grounds, I could not have been more wrong.

Jason allowed his mind to wander as he waited in the office. Since the 'episode' in his bedroom, the police had delivered the news of his parents' murder. When the Dean, along with two police officers, came to tell him, he simply replied, "I know." before anyone said a word, and then lapsed into silence. Both Quincy and Garth were led away for questioning. Jason saw the fear in their eyes as they left, fear of him.

There were no tears, no feelings of sadness or words left unsaid, just an unshakeable sense of inevitability. Jason knew no one else would understand because he did not understand.

The moment the Carsons entered his life, something told Jason this day would come. He liked the Carsons in his own way, but there was never any real love between them; at least not from him. They were nothing like Tony and Jin Chen, the young couple who adopted him soon after his abandonment at the hospital. Jason could not have wished for better parents than the Chens; adoptive or otherwise. In a sane world, they would have been his biological parents. They would never have left him to the mercy of an adoption system that, with all its safeguards and checks, was still an emotional lottery. When Jason was old enough, the Chens told him about the events surrounding his adoption. They believed he deserved to know the truth about his origins. It was a hard truth for Jason to accept, but the Chens were there to support him every step of the way. It was the Chens who had honoured the wish written on the note found when he was born, asking he be named Jason.

The Chens had died in a traffic accident ten years ago. Their deaths hit Jason hard, and even now he still mourned their passing. Perhaps this was why he never formed any real emotional connection with his new parents. Although John and Mary Carson were more concerned with themselves and their place in the world, he would still miss them. He would not, however, miss the secrets, the whispered and sometimes angry conversations between them and the strangers who would sometimes visit the house. These clandestine meetings would end if Jason entered the room. Whenever he broached the subject with his parents, he was met with excuses, silence, or was politely told to mind his own business. By the time he left for university, he was long past caring. They could keep their secrets, so long as they kept signing the cheques for his tuition fees. Only once did Jason catch a glimpse beneath the surface of his father. He had been going through one of his dad's drawers searching for a law book he promised to let Jason have for his studies. Instead of a volume on Consumer Law, Jason was shocked to find a gun. His father entered just as Jason was lifting the gun from its hiding place. His dad's usual, indifferent and distant demeanour shattered. He flew across the room at Jason, grabbed his arms and shoved him against the wall. Jason froze. His dad was far stronger than he imagined, and Jason doubted he could have broken free. He felt the gun torn from his grip as his father warned him to stay out of his affairs. Luckily for Jason, his mother came running into the room and was able to pry his father away. As he made a swift exit, Jason overheard his father whisper to his wife.

"He doesn't know we're doing this all for him."

"Are you, John?," Jason heard his mother reply.

"Of course I am, don't ever doubt it."

Jason saw his father look at the gun and smile sadly. "Like this is going to make any difference if they find us."

There was definitely more to his father's actions that night than just anger at a disobedient child, especially when he never expressed any strong feelings towards Jason, unless apathy counted for anything. Days later, he was packed off to university and no more was said about the incident, and until now, Jason had never given it any more thought.

The office door opened and Jason saw Bob Hunter, the Student Counsellor enter the room.

Student Counsellor, now there was a paradox, thought Jason. How does a man twice divorced and a none-too-secretive alcoholic operate under the misguided belief he can spout out advice like a greeting card?

Bob walked over to a large wooden cabinet behind his desk. He opened it and took a half-full bottle of whisky in one hand and two coffee mugs, held dangling by their handles, in the other. Smiling his thanks at him, Jason took the mug of whisky. He watched Bob fill his own mug before pulling his large armchair round to face him.

Bob's shaggy long hair and bleary, bloodshot eyes gave him the look of a man two steps away from living rough.

"Late night," said Bob. "I've got a ton of papers to be marked by the end of the week, guess it's finally beginning to show."

Jason nodded in agreement, failing to add the comment that Bob always looked like something the cat had dragged in then, after smelling the alcohol and stale nicotine, dragged him back out.

Bob pointed at Jason's mug whilst taking a sip from his own. "You looked like you could use that."

"You read my mind," said Jason, forcing a smile.

Not needing any more encouragement, Jason cupped the mug in both hands and took a drink. His body shuddered as the whisky forcibly introduced itself to his bloodstream.

"I take it the police have finished with you for the night?" said Bob.

Jason began shifting nervously in his chair. He was no more ready to deal with the night's events than he was two hours ago.

"They'll be back tomorrow,"

He lifted the mug for a second drink, this time steeling himself for the burning side effects.

Jason noticed Bob's eyes soften and knew he was about to launch into his professional 'I understand what you're going through' attitude. He weighed up the pros and cons of trying to make a quick exit. He was going to have a hard enough time once the lectures started and the gossip began. His original plan for the weekend would have placed him at home yesterday, and he would have been killed with his parents. It was something he had yet to work through. At least if he left now, he could try and grab a few hours sleep, if possible, and maybe clear his head a little.

"Listen, Jason, no one's going to force you to talk, certainly not me."

Too late; the first 'caring' salvo had been fired. There was no escape for him now.

Luther pulled up alongside the security window and saw a pair of boots propped up on the ledge. He rolled down his window and waited for a few seconds then coughed to try and attract some attention.

"What?" came a gruff reply.

"I'm here to see Mr. Hunter, I believe…"

"Name?"

Luther had not disobeyed orders, flown across the channel and driven non-stop to suffer fools gladly. He tossed his identification badge through the open window.

"Oh Christ," came a much more subdued voice. "You're with TORCH."

"Now, Mr. size nine, I've been told a Mr. Hunter is with a student whose life may be in danger. So unless you want to find yourself on the wrong end of a charge of obstructing a TORCH-sanctioned investigation, I suggest you open this gate and tell me where I can find Hunter."

A thin young man in a dark blue security uniform appeared at the window, hastily stubbing out his cigarette on the desk in front of him. In his shaking left hand, he held Luther's ID.

"Shit, Sorry mate…I mean, Agent Washington," he blurted out. "Didn't mean to …well, you know…"

Luther grinned, suddenly remembering Nelson. "No harm done, just get the gate open and point me in Hunter's direction."

"That's the weird thing, sir," said the guard, as he pressed the button to open the gates. "You won't find Mr. Hunter in his office."

"Why not?"

"Shouldn't really say, but I've seen him most nights this week passed out in his car, reckon he keeps a load of booze in there," said the guard. "I heard he didn't get the pay rise he'd been after, poor sod's been a wreck ever since. Funny thing is, he's usually stumbling back to his office by now but he's not moved for hours."

Luther loosened his pistol from its holster then swung open the passenger side door.

"Get in!"

"You what?"

"Now!"

The guard ran out of the booth and jumped in.

The car screeched through the gate where it sped down the road, veering left at the roundabout and skidding into the main car park.

"Show me where!"

"Over there!" said the guard, pointing. "Last one on the right!"

Luther pulled the car into a tight turn to bring it alongside a battered dark blue Ford Escort. He drew his gun, threw the door open and leapt out. Peering into the car, he saw, sprawled across the back seat, the naked body of a man with his throat torn out.

"Is that him?"

The guard nodded, his hand covering his mouth.

"Where's his office?"

The guard was silent, his eyes still on the corpse. Luther slammed him against the car door. "Where?"

The guard pointed to a large building in front of them.

"Main building…Third floor… A302 …,"

"Call the police," ordered Luther, sprinting towards the main building.

Bob leant forward in his armchair, displaying a willingness to listen. Jason tried to figure out what textbook Bob had gathered his tactics from. Whatever book it was, subtlety was obviously a chapter Bob missed.

"If you keep everything bottled up, it will only come back to haunt you in the long run," said Bob. "But then, you're not stupid, you already know that."

Jason said nothing at first, only the constant, almost hypnotic thudding sound from the rain steadily falling outside pervaded the silence.

"I saw it all."

"Go on," said Bob, his voice still keeping its reassuring tone.

"It was so real. I looked through its eyes, like I was there, like I was doing it, everything. I…it ripped them apart."

"Ripped who apart, Jason?"

"The bodyguards, my parents. It tore them to pieces like they were nothing and then it laughed, it just laughed." Jason's face was drained of colour, expressionless. "I know I was dreaming or something, but I couldn't wake up, then I heard the voice telling me to wake and remember."

"Voice, what voice?"

Jason looked at Bob. He was looking even worse than earlier. He was sweating and seemed to be having trouble breathing.

"You ok, Bob?" he said, genuinely concerned. "Should I call the campus nurse?"

"No, no," said Bob, dabbing his brow with a grey handkerchief. "I'm fine… go on, you were saying about hearing a voice?"

Something was wrong. Jason had already explained the disembodied voice to Bob. He had gone to see him straight after the incident in the lecture theatre. "It was a man's voice, and it's not my own."

"This voice, does it have a name?" Bob's manner was no longer full of reassurance, but sounded more like panic.

"Grey," Jason told him. "Joshua Grey."

"And what did this Grey tell you?"

"I can't remember."

"You're lying!"

Bob hurled his mug of whisky against the far wall. It broke into three pieces, staining the wall with alcohol.

Bob's behaviour was registering a high on Jason's weird-shit-o-meter. He had no idea what was wrong with Bob, but he was not waiting around for the encore performance.

Jason was halfway out of his seat when he was forced back into it by Bob. Jason struggled, but could not break free of the hand clamped on his shoulder. Bob was far stronger than his frail frame implied.

"You must…you must come with me, Jason," said Bob, sweat

pouring down his face.

Jason did not understand what was going on; this was not the Bob Hunter he knew. "Why?"

"I have no choice. The Cabal's will must and will be done."

Bob's hand snaked out. Seizing Jason by the throat, he lifted him out of the chair. Jason clung on to Bob's wrists with both hands. His legs lashed out in all directions, trying to strike his would-be kidnapper. Desperate to free himself, he sank his teeth into Bob's hand. The skin felt strange between his clenched teeth, like bitter-tasting dough, soft and spongy. Jason yanked his head backwards, tearing off a strip of skin in the process, only to find Bob's grip still as powerful. Jason thought he was going mad when he looked at the wound. The skin he had torn from Bob's hand was merely a covering; beneath it was a dark reptilian-like skin.

"Struggle all you want, boy. Like me, you will come to know your true place on this Earth." Bob smiled, baring all his teeth. "Who is this Joshua Grey? What has he told you?"

Jason stared, horrified as several of Bob's teeth began to elongate until they became black fangs. He was splattered with a foul smelling and sticky yellow substance as Bob's tongue split down the middle.

"Last chance, boy," rasped the creature Bob was fast becoming. "What did Grey tell you?"

"Are you going to kill me?"

Bob flexed the fingers of his right hand. The skin began to crack and peel away like dead leaves, revealing a scaled hand. His fingernails fell out, to be replaced by talons.

"Kill you," laughed Bob. "You are far more important than you realise. They tell me I must bring you alive, but they did not say how much alive."

Chapter Thirteen

Luther burst into Hunter's office, a Beretta in his right hand. He froze, staring at the half human, half... he had no idea what the other half was. Whatever it was, it had already killed in cold blood, and was about to do so again unless he did something.

"Let the boy go and you don't end up in a body bag."

The creature answered Luther's demand with a string of loud-pitched screeches and hisses that seemed to sound like laughter. One of the creature's claws hovered inches from Jason's chest.

"You have no idea who I am," it said.

"Now that's where you're wrong. I know exactly who you are."

Luther opened fire. The first two shots caught the creature in the head, causing it to drop Jason back into his seat. Another salvo hit it where Luther hoped its heart still was. The creature crashed backwards through the office window. Its screams were carried back into the room as it tumbled out of sight into the semi-darkness.

"You're a dead man," said Luther.

He discarded the empty ammo clip and reloaded. He went over to the silent teenager, now covered in inky black liquid; the creature's blood was Luther's first guess. As he moved to place a hand on Jason's shoulder, Jason recoiled in terror.

"Easy, easy."

Luther held up his hands and backed away.

"I'm one of the good guys."

"He was going to kill me, wasn't he?" said Jason. "Mr. Hunter was going to kill me?"

Luther sighed. He was reluctant to give the boy any more bad news.

"Whatever that thing was, it wasn't Hunter; I found him ten minutes ago."

"He's dead, isn't he?"

Luther nodded.

"Who are you?"

Luther was impressed the boy was able to think straight considering what had just happened.

"My name's Luther Washington." He flashed his ID at Jason. "I work for the United Nations."

"What are...?"

"Listen, son, I'd love to explain everything, and believe me, I could use a few explanations myself, but first, let's get someone to take a look at you, can you walk?"

Jason looked down at his clothes, stained with blood from the creature, then took a deep breath and lurched to his feet in one unsteady motion. Luther moved in to support him.

"I'll take that as a yes."

They had only taken took two steps towards the door when Luther heard a hissing noise behind him. Both of them stopped, neither man nor teenager turning.

"It's that thing," whispered Jason. "It's still alive."

"I unloaded a full clip into it, trust me, it's dead."

More hissing.

Luther pulled his gun from its holster. "Then again…"

He pushed Jason away, who immediately sought refuge behind a sofa. Luther turned and fired. This time, the creature was not caught off guard. It leapt into the air to land behind the office desk. Lifting the desk with one hand, it hurled it at Luther, who was barely able to throw himself out of the way. The desk flew past him and straight into a trophy cabinet, shattering the glass panels and peppering the air with shards of glass as it toppled forward. Luther rolled to avoid being crushed. Glancing upwards, he saw the creature scuttling across the ceiling. It sprang towards him, claws extended. Luther threw up his hands, managing to grab hold of the creature's wrists before it could strike. The creature's strength was formidable, and Luther could feel his own strength wane. His gun lay in front of him but was out of reach.

"Time to die, human."

The creature, able to break one of his claws free, plunged it into Luther's forearm.

Luther screamed, but the sound was born of rage, not fear or pain. He drove the palm of his injured arm into the creature's face, again and again. He then twisted the creature's other arm until he heard the bone snap. The creature fell. It lay, unmoving, in a pool of black ooze that was seeping out from under its skull.

Luther rose up and moved to retrieve his gun.

"Behind you!"

Upon hearing Jason's warning, Luther drove his heel back into the creature as it began to rise once more. It staggered, recovered its footing and then continued to rise, seemingly unbothered by the blow. The creature crouched low, its black eyes staring blankly out of a face battered beyond recognition. Luther felt the fear stir within him. It was an emotion that until now he thought he could control. A numbing, all-consuming terror struck him. As powerful as any physical blow, it swamped his limbs, stripping him of his will to move. A simple reality surfaced in Luther's rational, logical mind. What he faced was not human. It had never been human and no amount of rational thinking was going to change that.

The creature's laughter returned. "I can smell your fear, human," it said, sloping forward.

Luther pushed back the fear as best he could. He scanned the room for something he could use, anything that would give him a fighting chance. Perhaps he could not beat this thing, but maybe he could buy some time for Jason to escape.

"Time to die, human."

"Funny," said a voice. "That was going to be my line."

Both the creature and Luther turned to see a figure stood beside the shattered window. Luther had no idea who the man was or how he had been able to enter the room unnoticed. What he did see was a mixture of recognition and terror in the creature's eyes. Luther did not know if things were about to get better or a lot worse.

"This is none of your concern, Demon Stalker."

Two daggers sailed through the air and buried themselves deep within the creature's chest. Green flames burst from the wounds. The flames grew, enveloping the creature's entire body. It slumped to the floor, its screams filling the room. Luther watched as the green flames burned themselves out, leaving nothing but a small pile of black ash on the carpet. The bald-headed stranger; who wore a three-piece brown suit but no tie, brushed Luther aside and knelt beside the ashes of the creature. Luther noted the black eye patch the stranger wore over his left eye. Placing his face a few inches from the ashes, the man laid there for a moment sniffing, before he picked up his two daggers, the only things to have survived the flames intact.

"An Erogian," said the one-eyed man, without getting up. "You were lucky, they usually operate in threes."

"A what?" said Luther, retrieving his gun.

"A shape shifter."

The answer was no help to Luther. He stared at his gun or rather his hands; they were shaking, ever so slightly. He needed facts, cold indisputable logic, something he could rely on. This stranger was the closest he was going to get to some kind of explanation.

"Up slowly," he ordered, pointing the gun at the stranger's back. "Keep your hands where I can see them and no sudden movements."

The man did not move. Luther hoped he would not end up having to wound the man, who had just saved his life.

"You're in shock and acting irrationally, neither of which concerns me," said the man rising, keeping his back to Luther. "Now I am going

110

to check on my student, so you can either let me, or you can stop me," the man paused. "Trust me when I say, I would not take option two."

To the untrained observer, the stranger's body language showed a man unaware of the danger he was in. However, to Luther's eyes the man was centred, balance perfect, his body poised to deal with whatever happened next. Even with his gun trained on him, Luther did not feel he had the advantage, and for the second time tonight, he felt out of his depth.

"Professor Stone?" called Jason.

The one-eyed man leaned his head back and looked at the gun, then up into Luther's eyes. Smiling grimly at him, he moved to Jason. Luther was transfixed by the pile of ashes near his feet. As he stood staring at the carpet, a dozen explanations were evaluated and discarded. He looked across at the one-eyed man, who the boy seemed to know. Whoever he was, the creature had not fazed him in the slightest. Worse still, the creature had recognised him and shown fear.

He watched Stone take Jason's arm and help him up.

"It's ok, Jason," said Napoleon, the hard edge to his voice gone. "You're safe."

"It...It was...I mean I thought it was Bob, but it wasn't him."

"I know," said Napoleon. "But we have to go, now. Are you hurt?"

"No I..." Jason's answer was interrupted as he doubled over and vomited.

"I know how you feel," said Luther, still staring at the ashes.

Chapter Fourteen

Steph knew it was hopeless arguing with Ben once his mind was made up to do something. It had always been the same over their five-year partnership. Usually, she could ignore his inflated ego; after all, he was very good at what he did. This time was different.

There was no doubt in Steph's mind that they should have skipped the country the minute the Tokyo job went bad. Being wanted for theft was one thing; the mass murder of government personnel was a prison cell waiting to happen.

Ben had convinced her that they would be safe here, at their main hideout. Steph was not so sure. Elijah was not only smart, he was also well-financed and well-connected. They had bugged his office. Who was to say he had not returned the favour.

"Disc two, track five, volume level six," said Ben, cutting through her thoughts.

All around them, the sounds of seventies soul music blasted out from speakers concealed within the room.

Their subterranean apartment was designed to cater to Ben's obsession with having the best of everything. In the centre of the room was a large leather sofa, and in front of that, an oval glass table on which sat a wireless keyboard, mouse, and a pair of cordless headphones fitted with a microphone. Underneath the table were three games consoles. Ben's dream piece of hardware, swamping most of the wall facing Steph, was the huge plasma screen. Smaller monitors were fixed to the wall on either side of the screen.

Despite Ben's assurances, Steph did not feel safe. She recognised it as a by-product of her naval career. She needed to have things ordered, regimental, safe. She did not mind putting her ass on the line if the job called for it, but she did not subscribe to the unnecessary risk-taking Ben indulged in on an almost daily basis.

There were times when she could understand Ben's logic, or the lack of it, but right now, she would rather be arguing over his methods on a beach very far from here.

"Looking good, SC," said Ben as he walked into the room.

"Spare me."

"True, why waste my talents on my partner."

Partner. The word uncovered long-buried images that occasionally lapsed into Steph's conscious thought; images of a short and failed relationship she and Ben had shared several years ago.

112

A conflict of interest; the words that allowed Steph to end a relationship she should never have allowed to happen.

Ben, unlike her, could not see the problem and told her as much. It was fun, the sex was good, and it was all wrapped up with a commitment-free bow. The problem was they were professional thieves, not sex-starved teenagers. There was no place in a relationship like theirs for any feelings other than those borne from friendship or professional respect. For Steph, anything else was a distraction, and distractions, however nice, were pointless and dangerous.

"Hey." Ben was now seated in front of the keyboard. "You still with me over there or what?"

"Always," said Steph, with a knowing smile. She came over and joined him on the sofa as he put on the headset.

"Computer, this is Benjamin Ashodi. Request system access."

Several seconds passed as Ben's request was checked by the system. The plasma screen came to life, displaying the image of a white dove in the centre of the screen.

"Will Jessop."

Steph remembered the boring hours they had spent reading useless text into the microphone to enable the system to become familiar with their voice patterns.

The words 'Voice Recognition confirmed...connection being made' were displayed in large white letters across the top of the screen.

Steph stretched out on her half of the sofa and yawned.

"I hope Will's been able to make some sense of the disk," she said, wondering why Ben was looking at her so strangely. "Right now, it's the only leverage we've got."

"I hear you," agreed Ben. "But whatever's on that disk, it wasn't worth all those deaths."

"That's the thing, Ben." Stephanie shifted from her relaxed position and sat up. "What if it was? What then?"

Neither spoke for several seconds, each trying to form their own conclusions from Steph's words.

"Maybe we shouldn't have come here," said Ben at last.

"Bit late for an attack of conscience."

"I guess."

The beginnings of a smile broke Steph's stern demeanour. "I guess as lame ass apologies, go that was one of your better ones."

"That's big of you."

Before their conversation descended into the usual bout of name calling, the screen flickered and the image of a young man appeared. He wore a black T-shirt with the words 'There is no Truth only more Bullshit' printed in large defiant green lettering across it. The man was pretty unremarkable aside from the large silver-rimmed bifocals he wore, which threatened to slip off his stubby nose at any moment.

"Greetings all," the man beamed, pushing the glasses up onto his nose.

"How you doing, Will?" asked Ben.

"Great, check it out."

Steph saw Will's hand reaching towards something on top of his monitor, which judging from the sudden shifting on the screen could only be his web cam. The image on screen began to flicker and distort until Will's efforts were rewarded as the image of the black chrome and silver wheelchair he was sitting on appeared on the screen.

Ben let out an approving whistle. "Pretty sweet."

"Yeah, a lot better than the last ones we had."

The image on the screen changed back to Will.

"I heard that," said Ben. "Has everyone on the team got theirs now?"

Will nodded. "We tested them out at our last training session. You remember? The one you were supposed to be at."

"Sorry, Will, something came up."

"Yeah, like breaking into a UN research facility." Will shook his head, almost managing to pull off the impression of a displeased parent. "I told you to leave it alone. Something didn't feel right, but did you listen?"

"Does he ever?" said Steph.

"Do you have any idea how many people want a piece of your ass?"

"Well, I can tell you one person who doesn't."

"When everyone's finished with the 'I told you so's', maybe we can get to work," said Ben. "Tell me you got lucky with those files Steph sent you?"

Steph saw the anxiety on Will's face. He was not one to worry unnecessarily. Whatever Will was about to say, they were not going to like.

"You're not going to like this," said Will.

Ben shrugged his shoulders. "Figured as much."

"But it may be better hearing it from the man who caused all this."

"Pemrose?" said Steph.

"I found a video file buried under a ton of encryption."

"Run it," said Ben.

Steph watched as Will clicked his mouse and a window appeared over his web cam image. The grainy image of Pemrose's drawn and tired face appeared on the screen. His eyes depicted someone who had been deprived of sleep for far too long. His gaze kept darting around the darkened corners of what looked like a small basement. Steph did not

need to take a leap of major intuition from the shabby suit and five o'
clock shadow Pemrose was sporting to tell her that he was scared.

"I hope this thing is on," said Pemrose. "Never been good with
computers."

He smiled into the web cam, his haunted expression evident.

"Lisa, if you're watching, then the man helping me was able to get
this to you. Whatever they say about me, sis, I wanted you to know the
truth." Pemrose's eyes resumed a brief scan of the room before he
continued. "They're everywhere. I haven't slept in three, four
days...can't tell anymore..." Pemrose's head slumped into his hands, and
for several moments, all that could be heard was a faint sobbing.
Eventually, he lifted his head and started to speak again. "Shouldn't have
taken the assignment...stupid, stupid...wanted to make a difference for
once."

"Guy's strung out," said Steph, lighting up a cigar. "Borderline
nutcase, I'd say."

"I'd say shut up and let the man finish," said Ben, without looking at
her.

Steph's rebuttal took the form of a frosty silence and a funnel of
smoke directed in Ben's direction.

"I don't have much time, so listen carefully. You were right, the last
time I saw you, I was acting weird but there was a reason. I was a part of
something, a special task force set up by the Secretary General."
Pemrose's eyes flashed with a proud gleam. "Six years, sis, and finally I
get to head up my own operation. Our orders were to confirm or debunk
rumours about a rogue 'dirty tricks' agency working inside TORCH."

The enormity of Pemrose's statement was not lost on Steph.

"Apparently, this ghost agency had been siphoning off TORCH
resources for the last ten years, maybe more. I didn't believe any of that
conspiracy nonsense, but with a fifty percent pay rise, state of the art
surveillance equipment, my own hand-picked team of agents, and my
only boss being the Secretary General, I figured I could put my beliefs on
hold for a while. As it turned out, it wasn't such a waste of time after all."

"Here it comes," said Steph.

"What?"

"The part we're not going to like."

"One of our team, Hank Lazlo, started finding a lot of strange
discrepancies. Agents long thought dead were turning up alive and well,
unbeknownst to anyone within TORCH. We found hidden bank
accounts detailing coded payments totalling tens of millions. At first, we
couldn't figure out who these payments were being made to, but
eventually, we learned that the majority of them were made twenty-four
hours after a major international incident. Incidents like the kidnapping

of an oil magnate's two sons in eighty-five, the UN embassy bombings in two thousand, the assassinations of key figures in the global peace movements of the last decade.

"There was no doubt anymore. We were all believers now, but we lacked any real proof, that was until Hank stumbled across a file marked The Omega Project.

"The file was heavily protected, and when we tried to access it, a virus began to systematically delete the entire file. The only data Hank could extract from the file was a date, which is now less than a week away."

"Pause it," said Ben.

The screen froze.

"If what he's saying is true…"

"Then we've stepped in a much bigger pile of shit than I thought," said Ben.

Steph stubbed out the remains of the cigar in a nearby glass after seeing the withering look from Ben as she was about to flick it across the room.

"Now can I say I told you so," she said.

"Funny."

"Any chance of playing you the rest of this before I start drawing my pension?" cut in an impatient Will. "I've scrambled this signal using every trick in the CIA play book and a few of my own, but I still don't want to wear out my welcome."

"I hear you, Will, keep going."

Once more, Pemrose's image came to life.

"It was six months ago when things started to go wrong. I was heading home to finish up the report of our investigation. I was going to arrange a meeting with the Secretary General to discuss our findings. I was ten minutes from my house when my car was rear ended into a lamppost. When I came to, I was in a room with no windows, no furniture, just a speaker fitted to the ceiling."

Pemrose looked away from the camera. It was as though he was being forced to recall something he did not want his sister to hear, fearful of what new light that would put him in, in her eyes.

"After a few hours, I heard a voice through the speaker. It had been altered so I couldn't even tell if it was a man or a woman."

Pemrose began drumming his right hand on the desk. "The voice told me that they knew everything about the task force and our investigation. I thought they were bluffing, trying to scare the information out of me. I kept thinking that right up to when they threw Hank's body into the room." If it were possible, what little colour was left in Pemrose's cheeks was drained in an instant. "I suppose they

116

thought actions spoke louder than words: they were right. They told me I had to keep the task force running, but to make sure I only passed on information they had already seen and adjusted. They never threatened me directly; I guess they didn't need to after Hank." Pemrose's reluctance to look into the camera lens had become more pronounced. "You've got to understand me, sis. They didn't leave me any choice."

"Yeah, we understand," said Steph. "You're a gutless wonder who sold out his team to save his own ass. God, I hate bureaucrats."

"I stayed quiet about what I knew. I managed to convince the others not to pass on any information except through me. It was a lot easier to pull off than I thought. I guess Hank's disappearance shook them up enough to let me take all the risks."

"Disappearance?" said Steph. "He's downgraded a murder and then used it to make his lies a little bit easier to swallow."

"I know what you must think of me," said Pemrose, as if hearing Steph's disgust from beyond the grave. "It's no worse than what I think of myself right now. Maybe I don't deserve to make it out of this."

Any sympathy that Steph still had for Pemrose was now being aimed more toward his sister. Pemrose had betrayed his position and placed his own life above his team, and he had gotten exactly what he deserved.

"For three months, I passed on nothing but false information and kept my mouth shut. After a while, I nearly forgot I was falsifying reports; tampering with evidence, lying, it seemed, had become part of my job. A week ago, Hank's replacement left me a file before going home. He told me I should look it over and let him know what I thought in the morning, said it was important. What I found was a document detailing a theory he'd spent the last six months formulating, using his own research combined with notes Hank had left behind. He seemed to believe this group was planning some kind of attack against the UN itself, involving something called The Book of Cademus."

At that point, the video image went blank.

Ben and Steph exchanged shocked glances.

"What the hell happened to the video?"

"Sorry," replied Will, his face now once more displayed. "But like I said, the disk was full of encryption; that was all I could pull off....suppose I should have said something before."

"You think!"

"Enough," said Ben. "What about this Book of Cademus?"

"Still looking into it, but so far nothing, well not unless you count a couple of vague hits off the Net about some sort of cult set up around the time of the crusades."

"A cult?"

"Like I said, probably no link, they died out centuries ago."

"Ok, Will, keep digging."

"You got it. Look, I've been on too long already, I need to sign off."

Ben nodded. "Ok and thanks, Will."

"Whoever is running the show, they're major league players, my advice, get out of the country and keep going until you hit the North Pole."

"For once we're both on the same page," said Steph.

"Watch your back, Ben. It's no good having a rich sponsor if he's dead."

The screen went blank.

"Are you buying any of this?" said Steph.

"Pemrose did and now he's dead."

Steph wished she had not just smoked her last cigar. She could really use an infusion of nicotine about now. She headed over to the drinks cabinet, where she took out a bottle of whisky and two glasses.

"Ok, let's deal with what we know," she said, handing Ben a glass and filling it.

"Ok."

"It's a pretty good guess the disk contained enough information on this group to allow the Secretary General to start kicking down some doors."

"We know this group has something big planned a few days from now," said Ben, downing the contents of the glass in one. "But without knowing the target, that information is no good."

Steph sipped her drink, unlike Ben, she actually enjoyed savouring the taste of a fifteen-year-old single malt whisky.

"We could try and track down the other members of Pemrose's team," suggested Ben.

"No point. They're probably dead by now. I get the feeling these guys don't like loose ends."

Both of them fell silent, both knowing they were definitely a loose end.

Chapter Fifteen

Clancy knelt beside the woman and closed her eyes, which moments ago were so bright, so alive. He mouthed a single word before standing.

"Was that necessary?" he asked Kelly.

"Listen, sir," grinned Hammond, placing one of his oversized hands on Clancy's shoulder. "She was…"

"If you want to be eating your meals through a straw for the next six months, then by all means keep talking soldier."

Hammond removed his hand and took a step back, but Clancy could tell Hammond was struggling to keep his anger in check.

"Still waiting for that explanation, Kelly."

"She was watching us. We did what we had to," said Kelly.

Clancy had never been squeamish about killing a civilian, unarmed or otherwise. He never liked it, but back then, orders were orders. Things were different now. A few days ago, he had ordered the destruction of a building filled with civilians. He had not been concerned about casualties then, and that was what worried him; he had not been concerned.

"I don't know what the problem is," said Kelly. "All this pissing around is costing us time."

"My problem, Sergeant, is that you and laughing boy there just killed an innocent woman."

"When did we become the bloody Salvation Army?" threw back Kelly. "She was snooping. She could have compromised the mission. I made sure that didn't happen. Now we can carry on pissing around out here, or we can finish the job we were hired to do."

With that, Kelly stalked off down the alleyway.

Clancy watched him go. Kelly was right; the woman was a danger to the mission. How could he think to chastise him or anyone else in his unit for doing what they were trained to do? From now on, he would have to tread carefully. Any of the others, Kelly included, would put a bullet in him if they thought for one moment he was becoming too weak for command. He turned his attention to Hammond and Wheels, who had just arrived.

"Nice work, Hammond," said Wheels upon seeing the bodies.

"Hammond, you and Wheels hide the bodies and cover our exit. Now do you think you two screw-ups can handle that?" said Clancy.

"Yes, sir," both men answered, although the frown on Hammond's face showed he was less than happy about being left behind.

Hammond was a good solider, Clancy knew that. Hammond's

119

problem was that he was starting to like being paid a lot more than he liked following orders.

Leaving the two men, Clancy jogged to where Kelly and the others were waiting, gathered outside a small record shop. Clancy unclipped a radio from his belt as Kelly produced a small penlight. He nodded to Kelly, who switched on the light and directed its beam through the shop window whilst switching it on and off.

He stared into the shop, which was bereft of all light save that provided by Kelly's flickering torch. After a few seconds, a figure came out from behind one of the shelves and moved towards them.

"I hope we don't screw this one up," said Kelly, to no one in particular.

"Piece of piss, mate," shrugged Stony, who Clancy thought always had enough confidence for twenty people. "We get in, we get the disk, we kill the bastard, easy."

Everything Luther had come to know, believe and trust in the rational world had not merely been challenged, it had been devastated. How the hell was he going to explain all of this in a report in a way that would not get him committed?

"How bad are you hurt?"

Luther then remembered he had not endured this nightmare alone.

"I'm fine," he said, a little sharper than was necessary. "Thanks," he added, realising his gratitude sounded more like an afterthought. "I doubt I could've handled that thing on my own."

"You couldn't," said Napoleon, moving towards the broken window.

Luther watched Napoleon studying the window, then once again kneel to examine the creature's ashes. He then noticed for the first time the shotgun strapped to his back.

"Who the hell are you?"

"Stone," said the man, standing up. "Professor Napoleon Stone, I'm a lecturer here."

That's not all you are, thought Luther.

"Napoleon?" said Luther. "You're joking right?"

Stone's eyes narrowed.

"Ok then, Professor," said Luther. "Suppose you explained what just happened?"

"Why?"

Luther was caught off guard by Stone's reply. "Why…what do you mean why?"

"I mean, why would I waste my time explaining something we both know you are nowhere near ready to accept?"

"Trust me, Professor, you'd be surprised at what I'd believe after what I just saw."

Luther thought he saw the glimmer of a grudging respect crease Stone's face, accompanied by a raised eyebrow.

"Fair enough," said Napoleon. "As I explained earlier, this was an Erogian. They have the ability to take the form of any creature, human or otherwise, that they have been in direct contact with for more than an hour."

Luther listened, trying not to allow his own beliefs to cloud what he was being told.

"In the hour they are in contact with their victim, they create a mental link with them, siphoning off what aspects of that victim's personality they can use to make their performance more convincing."

"You said you were surprised it was on its own."

Luther looked over at Jason, who was slumped in the corner, a pool of vomit slowly drying a few feet in front of him.

"There are separate clans of Erogians. No one knows how many," said Napoleon. "Usually, they work in groups of two or three; where one fails, another appears to finish the job."

Luther pondered over Napoleon's explanation. "Seems like a logical plan of attack, so why," he pointed at the ashes, "did it…"

"He."

Luther decided against asking Napoleon how he was able to determine the creature's sex. "Ok, why did *he* come here alone?"

"Good question," said Napoleon. "Before I answer it, I have a few questions of my own, like who are you? What agency do you represent? And most importantly, what do want with one of my students?"

"My name is Luther Washington, and I never said I was working for a government agency."

Luther was unsure about revealing too much until he knew a lot more about the strange professor.

"Fine," said Napoleon, apparently unconcerned at Luther's blatant avoidance of his questions. He went over to Jason, who until now, had been largely ignored by the two men. Helping him to his feet, Napoleon placed the boy's arm over his shoulder and led him towards the door. Seeing Stone about to leave with the one link to his murder investigation acted like a shot of adrenaline to Luther's bloodstream, pushing the image of the creature from his mind.

"No one's going anywhere until I get some answers," he said, grabbing Napoleon's arm.

Napoleon turned his head and glared at Luther's hand. Luther took the hint, but chose to ignore it, instead his grip increased.

"Or else?" said Napoleon.

Two words spoken softly but each one filled with power, and the veiled promise of violence. Luther did not reply. There was no need. The fact that he still had not released Napoleon was answer enough.

"Listen to me, Washington. The longer we stand here arguing, the less chance we have of surviving the next ten minutes."

A part of Luther knew there was some sense in Stone's words, but his rational mind was clinging to his training. As long as it was there to fall back on, he would not have to force himself to find another way to rationalise the irrational.

"I work for TORCH, Professor. That means you're breaking enough laws to earn your ass a reserved seat in any prison of my choosing."

"TORCH?" said Napoleon, his voice sounding shocked.

Luther nodded and then, as if to hammer the point home, the sound of screeching tyres and car doors being opened and closed in succession carried into the room.

"You hear that?" Luther released his grip on Napoleon. "That, Professor is the back-up team I radioed for on my way here."

By now, Jason was coming to his senses. "What are they going to do?" he asked.

Luther heard the fear in Jason's wavering voice and sympathised with him. What a night he was having. First, his parents are murdered and then he's attacked by something masquerading as his guidance councillor. If there was a quota for bad luck, Jason Chen must have inherited a lifetime's supply of it.

"Don't worry, Jason. Those men are here to take you somewhere safe."

Seeing the pile of ashes, Luther wondered if Jason would ever feel safe again.

"Do you really think taking him to a safe house will stop whatever they send after him, or you?"

"Me?"

"You have seen something only a handful of people have seen," said Napoleon, leading Jason back into the room. "They cannot allow you to live with that knowledge."

"Who?"

Napoleon hesitated. "I'm not sure."

Now it was Luther's turn to go on the offensive. "You're lying, Professor, so I think I'll stick with my plan. Jason goes into protective custody and you, Professor Stone, are under arrest until you decide to become a little more truthful."

"I can't let you do that. There's too much at stake."

"I think the men with guns coming up the stairs will help to convince you," said Luther. He felt guilty for having to arrest the man who had just saved his life, but it was mixed with the relief of finally getting back to the reality of his world.

Jason was slouched against Hunter's overturned desk, hands stuffed in his pockets, watching the two men arguing over his eventual fate. How long would it be before they asked him what he wanted to do?

The strange thing was, he had sensed there was something not right about Bob from the moment he entered the office. Jason tried to focus his mind in an attempt to recall what was going through it during his conversation with Bob. The more he concentrated, the more the voices of the two men with him faded into the background like white noise.

He became aware of something else inside his head, a voice repeating something over and over again. He closed his eyes and focused on the word as hard as he could.

DANGER.

Then it struck him. A blinding, searing bolt of pain shot through his skull. Even as he could put his hand to his head, the pain was gone. He opened his eyes and found he was lying on the floor with no memory of having fallen over. Looking up, he saw Napoleon and Luther standing over him, both wearing expressions of concern.

"You all right?" asked Napoleon, helping him up.

Jason said nothing, his vision was still a little fuzzy but returning to normal, he staggered over to the door, kicked it shut and locked it. He picked up one of the fallen chairs and jammed it under the door.

"The men coming upstairs are not your men, Agent Washington." Jason's voice was strong and clear, with a tone of authority that surprised even him. "They're coming to kill us."

Chapter Sixteen

"Just sit down," said Ben. "You're doing my head in."

Steph, arms folded, continued to pace, only pausing for a nervous drag on the last embers of her cigar.

"Sorry, but sometimes little things make me nervous," said Steph. "You know, like finding out your supposedly secret hideout isn't so secret."

"It's not that…"

"Please don't insult my intelligence by telling me it's not that bad."

"How about…"

"No, Ben. We've never had it worse than this. We've never even come close to being worse than this."

Steph pointed at the monitor and the several figures making their way into the record shop across the street. The shop, which was also owned by Ben, housed their underground emergency exit.

"Samford's with them," said Steph. "Now why am I not surprised?"

Ben hired Samford to run the record shop after he had approached Ben after getting out of prison. Knowing how hard it was to get work on the outside, Ben had taken a chance on him. He figured he could keep Samford away from their real operation. He was wrong.

"Thanks to your prison buddy, Clancy and his men will be here in less than ten minutes, so forgive me if I'm a little stressed."

"Take it easy, Steph, I have a plan."

"Which is?"

Ben went silent.

"You don't really have a plan, do you?"

"No."

"Give me one reason why I don't kick your ass into next year?"

"My award winning personality?"

Steph shot him an angry glance before moving to one of the walls. Touching the hidden pressure pad, she stepped back as a section of the wall slid away to reveal an assortment of weapons and equipment.

"I'm assuming you're going to do something really stupid when they get here?" asked Steph, lifting a weapon from the compartment.

"I was thinking more insanely clever."

"Really, really stupid then," said Steph. "I'll see if I can slim the odds down a bit. I would tell you to be careful, but I'd be wasting my breath, wouldn't I?"

"The last time, I wasn't ready for them. This time, Clancy and his boys are about to find out what it means to get on my bad side."

"I'm sure they're quaking in their boots."

"Thanks for the confidence boost."

"No problem. Besides you still owe me my cut for this job, and if we live through this, I expect a bonus, otherwise mercenaries will be the least of your problems!"

Ben began quietly counting to himself.

"What are you doing now?"

"Figuring out what day of the month it is, you're usually only this cranky when…"

Steph threw the safety off the MP5 submachine gun she was holding. "Don't start with me, Ashodi."

A glaring truth became apparent to Samford the moment he unlocked the door and allowed the figures clad in black to move past him. He was a traitor, one that had been years in the making. He had been approached a few months after he left prison by associates of an anonymous and wealthy benefactor. All Samford had to do was approach Ben, get close, sit tight, watch and wait for when he was needed. Over the years, he all but forgot about the arrangement; last's night phone call changed all that.

They were offering a clean slate for all his gambling debts he owed, both before and after prison, and some nice change in the tune of ten grand for a few minutes work.

Samford wished he was the kind of man who would not sell out a friend, but it was no use. Any outdated notions of doing the right thing were overshadowed by his desire for self-preservation and wealth, which were far greater motivators than friendship and loyalty.

He felt two taps on his shoulder. It was the leader. He was pointing at Samford's torch. Taking the hint, Samford switched it off. Moving to the head of the group, Samford led them past the many cluttered shelves of junk, through another door, which took then into a storeroom. It was a cramped fit for everyone, but they somehow managed it. The only light on offer was from a small window high up on the wall that faced the storeroom entrance. On the floor, in the centre of the room was a flat, square-shaped metal hatch. No turning back now, Samford told himself. Considering the amount of cash they had paid him over the last year for just keeping an eye on Ben, he was sure they could not be doing anything one hundred percent legal. Looking into the expressions surrounding him, each one illuminated by the streaks of moonlight criss-crossing the room, he was even more sure.

"We're here," the leader whispered. "Now what?"

"What about my cash?" said Samford, surprised at his own bravery, or rather his stupidity in the face of so many loaded weapons. "You said I'd get it up front."

The leader smiled and Samford felt like someone had reached into his trousers and grabbed his testicles.

"Don't worry, you'll get your payment."

Samford did not like the way the man was cradling the gun in his arms. "But if you need some incentive…" he gestured with his eyes to something behind Samford. Following the leader's direction, Samford saw a metallic briefcase lying on the ground. The case was secured by two combination locks on either side of the handle.

"Tell us what we need to know to breach Ashodi's security measures, and I'll give you the combination to the briefcase right now."

"What and you'll just let me walk out of here?" said Samford, unconvinced. "Man, you must think I'm crazy."

The leader stepped forward until he was inches from Samford's face. "We're not cheap thugs, Mr. Brown. We are professionals. The question is, are you?"

Samford considered his alternatives. It did not take him long to realise there were none. He had backed himself into a corner. Nothing to do now except play out the hand. He walked up to the hatch, knelt down in front of it and took out a small knife. With the others looking on, he tapped out a sequence of sounds onto the surface of the panel with the knife, before sitting back. The hatch slid back revealing steps leading down into the darkness.

"Head down the stairs. They will lead you into a tunnel," explained Samford. "At the end is a wall. There must be a way past it 'cause I've seen Ben and Steph go in and out of there loads of times."

"Security measures?"

"I told you before, I don't know if he's got any, I don't even know what he's into, and I don't want to."

Samford caught the shocked look on the man standing closest to the leader; obviously it was news to him.

"So we could have already tipped him off just by opening this thing. Great, that's just great," said one of the men.

"There's nowhere for him to go. We've got a sniper watching the record shop entrance," said the leader. "There are only two of them and the only one with any kind of military training is the woman. So we put her down first."

The leader turned to Samford, providing him with an assuring smile.

"Well, Mr. Brown, as promised." Even as he spoke, Samford was already scrambling across the storeroom to the attaché case, his thumbs resting on the tumblers of the case's two combination locks.

"The left combination is three, two, four and the right is seven, one, nine. Enjoy your reward, Mr. Brown. You've earned it."

The leader started down the steps, his men following. Samford did not hear or see them go. All his attention was focused on the attaché case. After fumbling with the combinations, the clasps on the case finally sprang open. Licking his lips in anticipation, he carefully opened the case; he wanted to ensure not one dollar bill escaped.

"What the....?"

The interior of the case was empty except for a small piece of paper neatly folded in two.

"It's a cheque," said Samford, trying to convince himself. "It has to be a cheque."

He opened the paper and read the single phrase written in large black ink.

WE DON'T LIKE TRAITORS

Samford turned too late to see the leader, who had obviously sneaked back up the stairs while he had been focused on the case.

"Why?" said Samford, tears already beginning to fall as he watched the man fit a silencer to the Beretta he was holding.

"Can't you read?" he replied, firing a single round into Samford's forehead. Samford fell backwards, one hand still clutching the attaché case, the other, the now blood-stained message.

"Unlock the door, Jason," said Luther, keeping his tone light. "You're in shock. You need help."

Luther glanced at Napoleon, hoping he took the hint.

"You know me, Jason," said Napoleon, his tone matching Luther's. "He's right. You have to open the door. Those people you heard, they're coming to help you."

Jason shook his head. "No, you're wrong; they're coming to kill us!"

Luther knew enough about the effects of shock to know that the best way to deal with it was to be as gentle and compassionate as possible. The heavy booted footsteps coming up the corridor outside were not helping the situation. If he pushed too hard, Jason's mind could close in on itself and he could kiss goodbye to getting anything useful out of him for a very long time.

"Listen, son."

"I'm not your son!" Jason shot back, glaring at him. "I don't have a father anymore, remember? He's dead. They're both dead!"

Luther started towards Jason, one cautious step at a time. He held his hands out in front of him, showing he was no threat. The sudden banging on the door caused him to freeze.

"Stand fast," ordered Luther. "We have a small situation here."

There was no reply and the banging increased. Now it was Luther's turn to experience a feeling of uneasiness.

"I hate to say this," whispered Napoleon, pulling his colt .45 from its side holster. "But I think Jason may have a point."

"Come off it! How can he be …?"

Luther then heard something that demanded immediate action. He sprang forward, tackling Jason. Napoleon was already halfway over the desk as Luther moved. With Jason struggling to break Luther's grip, they tumbled into a book cabinet. The next thing they heard was a sound not unlike a shower of hailstones, only softer. All through the room, pieces of wood were catapulted through the air like tiny darts as the furniture was hit. Luther saw Napoleon dip his head down behind an oak desk as it too was riddled with suppressed gunfire.

Luther shelved the notion that his back up team were trying to kill him, and allowed the cold and rational part of his psyche to take hold.

"Stone!" he called out, whilst shoving Jason back further into the corner. "Stone! You hit?"

Luther saw a hand appear from behind the desk, the fingers forming an OK sign, then there were four fingers held aloft.

"Stay down," he told Jason.

Luther edged closer to the door, ignoring a splinter as it struck his left cheek, drawing blood. He focused on the four fingers.

Three fingers now, Luther took the safety off his gun.

Two fingers, he took a deep cleansing breath.

One finger then a single clenched fist. Napoleon's other hand appeared over the top of the desk clutching his colt. It roared into life, blasting large chunks out of the barricaded door. Luther twisted his arm so that he was able to fire into the door without exposing himself.

"The window!" shouted Jason.

Napoleon swung round to see two sets of boots appear at the window. He threw himself sideways, dodging gunfire that nearly ripped the desk in two. Colliding into a bookcase, Napoleon was stunned but managed to return fire. One of the men was blasted from his feet and fell screaming from the window. The second man dropped into the room firing. Napoleon was covered by paper as the row of books above his head were reduced to confetti by gunfire. Unlike the aim of his attacker, Napoleon's aim was accurate and unhampered by panic. A shot rang out, removing the attacker's right knee. The man fell, his automatic rifle flying out of his hands and towards Luther.

The door burst open, and three men entered the room. Discarding his gun, Luther ran forward, caught the rifle turned and fired. The result was bloody but conclusive. Another four men appeared at the doorway, stepping over the bodies of the fallen, their weapons trained on Luther.

"Down!"

Luther dropped as Napoleon, a gun in each hand, dived over him, firing. One man was killed instantly, the others scattered.

"Jason, the door!" shouted Napoleon.

Jason kicked the door shut.

"Help me," ordered Napoleon, who was beginning to drag a desk. Luther came over and together they shoved it against the door.

Luther saw the wounded man was crawling towards a gun. He was about to shout a warning when Napoleon fired once.

The man did not move a second time.

"You didn't have to kill him," said a horrified Luther. "You could have fired a warning shot."

"He had his warning shot," said Napoleon. "He chose to ignore it."

Luther would have to watch Napoleon carefully. This was not a man to be crossed lightly.

"Jason," called out Napoleon. "You Ok?"

"No."

"Just stay calm and keep your head down," Napoleon told him.

Napoleon bent over one of the corpses and tore open the man's sleeve.

"What's that?"

Luther pointed at an intricate tattoo, which decorated the inner part of the man's right bicep, just below his armpit.

"I've seen it before," said Jason.

Napoleon grabbed Jason's arms. "Where?"

"In my nightmares," said Jason, who was staring at the tattoo of the flaming sword and the orange bird. "But I didn't think it actually existed. What is it?"

"A coat of arms," sighed Napoleon, letting go of Jason.

"A coat of arms?" repeated Luther.

"The Knights of Cademus," said Napoleon. "If you thought we were in trouble before, you can multiply that by a hundred now."

Luther had been in more than his fair share of scrapes and near death situations. He was not about to be spooked by a tattoo and a cryptic warning.

"Who are we dealing with?."

"Fanatics," said Napoleon. "They'll keep coming. It won't matter how many of them we kill. Death holds no terror for them."

To add weight to his words, sounds could be heard of something being slammed repeatedly against the door. Luther did not know how many men were on the other side of the door, but there were too many for the two of them and a terrified teenager to handle. He flipped the catch, allowing the ammo clip to slide out into his waiting palm. Six rounds: not enough, not nearly enough.

129

"All we want is the boy," a voice shouted. "Give us Jason Chen and the two of you can go free. Stand against us and die."

"Original," said Napoleon.

"I've got six shots." Luther pointed at Napoleon's shotgun. "How many you got in there?"

Napoleon slid his arm over his shoulder and pulled the shotgun from its holster. "Enough to get us out of here," he said, moving to the wall that was facing them. "Be ready to move," Napoleon told them, closing his eyes.

Luther frowned. "Get ready for what, Stone? Stone?"

A moment later, everything changed again for Luther. Like the creature he had fought earlier, this was another of those 'my life will never be the same' moments. His half-formed suppositions about Professor Stone were thrown into disarray. He gazed, struck dumb at the luminous glow now surrounding the shotgun Napoleon held. The eerie yellowish light suffused the room in an extraordinary hue, as if it was trapped inside a glass jar with a million fireflies.

Even stranger than the light was the energy that defied description emanating out of Napoleon's chest and down his right arm. A thin layer of sweat had formed on the Professor's brow, his eyes remained tightly shut. Whatever Napoleon was attempting, it was clear to Luther that it was taking its toll on him.

Napoleon knew the risk he was taking using his power again so soon after the battle with Alvarez. His mind and body needed time to recharge from the mental and physical strain placed upon him every time he called forth the power. He could already feel his pulse and heartbeat quickening beyond acceptable levels. There were others who shared his strange vocation, others who had died attempting a similar feat. There was no choice, Napoleon told himself. All he could do now was steel himself for what was to come.

Napoleon heard another crash against the door and guessed one more would be enough for the door to give way.

"Stone!" yelled Luther. "If you're going to do something, now's the time!"

Luther's words had the desired effect. Napoleon raised his shotgun and aimed it at the solid wall in front of him. His heart was bursting against his chest, the blood raced through his veins, *focus, breathe*, find the quiet place, the place where anything is possible.

Napoleon opened his eyes and spoke the word. He could not stop the others from hearing the word, but that did not matter. Even if the TORCH agent spoke a dozen languages, he would never understand it. The surrounding energy was pulled into the shotgun then discharged in one column of pure focused energy. It tore through the wall, leaving a hole at least seven feet high in its wake. The force of the blast knocked Jason off his feet. Luther stumbled, but somehow stayed upright. The energy did not disperse, but instead continued forward, blasting another hole in the far wall of the adjoining room, and causing the same damage to two more rooms before it eventually dissipated. It was then the office door finally gave way, allowing several men into the room. Napoleon was exhausted, but still was able to grab Jason by the scruff of his t-shirt and haul him over to the hole. He could barely lift his head, and his legs threatened to buckle at any second.

"Go!" ordered Luther, hoisting a man who was unfortunate enough to enter the room first off his feet and pitching him back into his comrades. Luther scooped up the attacker's weapon and again the room was alive with gunfire.

Drawing on what little strength remained, Napoleon shoved Jason into the next room, yelling at him to keep moving. Hearing the gunfire behind him, he thought about going back to help the TORCH agent. He knew he would be of little use; it was taking everything he had to keep himself from blacking out, let alone plunging back into a second gun battle. He had to concentrate on getting Jason to safety and hope the TORCH agent would not be far behind, or at the least, died quickly. The Knights of Cademus utilized methods for gaining information that were far less humane than a bullet through the brain.

As he entered the second room, the toll of his actions began exacting their due on him; his vision began to fail him, along with his legs. He sagged against a wall, where he tried unsuccessfully to rally his strength, even the simplest bodily function had now become a lesson in willpower.

Jason reached the last hole. He had not needed much prompting from Professor Stone to make a break for it. He recognised the deserted and darkened room now littered with dust and debris as one of the staff common rooms. Even through his fear, Jason wished he could be here when the teaching staff saw the remains of their room. Jason dismissed his first pleasant thought in ages, and sprinted for the door that would lead to a small balcony and a flight of stairs, which would lead him downwards and out to the relative safety of the college grounds. Wasting no more time, he grabbed the door handle, and with it, the promise of more safety than he had known in the last thirty minutes. He looked round, realising for the first time he was completely alone.

Reluctantly, he looked back through the holes and saw Luther embroiled in a brutal hand to hand battle with at least six other men. Clutching a rifle in his large hands, Luther had turned it from a sophisticated piece of weaponry into a makeshift but effective club. Jason then caught sight of Professor Stone, slumped on the ground, legs stretched out in front of him, clutching his chest. Napoleon looked up and saw Jason; lifting his hand, he kept pointing to the door. Jason shared the sentiment; right now there was nothing more he would have liked than to follow his lecturer's advice. After one last look at the closed door, Jason took a deep breath and ran back towards Napoleon.

"Bloody conscience," he mumbled as he ran.

Chapter Seventeen

If there was one thing Hammond hated more than watching his basketball team lose on those rare occasions when he actually got to see them play, it was rear guard duty. To make matters worse, he was left with 'Wheels' for company, who was about as much use as…well, he could not even come up with a close comparison.

He leant against the side of the van, listening to the rain on its roof. It sounded like a major downpour was on the way, a downpour he had no intention of being caught in. He walked round to the rear of the van, where he found Wheels inside, checking over his gun. Rookies, nothing but an accident waiting to happen.

"Hey, Wheels," he said, leaning through the open van doors.

Wheels sat bolt upright, waving his gun in Hammond's direction.

"Get that weapon out of my face, boy!"

"Sorry, Hammond, I must have…"

"Let's get one thing straight. I ain't interested in being your daddy or your long lost buddy, you get me, boy?"

Hammond leaned in further, allowing Wheels to the see expression on his face.

"I'll make a deal with you. You don't screw up before the others get back, and I won't gut you like a fish. Deal?"

Wheels nodded sharply.

"Good," said Hammond, satisfied his point had been made. "Now, I'm gonna check the alleyway again. You stay put and stay alert."

Without another word, Hammond set off, slowly making his way down the alleyway. His eyes took in every rooftop, every window, anywhere someone could conceal themselves. The prospect was unlikely, but he also knew unlikely prospects were the sort of thing that earned you a bullet in the ass.

Hammond moved further down the street, past the last run down apartment building until he reached the bottom of the alley. At this point, the alley opened out into a much wider street. All he saw, looking around, were a few tramps and hookers, nothing to worry about. The rain was beginning to fall by this time, and he decided Wheels could take the next turn as sentry. Why should he get himself and his equipment soaked when there was a rookie he could exploit? Smiling at the idea, he started back to the van. He stopped when he was halfway and turned into the alcove of a small shop. The flashing neon sign above the shop read Sam's Café, although this was not clear, at first, as several of the letters had ceased to flash.

Hammond placed his rifle up against the wall and moved his hands down to his trouser zip. He thought it best to relieve himself now before the rain got too heavy. As he stood there, he became aware of the sensation of being watched. Tilting his head slightly to the right, he gave the impression of scratching his nose. His suspicions were confirmed when he caught a glimpse of a laser sight resting on the wall in front of him, before it lurched left and disappeared. There was no doubt in Hammond's mind the sight was now fixed on the base of his skull. As he planned his next move, the heavens opened and sheets of rain poured down onto the street, accompanied by a flash of lightning. Hammond reacted instantly, fifteen years in the military were not about to end in an alley. He dived to his left, snatched the rifle and as he fell, twisted in mid-air to face his attacker, the anticipated gunfire harmlessly clattering against the wall. He landed hard on his side and slid down the rain-soaked street, his gun blasting away at the flash of gunfire coming from across the street on one of the building's fire escapes. Hammond was peppered with rainwater and pavement chippings as automatic weapons fire tore into the street around him. Luckily, the downpour was making it difficult for his attacker to get a clear shot at him. Vaulting to his feet, Hammond sprinted back the way he had come, firing up at the fire escape as he ran. He caught a glimpse of someone running along the fire escape, but his bullets were unable to find their mark. Upon reaching the end of the fire escape, the figure leapt over the rail. The attacker levelled their gun and fired, catching Hammond high in the chest, catapulting him through a shop window and into the darkness beyond.

Despite landing hard, Steph's only injury was a slight twinge of pain as she rested her weight onto her right leg. She switched on the torch attached to the underside of her gun and pointed it to where she had seen the big man fall. Cautiously, she edged forward, the torch cutting a path through the rain. The sound of broken glass underfoot greeted her ears, and she stopped in front of what remained of the shop window. Steph moved inside and cast her light over the unmoving body, covered in glass. She moved closer, making sure the laser sight was kept trained on his forehead. Kicking the gun out of the man's right hand, she knelt beside him. She placed two fingers against his throat and felt for a pulse.

"His overconfidence cost him his life."

Steph turned to see a young man, who the dead man had called Wheels, barring her exit from the shop.

"Stand fast, soldier," she ordered, training her gun on Wheels. "Let me see those hands."

"Impressive reflexes, Stephanie. Can I assume if you're here, then

Benjamin has either already escaped, or is somewhere in the vicinity? Which is it?"

"This is the part where you offer me my life in exchange for Ben and the disk, right? "

"You misunderstand me, Stephanie. I have no intention of allowing either of you to live; my employers were very specific on that."

"And your employers are?"

Wheels smiled malevolently. "You are not ready for that kind of truth; now where is the disk?"

"You're forgetting who's holding the gun."

"Not at all."

Wheels lunged at Steph, who unloaded several rounds into his chest. She heard the bullets tear through cloth then skin. Wheels staggered back a few steps, his advance halted. She then watched as the wounds sealed themselves as if the skin had never been broken.

"What the hell are you?" she said at last, realising the question was probably the most understated phrase she had ever uttered.

"Your executioner," said Wheels, grabbing her by the throat.

His fingers began to stretch, tearing the skin to reveal claws where his hand had once been.

He hefted Steph over his head with one arm, and threw her as if she weighed nothing. Steph hit the pavement hard on the far side of the street. As she spat out a mouthful of blood, she felt a stabbing pain in her ribs and guessed one of them was badly bruised, perhaps broken. The warm sensation moving down the right side of her head told her she was bleeding. She touched her jaw, it was not broken, but it hurt like a bitch. She looked across at the shop window and saw Wheels step out into the street.

Steph pulled herself up, looked at her gun and then tossed it away.

"That is the first sensible thing you have done, Stephanie."

The clever combatant imposes his will on the enemy, but does not allow the enemy's will to be imposed on him.
Sun Tzu

Forcing a defiant grin, Steph reached into her jacket. She produced a combat knife in one hand and a small metal tube in the other. Flicking her wrist downward, the tube extended like a telescope and locked itself into place. It now resembled a police baton.

Wheels advanced towards Steph, matching her smile with one full of malice and dark intent.

The good fighters of old first put themselves beyond the possibility of defeat, and

then waited for an opportunity of defeating the enemy. To secure ourselves against defeat lies in our own hands, but the opportunity of defeating the enemy is provided by the enemy himself. Thus the good fighter is able to secure himself against defeat, but cannot make certain of defeating the enemy.
Sun Tzu

A sense of calm settled over Steph's mind, an impossible battle against an enemy more powerful than herself was not a new position for her. Yes, bullets were no good, but he breathed the same air she did and that meant he could be killed. Only one of them would leave the alley alive, and Steph planned on it being her.

If he is secure at all points, be prepared for him. If he is in superior strength, evade him.
Sun Tzu

Wheels came in fast and hard. Steph was ready; her opponent was arrogant and overconfident, relying on brute strength to win the day. She ducked under the first blow, recovering in time to deflect Wheels' clawed hand with her baton, whilst slicing along his open palm with her blade. Her mind was honed on one thing, survival. She rolled right and came up into a kneeling position, her baton blocking Wheels as he smashed down with both hands. The pain from the blow and the power behind it was unbelievable, but Steph buried it. She slashed out at Wheels' midriff, span round and smashed the baton into his spine, slamming him into the wall behind her.

Wheels looked down at the six-inch gash now running along his stomach. Steph stood. Her knife was now stained with a black and sticky liquid she guessed was the creature's blood. Wheels came forward again, only this time, more cautiously. Steph knew he would not be so cocky now she had drawn blood.

"You cannot win, human," Wheels told her. "Throw down your weapons and your death will be quick."

In battle, there are not more than two methods of attack - the direct and the indirect; yet these two in combination give rise to an endless series of manoeuvres.
Sun Tzu

Steph did not answer. She was studying her opponent's every movement, no matter how subtle. She saw his right shoulder tense and at once knew what was coming. She dropped to the floor, in a splits position, leaving Wheels swinging at thin air.

The direct and the indirect lead on to each other in turn. It is like moving in a circle - you never come to an end. Who can exhaust the possibilities of their combination?
Sun Tzu

Steph's baton cracked against Wheels' right knee, whilst burying her dagger deep into his left. Wheels howled in pain, the sound unlike anything Steph had ever heard. Wheels dropped onto his ruined knees before Steph, who had produced a second dagger.

"You think to kill me, girl. I have existed since before..."

"Please," said Steph, plunging the dagger into his throat. "Give it a rest."

Instead of finishing him off, the strike only seemed to anger Wheels further. He leapt onto Steph, his hands clamped around her throat.

Steph head-butted him, grabbed the dagger lodged in his throat and pushed down on it with what little strength she had left. She could feel herself slipping away and Wheels' grip around her throat grew tighter.

"Tell me where the disk is!"

"Screw you!"

As Steph's vision began to give way to a tiredness from which she knew there would be no waking, a crossbow bolt buried itself deep within Wheels' left temple. He screamed, causing Steph to clamp her hands over her ears, before he disintegrated before her eyes. For what seemed like an age, Steph lay on her back covered in black ash, breathing hard. She did not say anything; she just stared up at the night sky and took a moment to fully appreciate that she was still alive. A gloved hand extended towards her, which she grasped and it pulled her to her feet. She stumbled but was supported by another gloved hand. Looking into the man's face, she saw not only a hardness born of a deep-seated ruthlessness she knew only too well, but also a sincere look of concern.

"You sure know how to make an entrance, Reverend," she smiled weakly at the man, whose real name she had never discovered. "Thanks."

The Reverend nodded, wearing his usual distant, almost uninterested expression, made more pronounced by his gaunt and weather-beaten face.

"It's good to see you again, Steph," said the Reverend.

He cast an inquiring eye over the remains of Wheels still covering Steph's clothes. "I would be grateful if you could tell me what I just killed?"

"Right now, Rev, I know about as much as you do," she said,

dusting the ash from her clothes. She bent down and retrieved her gun.

"I know nothing."

"Like I said, as much as I do. How did you know where its weak spot was?"

"Because I placed the thought inside his limited and somewhat disturbed mind," a voice said.

The Reverend and Stephanie moved as one, each of them making the decision to shoot first, identify bodies later. Steph, who was still kneeling, span and fired. The Reverend mirrored her actions with his Uzi pistols. Some distance away in the middle of the street was their intended target. A man, dressed in an immaculate, charcoal-coloured, three-piece suit and an unbuttoned black raincoat, did not flinch. The bullets did not strike him, instead they paused in front of him as if considering their next move, before flying around him and continuing on their original path.

"Impossible," said the Reverend.

"State the bloody obvious, why don't you!" yelled Steph, still firing.

The man strode towards them, each step measured, his hands clasped behind his back. The raincoat he wore now resembled a cloak as it flowed out behind him. Closer now, Steph was able to get a better look at him, the tailored suit, the neatly combed dark brown hair, the expensive-looking footwear. This was someone who took great pride in his appearance, and he expected others to notice the effort. Apart from an expensive taste in clothing, there was nothing unusual about the man's appearance. He was attractive in a clean cut, older man kind of way, not Steph's usual type as he looked old enough to be her father. There was, nevertheless, something unsettling about him, though she put that down to his little trick with the bullets.

"Please lower your weapons," the man's voice radiated power.

Steph hesitated, unsure what to do next.

I WILL NOT ASK YOU A SECOND TIME.

The voice boomed through Steph's mind, blocking out all other thoughts. She dropped her gun at once. The Reverend also relinquished his weapons, no doubt the result of a similar mental tongue lashing, she guessed.

The man stared at the discarded weapons and sighed.

"Never ceases to amaze me just how many new and more efficient ways we can find to take another life."

"How did you do that?" said Steph. "How did you get inside my head?"

The man smiled. "Well, it was not difficult, there was a lot of space for me to fill."

Steph disregarded the man's attempt at humour; invading her mind was not something she found funny. To be honest, right now, she did not know what she thought about it.

"I don't suppose you'd like to tell us what the hell is going on and while you're about it, who the hell you are?"

"And perhaps you could explain how it is that gunfire has no effect on you?" added the Reverend.

"Perhaps it was a miracle, Jonathan," the man said quietly. "You still believe in those, don't you? Or have you forgotten that, as well as the commandments you conveniently misplace each time you take another life?"

For the first time since she had known him, Steph saw shock on the Reverend's face. She guessed it was a relatively new experience for him too. It was also the first time she had heard someone call him anything other than Reverend.

"How do you know my name?"

"Hmm," mused the strange man. He turned and pointed at Steph. "That's one what and one who from Stephanie. And two how's from Jonathan. I hope you don't mind being called Jonathan. I cannot abide nicknames, and 'The Reverend' seems rather silly, don't you think?"

The Reverend said nothing.

The man clapped his hands together and began rubbing them as if trying to banish the cold night air. "Well, let's see, what, who, how...yes, all good questions. Perhaps if you started with good solid questions like those, I would not have had to resort to such cheap theatrics to get your attention," he raised an eyebrow at them both. "No matter, well the what and the two how's are best left for a more appropriate time, but the who, the who I can definitely answer. My name is Joshua Grey."

Chapter Eighteen

Jason ran back into Mr. Hunter's office, or at least what was left of it. The office was in ruins, furniture everywhere, mixed with the dead or dying who were scattered throughout the room. Standing by the door, he saw Luther Washington, transformed. No longer was he the well-groomed government operative from TORCH, he was now a throwback to days long past, a gladiator, a warrior. His jacket gone, Luther's shirt was torn and covered in blood, most of which Jason guessed was not his own. Luther's frame filled the entranceway, making it impossible for any of his attackers to approach him from either side, forcing them into a reckless frontal assault. Even without any weapons, the government agent was somehow holding his own. Jason watched the battle unfold, mesmerised by the sheer ferocity of the attackers, a ferocity matched only by the pig-headed resolve of the man keeping them at bay. Jason crouched beside Napoleon and felt for a pulse, a wave of relief washed over him as he found one.

"Professor Stone! Come on, Professor, wake up!"

Jason slapped Napoleon hard across the face, in an effort to rouse him back to consciousness. Napoleon groaned, but his eyes remained closed.

He hit Napoleon again, this time harder. "Come on! Come on, get up."

Another slap, nothing, another, this time drawing blood.

Jason raised his hand again. "I'm not going to die here because of you!"

He brought his hand down with all the strength, fear and anger he could drag from inside himself, only to find his wrist caught in a powerful grip before it could strike flesh.

"I thought I told you to get out?"

"You did, Professor," said Jason, hoping he was not about to receive his share of backhands. "How about we argue about it outside?"

"Point well made, Mr. Chen."

With Jason's help, both of them started back towards the exit.

"Washington, give us two minutes then follow if you can!" Napoleon called back.

Two minutes. Jason saw Luther smash his right heel into someone's chest, hurling him back into the others. He figured the TORCH agent would be lucky if he lasted another twenty seconds.

"Come on, Professor, we're nearly out," said Jason.

Seeing the door once again, and the freedom it offered, Jason forgot his fears and his hold on Napoleon and made a bolt for the door. A firm hand clamped down on his shoulder, leaving his hand outstretched, the door a few tantalising inches out of reach.

"What are you doing? We've got to get out!"

Napoleon pushed Jason out of the way and held his gun out in front of him.

"What...what's wrong?"

"Something, something doesn't feel right."

Before Jason could get Napoleon to explain himself, the door exploded inwards as if it torn from its hinges.

"Get behind me!" ordered Napoleon, as a deafening roar sounded from the other room. These were the only words Jason heard as something struck him and everything went black.

The more Clancy thought about the number of lives taken during his command, the more the numbers blurred into incomprehensible figures. All those years spent clearing up other people's messes had taught him that only three things mattered in the final analysis. Am I still alive? Was the mission objective achieved? And when do I get paid? Clancy considered the notion of payment and success as Stony placed the C4 charges against the wall, which, according to the late Samford Brown, would lead them into the underground lair of The Hand.

Clancy had decided to disappear for a while when the mission was over, maybe try his hand at some fishing. The last time he held a fishing rod, he was twelve and out with his dad. It turned out his dad was even worse at fishing than he was, still though, it had been a good day spent in the company of one of the few people who still held his respect. Some beers, some fishing, and the sea; it sounded like the perfect vacation. Even if it lasted a single sunny afternoon, it might help wash some of the blood from his hands.

Stony gave Clancy a thumbs up. Clancy nodded in return then began signalling to the others, who followed the silent orders without argument. Crouching low, they split into two teams of three, flattening themselves against either side of the tunnel. Clancy was at the head of one team, Kelly the other. Once the charges went off, they would be heard, that was unavoidable. There was no time for a stealth entry. The incursion needed to be swift, sudden and decisive. Signalling his readiness, Clancy waited. Stony held up the small detonator, counted to three and then activated it. The explosion was deafening, made worse by the cramped conditions, but Stony's expertise with explosives paid off. A large hole was now visible and artificial light streamed in from the room beyond. That was all the confirmation Clancy needed.

"Bravo team go!" he ordered, switching off his night vision goggles.

Kelly was already moving through the hole, covered by Stony and another man; all were covered in dust, water and mud thrown up by the blast.

"Alpha team on me!" Clancy led his men through the hole and into the room.

All six men trained their weapons on Benjamin Ashodi, who stood in the centre of the room, his hands raised. Clancy could not help smiling when he saw the gold disk in Ashodi's left hand.

"Mission accomplished."

Steph faced a man she was not sure was even human, arms crossed, waiting for what she called the 'things are about to get a whole lot worse' principle to make itself known.

"This is wasting time. I have a friend that needs our help I don't have time to..."

Steph clutched her throat in both hands. Her mouth was moving, but there was no sound, as if the words were ripped from her as they left her mouth.

"That's better," said Joshua. "I can hardly hear myself think with your constant chattering. Don't worry, it's not permanent, more's the pity."

Steph voiced her disgust through the use of sign language.

"Quaint," said Joshua, staring at the single middle finger being thrust in his direction. "Perhaps I should allow the Book of Cademus to have its little apocalypse. Maybe it might help thin the herd, so to speak."

Hearing Grey mention the Book of Cademus was enough for Steph to put her anger in check and lower her finger.

"Ah, common sense finally prevails in the fairer sex," said Joshua. "The Book of Cademus is the cult Stephanie here believes does not exist. Their doctrine is one of chaos and despair. They revel in the misery and pain of their fellow man, much like you, Jonathan."

"How did…" began the Reverend.

"I know, you were going to ask who the Book of Cademus are?" finished Joshua. He tapped the side of his temple. "Magic, dear boy, magic, although I prefer the term Elemental Science."

"Magic?"

"One man's science is another man's magic."

The Reverend and Steph's expressions reflected their confusion.

"You still cannot believe after everything you both have seen tonight?" Joshua sighed. "I suppose it's to be expected, and it's going to make what I have to say even harder; no matter, it still has to be said."

"Which is?"

"When our little friend there regains the power of speech, she will explain to you that she and Benjamin have unwittingly become involved in the Book of Cademus' grandest scheme. If they are not prevented from achieving their goal, the cost to the world will be immeasurable."

"Let us suppose I believe you. How…"

"Jason Chen. He is the key. The others failed to protect him and the enemy have him now; though I cannot see where. I can tell you no more. You are all already on the path, as are the others. Where it will lead, even I cannot see."

"What can you see?"

"That if you fail, the world will become a very different place."

Steph blinked and was staring at an empty space in front of the Reverend: Joshua was gone.

"Incredible," said the Reverend.

"Yeah, incredible."

Although her voice sounded as though she was suffering from a severe sore throat, she was glad to have it back.

"Reverend?"

"Yes, Stephanie."

"Remind me to smash that guy's face in the next time I see him."

Pain. He was alive. A surprise, but not an unwelcome one. His body was being jarred, shaken in all directions and he had no control over the sensations. Napoleon opened his eyes. He was in the passenger seat of a car travelling at high speed down a badly lit road. He had driven the road enough times to know it was the main one leading away from the university. He was also handcuffed.

"Good. I was starting to think you might do something stupid like die on me."

Napoleon looked into the driver's face beside him and groaned.

"Vincent, what are you doing here?" He lifted up his handcuffed arms. "And you better throw in a dammed good explanation for these."

"First, you might try thanking him for saving your life."

Looking behind him, Napoleon saw Luther. His shirt, what there was of it, was stained with dried blood, rendering the dark crimson tie he still wore not just inappropriate, but also highly comical. Other than a bandaged forearm and some shallow cuts on his torso, Luther was unharmed.

Vincent lifted a pair of keys from the dash board and handed them to Napoleon. "I headed back to the foundation with the boy. I told the board of trustees what happened, and guess what?"

Napoleon frowned as he unlocked the handcuffs. He was not in the mood for games. "I have no idea."

143

"An hour before I got there, they had a visit in person from that voice inside your head."

"Grey?"

Vincent nodded. "Seems he'd come to give the 'we're all in danger, the world's going to end' speech and how Jason was the key."

"The board took him seriously?"

"Difficult not to. The man did appear out of thin air. Anyway, they sent me back to help out, must say I didn't expect to walk into a war zone. I hadn't even unpacked yet."

"That explains why you're in England, but it does not explain the handcuffs."

"You were delirious," said Luther from the back seat. "Babbling something about an invisible enemy, you attacked your friend here, so I had to restrain you."

A timely spasm of pain coming from the right side of his jaw left no doubt in Napoleon's mind as to the method used for his restraint.

"And I suppose you took no pleasure in that."

"Would you believe me if I said I no?"

"No."

Luther grinned. "At last we agree on something."

A horrifying question entered Napoleon's mind. Even though he knew the answer, the question still needed to be asked.

"Where's Jason?"

At first, the question was met with the sounds of the car engine.

"He's gone," said Luther at last.

"What do you mean he's gone? We were supposed to protect him! Where were you?"

"Easy, boss, it's not his fault," put in Vincent. "By the time we were able to get to you, Jason was gone."

"So instead of laying blame," said Luther. "How about you start filling in a few blanks for me, like who you really are, who those guys back at the university were, and why they kidnapped the only link to my investigation?"

"That link had a name."

"Ok, wrong choice of words," admitted Luther. "You can take it up with me after we find Jason, but now I want answers."

"You've asked a lot of questions," said Napoleon, relieved to find his shotgun resting comfortably under his right foot.

"We owe him some answers, boss. If it wasn't for our friend back there, you'd be dead."

"Your point?"

"He's earned the right to hear the truth, whether he believes it or not."

144

"Earned the right? You want me to break an oath of secrecy that has existed before you and I were born because some pencil pusher saves my life…not good enough… not by a long way. Besides, you know the rules, Vincent. If they found out we had told an outsider," Napoleon did not finish, hoping to let his silence make the point for him.

"I don't buy that crap and neither do you. It's easy for them to talk about rules and tradition. They're not the ones knee deep in shit, fighting this war."

"We've only just met this man, we don't know anything about him."

"I know he went toe to toe with an Erogian, and single-handedly took on the knights of Cademus long enough to keep you alive. What more do we need to know?"

Napoleon could see Vincent's mind was set. He wondered not if, but when the decision he was about to make would decide to repay him for his act of betrayal.

"The people that attacked us were part of a group we've been investigating for years."

"Investigating?" asked Luther. "What kind of investigators deal with what went on back there? I don't believe most of it, and I was there."

"The Icarus Foundation," put in Vincent.

"Never heard of you."

"Most people haven't, at least not until they need us, and by then it's usually too late," said Napoleon. "We have no official ties to any country or law enforcement agency, even though some of our members come from that background. To the outside world, we're a think tank. We investigate and research paranormal occurrences on a global scale. We also conduct studies into many of the cults and religious sects in existence today. Unofficially, some of us have been trained to intervene if said phenomenon turns out to not only be real, but also threatens or takes human life."

Napoleon almost felt a measure of sympathy for Luther clinging to his quaint idea of his reality. His response was much the same as when he first came in contact with The Icarus foundation.

"You're faced with two options Agent Washington. Option one. You run back to the world of the rational, the sane. You grab any shred of evidence that will help dismiss the idea that there is a lot more going on in the world than you know."

"And option two?"

"You accept that for a moment you stared into the unknown and it smiled back at you."

Chapter Nineteen

Luther did not like the way things were going. Everything he had come to rely on as the truth was unravelling before his eyes. He was tired, in pain and on his last nerve. Napoleon was convincing, but then he had met his fair share of convincing nutcases in his time. He could not forget what he had seen, but he was not about to be swayed into believing Napoleon's outlandish story with a few well chosen words.

"How can any of this be real? How does someone blast a seven-foot hole through two walls?" Luther asked

"It will take time for you to accept everything you've seen tonight, so deal with this for now. The people who attacked us were human, not monsters, at least not in the literal sense," explained Napoleon.

Luther leaned forward in his seat.

"You said something about them before, who are they?"

Reaching down, Napoleon lifted up his shotgun, took a handful of shells from his pocket and began reloading his gun.

"The knights of Cademus are a highly trained secret army. They protect and enforce the doctrines of The Book of Cademus." Napoleon cocked the shotgun, before placing it back under his feet.

"The what?" said Luther, once again feeling out of his depth.

"The Book of Cademus is what we call an apocalyptic cult," said Napoleon.

"These types of cult have a belief system that is sometimes based in religion, and bordering on the fanatical. In most cases, they are led by a charismatic leader or leaders."

"I know cults can be dangerous, but mainly to themselves. Usually, they are badly equipped and too small to cause any real damage," said Luther.

"The Aum Shinrikyo cult had a worldwide membership estimated at forty thousand at its peak in the nineties. Some of their followers were responsible for a gas attack on several Tokyo subway lines that left twelve people dead and many more injured, should I go on?"

"Ok, I take your point. So what can you tell me about the Book of Cademus."

"We believe it was founded ten years after the first crusades."

"The crusades?" said Luther. "As in Richard the Lionheart?"

"That was the third crusade, we're talking about the first," put in Vincent.

Luther was slammed against the car door as Vincent swerved to avoid a motorcycle, who obviously had better things to do than drive on the right side of the road. "Stupid…" Vincent's voice trailed off. "Sorry, where was I? Oh yeah, The Book of Cademus was led by an English knight called Sir Oliver Cademus, who had fought in the first crusade. If the legend is to be believed, Sir Oliver formed the cult after he experienced a spiritual awakening from beings he called The Unseen."

"What happened to him?"

"Back then, they'd burn you at the drop of a hat so you can imagine how they felt about someone setting up their own sect. There were also rumours circulating that Sir Oliver was planning to use the cult to overthrow the monarchy."

"Although," said Napoleon, taking back the reins of the conversation, "that plan was never proven to have existed. Some historians believed it was merely an excuse to remove Sir Oliver and his followers before they became too big a threat."

"Makes for good sense," Luther admitted.

"Many atrocities committed back then were carried out under the banner of good sense," Napoleon pointed out. "Anyway, an army laid siege to Cademus' castle, but before they could breach the castle walls, Sir Oliver ordered his followers, who included his mother, wife and twelve-year-old daughter to take a draft of poison that he had prepared. When the army finally breeched the castle, there was no sign of Sir Oliver amongst the dead. He had instigated the mass suicide as a smokescreen to cover his escape."

"He did that to his own followers, his family?" asked Luther.

"You need to understand that Oliver Cademus was not only a homicidal mass murderer, he also believed he was chosen to save the Earth. A destiny which he would let nothing interfere with."

"Ok, Ok," said Luther, raising his hands. "You said deal with facts, so tell me why a cult that died out centuries ago would kidnap…" Luther's voice faltered. His eyes widened in the twilight brought on by the coming dawn.

"What is it?" said Napoleon, following Luther's dumbfounded gaze to a series of photos spread out on the car's dashboard. "What do you see?"

"The photo in the middle," said Luther, pointing to it. "Give it to me."

Napoleon handed the photo to him.

"What is this?" he said studying the photo.

"A sacrificial dagger thought to belong to Cademus himself. Why?"

"You see these markings on the dagger?" Luther traced his finger along the image. "I saw similar markings written in blood where Jason's parents were killed."

"Did you decipher them?"

"I've a friend working on that now."

"According to the Archivist," said Vincent. "The markings on the dagger are so rare, he's only seen it a handful of times. They were first used by some of Cademus' earliest converts. Apparently, Cademus designed the code so that his followers could communicate in secret with each other. The markings refer to a prophecy."

"Prophecy?" said Luther.

"That which was stolen shall be found, the sleeper shall awake," said Napoleon, sliding the photos back into the file.

"That's right," said Vincent, looking confused. "How did you know?"

"I examined the dagger whilst we where in Mexico."

"Then…"

"Why send you back with the photos? I was not one hundred percent sure of my interpretation of the inscription, and on something like this, I needed a second opinion."

"You could have told me."

"I just have."

"What does it mean?" said Luther.

"One of the cult's enduring prophecies is that Sir Oliver will return to lead them. My guess is they believe Jason has something to do with that prophecy."

"This is insane, Cademus would have died centuries ago."

"There's seldom anything sane about a prophecy," said Napoleon. "But don't let that fool you. The Book of Cademus have a purpose, a clear goal from which they never waver. Yes, they are ruthless and will act without a second thought for the lives they ruin, but they also do not kill for the fun of it. Believe me, the murder of Jason's parents was for a specific reason."

"We found an appointment book at the crime scene," said Luther. "On the night they were murdered, Jason's parents were expecting him home from university but he never showed up."

"You think they came for Jason and instead found his parents?" said Vincent.

Luther gave a non-committal shrug of his shoulders. He could not believe he was buying into any of this. It sounded like the plot for a bad movie.

A bleeping noise from Luther's seat pulled their focus away from the topic at hand.

"It's just my PDA."

Luther picked up his palm-sized, personal digital assistant. He took the small light pen attached to the side of the device and began using it to access his email. The first was from Nelson, not to be unexpected he thought, but still unusual, he expected any updates on the investigation to come from Eve. The second message was an encrypted email to all TORCH field operatives from Chardon. Luther decided to open Nelson's email first; after all, he could always wait a little longer for bad news. He tapped his light pen twice on Nelson's name to display the contents of the message.

As per your instructions, we flew out to Tokyo and began examining the eyewitness reports. The common theory here is that the destruction of the centre was carried out by The Hand, however, further investigation of the evidence suggests otherwise. Security logs, in compliance with TORCH protocol for disaster recovery, were retrieved from a secure remote access site, several miles from the research facility. The logs show a small electrical spike in the system approximately twenty-five minutes before the explosion; further investigation found this spike may be the result of someone gaining unauthorised access to the security measures on the ventilation shaft, which would suggest this was The Hand's point of entry.

Agent Appleton uncovered new evidence via a covert camera installed within the conference room. The footage showed a meeting taking place between two men, one later identified as Giles Pemrose, a UN official, the other man was unknown, but I would submit the second individual was The Hand. During the meeting, Pemrose was shot and killed by a sniper and The Hand was taken captive by a force of armed men. We attempted to access Pemrose's files to see if it would shed any light as to his meeting with a known criminal, unfortunately we found the files were protected with the highest UN security protocols. We do know that it was Pemrose himself who had requested the camera be installed in the conference room a week earlier. We were also able to trace Pemrose's last movements before his death. He had a breakfast meeting with a John Carson before flying out to Tokyo. A check into his flight plan showed he was due to fly to Switzerland on the night of his death. One last piece of the puzzle that may interest you is that booked on the exact same flight in the seat next to Pemrose was Elijah Barrington.

Nothing more to do here. Will be catching the first flight home.

Nelson

Luther read through the contents of the email again to make sure he had read it correctly. There was no mistake. Looking up from his PDA, he realised from the questioning look he was getting from Napoleon that he had not done a very good job in hiding his surprise at the revelations contained within Nelson's email.
"Anything you want to share with the rest of us?"
The polite request was no more than a courtesy. Luther had a feeling

Napoleon had no intention of taking no for an answer.

"You're civilians. This has nothing to do with you. This is official TORCH business."

Napoleon nodded, and for a moment, Luther thought he might actually settle for the answer he was given.

"Stop the car."

Then again.

Vincent applied the brakes and pulled the car off the road and up onto a grassy verge, ignoring the large bakery van that hurtled past, its horn blaring, which served to muffle the stream of abuse being spewed out by the van's driver.

"Keep an eye out," said Napoleon, stepping out of the car.

"I hear you," Vincent replied. He removed his two guns and laid them on the dashboard. "If the boys and I see anything, you'll know about it."

Never one to shy away from a confrontation, Luther got out and followed Napoleon up onto the grassy verge. Glancing up, he saw the first signs of dawn, the twilight giving way to a tinge of orange, heralding the coming day.

"Ok," said Luther. "You've got something to say. Fine, let's hear it."

Luther was confident in his initial assessment of Napoleon Stone: a paranoid bully, nothing more. Although he believed he was not in any immediate danger, he kept his hands by his side and close to his holstered gun.

"That email has something to do with Jason, doesn't it?"

"I told you before, this is an internal matter and it's confidential. Sorry, but I can't break protocol, no matter how good the reason."

The moment Luther stopped speaking, he caught the subtle weight shift in Napoleon's stance and realized he had misread him. He went for his gun but the movement came too late. Napoleon's colt was now inches from Luther's temple, whilst Luther's own gun had barely cleared its holster.

"If you think some outdated sense of fair play is going to stop me from putting a bullet between your eyes if you don't tell me exactly what I want to hear," Napoleon pulled back the hammer on the gun, "think again."

Luther knew when someone was bluffing or trying to scare him, and this was neither.

"The Book of Cademus are very real and very dangerous. They are also not stupid. They would not launch an all out assault on a university after spending centuries working in secret just to kidnap one boy, unless that boy was pivotal to their plans."

"And you're trying to convince me by sticking a gun in my face?"

As he spoke, Luther weighed the odds of tackling Napoleon before his brains were splattered over the grass. "From where I'm standing, I can't see much difference between you and them."

"If I were anything like the Book of Cademus, we would not be having this conversation," said Napoleon. "I simply prefer the direct approach to dealing with a situation rather than wasting time, time Jason is fast running out of."

Then, to Luther's surprise, Napoleon lowered his gun and stood waiting. Luther repressed his first instinct, to wrestle the gun from Napoleon's grip before placing him and his partner under arrest. The rules and protocols he lived by were of little help in this situation. His duty to the law and the government he served had already come at too high a price. He was not going to make that mistake again, even if it meant breaking every rule in the book. He related the contents of the email to Napoleon, leaving nothing out.

"So, Jason's father met with this Pemrose, who then flew out for Tokyo. Less than forty-eight hours later, Pemrose is killed and twenty-four hours after that, Jason's parents are murdered."

"Coincidence?" suggested Luther.

"I don't believe in coincidences."

"Me neither."

"What information was Pemrose passing on?" Napoleon asked.

Luther shrugged. "No idea, but he was booked on a nine am flight out of Tokyo. On the same flight was Elijah Barrington."

Napoleon nodded. Luther saw no need for further explanation as to Barrington's identity. His, or to be more correct, his late mother's business partner, Justine Hillman's company was a multinational giant that had made the Hillman family amongst the wealthiest people on the planet.

"Obviously, you know Elijah Barrington is a respected businessman, but what you may not know about is the neat little sideline he runs."

"Sideline?"

"Interested clients who need special jobs doing, such as surveillance or protection, as well as some more illegal enterprises, and are willing to pay the Earth for that service, go to Barrington. He handles all the arrangements to facilitate the request, for which he takes a percentage."

Luther's last sentence had broken enough TORCH protocols to earn him the suite of his choice in any prisons.

"Think of it as a recruitment agency for mercenaries. His books are allegedly filled with ex-spies, professional assassins, soldiers, or in this case, a professional thief who calls himself 'The Hand'."

Napoleon was silent for moment, taking in everything he had heard. "For years, we've been sure the Book of Cademus had to be getting some serious financial support, as well as skilled mercenaries to train new recruits for the Knights of Cademus. Maybe Mr. Barrington was picking up the bill for this."

Luther thought it was still early for conclusion jumping, but he kept the thought to himself.

"Whether or not there is a connection between Barrington and Cademus, there is a link between the murders of Pemrose, Jason's parents and his kidnapping," said Napoleon.

"So what now?" said Luther, pointing at the gun.

"We need to find out what Barrington's connection is to all this. We need him to lead us to his associate, this thief who has the information Pemrose was killed for," Napoleon replied. "They could have killed Pemrose at any time, but they were waiting to make sure he had the information in his possession before moving against him."

Luther was impressed. Napoleon's conclusion was logical and it made sense. An impromptu moment of silence passed between the two men, each one making up their mind as to their next course of action and what that choice would mean for the other man.

"For the time being, it seems our goals lie in the same direction," Luther said, offering his hand.

Napoleon holstered his colt, nodded, and ignoring Luther's hand, started back to the car.

"Agreed," he called back, the words sounding more like an afterthought to Luther.

The conversation left Luther beginning to wish he had left Stone back at the university. He was far too ruthless, too quick to solve a situation with the wrong end of a gun for Luther's liking. However, in the last few minutes, events had taken a disastrous turn, leaving the two men his only allies. It had been a risk not telling Napoleon everything, but Luther figured that Stone would be only interested in hearing about any connection to Jason; the second email was of no concern to him at the moment and Luther hoped to have the situation resolved before Napoleon pushed him for any more information. After all, what was there to worry about? Only a global bulletin to all field operatives that one Luther Washington was wanted in connection with the murder of one trainee agent found dead in his hotel room, whilst on an unsanctioned operation. An attack on the agent accompanying the trainee had left her in a coma.

Luther fought to keep the flood of emotions at bay: guilt, loss, grief, and anger; they all wanted their pound of flesh. His feelings would have to take a back seat until he found the people responsible.

Chapter Twenty

Overconfidence had always been Ben's curse. No matter how much planning he put into something, he always managed to end up feeling like he had just been hit by a lorry, with overconfidence grinning behind the wheel. With six laser sights now resting on various vital organs, he could almost hear Steph giving him an unneeded 'I told you so'.

"Which one of you is Clancy?" he said, addressing the masked men.

One of the men stepped forward and removed his goggles and balaclava. Ben recognised him straight away.

"Good, you've done your homework," said Clancy. "That should help things run smoother."

Clancy gestured to Kelly, who held out his hand.

"Let's have the disk. You don't have all day," said Kelly.

Without a word of protest, Ben tossed the disk to Kelly. He watched the man with the heavy Irish accent unhook his backpack and lay it in front of him.

"You made a simple snatch and grab into something far more complicated. I don't like complicated," said Clancy.

"My heart bleeds."

Before another smart remark could leave Ben's mouth, Clancy's right fist smashed into his face, knocking him to the floor.

"Don't worry, it will," promised Clancy.

Ben wiped the blood from his mouth and got up, his smile gone.

"I owe you one."

Now it was Clancy's turn to smile. "Don't bother, Ben, I've been threatened by bigger and better men than you."

Ben tried to hide his shock at the use of his name. Clancy had also been busy.

"Please," said Clancy, "did you really think I was going to come in here without knowing exactly who I was dealing with?"

"Well, you should have done your homework better because…"

"Because you're not Benjamin Ashodi, former inmate of Beauford Maximum security prison?"

"Don't know what you're on about."

Ben felt stupid fighting to maintain a cover that was already blown, but he saw no reason to offer Clancy any more information than he already had.

"Must have been a real kick in the guts that the people who framed you were not even after you; they were just the leverage to get your big

153

brother to back down, but he didn't, did he?" asked Clancy. "Instead, he watched you get sent down. Now that would piss me off big time."

Ben did not reply. Clancy was trying to get under his skin and it was working. Ben wanted to slam him against the wall and make him understand. He had paid for his brother's betrayal every day during those seven years, and every day since. He never asked for this life. He never wanted to be a thief.

"We're hot," said Kelly.

Ben now had a clear view of Kelly, who was hunched over a laptop, no doubt checking the disk's authenticity. Time was running out.

"Betrayal hurts, doesn't it, Ben?" said Clancy. "Believe me, I know."

Kelly placed the laptop back in his backpack along with the disk, stood up and returned to pointing his gun at Ben.

"Wish I had the time to pay you back for the trouble you caused," Kelly told him. "Guess I'll just have to take it up with your little navy bitch when we find her."

Ben smiled back at him. "Trust me, man, you better hope you don't find her."

"Thanks for the advice," replied Kelly, his finger tightening around the trigger.

"Stand down," ordered Clancy.

"What? We put this guy down now and it's game over."

"You heard the order. I won't give it a second time."

Kelly mumbled something under his breath before lowering the gun. Ben was impressed at the amount of control Clancy could exert over his men.

"What's on the disk, Ben?" asked Clancy.

"Come again?" said Ben, feigning ignorance.

"I've read your file, Ben. The minute you got that disk, you would have been trying to access it, my guess is you succeeded."

"Whoa, easy there, chief," Kelly stepped in. "In case it's slipped your mind, sir, we are being paid a lot of money to get this disk back to our employers. Let's just put a bullet in this joker and be on our way, before the FBI or TORCH find their way down here."

"Good point," said Clancy. "Now here's another one. Do you really think our employers plan to keep us alive once this mission is over, after we screwed up in Tokyo? Right now, what's on that disk is the only leverage we have."

"Ok, I never looked at it that way."

"You never do." Clancy turned back to Ben. "So how about letting us in on the big secret, Ben?"

Ben shrugged. "Why should I tell you anything, you're going to kill me anyway?"

154

Ben did not like the way Clancy grinned at his question. Laying his gun on the glass table, Clancy drew out his knife and moved forward until he stood inches from Ben's face. He held up the knife between them.

"True, we're going to kill you whether you talk or not," said Clancy, running his thumb down the serrated edge of the blade. "But there are many ways to die, Ben, and if you don't tell me what's on that disk, I'll make sure that they'll be talking about what they find down here for years."

"Now that I think about it, I was able to access some of the files," said Ben, pointing at the keyboard. "They're stored in the system, I'll access them for you."

Ben took a few steps then froze as all the men in the room brought their weapons to bear.

"Easy there, boy," said Kelly. "You move again and we'll rip you a new one."

"I was going to access the records for you."

"No worries," said Clancy, nodding to one of his men. "We can handle it."

Ben felt a gun shoved into the small of his back by Kelly, who was now stood behind him.

The other man, whom Clancy had signalled, seated himself in front of the keyboard.

"I'll need the access code to log onto his system," said the man.

All eyes fell on Ben.

"Nine, Nine, Nine, Houdini," said Ben.

The soldier began entering the access code. Ben's eyes met Clancy's, and then he watched as the mercenary's confident visage changed to one of realisation.

"No, Wait!"

But Clancy's warning came too late as a finger pressed the return key and the room was plunged into darkness.

Kathryn sat up on her bed, wiping away the last of her tears. She could endure horrific autopsies, but a ten-minute phone conversation with her daughter, Emily, left her an emotional train wreck.

Her ex-husband, Marvin, on the other hand, had little problems getting in touch with his emotions. Two minutes of his incessant and characteristic worrying was more than Kathryn's nerves could stand. Their strained conversation only served as another reminder that divorce was so much more preferable than a lifetime of misery spent in each other's company. She had quietly suggested to Marvin that he shut up, quit worrying about everything, and put their daughter on the phone.

Emily, who often displayed a maturity greater than both her parents put together, was far more interested in France than her mother's health. It was only when Kathryn promised to take her to Paris did Emily finally focus on her mother's accident.

Kathryn had lied and told Emily she had fallen over while at work. It was not a complete lie, more of a half-truth; besides how could she tell her eight-year-old daughter that someone had tried to kill her mother?

Emily had taken the lie in her stride. She told Kathryn to get better and she was making a get well soon card that Daddy was going to send when she was finished. Kathryn had made Marvin promise he would not bring Emily to see her whilst she was in hospital. Kathryn did not want her seeing just how freaked out she was by being here, her daughter had already seen enough of her mother's demons.

Sure all the tears were gone, Kathryn picked up her mobile phone and pressed redial, hoping Luther would pick up this time. She had got his voice mail seven times already. She kept one eye on the door on the lookout for any hospital staff. Earlier, they had warned her about using her mobile within the hospital.

She ran her thoughts over her discoveries. They had left her stunned, with as many questions as the answers she had found. She would feel better when she could share that sensation with someone else.

The phone rang four times; the next ring would take her through to voice mail again. "Hello?"

Kathryn stopped herself from pushing the end call button.

"Luther?"

"It's me. You ok?" Kathryn could hear Luther's concern, despite the poor reception.

"I'm fine. Can you talk?"

There was a pause.

"Hello, you still there?"

"Sorry, my friend here has just come to the decision not to blow my head off."

"What?"

"Ignore me, rough night."

"I don't see you laid up in hospital with nothing but bed sores to look forward to," said Kathryn.

"Much as I'm enjoying being given the third degree, I'm assuming there is a point to this conversation?"

"I had some TORCH agents here earlier. They were asking me where you were, they wouldn't tell me why though."

"I bet they didn't."

"They also told me that if I passed any information to you, it would be considered a criminal offence and that anything I had was to go

156

through Chardon. So please feel free to tell me what the hell is going on?"

Kathryn listened, not saying a word as Luther related his movements. Kidnapping, murder, and a warrant for his arrest; Kathryn found it hard to believe so much could have happened to her friend in such a short space of time.

"I'm sorry about Eve," she said at last. "I only met her a few times; she seemed nice and from what I hear, was a good agent."

"She is a good agent."

"Right, the coma…they said…sorry…I didn't mean…"

"Forget it."

Kathryn was not expecting Luther to open up any further on that subject. He was never one for wearing his heart on his sleeve. He would deal with it in time, in his own way and as always, alone.

"What did you tell the agents?"

"Nothing they didn't already know," said Kathryn. "I said you were on your way to interview Jason. I take it they don't know he's been kidnapped?"

"I'm sure they will by now. They weren't exactly the most subtle of kidnappers."

"Any idea who took him?"

"A very good idea; I just don't know anyone else who will believe it."

"Try me."

"Ok. How about a cult founded by a knight of the first crusade, who apparently had designs on rewriting the world in his image."

"So the Book of Cademus really does exist," said Kathryn.

"How did you…"

"Expert on the occult, remember?"

Kathryn looked at the sea of documents, photos and other assorted paraphernalia scattered around her laptop. She had hoped she was wrong about all of this, that it was nothing more then an overactive imagination mixed in with too many painkillers.

"Thanks to you, I was given complete access to all the crime scene documentation concerning the murder of Jason Chen's adoptive parents."

"It's bad, isn't it?"

"You have no idea," replied Kathryn. "Forensics found several latent prints inside the symbols written in blood. The prints belonged to John Carson."

"Jason's father?"

"Oh, if you think that's weird, they ran a check on the blood, it was also Carson's."

"He used his own blood to make those drawings?"

"Not drawings; phrases, badly drawn ones, which was why I didn't recognise them at first. I had forensics fax copies of the symbols to a few trusted experts I had worked with in the past. Although my knowledge of the occult is pretty big, this was out of my league," Kathryn admitted. "Apparently, it was written using a code created by followers of the Book of Cademus."

"How did you find out about the cult?"

"According to my source, an excavation in 1935 of what was thought to be the ruins of a monastery discovered several documents suggesting the site was once a meeting place to one of the offshoots of this cult."

"They're called chapters, I think."

This time, it was Kathryn's turn to be on the receiving end of a shock. "How the hell did you know that?"

"You really don't want to know. What else did you get?"

"A linguist expert, who's been helping me with my research, examined the text and with some help was able to break the code. The basic translation reads, 'protect the boy.'"

"So they were after Jason then, not his parents. But why?"

"God knows, but I managed to convince a friend who owed me a favour to do a background check on John Carson. I figured TORCH were monitoring my activities at the hospital so I had to do a little behind the scenes work to get you something useful to work with."

"Your friend must have some connections."

"Should do, he works for the CIA. Nice man, poor in bed, but still a very nice man."

Kathryn laughed as she listened to Luther's weary sigh from the end of the phone line. She had forgotten how easy it was to embarrass him.

"Thanks for the image; what did this friend turn up?"

"Seems that John, during his college years, was quite the little radical. You know, the whole 'I'm going to change the world' deal. He was a history buff and was thought by his personal tutor to be a little too interested in things that go bump in the night, if you get my meaning."

"The occult."

"In a big way, apparently," went on Kathryn. "He was a member of a society at college that used to meet to discuss all things paranormal. One of the other members was one Mary Schofield, who became John's girlfriend and future wife. The society was disbanded after the accidental death of a student during a ritual carried out at one of the meetings."

"How is it Carson was able to end up working for the UN with a past like that?"

"Both John and Mary's parents were wealthy and well connected.

The whole thing was brushed under the carpet before the media could get hold of it. I doubt the UN even knows about it."

"What happened to John and Mary?"

"They both dropped out of college and sight soon afterwards. Aside from the occasional phone call at the holidays, none of their families saw them again until six years later, when they returned, married and with no explanation for where they had been all those years."

"I'm guessing you've got a theory on that, right?"

"Well, given their past activities…"

"You think they joined the Book of Cademus?"

"I do, but my instincts tell me when they returned home, they had parted ways with the Book of Cademus for reason or reasons unknown."

Luther's silence told Kathryn he was mulling over her theory but knowing Luther, he was going to need more.

"My guess is they got scared," she said. "If half the things I've read about this cult were true, they were lucky to get out with their lives and sanity intact."

"So writing cryptic notes in your own blood is what's passing for sane these days?"

Kathryn was not ready to relinquish her theory so quickly. "They were young, rich, arrogant and obsessed with the occult. They were already indirectly responsible for the death of a fellow student. I can't think of better candidates for the Book of Cademus, can you?"

"It does make sense when you put it that way," Luther admitted. "But …"

"Now think about the message John left. If this cult has taken Jason, then it makes sense that they were the ones John and Mary were trying to protect him from."

"If that's true, why would Carson leave a message only members of the cult could read."

"Last act of a desperate man. He wanted to make sure the message would be seen and taken seriously, hence the blood," said Kathryn. "He knew anyone with knowledge of the Book of Cademus would eventually decipher the code. I guess he hoped it would be the good guys."

Kathryn saw two men coming towards the door, the expensive yet unremarkable suits and the regulation haircuts left no doubt in her mind as to their identity.

"Listen, Luther, I need to get off the line. Looks like TORCH are back for a return visit. I'll get word to you somehow if I find anything more."

"You concentrate on getting better," said Luther.

"You concentrate on staying alive," said Kathryn as she hung up.

Chapter Twenty-One

A single burst of automatic weapons fire punctured the darkness.

"Stand down!" ordered Clancy. "We need him alive!"

The firing stopped and silence was restored to the room. Seconds later, the lights came back on. Benjamin Ashodi was nowhere to be seen. Worse still, the solider that moments ago had been aiming his gun at Ashodi, now wore a horrified expression. Clancy then saw Kelly. Blood flowed from several gunshot wounds on Kelly's chest. It was clear the solider had fired in an attempt to stop Ashodi from escaping, without success. Kelly placed his hand against his chest, stared at his bloodied palm, and then at the soldier.

"You stupid wanker," he managed to blurt out, before his legs gave way.

Clancy rushed in, catching his friend before he hit the floor.

"Hang on, Sergeant, we'll get you back to the rendezvous."

"How bad?"

"You've taken four shots to the chest. It's a miracle you're still breathing."

"They breed us Irish tough," coughed Kelly, blood spilling from his mouth. He looked at Clancy, no fear in his eyes as he spoke. "I'm not walking out of here, am I?"

Clancy shook his head. There was no use in lying. They had both seen enough death to know what signs to look for.

"Don't let me die like this, chief, like a rookie."

With Clancy helping him into a sitting position, Kelly, whose every movement seemed to be agony, held out a trembling right hand.

"Safety's off and the round's already chambered," Clancy explained, whilst pressing his gun into Kelly's sweating palm and closing his fingers around it.

Kelly took aim and fired. The single shot tore a bloody swathe through the forehead of the solider who had fired, exiting out the back of his head along with most of his brain. A grisly end to the soldier's first contract as a mercenary, thought Clancy.

"Bloody amateurs!" yelled Kelly spitting on the corpse before forcing a grin. "Least I'll have company for the trip downstairs, eh, chief?"

Kelly's head slumped forward; the gun fell from his grasp.

Clancy laid Kelly's body on the floor and got up. There was no sadness. The honourable soldier and friend Clancy had fought alongside had been dying a little each day for years.

"Would someone mind telling me how that bastard got out of here?" asked Stony. Clancy was not surprised by Stony's lack of emotion over Kelly. He would now, no doubt, be hoping for a bigger share of the cash once the mission was over.

Clancy stared at the keyboard and then the floor. His eyes narrowed until they were little more than slits. He tried to keep calm, despite the wave of anger pushing at him. Twice now, Ashodi had made him look a fool, and now he had cost the life of one of the founding members of their unit. He promised himself he would carve Kelly's name into Ashodi's chest when they found him. "The son of a bitch had this planned from the start." Clancy took out his radio. "This is Blacklight one, Blacklight four, do you read, over?"

Static.

"Hammond....Wheels... come in."

"Why don't they answer?" asked Stony.

Clancy switched off the radio. "Because they're dead."

"Sir?"

"That's why Connisbee wasn't here. She was taking out the rear guard, clearing the way.

"This is crazy..." said Stony. "You think a skirt took out Hammond? Wheels maybe, he was a tosser, my mum could have him, but Hammond? No way, no bloody way."

"I don't give a damn what you believe. I'm telling you they played us from the minute we got here," said Clancy. "You still don't see it, do you? He wanted us to get in here."

"Doesn't make any sense. If he knew we were coming, why stay, and why give us the disk?"

"First rule of war, know your enemy. He wanted to know who he was up against, and at the same time, show us just how good he is."

"Arrogant little shit," said Stony.

"That arrogant little shit just outmanoeuvred a room full of armed men. Remember that when we find him."

"And how do we do that, sir?"

Clancy was not listening, he was checking his watch. "Time to move out. The explosion will have tipped off the police by now." He started back for the hole. "We can't afford to be compromised down here."

"What about the bodies?" asked Stony, upon reaching the hole.

"Leave them. According to military records, Kelly died serving his country years ago. Let them figure out what him and Johnson are doing here."

Without a backward glance or another word to his men, Clancy began leading them back through the tunnel. He shut out the image of his friend lying dead, killed by friendly fire; not much of an epitaph for a man like Kelly. If his friend were here now and sober, he would be thinking of a way to ensure they all survived the night. Their employers were not the kind of people who forgave failure. He ran his hand over the disk in his pocket, the primary objective was accomplished, but Ashodi had escaped again, along with any information he had obtained from the disk. Clancy was not out of ideas yet. He still had one more chance to ensure his men got paid and Ashodi got what he deserved.

A small panel in the floor, a few metres from where Kelly's body lay, slid open. Ben pulled himself out of his tiny hiding space, grinning from ear to ear. Turning, he almost fell over Kelly's body, then again as he saw the body of a second man. From his hiding place, he had heard the gunfire. He stepped over the bodies and moved to the keyboard. He decided against searching the bodies. There was nothing he did not already know about the mercenaries that would give him a further edge than he already had.

"Acknowledge voice activation request," he said, once more putting on the headset.

Voice activation confirmed…awaiting command.

"Display Street Exit Camera."

The screens responded by displaying nothing but static. Not good, thought Ben, his concern for Steph growing.

"Load Street Exit Camera footage time index twenty minutes."

The screen flashed then this time, scenes of the street where the not-so-secret exit from his base appeared. What he saw on the screen was an image he would never forget.

"What the…?" The rest of the sentence was caught in his mouth as the shock at what was on the screen sunk in.

He stared at the strange human-like creature in a fierce hand-to-hand fight with Steph. He watched the fight unfold, holding back his fears concerning the eventual outcome, but allowing the relief to wash over him as the Reverend made an appearance.

Ben watched them exchange words, but for some reason, the camera was not able to pick up the conversation. He then saw a slight distortion, like a shimmer in the air behind them before the screen became static once more.

All of Ben's trademark witticisms had deserted him. He had no idea what had just tried to kill Steph; it was unlike anything he had ever seen. He put aside his fears and questions and concentrated on his own survival. There was little he could do to help Steph if he was behind bars or dead.

"Initiate Phoenix, code alpha two echo zero."

He watched as the image of the dove was overwritten by lines of program code. After downloading all his data to a computer located at one of his safe houses, the program would load a virus into the operating system, destroying everything, or so Will had assured him.

Grabbing his leather jacket from the edge of the sofa, he threw it on as he ran to the elevator. It was risky walking out the front door, but Ben was gambling that Clancy and his men would be on their way to deliver the disk to their employers. He hoped that whoever was paying Clancy would not be happy to discover his failure to kill him a second time, and hopefully that would keep the mercenaries off his back permanently.

The lift doors closed behind him. Ben did not bother taking a last look at the place that had started out as a hideout and had become his home. He always knew he was living on borrowed time there. The lift slowed, the doors opened and Ben stepped out. He was grabbed by the arms as something was thrown over his head, plunging his vision into darkness.

"Keep that big mouth of yours shut, and you might just live through this," said a voice.

"Man, this night just keeps getting better and better."

The restraints around his wrists and the blindfold told Jason he was not in the university anymore. He remembered Professor Stone yelling at him to get down, a request he had no problem following. Jason did not understand what happened next. It was the strangest sensation, like being struck by an invisible fist that drove him onto his knees, his vision a blur. The last thing he saw before darkness took him was Professor Stone firing at thin air one moment, and in the next being hurled across the room.

"He's awake," said a man's voice. "Shall I give him another dose?"

"Hang on," answered a second voice, another man. "I'll check with the boss."

Footsteps, a door opening and closing, Jason tried to take in every sound and smell, anything that might give him a clue as to where he was. Professor Stone was at the forefront of his mind. He was forced to consider the possibility that both the Professor and the government agent were dead, and with them any chance of help. If he was going to get out of this, it would be down to him.

It was not the first time events had conspired to force Jason to cope alone. In one way or another, he had been doing it all his life.

You really should stop all this self-obsessing Jason, it's actually quite tiresome to listen to.

"Grey," said Jason aloud.

He heard shuffling behind him and then felt a sharp pain to the back of his head. "Keep it shut."

Jason nodded vigorously.

"Better."

Jason berated himself for not realising Grey had again tapped into his subconscious. The weird thing was he was not shocked or surprised at this latest mental intrusion, just increasingly more annoyed.

Quite the predicament .

Jason could almost taste the sarcasm in Grey's words.

One of these days, you should listen to yourself…quite the predicament, please spare me the olde English chat.

I wish I had the time or fortitude to indulge in meaningless banter with you, but soon I will no longer be able to reach your mind.

The sudden idea that he might not be able to speak to anyone remotely on his side began to unnerve him. The seriousness of the situation began to sink in.

Jason, no matter what happens you must stay strong. Stone is…

I know. He's dead.

If you could control your bad manners for one minute more, you would learn that Stone and Washington are alive.

Jason did not know if he should believe what he was hearing. How could they have survived after what he had seen take place at the university?

Whatever happens, you must stay strong and have faith. Help is coming…help is…

Jason sensed Grey's voice slip out of his mind at the same time he was thrown forward in his seat; something across his stomach drew tight preventing him from falling forward any further. A loud rumbling filled his ears and it came to Jason exactly where he was.

"A plane!" he shouted, before he realised what he was saying. "I'm on a plane!"

Jason felt something damp pressed against his mouth and nose, its unpleasant odour filling his nostrils. It did not take long for him to succumb again to unconsciousness.

Clancy watched down in the street across from them as Ashodi was hooded and handcuffed.

"Well?" Clancy asked, as he knelt beside Stony.

The other members of the team were also in crouched positions, observing the arrest that was taking place in the street below.

"Nothing," Stony grunted, one eye closed, his remaining one focused on the images being fed to him through the telescopic sight of the sniper rifle. "If I didn't know better, I'd swear Ashodi knows someone's trying to get a bead on him."

"Explain."

"He's hooded, but he's still managing to keep one guy in front and to the side of him at all times. I could risk a shot, but chances are it would hit one of them first, giving the others time to get our boy to cover, as well as revealing our position."

Clancy was forced to watch, helpless to act, as Ashodi was bundled into a car.

"We've got one Law rocket launcher with us," put in one of the other men. "I say we take out the car and everyone in it."

"Unless you've got something sensible to offer, I suggest you keep your mouth shut," said Clancy.

"I just thought..."

"That's just it, soldier, you didn't think," snapped Clancy, trying to keep a lid on his frustration. He pointed at the car, which was starting to pull away. "We don't know who those men were. They could be TORCH, FBI, or even a backup team from our employers. Now, we came here to take out one man and retrieve our client's merchandise, not to start a war with the intelligence community. We have the disk and The Hand will keep for now. He isn't going anywhere except prison, if he's lucky."

He patted Stony on the shoulder. "Pack it up. It's time to cut our losses and move out."

Stony got to his feet, cradling the sniper rifle in his arms. "Where to now, sir?"

"We make for the exchange point, hand over the disk and get paid, though I doubt there'll be any bonus this time."

"Then what?"

"Fishing," Clancy announced, staring up into sky. "I'm going fishing."

Chapter Twenty-Two

"We should be far enough now," Ben heard a voice say. "You know what to do."

Ben's handcuffs were removed, followed by the hood. Ben blinked twice then grinned at the man in the seat beside him. Heavily tanned, the man's stern gaze radiated confidence in every direction. Flecks of grey prominently featured in several places within his thick, brown hair.

"Assistant Director Davies. Good to see you, man," smiled Ben. "How long has it been? Two years?"

Frank Davies frowned. He looked anything but happy. "Not long enough, Ashodi, not by a long shot."

Ben sank back into the leather interior. "Frank, that hurts me, after all we've been through."

Davies' frown broke into a tight-lipped grin. "Why is it when Steph calls, it's never social, it's always to bail you two out of trouble?"

"I take it you never got the Christmas and birthday cards we've sent, then?"

"If it weren't for the work you occasionally perform for the agency, I would have had you both behind bars years ago. It would certainly go a long way to curing my ulcer."

Ben began rubbing the circulation back into his wrists; one of the overzealous agents had fastened the handcuffs a little tighter than was necessary. "Look at it this way, Frank, you've lost a prisoner and gained two patriots."

"You may not take the security of this country seriously, Ashodi, but I do. One more crack like that, and I'll personally hand your ass back to Wallencheck."

Davies' knowledge of Wallencheck did not surprise Ben; he knew who he was dealing with. The assistant director of the CIA had tracked him down some time ago, fortunately, his goal had been to recruit him for some lucrative off the books missions.

"You must be in trouble," said Davies. "Steph usually does a far better job at covering your tracks. I don't suppose you want to tell me why Blacklight is after you?"

"I could but…"

"You're not going to?"

Ben grinned. "It's like you're psychic." He paused for a second, becoming serious.

"Where's Steph?" The images Ben had seen on the camera broke into his mind.

"She's fine," said Davies, as he reached forward to tap the driver on the shoulder. "Here's good."

The driver complied and brought the car to a stop outside a small coffee shop. A grey van pulled up behind it.

Davies and Ben got out and walked over to the van. Its doors opened and out stepped Steph.

Ben noticed the large gash on her forehead and the swelling on the right side of her mouth. She had also acquired a slight limp.

Ben tried reading her emotions as she came up to him; as usual it was a futile exercise. Trying to read Steph was like reading a book with blank pages.

"Steph, it's good to…"

The last part of Ben's sentence was interrupted by a right hook. He landed hard on the rain-soaked street. As he sat up, he wondered if Steph was going to conclude her performance with a boot planted firmly in his groin.

"You see what happens when you don't listen to me," said Steph, offering Ben her hand.

"And you couldn't say that without smacking me in the face?"

Steph pulled him to his feet. "Probably."

Ben moved his tongue around the inside of his mouth to check all his teeth were present and accounted for. "Consider me reminded."

"Hate to interrupt the tearful reunion, but some of us have careers to try and save," put in Davies.

"Thanks for the assist, Frank," said Steph. "We owe you one."

"And I mean to collect, believe me."

Everything with Frank Davies came with a price tag. Sooner or later, he would make good on his marker. Ben expected nothing less from him; after all he was CIA.

"How are you going to clear this with the people upstairs?" asked Ben.

"It's better you don't know," Davies answered, starting back to the car. "If you two manage to dig yourself out of this mess in one piece, I have some work for you."

"And if we can't?" asked Steph.

"Then the next time I see you will be behind bars. No more favours."

"Always a pleasure, Frank," Ben called after Davies as he reached the car.

Davies paused, the driver holding the door open. He opened his mouth to say something then instead, he raised his middle finger before getting into the car.

"Did you really have to wind him up like that?" said Steph as the car drove past. "He did just save your life."

"I had everything under control. I was on my way out the front door."

"You do realise Clancy would've been waiting for you to come out. He probably had a sniper waiting to pick you off. It's what I would do," Steph pointed out. "You were lucky."

But Ben had come to a different conclusion regarding his actions. "From where I was standing, I handled the situation like a professional."

"A professional amateur. If Clancy had stuck to the mission, he would have killed you the second he had the disk."

"Yeah but…"

"I'm not going to argue about this. You were lucky, they were sloppy: end of story."

"But..."

"No."

"No, listen I..."

"How about you just thank me for saving your ass for the twentieth time this year," said Steph, storming off towards the coffee shop entrance.

"I thank you, and more importantly, my ass thanks you," grinned Ben, following her.

They entered the coffee shop together. There were only two people in the place and one of those was a waitress who was already scuttling over to intercept them. The other person sat in the far corner booth, allowing him a full view of the entire shop. Ben's pulse quickened as he locked eyes with the Reverend, who replied with a nod. Ben hoped the reason the place was so dead tonight was not because his new ally had decided to eliminate the other customers whilst waiting for his salad.

"Can I take your order, please?" the waitress said in her best, 'it's not really my first day' voice. She appeared transfixed by the dried blood on Steph's face.

"Can you give us a minute?" said Steph.

"Can I get two ham and cheese bagels please?" said Ben, then pointing to a large tray of chocolate muffins. "And a couple of those bad boys, a large orange juice and a coffee please."

The waitress nodded, smiled and turned to leave.

"Are you crazy?" snapped Steph under her breath. "We don't have time for this."

"You're right, Steph,"

The waitress paused, aiming a fierce scowl at Steph.

Ben smiled at her. "Could you make that coffee a decaf, please?"

The waitress nodded and hurried away.

"What?" said Ben, seeing the disgusted look on his partner's face. "Near death always gives me an appetite."

Steph shook her head and headed for the corner booth. As Ben approached, the Reverend got to his feet and held out his gloved hand.

"It's good to see you again, Benjamin."

Ben shook his hand; it was like shaking hands with a brick, only slightly more solid. "Rev, always a pleasure."

"Lying is a sin, Benjamin."

The tension Ben was feeling began to ease. "Comedy from the one-man demolition squad. There's hope for you yet, Rev."

Ben took a seat, as did the others.

"Thanks for looking out for Steph," said Ben, becoming serious.

"I'm glad I was there in time, though I'm still not exactly sure what it was I killed."

"Grey called it an Erogian. It was sent to retrieve the disk and to take us out."

Ben was fast becoming lost listening to the exchange. "I guess you're talking about that thing with the big ass claws that tried to slice and dice you?"

Steph's surprised look immediately turned to one of sudden realisation. "The street camera?"

Ben nodded. "So how about you tell me who this Grey is, what the hell an Erogian is, and where the hell those bagels are? I'm starving."

A jarring impact, accompanied by the screeching of tires woke Jason from his forced unconsciousness. He was still blindfolded, but his hearing was unimpaired. He guessed from the sound, they were landing at last, whether that was an improvement in his situation was debateable. At least, he reasoned, there would be more chances for escape on the ground than in the air. He felt something sharp, probably a knife, inserted into the side of the blindfold. He tensed instinctively, but a large hand held his chin as the blindfold was cut from him. Blinking several times as his eyes struggled to become accustomed to the sunlight streaming in through the cabin window, Jason's vision became filled by a giant of a man who held the remains of the blindfold in one hand, a knife in the other. Wearing a short-sleeved khaki shirt and brown trousers tucked into black boots, the man sneered at him, displaying two gold front teeth.

"What is it with you?" said the man, looking surprised. "That last dose I gave you should have knocked you out for another day at least."

Barry Nugent

"How should I know?"

Staring out of the window, Jason saw a few buildings, but beyond that, stretching back into the horizon was an unfriendly-looking jungle landscape. "I don't even know where the hell I am."

"You're nowhere," the man told him as he untied Jason's wrists. "And just so we both know where we stand, you try anything, and you'll regret it."

Jason said nothing as the giant untied him. As he was pulled to his feet, he realised there was barely feeling in his legs. It was a strange sensation like floating on a cushion of air. Supported by the giant, who opened the plane's exit hatch, Jason was led outside. The first thing that struck him was how effective the plane's air conditioning had been in shielding him from the oppressive, stifling heat now assaulting his senses. The after effects of the drug combined with the heat were almost too much for him and he fought to push back the rising nausea in his throat.

"That's what you get for being resistant to the drug," said the giant, grinning. "Don't worry, it'll pass."

The giant helped Jason down the steps to where three jeeps were waiting for them. Two of the jeeps were manned by armed men. Jason tried not to focus on the weapons, but the nausea he felt once more threatened to erupt.

"Welcome, Monsieur Chen," said a slim man who wore a white collarless silk shirt and black trousers. "My name is Philippe Chardon. It is an honour to finally meet you."

170

Chapter Twenty-Three

Clancy sat watching the rain running down the windshield. He took a drag on his cigarette and wondered if the downpour, which had been lashing the city all night, would ever let up.

"Picked a great time to take up smoking again," he muttered to himself. Opening his window, he flicked the cigarette butt out into the rainstorm. He stared across the street at the hotel that housed the restaurant where he was to deliver the disk. Nearly a day had passed before he received the location for the exchange.

Clancy was a realist. The news of Ashodi's second escape would not have been well received. The fact Ashodi might have circumvented the disk's encryption and read its contents was something Clancy had decided was best not to mention.

Then there was Ashodi himself, who Clancy had last seen being led away hooded and handcuffed. After arriving back at the safe house, Clancy had made a few calls and discovered through his contacts that there was no record of any arrest. Clancy was not concerned. He had found Ashodi before, and would do so again.

By now, Clancy hoped the remainder of his team were well on their separate ways out of the country. The plan was to lay low until he made contact. The others were none too happy about running from a fight. The main thrust of the objection stemmed from the belief that they were stronger as a unit. They were right, to a certain extent, but if there was one thing all Clancy's years of soldiering had taught him, it was knowing when to stand your ground, and when to run.

Neither Clancy nor his team had any idea who their employers were, let alone where to find them. In their world, any scrap of useful intelligence was a priceless commodity, and the lack of it a dangerous mistress they could ill afford to entertain. So despite their misgivings, they had run, all save Clancy who had announced that he alone would perform the exchange. It was more than a desire to see out his contract that had bought him here. If he failed to attend, it would bring the wrath of his employers down upon them all that much sooner.

Once again, voices were raised, objections made, but they fell on deaf ears. Clancy's mind was made up. He allowed his men some latitude to comment on decisions concerning the safety of the team, but the final say was always his.

Now, hours later, the plan seemed less effective and, as he sat waiting for the signal from his contact to enter the restaurant, Clancy's silent misgivings were beginning to surface. His team had recovered the disk: that would have to be enough for their employers. He patted the automatic pistol nestled in his inside pocket; if not, then they would have a problem.

Perched on top of the dashboard, his mobile let out two sharp, high pitched tones. This was it: snatching up the phone, Clancy saw the small flashing, envelope symbol on the phone's main display screen, indicating there was a new text message. He quickly went through a short code sequence of key presses to bring up the message.

Right corner table, large bay window.

Clancy stepped out of the car, and felt the rain was beginning to ease off. He would have taken that as an omen, if he believed in such things. Crossing over the road, he walked towards a large revolving door that led into the lobby of the hotel, nodding a brief acknowledgment to a waterlogged doorman, who was probably praying for his shift to end and the welcome release from the constant onslaught of rain. The man delivered his best fake smile at Clancy before moving to a large limo that had just pulled up. Not breaking his stride, Clancy made his way through the revolving doors and into the hotel lobby.

Even though the hour was late, the lobby was a hub of activity. Queues of people stood at the front desk waiting to be checked in. Clancy headed for the glass double doors that led into the restaurant. Two young men were stood on either side of the door and seeing Clancy approach, they hurried to open the doors for him.

"Can I get you a table, sir?" said one of the men eagerly.

"No thanks, I'm good."

Clancy's eyes swept the room. Seeing his target, he made his way to the table at the far end of the room, and the three men sitting at it. Two of the men were tall, determined-looking, and both wore dark, two-piece suits. Clancy ignored them, they were just hired muscle. His business tonight was with the man who sat sandwiched between them, finishing his meal. Clancy walked towards him, the man showed little interest in Clancy and seemed more concerned with the last portions of meat he was shovelling into his mouth.

"Nothing like a medium rare steak," said the man, without looking up.

Taking up a half filled glass of red wine, he passed it three times under his nose before swallowing the last mouthful. "Much like a good wine."

The man picked up his napkin, which had been draped over his lap, and dabbed the remains of his dinner from the corners of his mouth. Dropping the napkin onto his plate, he leaned back and finally acknowledged Clancy's presence.

"Where's the rest of your entourage Mr. Wallencheck?" he said, looking past Clancy.

"I'm here to do business, not talk about my men."

"I can assume you are alone then?"

"I'm alone."

The man studied Clancy intensely. "You're armed."

"I said I'm alone, not stupid."

A thin smile creased the man's lips and he gestured to the seat in front of Clancy.

"I take it you've been briefed on the situation?" said Clancy, as he sat down.

The man held back his reply as a waiter moved to clear the table. "Can I get you anything, sir?" the waiter asked Clancy, whilst balancing the soiled crockery in one hand.

Clancy shook his head and the waiter once more disappeared from sight.

"If you're referring to your continued failure, then the answer is yes."

"We secured the disk," Clancy pointed out, ignoring the insinuations behind the man's words. "That was the main objective."

"Seeing that all you have to show for your work is the disk, I would expect you to say that."

"Do we have a problem here?"

The man held out his hand. "The disk, Mr. Wallencheck, and then I'll decide if there's a problem."

"I want assurances that my men will not be held responsible for my actions," said Clancy. "I underestimated Ashodi, but that mistake was mine, not my men's. You leave them out of any reprisals, and then we can talk about me giving you the disk."

The man reached down and lifted up a small attaché case that had been leaning against his chair. Opening it, he pulled out a small white envelope and slid it across the table and into Clancy's hand.

"I'm afraid it's too late for excuses, Mr. Wallencheck."

Clancy opened the envelope, all the while, hoping his instincts were wrong.

A passing waiter refilled the man's wine glass before moving on.

Clancy looked at the first photo. The blood-soaked body of a man lay slumped against the bonnet of a car, which was riddled with bullet holes.

"Jesus!"

"Stony, wasn't it?" said the man, sipping more of his wine. "You really should try this," he held the glass towards Clancy. "I think even your rudimentary palette would appreciate its subtle merits."

"You had him killed."

"Please take your time and look at the other photos. I think you will find them enlightening as to your current bargaining position."

Clancy's rage swelled as he held up each photo, studied each death, captured and frozen for posterity. One gunned down inside a phone booth, another reduced to charred remains that lay beside the smouldering wreckage of a car. A ruined and broken body, the result of being pushed from a great height; there were other images, all depicting the same grisly end. Death was always an occupational hazard in their line of work, but not like this, this was no way for a solider to die.

Clancy could hear the voices of the dead demanding retribution from the confines of the photos.

"I trust you understand your position now, Mr. Wallencheck?"

"Explain it to me."

"You hand over the disk and then we can discuss how you can leave this table alive."

Clancy noticed the bodyguards' increased agitation. Whatever was going to happen, it would be soon.

He pushed his hand slowly into his jacket pocket, making sure the movements were slow, so as not to provoke any kind of violent reaction from the bodyguards.

Clancy placed the case containing the disk on the table.

"A wise decision, Mr. Wallencheck."

The man picked up the disk and placed it inside the attaché case before returning the case to the floor.

Clancy slid his hands under the table.

"I can assume that now our business is concluded, you are about to do something foolish?"

"That depends on whether you're going to let me walk out of here."

The man did not reply. Instead, he picked up his glass of wine and pressed it to his lips.

"Kill him," he said, in between sips.

The two bodyguards reached into their jackets. Clancy threw himself back against his chair, toppling backwards as the bodyguards' guns cleared their holsters. Midway through the fall, Clancy's hands came up, each one holding a gun. He got off a few shots before his chair hit the ground. The bullets found their mark, shattering the kneecaps of the bodyguards. As one of them screamed in pain, he fired a shot that missed Clancy but ploughed into the chest of a nearby waiter. Through his now reversed vision, Clancy saw a couple sitting a few tables back pull weapons from under their table. He should have guessed there would be more than two assassins. He brought the guns over his head and fired. The first bullet caught the man between the eyes. He crashed backwards onto the table, scattering the remains of their desert, showering the fleeing guests with a mixture of blood and chocolate soufflé. The second bullet caught the woman in her right shoulder causing her to spin round as she fired a burst of gunfire that, by some miracle, managed to avoid the screaming, terrified patrons in her wake. Her pain was short-lived as a second bullet silenced her screams forever.

Clancy rolled backwards and came up firing, killing both bodyguards. Clancy's contact threw himself down. The case tumbled away from his reach, its clasps open, the contents spilling out over the floor. He reached out for the disk, only to watch his hand erupt in blood, flesh and bone as a bullet smashed through it.

He lay there screaming, his other hand clasped around the injured one. Clancy saw him looking at the gun a few feet from one of his dead bodyguards.

"Unless you want to lose the other hand, I suggest you forget about that gun."

Clancy crouched beside the man, his gun hovering in front of the man's terror-filled eyes, his former composure and self assurance a distant memory.

"I'm going to let you live. I want you to run back to whoever pulls your strings and give them a message. You tell them…"

Clancy fired three times into the man's chest. "On second thoughts, I'll tell them myself."

Zurich.

Elijah Barrington allowed the freezing water from the shower to blast onto his shaven head, refreshing his senses as it ran down the length of his body. He began massaging his temples in an effort to soothe the migraine that still lingered from last night. Even an hour's exercise in his largely unused personal gym did not manage to fully ease the headache.

The sound of his mobile phone ringing cut through the noise of the shower.

"The pressures of success," he told himself, as he stepped from the shower.

He paused to grab his dressing gown from the back of the bathroom door. He picked the phone up from the top of the bathroom sink. Before answering, he checked the number on the caller ID, to make sure it was a call worth taking. The caller was Harold Lambert, his personal assistant and a man with no understanding of the concept of time. Elijah let out a heavy sigh and flipped open the receiver on the phone.

"Sorry to disturb you, Mr. Barrington," began Lambert, with his usual air of annoyance.

"Lambert, my friend, if you were sorry, you wouldn't be dragging my ass out of the shower at four a.m. on a Sunday."

"Good point, Mr. Barrington," Lambert conceded. "But there's a situation here that demands your immediate attention."

"A situation? You need to do a lot better than that if you want to keep your job longer than this conversation."

There was silence for a few seconds before Lambert answered, probably after silently mouthing every foul name under the sun at him, guessed Elijah. "The situation regarding your overseas development plan in New York has taken a turn for the worse."

There was no overseas development in New York, thought Elijah. Whatever was going on, Lambert did not want to discuss it over the phone.

"I'll be ten minutes."

"Thank you, Mr. Barrington."

"Lambert?" said Elijah. "You know no one disturbs me on a Sunday morning?"

"Yes sir."

"Is your PC powered up?" Elijah asked, picking up a dark blue, double-breasted suit that was draped across the bed.

"Yes," said Lambert, his voice sounding slightly unsure.

"Good. Log in and pull up a letter of resignation," Elijah told him. "There's one saved onto your hard drive, print it off and have it waiting for me when I get there."

"May I ask for what purpose?"

"Because if I find out I've come in to baby-sit a PA who's more than capable of doing his job, then you'll be looking for a new one," said Elijah, turning off the phone.

Christ, he worked around the clock for the company, six and a half days a week, his only vice was Sunday morning. No matter where he was or what he was doing, he always spent his Sunday mornings relaxing. This involved a workout, when he could be bothered, then a shower, followed by a large fried breakfast and the morning paper whilst listening to music. Too many men his age burned out way before their time because they had forgotten the art of relaxation, and Elijah planned to be around for a very long time. He had Justine to thank for his healthier lifestyle. Justine Hillman was the co-owner of Barrington Inc. along with Elijah's mother, Lucille. Ten years after Lucille's death, Justine had taken the twenty-five-year-old Elijah under her wing and mentored him until he was ready to assume his mother's responsibilities in the running of the company. Ten years on, and Elijah was pretty much running the company during Justine's frequent absences.

Elijah pictured his mother's smiling face as he often found himself doing. He thought about some of the stories Justine would tell him about his mother, and some of the crazy things they used to get up to when they were younger. Having Justine around was like having a part of his mum with him, and he was always grateful to Justine for that. It did not take long for the sadness to creep in. Deciding it would do him no good to dwell on it, Elijah finished dressing and left his flat. His home was located on the twentieth floor of Barrington Tower, the heart of the company's operations. Elijah had rented the entire floor for himself. He always joked that as he spent so much time in the office, it seemed a good idea to sleep there as well.

Elijah headed down the corridor to his private elevator. It opened immediately, courtesy of the sensors built into the door. As the door closed behind him, he paused to check his reflection in the metallic surface of the elevator wall facing him.

"Twenty-four," he said, straightening his tie.

The lift, triggered by Elijah's voice, started to move. Only his closest business advisers and friends had access to the elevator. The stairs to the floor were blocked by a security door that could only be opened with the aid of a special swipe card and a five-digit code. Elijah prized his own privacy over all other things, with the notable exception of money.

The lift announced its arrival to the twenty-fourth level with a sequence of chimes. Elijah stepped out into a long hallway, which led him to a pair of glass doors. As he approached the doors, he could already see Lambert's nervous slender frame, filling a badly-tailored, dark grey suit, waiting on the other side. Lambert, upon seeing Elijah, scurried forward to open the door as Elijah reached it.

"Thank you for coming in so promptly, sir," said Lambert.

Elijah did not miss the sweat decorating Lambert's forehead and bottom lip.

He held out his hand. "Do you have that item we talked about?"

Lambert leaned over the desk behind him and snatched a copy of his resignation from the printer and handed it to Elijah, who briefly scanned the document before folding it carefully and placing it in his jacket pocket.

"So what's so important you had to drag me up here?"

"The person to answer that question is waiting in your office, sir."

Elijah's restraint shattered. "What's the point paying out for a security system that costs more than most third world countries make in a year, if you go around inviting people into my office? Do you have any idea how many ways I'm thinking of ruining your career about now?"

"Sir...I."

"Twenty!" said Elijah. "And that's off the top of my head, you keep talking and I'm sure I can double it."

"I did not let anyone into your office, he was already there when I came in. He said he was here to discuss the Tokyo contract, and that you would know what he meant."

"Get to the security station and get them up here, now!"

"Wouldn't do that, Elijah," said a voice coming from the speakerphone by Lambert's desk. "If your boy even scratches his ass the wrong way, my friend promises me he can destroy fifty percent of your company's data before you can sever his connection."

Elijah opened his mouth to say something when the voice spoke again.

"Now, before you come up with more ways to piss me off, just get your ass in here. You know I can do everything I say. I'll ruin this company in a heartbeat, go home, and sleep peacefully tonight, your choice."

Elijah's shoulders slumped in defeat as he headed toward his office. He knew exactly who was in his office, and what kind of reception he could expect. The door unlocked as he neared it.

"What should I do?" asked Lambert.

Elijah stopped, his hand on the door handle.

"This meeting should be over in ten minutes." He took the letter of resignation out of his pocket and dropped it behind him. "It's already signed, have a nice life, Mr. Lambert."

Elijah opened the door and walked into the office, leaving Lambert alone, the letter of resignation mocking him from the floor.

Chapter Twenty-Four

As he watched Philippe cast a critical eye over his sweat-drenched shirt, Jason wished the only worry on his mind was the ruination of an expensive silk shirt.

They had been travelling for hours, and so far, Jason had learnt nothing regarding their destination or the purpose behind his abduction.

The dreams, Joshua Grey, the Carsons' murder, and his kidnap had all happened so fast that this was the first time Jason had been able to stop and begin processing everything. The knowledge that he was the single thread somehow tied to everything was as frightening as was his lack of understanding why.

The journey had been without incident, so far. There was the occasional shove or harsh word when he tried to probe his captors for more information, but that was it.

Jason examined his position. He was outnumbered with no chance of escape, at least not for the moment. He had no idea what was in store for him, but he knew he was not going to accept it without a fight. He promised himself that was one lesson his kidnappers would learn the hard way.

The hours passed slowly, allowing the monotony to sink in. Jason was given food and water when the convoy stopped, and was allowed to get out and stretch his legs, although the two men guarding him, who he nicknamed Eric and Ernie, were never far from his side.

Over time, the jungle, which at first had depicted an inescapable and inhospitable environment, became more intriguing to Jason the further they travelled. All his life had been spent living in the city with little contact with nature except what he saw on TV. It was impossible for him to not become immersed in the breathtaking landscape of sights, sounds and colours that surrounded him. It was as if he had woken from the most vivid of dreams only to find it was now a reality.

Eventually, the jungle opened out into a large clearing, allowing shafts of sunlight to cut through the foliage, creating spheres of light on the ground. As fascinating as watching the sunlight bounce from leaf to leaf was, it was the impossible sight before Jason's eyes that held his attention. There, in the middle of the rainforest stood a castle. The towering edifice of stone and metal appeared as if it had been torn from history and placed here. Jason counted five semi-circular turrets of varying heights, at regular intervals along the walls. Even from this distance, he could make out tiny figures manning the battlements. Great, he thought, more Knights of Cademus.

The forest seemed content to keep a safe distance, making the castle seem even more at odds with the environment. Jason could not even begin to comprehend how such a place could come to exist here.

"Magnificent, isn't it?" said Philippe, his words mirroring Jason's thoughts. "I was about your age when I first saw it. I wonder if the look on my face was the same as yours."

In spite of the danger he was in, Jason was overwhelmed by the splendour of the castle.

"Where are we?"

"This is the Cabal's seat of power," said Philippe. "Our founder was a man who believed in being prepared. Our history tells us that he foresaw the destruction of his home and the death of his followers, and so, in secret, he commissioned the construction of this castle, to serve as his new home and that of his Cabal."

"The Cabal?"

"The Cabal is the heart of our order. But don't worry, you will see them soon enough."

Jason got the impression that meeting this Cabal was not going to be a pleasant experience, but perhaps, at least, he would get some answers.

"How come this place hasn't ended up all over the news?"

Philippe placed his hand on Jason's shoulder and gently guided him forwards. "The answer is a simple one. It has already been discovered, several times, in fact, before you or I were born."

"Then how..."

"Has the discovery never received any media attention? Because the Book of Cademus and the Cabal have a far longer reach than you know."

Philippe pulled an apple from his pocket and, after producing a pocketknife, proceeded to cut a slice. "Since I first came here, at least seven archaeological expeditions have stood on this spot."

Jason suddenly felt all the wonder and amazement drain away as he asked his next question. "Where are they now?"

"They were killed, their research destroyed," said Philippe, as if discussing the most trivial of matters. "Apple?" he smiled, offering Jason a slice.

Elijah was not a man prone to fear. He believed in facing problems head on. However, the handgun pressing against his left temple was forcing him to rethink that stance.

"I'd find it a lot easier to talk without the gun, Ben." Elijah was directing his words to the occupant of his large leather chair behind his desk.

"Good brandy," said Ben, swirling the glass.

Elijah tried to turn his head, only to find the gun pushed even harder.

"Eyes forward, if you want to keep that bald head of yours in one piece."

Elijah recognised the voice straight away. Where Ben Ashodi was, Stephanie Connisbee was never too far behind.

"Look, there's no need for any of this."

Elijah heard the gun's hammer pull back. He flinched, but gave no other indication he was scared, merely concerned.

"Now that's where you're wrong, Elijah, there's every need for this," said Steph. "Believe me, if I had my way, we'd be having a lot shorter conversation."

"I don't doubt that for a second, but for now, I can assume you're not here to kill me."

Ben swivelled around on the chair. "What makes you think we're not here to kill you?"

Elijah smiled. "You're thieves, not murderers, so how about we cut the crap and start having a real conversation?"

Ben hurled the glass at Elijah, missing his head, but not the door it shattered against, showering Elijah with brandy. Elijah looked back at the brandy-stained door and said nothing.

"You sold us out!" said Ben.

He rose from the chair until he was face to face with Elijah.

"Anyone who can carry a badge is on our asses. We've got mercs looking to put a bullet in us, and that's all down to you."

"What Ben's saying is that we have no problem ending you right here."

"I believe you, but I'm still going to find it hard to explain myself with a gun shoved in my face."

"You're going to find it a lot harder with half a brain missing."

"Think of it as a motivational aid," said Ben. "Now, I want to know the why and the who, because I know you didn't set this up on your own, not your style."

"That's going to be hard to explain."

Elijah winced as the gun barrel was tapped hard against the side of his head.

"Try real hard," said Steph.

"Can I get to my desk without being shot?" asked Elijah. "There's something I need to show you."

Elijah saw Ben nod and then the pressure from the gun was gone. He walked past Ben, who had relinquished the chair, and took his seat. Elijah knew there were a number of security measures installed within the desk. Any one of them would activate a silent alarm, alerting one of the nearby security teams.

"Please don't insult our intelligence by assuming we haven't taken out every little trick in that desk of yours," said Steph, who seemed to Elijah to be taking far too much pleasure in watching him squirm. He was not really surprised, she had never liked him. Succumbing to his fate with a sigh, Elijah leaned to the right and pressed his thumb against a small pressure pad attached to his drawer, a second later the red light next to the pad flickered then flashed green. Elijah opened the drawer, took out a large manila envelope and threw it onto the desk.

"This is why I set you up."

Ben picked up the envelope and reached inside. Steph came over in time to see him take out a large black and white photograph.

"Ah hell," said Ben.

The picture showed a woman gagged and bound to a chair. One look at the dried blood that matted her hair, and the bruises that covered half of her face confirmed her poor treatment. Resting on her lap was a piece of cardboard with writing on it in thick black letters.

"Help us or she dies," said Elijah, closing his eyes, the words from the picture as clear now as when he had first seen them.

"Who is she?" asked Steph.

"Justine Hillman, the CEO of this company."

"You're kidding me, right?"

"It happened six months ago," began Elijah. "She was travelling home on the company jet when it disappeared. The common theory was the plane went down."

"Hang on," said Stephanie, returning her gun to her holster. "A plane carrying the head of a large multinational crashes and no one hears about it?"

"If the shareholders got wind that Justine was missing, presumed dead, our stocks wouldn't be worth shit. It would leave us open to takeover bids, or this company would rip itself apart with everyone wanting to be top dog."

"So you covered it up," said Ben.

"It was easy enough to do, Justine was always away on business, so no one really questioned where she was, and when they did, it wasn't too difficult to come up with a cover story."

"But the plane didn't crash, I'm guessing hijack, right?"

Elijah nodded. "About a month after the crash, I was sent that photo and a hand-written note. I had the letter authenticated; it's definitely Justine's handwriting.

"Her note said that if I didn't carry out the kidnappers' instructions, she would be killed. Two days later, she called to give me their first set of instructions. Over the next few months, they had me siphon off Justine's private bank accounts into account numbers they sent me, and then I was told to begin recruiting."

"Recruiting?"

"Mercenaries, the best I could find."

"Recruit them for what?"

"No idea."

"Didn't you think it was worth finding out what you were bankrolling?" said Steph.

"Look, they had Justine. I wasn't about to start asking questions," snapped Elijah. "Besides, that's not the way I do business."

"Yeah, and look where that life philosophy has got you," said Steph, glaring at him.

Elijah ignored Steph's outburst and continued. "About two months ago, they asked me for information on you two. They said they'd know if I held anything back so I had to come up with the goods."

"Boy, did you come up with the goods," said Ben.

"You think I had a choice?" said Elijah. "Justine and Mum were the best of friends, and when she died, Justine was the closest thing to family I had."

"It's not like she's blood or anything…what, were you afraid with your meal ticket gone, you might lose all of this?" Steph waved her hand around the large office. "Now that would be a shame."

"You've got a big mouth, bitch," said Elijah, moving round his desk to face her. "How would you like to see how fast I can close it for you?"

Steph smiled malevolently back at him, beckoning with her left hand. "Bring it on, big man."

As Elijah started forward, Ben grabbed his arm. "You know smacking her is only going to piss her off," said Ben. "And I know you don't want to do that."

Elijah was no coward, but he was a realist. He could handle himself, but Steph, he had seen Steph fight. She could take him without breaking a sweat. He felt his pride take a severe body blow as he stepped back behind his desk; but better a wounded pride then a broken arm, he told himself.

Ben perched himself on one of the corners of Elijah's desk. "So Tokyo was a trap: you set up the meeting with Pemrose, promising him to help him disappear, so that Justine's kidnappers could get the disk and take out Pemrose, that bit I understand."

"If you arranged the meeting between us and Pemrose, then you could have got to him anytime you wanted to, why drag us in?" said Steph.

"There was no one else, they wanted The Hand."

"Who?" said Ben. "Who wants me?"

"My guess would be the Book of Cademus."

The words had come from behind; Ben turned, gun in hand, together with Steph, and found three armed men standing in the open doorway.

Elijah looked at the handsome, well-dressed and well-built man standing in the centre. He knew exactly who he was, and once Ben recognised him, his office would become a shooting gallery.

"Put your guns down, it's ok," ordered the big man.

"I don't think so," said the one-eyed man, who stood beside him. Whoever he was, Elijah knew a serious player when he saw one.

Ben walked towards the big man. Elijah saw the anger in his eyes and wished more than anything that his alarm system was intact.

"Ben, what's going on? Do you know this guy?" asked Steph.

Ben did not reply. His attention was on the man whose nose was now supporting the tip of his gun.

"You better back up, friend," advised the third man, whose accent Elijah recognised as Italian.

"Napoleon, Vincent, put your guns down," the big man said again. "Trust me, we're in no danger."

"I think the man with the gun in your face would disagree with you," said the one-eyed man. "So give me a reason, any reason why I shouldn't start shooting?"

"He's my brother."

Chapter Twenty-Five

The bleak and barren wasteland stretched out before Jason. He knew he was dreaming again, he just did not know if this was to become another of his vivid nightmares. Like his first nightmare, he was standing amidst the ruins of a city.

Jason whipped his head round as something whispered in his ears. The sound was too faint to tell what it was.

"Hello," he called out, his voice echoing through the ruins. "Is anyone there?"

There was no reply, but the sound was growing louder. Jason recognised the sound as footsteps, but he could see no one.

"Where are you?" he screamed, starting to run. "Who are you?"

Jason ran from the city and into the desert beyond, not knowing where he was going and not caring. The desire to be free of the nightmare drove him forwards.

The footsteps had become deafening, forcing Jason to cover his ears as he ran. The ground shook with each footstep, each one drawing closer to Jason. Panic took hold. Jason lost his footing as he reached a rise, causing him to tumble headlong down the slope and landing face first in the sand. Lifting his head, he found himself back in the city, as if he had never left it. He got onto his knees, coughing out mouthfuls of dirt and sand.

"What do you want?" shouted Jason.

The sleeper shall awake.

For a second, everything became blurry, and then the scene shifted. Jason was now standing at the top of a spiral staircase, its steps made from huge stone slabs. In front of him lay a long passageway lit on both sides by flaming torches. Jason could hear the sound of talking coming from the far end of the passage. Pushing his fears aside, he started to walk forwards. He armoured himself with the fragile belief that things could not possibly get much worse. Famous last words, his overactive imagination whispered back at him. With caution dogging his every step, Jason edged closer to the opening of the corridor. The strange thing was that the closer he came to the opening, the lower the voices became. Jason fought to calm his growing fear. Get a grip; he told himself, you'll never get out of this if you lose it now. He took a few more deep breaths before he strode out of the corridor. The room he moved into was immense, far larger than he would have imagined given that he assumed he was inside what he thought to be a castle tower. Jason went quietly into the chamber, which at first glance was not much to look at after all the strangeness he had already encountered. What grabbed his interest were the six robed and hooded figures standing in the centre of the room. In front of them, suspended in mid-air was what looked like a glass coffin. Jason was too far away to make out who or what was inside. All was silent now, the voices he had heard earlier now rendered dormant. As Jason contemplated his next move, the figure who was standing closest to the coffin started to move. The figure turned and faced Jason before seeming to glide across the floor towards him, making no sound as it moved. Instinctively, Jason took a step back but as the hooded figure reached out to touch him, Jason felt something. He could not explain what the feeling was, but he had experienced something similar whilst standing in the wasteland. The robed figure did not raise its head, so Jason was unable to see its face, a fact he was glad of.

"Who are you?" said Jason, moving further back as the figure continued towards him.

The sleeper shall awake.

"What are you?"

You cannot stop it, the sleeper shall awake.

Everything went black, and Jason realised the dream had ended as abruptly as it had begun.

"Good, he's coming round."

Jason heard Philippe's voice and slowly sat up. He looked around; he was sitting on a four-poster bed in a large bedroom. Two stained glass windows allowed the sunlight to stream into the room, where the images on the glass decorated the stone floor. The images depicted a lone knight, clad in white, fighting against a horde of creatures. Jason thought the creatures in the painting resembled the one that had tried to kidnap him at the university. On the wall opposite hung a portrait of a man. Closer examination revealed the man to be the same one gracing the stained glass window. Long blond hair flowed to the man's shoulders, and he had blue eyes that seemed to betray a softness, which was in direct conflict to the huge battle sword he held and the silver armour he wore. Even though Jason had never seen the portrait or the man depicted within it before, he felt strangely drawn to the painting.

"You seem intrigued by the portrait," said a female voice. "But then given your history, I suppose it's to be expected."

To Philippe's left, Jason saw a woman in her late forties, wearing a black trouser suit. Her curly blond hair was cut short, resting just below her ears. The fierceness in her hazel eyes told Jason that whoever she was, she was someone who demanded respect from those around her.

She smiled at Jason, but it was a smile that failed to convey any genuine warmth.

"Who was he? he asked.

"Our founder, Sir Oliver Cademus."

"He was a Knight?"

"Yes, he journeyed to the crusades with his father, but there will be plenty of time to discuss history later."

The woman held out her hand. "After all these years I was beginning to think we would never find you."

Jason stared at her hand, unimpressed. "And you would be?"

The woman's smile was gone as quickly as the stinging back hand she delivered across Jason's face. Rubbing the sore red patch on his left cheek, Jason was surprised such a slightly built woman could hit so hard. The woman leaned in closer.

"Just so we understand one another. I am one of the people who ordered the deaths of your adoptive parents, and arranged for your abduction. So I would advise a little less attitude and a lot more respect."

The words sunk in. Jason's mask of bravado was gone. It was if she could see him for what he was, a scared teenager doing everything he could to stay alive.

"Your only value is what you may carry inside you, and once we have that, there will be no more use of you."

Although he was afraid, Jason still had to force himself not to spit on the woman's no doubt wildly expensive footwear.

"You have been brought here for the ritual of restoration."

"The what?"

"I know, it all sounds quite archaic, doesn't it? Castles, ancient rituals, and the like," sighed the woman. "I don't subscribe to all the trappings of our little community, but I am willing to put up with some of its eccentricities for what I receive in return."

"Which is?"

The woman smiled, and Jason was lifted from the bed by unseen hands, and hurled against the wall.

"Power, Jason," said the woman, walking towards him. "A great deal of power."

"The boy is not to be harmed," said Philippe, following the woman close behind.

"And you forget who you're talking to, Philippe, besides we're just getting acquainted, aren't we, Jason?"

The woman leant forward and kissed Jason lightly on the cheek.

"Time to go," she said. "The Cabal don't like to be kept waiting."

The woman clicked her fingers and two men dressed in white laboratory coats came into the room. They grabbed hold of Jason and pulled him to his feet.

"Wait!" said Jason, as he struggled with the two men, one of whom was rolling up Jason's right sleeve. "Please...wait, you don't need to do this ...please...I'll..."

There was a sharp but brief pain, and then Jason felt his limbs grow heavy. He did not fight the sensation: suddenly he wanted the numbness, the momentary oblivion the drugs offered. He collapsed into the arms of the two men; he was conscious but unable to move.

Philippe watched the men throw a hood over the boy's head and drag him from the room. Once they were alone, the woman grabbed the back of his head and pulled him into a passionate kiss, breaking it off almost as soon as she had begun.

"You should not be here, Philippe. It's crucial that you be at the meeting to avoid suspicions being raised."

"I will be leaving within the hour, I have plenty of time to make the rendezvous," Philippe assured her. "I thought it best to handle the boy's transfer here personally."

"You're a very lucky man, Philippe," she said, whilst stroking the back of his neck. "The Cabal are not happy with your performance to date."

"So I have been told," replied Philippe. He had not forgotten his last encounter with the Cabal.

"If the Knights of Cademus had failed to secure the boy, I would be feeding you your intestines," the woman told him.

Philippe, angry at the way he was being spoken to, pulled away. "Is it my fault I am surrounded by incompetents who cannot follow a simple order?"

The woman tutted disapprovingly. "That's always been your problem, Philippe; you blame everyone except yourself."

"They were your orders, maybe if you..."

The woman placed a finger against Philippe's lips. "Be careful, my dear. You're good in bed, but not that good, I'm sure I could learn to live without you."

Philippe had no illusions about what place he held in her affections. Their arrangement was something they both enjoyed, but the moment she tired of the relationship, whatever slim protection she offered would be gone.

"Where are Washington and Stone?" she asked

"I have several leads, which my operatives are following up."

"I would be far more impressed if you just said you have no idea."

"Along with Stone's assistant, there are only three of them. Washington's a wanted man and now we have the boy, the timetable is set," said Philippe. "There is nothing they can do."·

"It amazes me how you managed to end up as head of TORCH even with the Cabal's help," remarked the woman. "Has it slipped your mind that Stone has intimate knowledge of our organisation? And he single-handedly crippled our Mexico chapter in one night."

She let out an exasperated sigh. "At least Ashodi and his partner are dead, that's one less thing we have to worry about."

Philippe averted his gaze to anywhere but the woman.

"Please tell me they're dead, Philippe."

"They evaded Wallencheck's team and killed the Erogian you sent after them."

Philippe could see the woman fighting to control her temper. "And you did not think this was the kind of information the Cabal would want to hear as soon as possible?"

"They're career criminals. They'll go to ground and wait until the dust has settled. It would serve them no purpose to come after us."

"They're wanted for terrorism and mass murder; if they're caught, it will mean the death penalty. They have no choice but to come after us and should they manage to ally themselves with Stone and the others, our problems will be compounded."

Philippe could not understand why she was so concerned. The Book of Cademus commanded the loyalty of thousands, each one ready to sacrifice themselves for the cause. What possible threat could be posed by a rag tag group of criminals and fallen heroes?

"These are not ordinary individuals we're dealing with, therefore, we must accord them the respect they deserve. Find them, Philippe, find them and kill them, no more mistakes."

"This is a wind up, right?" asked Steph. "You can't be his brother, his brother's dead."

"Is that what he told you?" said Luther, placing a hand over the gun Ben was holding. "Sorry to disappoint, Ben, or would you prefer The Hand?"

Ben was not listening. The recurring fantasy that had got him through those first years in prison was now a reality. The others in the room were reduced to bystanders as the explosive family reunion unfolded before their eyes.

"Can you do it, Ben?" Luther's hand was still on the gun barrel, a look of disappointment in his eyes. "Do you really hate me that much?"

"You have no idea."

Ben could barely contain the rage. His brother, the words stung. Now Luther was nothing more than the man who destroyed any hope he harboured for a normal life.

"Remember the last time I saw you, what was it? Five years ago?"

"More like seven," said Luther.

"It was Mum's funeral. You were wearing a three-hundred dollar suit and I was in an orange jumpsuit handcuffed to a prison guard. Do you remember what I said?"

"You said I was a dead man."

Vincent edged closer to Napoleon. "We better do something, looks like brotherly love has long since left the building."

"I'll take the brother, you go for the girl."

"It would be better if neither of you make any such movements," said the Reverend, who, from out of nowhere, had taken up position in the open doorway brandishing his Uzi pistols. "I don't know who you are, but if you move again, make no mistake, I will kill you."

Napoleon raised his hands and kept them in plain sight, as did Vincent.

"So here we are, bro, seven years on," said Ben, moving his gun until it was resting under Luther's chin. "How does it feel to be the one in the shit for a change, huh?"

"Prison may have changed you, Ben, but I can't believe it's made you a killer." "You're right," said Ben, smashing the gun butt across his brother's face.

Luther staggered under the weight of the blow, but did not go down. He righted himself, a large gash now evident across his left cheek.

"I suppose I had that coming."

"You've had that coming since we were kids and I'm just getting warmed up."

"Will you two give it a rest!" shouted Elijah, standing up from behind his desk. "We don't have time for this bullshit."

The room fell silent, all eyes turning to Elijah. "You both need to calm down before someone, namely me, gets his head blown off!" he advised. "I'm assuming you're here for information as well, Luther?"

Now it was Ben's turn to look surprised. "Please, don't tell me you know him?"

"Only by reputation; I get a lot of work from TORCH so I make it my business to know who I'm dealing with. You must be insane coming here, Washington. I could get twenty years for just talking to you."

"What's he talking about?" demanded Napoleon.

"Yeah, Mr. big shot secret agent," said Ben, who was now grinning at the prospect of his brother in trouble. "Tell us what's going on?"

"Two agents who were working for me on an off-the-books operation were attacked. One's dead, the other's in a coma, and I'm being held responsible."

Ben shook his head, sighing. "Why is it everyone around you ends up taking the fall for your mistakes?"

Ben did not get the chance to hear Luther's reply or enjoy the pained expression on his brother's face. Luther's left hand, moving with blurring speed, snatched the gun out of Ben's hand. His right fist came up, cracking against Ben's chin, lifting him up onto Elijah's desk and sending files and stationery everywhere.

"You want to blame me for what happened to you, fine, you want to kill me, that's your choice, but we deal with this situation first, you got that?"

Ben opened his mouth to say something, then relaxed. "Yeah, I got that."

Luther tossed the gun back to Ben before turning to the others. "Something tells me we're all here for the same reason; someone, somewhere is playing with us and I'm sick of it."

"Agreed," said the Reverend. "And your suggestion for resolving this situation is?"

"We need to start afresh, hear everyone's side of the story. Barrington, do you have a conference room or something, we can use?"

"No," snapped Elijah. "Look, this mess has nothing to do with me. I'm a businessman, which means I don't put my ass on the line for anyone or anything that isn't in my or the company's best interests."

Napoleon strode past Luther and up to Elijah's desk, slamming his hands down on it.

"You're in this, Barrington, you're in this up to your corporate neck."

Elijah leaned forward. "Now you listen, no one comes into my office, my home and starts threatening me, certainly not some one-eyed guy dressed like a bum. So unless you're going to ask me where the nearest soup kitchen is, then back off."

"You remember Pemrose don't you?" asked Napoleon.

"Who?"

"Pemrose tried to escape the Book of Cademus and they killed him. How long do you think it will be before they come after you?"

At the mention of the Book of Cademus, Ben realised that right now, answers were more important than vengeance. "The Book of Cademus?"

"Elijah, tell the man what he wants to know," said Steph. "You do not want these people on your case, believe me."

Elijah began rubbing his chin and went silent. Ben figured Elijah was mulling over his options, looking for the one that benefited him the most.

"The main conference room's the second door on the left," Elijah said, leading the way past the Reverend.

"You coming?" said Steph, pausing at the door, her eyes fixed on

Luther.

"It's all good, Steph," said Ben. "We're right behind you."

She stood in the doorway a few seconds more then walked away, leaving the two brothers alone.

Ben adjusted his clothes and took up his leather jacket, which had been resting on a chair.

"Listen, Ben, I…"

"Just so we're clear, I'm going to back off and play happy families for now, but once this is all over, we're going to pick up were we left off five minutes ago."

With that, Ben shoved past Luther.

"I thought you said you couldn't kill me?" Luther called after him.

"Not yet," Ben answered without turning. "But things change."

Ben caught up with the others as Elijah finished typing in a key code and swiping his key card through the sensor. Hearing the doors unlock themselves, he pushed them open and they all stepped inside.

"So you finally got here," smiled Joshua Grey, who was seated at the head of a conference table. "Now, would one of you be so kind as to fetch me a cup of tea before I die of thirst?"

Chapter Twenty-Six

After Steph's description of her meeting with the mysterious Joshua Grey, Ben was a little underwhelmed at the man who now sat before him. Joshua was preoccupied with the small, caramel-coloured plastic cup containing his tea. Anyone seeing the look on his face would think he was about to swallow his own urine.

"Problem?" said Elijah, who had earlier expressed his disgust at having to play Tea boy in his own building.

"The fact you call this tea is more than problem enough thank you, Elijah." Joshua 's eyes never left the cup as he spoke.

"How do you know my name?"

"Why the concern, Elijah?" said Joshua, taking up the cup at the last. "Do you think I would waste time reading your grubby little mind when I need only look at the sign on your office door?"

Ben chuckled behind Elijah and kept doing so even when Elijah was staring straight at him.

Joshua swallowed his tea in one mouthful. "Now that my taste buds have been sufficiently ruined, we can move to the business at hand."

"And what business is that, Joshua Grey?" said the Reverend. "It seems that you have had business with all of us over these past days, how is it that one man can travel to so many places in so short a time?"

"Irrelevant," Grey said, with a dismissive snort. "You can do better than that."

Ben wondered if Grey realised just how little it would take for the Reverend to put a bullet in him. He figured he should at least try to defuse the situation before things got ugly.

"Here's an idea, Josh. How about you stop pissing about and tell us something useful?"

Ben thought his question might have pushed Grey too far, and if half of what Steph had told him was to be believed, that could be a problem. Joshua slid his chair back and stood. Not a word was spoken as he made his way over to where Ben was perched on the edge of the conference table.

"Finally." He slapped Ben hard on the back. "There is nothing I find more refreshing than a bout of plain speaking, don't you agree?"

"Guess so," said Ben, who was unsure whether the conversation was actually going anywhere. "Depends who's doing the speaking."

"A valid point, Benjamin," said Grey, returning to his seat without a second look at Ben. "Maybe it's time you all indulged in some plain speaking."

Grey's suggestion was met by silence and looks of distrust. Ben did not know if the silence came from the unwillingness of the others to share information, or that no wanted to go first and show their hand too early.

"Difficult to the last," sighed Grey, once more getting out of his seat. "Well, it seems then, it is up to me to fill in the blanks none of you seem willing to, despite the fact that your failure to put aside your petty squabbling will cost a young man his life."

Ben did not know who the young man was, but the disapproving glance Grey aimed in Napoleon's direction told him who did.

"Now, let me see if I get this right," said Grey. "Several days ago, Benjamin and Stephanie here break into the head research centre for TORCH, where Ben is met by…"

"Hang on, hang on," Ben cut in, holding up his hands, mentally committing himself to his next course of action. "If anyone's going to tell this, it might as well be me."

"By all means, Benjamin," said Grey, who appeared unperturbed by the interruption.

"Cheers, Josh."

"I would prefer to be called Joshua if you please."

"Whatever, Josh," said Ben. "We were hired to make contact with Pemrose, buy the disk from him, and then deliver it to Elijah."

"And thanks to our employer over there," said Steph, pointing at Elijah, "Pemrose ended up dead and we were public enemies one and two."

"I've already explained why I had to do it," said Elijah.

"That explanation doesn't cover why you needed us to break into the centre in the first place?"

"The kidnappers wanted you in that building, so I made sure you were."

"How did you manage to convince Pemrose?" asked the Reverend. "Surely he must have suspected something."

"The man was beyond the ability to think rationally. It wasn't hard to convince him that I needed to change the original plan."

"A plan that got a lot of people killed," Luther put in.

Elijah pounded his fist down on the table, spilling his cup of coffee across it.

"Don't you think I know that?! I swear I didn't know what Clancy and his team were planning "

"You can swear all you want, Barrington, but those people will still be dead and it will still be your fault," said Luther.

"A lecture on ethics from you, that's rich. At least I've never let a member of my family rot in prison for something he didn't do. What, didn't you think I knew? I make it my business to know all the dirt on people I may have to deal with."

"This isn't the time, Elijah," warned Steph. "Let it go, we've got more important things to worry about."

"No, I won't. Look at him, Steph. The big TORCH agent ordering us around, who put him in charge?"

"Leave it, Elijah," this time it was Ben who was speaking. "Steph's right, now is not the time."

"Not the time, Ben? They gave him a choice, did you know that? A choice: back off or watch you go to prison. I don't know how you can stand to be in the same room with him."

"You know, Elijah that's all true," said Luther. "But I did what I thought was right to protect hundreds of lives, what's your excuse? You used and betrayed a frightened man, sent him off to be murdered. I don't care if you were trying to save a life, murder is murder, and when this is over, you'll answer for your part in it."

"And who will you answer to?" shot back Elijah. "Who will be there to make you pay for what you've done?"

No one was looking in his direction, but Ben knew whose name was on everyone's lips.

"This is getting us nowhere!" shouted Vincent. "The disk? What was on it?"

"It was encrypted but we were able to access a video file made by Pemrose. It seems he was part of an undercover task force investigating a rogue agency operating inside TORCH."

Ben could not smile fast enough at the disbelieving look now on Luther's face. He went on to explain what Will had discovered about the rogue agency's connection to the Book of Cademus.

"So Pemrose found out this group, and the Book of Cademus were planning an attack against the UN?" said Vincent. "Did you believe him?"

"These people destroyed a building to get that disk back, and they've been trying to kill us ever since, on the off chance we may have accessed it. That's convincing enough for me."

Vincent exchanged looks with Napoleon, who nodded, as if giving his consent. Ben hoped this meant they were about to provide another piece to a puzzle that was becoming more twisted by the second.

"The organisation we work for has always believed the Book of Cademus had an agenda, but to move against the UN itself and risk worldwide exposure? I don't think so."

"Explain?" asked the Reverend.

Vincent went to reply, but Napoleon got there first.

"We are talking about a cult that has existed for centuries. Its continued survival is thanks to the veil of secrecy they operate under. They would not risk that anonymity on a single attack."

"Unless that attack was to protect themselves," said Elijah. "When Pemrose contacted me, he said that he had spoken with Secretary General Morton and told her everything about this group's involvement with the Book of Cademus." Elijah held up his hands when he saw the anger on Ben's face. "Yes, I knew about them when you came in here, but I decided to keep a few cards up my sleeve just in case."

"One of these days, Elijah," promised Ben, not bothering to finish the threat. "She must have thought he was crazy."

Steph took out a cigar and lit up, despite the stern looks from both Elijah and Ben.

"On the contrary, Pemrose said she believed every word."

"A man with nothing to lose can be very convincing," said the Reverend.

"Morton agreed to arrange a secret meeting with several of the more open-minded members of the UN Security Council."

"I find it hard to believe that the Secretary General of the United Nations would walk into a room and announce how a cult few people have even heard of has infiltrated the world's foremost security agency and now poses a global threat. She'd be laughed out of office," said Napoleon.

"According to Pemrose, the plan was to handle the release of the information in stages," said Elijah. "The first being to inform some of the Security Council members of the task force's existence, and their mandate to investigate claims of corruption within TORCH. Morton's goal was to get approval for the task force to be expanded and more resources put at their disposal. In the meantime, Pemrose was to go into hiding with whatever information he had discovered, until he could present it in person before the council once they believed in the reality of the threat the Book of Cademus represented."

"Makes sense," agreed Steph, who had now opened a window a fraction and was blowing smoke rings out into the early morning sky. "The members would be pretty pissed if they found out about a task force set up behind their backs, much better to spoonfeed them the information over a couple months, build up a case before hitting them with the Book of Cademus."

"Pemrose was probably her ace," said Ben, as he slid an ashtray down the table to Steph's waiting free hand. "His testimony combined with the information on the disk might have forced the Security Council to take action."

"And who knows the amount of information a new and improved task force could uncover," finished Steph, smiling her thanks to Ben for the ashtray.

"If what you say about them is true, would this cult risk that kind of exposure?"

"No," admitted Napoleon. "But I still think we're missing something. They went to great lengths to kidnap Jason Chen; why? We know his adoptive father, John Carson was linked to Pemrose, but we don't know for what reason."

"I'm sorry? Jason Chen?" said Ben "Who's Jason Chen ?"

Ben and the others listened as Napoleon related what had taken place at the university. His explanation was interrupted by Luther, with his revelation regarding Pemrose's meeting with Jason's father. Luther also threw in what Kathryn had told him about John and Mary Carson's dubious past. Ben was trying to take it all in, but he was pretty sure some of the finer points were lost on him.

"So you're a history teacher, then?" remarked Steph, looking Napoleon up and down.

"Kind of."

"That university you work for must be one rough place if they hire people like you two," she smirked, relieving her cigar of a large build up of ash.

Napoleon gave a slight smile. "You have no idea."

"If Jason's parents were killed by this cult, then what's the link to Pemrose?"

"If we work under the assumption that the Carsons were former cult members, then maybe John was Pemrose's source of information on all matters regarding the cult," said Luther.

"There was something else on the disk." Steph flicked what was left of her cigar out of the window before closing it. "Does the phrase 'The Cabal' mean anything to you?"

Napoleon's expression darkened. "Now, that's information they would kill to keep hidden."

"What's the Cabal?" said Elijah.

"They are the heart of the cult, its ruling council. There are always six members, three men and three women, originally they were Sir Oliver's chief advisers and closest friends. After his disappearance, they continued to lead the cult in his name. The Cabal that exists today are the direct descendants of the original six. It's possible that Pemrose learned the names of the Cabal from Carson."

"Don't you know who the Cabal are?" asked the Reverend.

"No one outside of the cult does, and even then, most of its members will have never laid eyes on the Cabal. If Carson did have that knowledge, he would have to have been very close to the Cabal, which makes any information he passed on even more damaging."

"How so?" asked Luther.

"Removing the Cabal would be a blow the cult would take years to recover from. To protect themselves, the Cabal would kill every person who attends that meeting with Morton."

"Hang on a sec," Steph put in. "There's one thing that doesn't add up."

"Only one?" said Ben, wondering what story she had been listening to.

Steph did not acknowledge Ben's wisecrack, and continued undeterred. "Seems a little convenient that this teenager ends up at your university," she said to Napoleon, eying him suspiciously. "As you seem to be an expert on this Book of Cademus. A lucky coincidence?"

It did not take long for the logic of Steph's statement to filter through the group.

"Is it possible Jason's parents knew who you were?" asked Luther.

"If they were once close to the Cabal, then yes, it would be possible," said Napoleon. "You believe Jason's parents placed him at that university for his protection?"

"Makes sense, they couldn't stop him going to university, but as they were probably footing the bill, they would have some control over where he went. What better place to send him for protection from the Book of Cademus than where two of its enemies worked?"

"The enemy of my enemy is my friend," said Steph.

"Exactly," Luther got to his feet and made for the door. "Now we've settled that mystery, I need to get word to Morton and stop the meeting before it takes place."

Vincent grabbed his arm. "You're a wanted man, even if you could get to her, she's not going to listen to you."

Luther shrugged the hand off. "Well, I don't see anyone else offering up help, so I guess it's down to me."

"You haven't changed a bit," said Ben. "Still trying to play the martyr."

"You're also forgetting about Jason," Napoleon pointed out. "He's in as much danger as Morton."

"Actually," said Joshua, who had stayed quiet up until now. "That is something of an understatement."

"You know why they grabbed the boy, don't you?" asked Napoleon.

"Of course I do."

Chapter Twenty-Seven

Ben could see how much Grey was enjoying the suspense he was creating. It was as if the current situation served only as a pleasant diversion for him.

"Jason's adoptive parents were killed as a warning to anyone else harbouring thoughts of betraying the Book of Cademus," said Joshua. "I believe John Carson hoped to engineer their downfall by passing information to Pemrose."

"What does this have to do with the boy?" asked the Reverend.

"If you stay silent, you may just discover that information," snapped Grey, obviously angered at the interruption.

The Reverend's hand brushed the handle of one his pistols that was poking out from under his jacket. Ben hoped the movement was an involuntary response.

"After his escape from the army sent to execute him, Oliver put into motion a plan to cheat death itself."

"Immortality," whispered Vincent, almost afraid to utter the concept. "I say this for him, he doesn't think small, does he?"

Joshua nodded in solemn agreement. "Oliver told the Cabal that the same higher powers who had tasked him with the mission of creating the Book of Cademus had placed the knowledge necessary to achieve this within his mind. At first, the Cabal were reluctant to go along with his plan, but the promise of more power was enough to alleviate their doubts."

"Greed can be a powerful motivator," said the Reverend.

"Indeed, although the Cabal were equally afraid of what may happen to them should Oliver's dream become a reality."

"I thought they were all on the same side?" asked Ben, who was trying his best to keep an open mind, but finding it hard.

"Same side," chuckled Grey, his laugh cold and humourless. "Power has no sides, Benjamin. A man like Oliver Cademus does not share absolute power, that is why it is absolute."

"Even if I believed this, which I don't, what you're suggesting goes against everything known to medical science," said Elijah.

"Fortunately, I do not seek your belief. I am here to explain what has happened and what will happen if you do nothing."

"The fact that this Cademus bloke isn't still leading the Book of Cademus today tells me that this ritual thing cocked up," guessed Steph.

"Not exactly, Oliver did achieve the immortality he sought, but not the way he imagined."

"He was double crossed, wasn't he?" asked Steph.

"Yes, there was one among the Cabal who saw the chance for power and took it."

"How?"

"For the ritual to succeed, Cademus needed several minds joined in meditation with his own."

Joshua caught the questioning look from Napoleon.

"To make a human immortal is not as implausible as it sounds, the real difficulty lay in ensuring the mind is able to comprehend the transformation, otherwise it will reject the process."

"Like an organ transplant being rejected by the host body?" said Steph.

"Exactly," replied Grey, raising an eyebrow at Steph. "You have a keen mind."

"And a fine..."

"Shut it, Ben."

"The role of the Cabal was to remove Cademus' mind from his body and house it in six equal parts within their own."

"Time out people!" shouted Ben, making the letter T with his hands. "Come on, are we really buying this rubbish?"

"I've seen enough doing this job to know not to rule anything out," said Vincent. "So why don't you give that mouth of yours a rest? Who knows, you may learn something."

"Oh, that's real funny," snarled Ben, feigning a grin. "How would you like to be eating the rest of your meals through a straw, pretty boy?"

Vincent rolled his eyes in exasperation. "Please, what are you, five? All I'm saying is let the man finish, then make a judgement call, that's if your attention span can stretch that far."

Ben took his seat, deciding that Vincent was right, and also deciding he had no intention of voicing that fact out loud. "Fine, go ahead, but I'm telling you this is a waste of time."

"Quite finished?" asked Joshua, arms now folded, eyes blazing with barely contained contempt.

"All yours, Josh."

Ben wondered if behind the irritated look on his face, Grey was suppressing the urge to levitate him out of the window before introducing him, face first to the pavement below.

"After housing Oliver's mind within their own, the Cabal was to infuse his body with the energies needed to achieve his goal of immortality. They could then safely reform and re-implant the mind fragments."

"What went wrong?" asked Vincent.

"Jacob Covenant, who until that night was a trusted member of the Cabal, saw his chance for power; he broke free of the ritual and escaped, taking a portion of Cademus' mind with him, locked deep within his own subconscious. In its incomplete state, the remaining members of the Cabal could not re-implant the mind. The irony is that the first part of the ritual was a success, and Cademus' body had indeed been made immortal, unfortunately, it was little more than an empty shell."

"You say this guy got away?" said Steph. "Surely, if this Cabal was as powerful as you say, then…"

"Why couldn't they find one man?"

Steph nodded.

"As well as disrupting the ritual, Covenant was able to tap into the portion of Cademus' mind that he possessed."

"Sounds painful," threw in Ben, who could not resist the chance to have a bit of fun, but was disappointed when Joshua did not take the bait.

"He was able to use the stolen mind fragment to enhance his own abilities and in doing so, mask his presence from the remaining members of the Cabal."

Napoleon had listened to every word, all the while studying Joshua Grey. How was it he knew so much about the cult? It was as if he had first-hand knowledge, which in itself was dangerous. It was possible Grey was working with the cult in some way to steer them away from the real threat. No, he felt sure Joshua was telling the truth; he was, however, equally sure Grey was also following his own agenda.

"All this happened centuries ago, Grey, what bearing can this have on…of course; the body's immortal." A grim realization dawned on Napoleon. "The Cabal! They still have Cademus' body, don't they?"

"Come on, Stone, that's a stretch even from you," said Luther

"Very perceptive of you, Demon Stalker," said Joshua. "Down through the centuries, each new incarnation of the Cabal was charged with the protection of Oliver's body. They also pledged themselves to discovering the whereabouts of the stolen mind fragment and using it to restore Cademus back to life."

"How were they supposed to achieve that?" asked Napoleon, his suspicion walking hand in hand with his curiosity. "Even if Cademus' body were immortal, the original members of the Cabal were not."

"The mind of Oliver Cademus is not so easily destroyed. It survived by being transferred to each descendant of the Cabal. It is my belief that Covenant did the same thing with the mind portion in his possession. Why he would choose to do this is beyond my knowledge, possibly to pass his power onto his heirs and in doing so, achieve a kind of immortality."

Napoleon heard a chuckle come from Ben's direction, his scepticism, though annoying was at least honest.

"You believe Jason's a direct descendant of Jacob Covenant, don't you?" asked Napoleon. "That's why the Carsons adopted him in the first place, somehow they must have known who he was all along."

"We will never know why the Carsons took the boy in; either to protect him from the evil they themselves had fled from, or to use him for their own ends," speculated Joshua. "One thing is certain: Jason, although unaware of it, carries within him the last piece of Cademus' fragmented mind. If you do not reach him in time, the Cabal will rip the fragment from Jason's mind and use it to revive Oliver."

"Or what?"

All eyes now turned to Luther, who had his arms crossed and looked every inch the non-believer. "Nine hundred years ago, he might have been big news, but mankind has moved on a bit since his day; I'm sure we can deal with one resurrected knight."

Joshua Grey sighed. "Ignore my warning at your peril,"

"Ignore my warning at your peril," echoed Ben in a low whisper. "Are you getting this from the idiots guide to clichés'?"

"Whilst his body has lain dormant, it has stored the energies of the Earth within him. If he rises, he will have power and abilities that would dwarf my own. But aside from this, Cademus' real gift lay in his words, many would flock to his cause."

"I take it flocking is bad?" asked Ben.

"Given enough time, he would sweep away the old world order in favour of his own; remember, generations of the Cabal have had centuries to plan, awaiting his rebirth."

"Wait a minute, I thought he was in some kind of a coma."

"After a fashion, in truth, the Cabal were able to communicate with Cademus by means of a joining spell whereby they could use the five mind fragments still in their possession to create a being that was, for want of a better term, the essence of Cademus, his spirit if you will, for short periods of time. Over the years, Cademus was able to direct and rule the Cabal seemingly from beyond the grave. But the years took their toll on the mind fragments, and soon Cademus' spirit began to lose all sense of reason and memory of who he was. It became a creature that revelled in destruction. So, until such time as they found the last piece, the Cabal used the mind creature for their own devices."

"An invisible monster," mused Ben, "Now there's something you don't see everyday."

Luther and Napoleon exchanged looks.

"I'm guessing that was what you sensed back at the university?" suggested Luther.

Napoleon nodded, "A creature created by the fragmented mind of an already insane and now, it would seem, immortal cult leader."

"But if these mind fragments are so degraded, what's the point of trying to put them back into Cademus' body?" asked Vincent, who had been trying to catch Steph's eye for the last few minutes.

Steph caught the look and rolled her eyes. He was probably wondering what side of the bed she liked to sleep on, she thought. Typical man, all the world's going to hell and yet he's still got time to think with the lower end of his anatomy.

"Once Cademus' mind is placed back within the body, it would be healed by those same energies used to make the body immortal."

"And the boy?" asked the Reverend. "What will become of him?"

"First, they must make sure that he possesses the mind fragment," explained Grey. "They will only get one chance to perform the ritual to reintegrate Oliver's mind back into his immortal body; should they fail, then both would be destroyed."

"I thought you said his body is immortal."

"Immortal from everything but the spell needed to reintegrate his mind,"

said Ben. "That's unlucky."

"If the ritual is successful, Jason will no longer be of any use to them."

"You mean they'll kill him," said Steph.

"I believe, Miss Connisbee, that is exactly what I said."

"I can't believe we're still listening to this bullshit. Ancient cults and magic? It's the twenty-first century, for Christ's sake," said Ben.

"None of that is important," said Napoleon.

"What the hell does that mean?" asked a bemused Steph.

"The Book of Cademus have manipulated and murdered to achieve their own ends for centuries, and will continue to do so for centuries to come, if not stopped. They will not back down, they will hunt you one by one, and then they will kill you."

"So either we run or we make a stand?" said Steph.

"I will not run," said the Reverend, folding his arms.

Ben got the impression that was all they were going to hear from the Reverend on the subject. He coughed for attention and got to his feet.

"Don't mean to put a dampener on all this gung ho bullshit, but I'm not getting myself killed over this, and certainly not to help out TORCH's finest over there. My ass is on the next plane out of harm's way."

"There's a surprise," said Luther. "Bailing at the first sign of trouble, you haven't changed; you were always looking for the easy way out."

"You go on cracking jokes," smiled Ben, his eyes burning with contempt. "I'll be sipping piña coladas on a beach with no extradition rights when one of those Erogian things is using your collar bone for a tooth pick."

"What about you, Steph? You a runner too?" said Luther.

"Look, I don't know you. I do know Ben, and for a change he's actually making sense." Steph moved to stand beside Ben. "By the way, after what happened at the research centre, it was Ben who stood his ground when I wanted to run, so maybe you don't know him as well as you think, TORCH boy."

"Well it's been fun, people, and I wish you every success in your soon-to-be over lives," said Ben.

"You're just going to walk out on this?" shouted Luther, as they reached the door.

"No, I'm going to run my ass off. I'm going to put as much distance between me and your little suicide club before the Book of Cademus catches up with you."

Without saying another word, Ben and Steph walked out of the room.

Chapter Twenty-Eight

"Where are you taking me?" Jason called out from beneath the hood.

He felt a sharp pain to the back of his head.

"Keep it shut," a gruff voice ordered. "Unless you want another one."

Jason felt himself dragged forwards, forced to rely on the guards to be his eyes. He tried to make his other senses work for him; he had heard it said that when one sense is lost, the others can compensate for the loss. There was no such heightened affinity for his other senses; he was as much in the dark both physically and emotionally as he was when this nightmare had begun. He heard his footsteps echoing across the stone floor of the castle as he was marched across it.

"Watch your step, we're heading down," came the gruff voice again.

Jason gingerly lowered his right foot, realised there was no ground beneath it and adjusted his balance, relaxing when his foot touched stone. With one of his captors supporting him, they walked downward. The surrounding area was thick with a foul odour assaulting his nostrils, threatening to make him gag with every step.

Jason's unfettered imagination was taking great delight in conjuring up a suitably horrific scenario whenever he considered his final destination.

Hopes of the journey nearing its end upon reaching the bottom step were swiftly quashed when he was pulled forwards. Only the sounds of footsteps, laboured breathing and the firm grip on his arm told him he was not alone. After a few more minutes of walking, they stopped and Jason's arm was released. He began to rub his bicep, attempting to force some circulation back into it.

"This is as far as we go," said the voice.

Jason heard grinding sounds coming from in front of him, like doors being opened, and judging by the volume of the sounds, they were large.

"Tell them what they want to hear and you might live through this," said the voice. Footsteps were heard again; this time they grew fainter as Jason's guards moved away, their duty done.

The next touch Jason felt was far gentler than his earlier manhandling, as someone took his hand and guided him forward.

"Remove the hood."

The voice had come from somewhere in front of Jason.

The hood was torn from Jason's head. He was in a large chamber, at the far end of which was a long oak table. Seated behind the table in high-backed chairs were two men and three women of varying ages.

Jason recognised the woman who had earlier claimed responsibility for the Carsons' murder and his kidnap.

Seeing Jason, the woman stood, opened her arms out and smiled.

"My name is Justine Hillman, the Cabal welcomes you, Jason."

"One hundred grand!" said Elijah, his deafening voice silencing the conference room.

Ben's smiling face peered round the corner of the door. "I'm listening."

Steph followed Ben back into the room. Her shoulders sagged as she rolled her eyes.

"So close," she muttered to herself.

The plan was still forming in Elijah's mind. Justine's safety was a main concern, as was the need to keep himself out of prison. Organising a rescue attempt to save the Secretary General and members of the Security Council would be a good start.

"You see this through to the end, and I'll pay you one hundred grand. Come on, Ben, that's got to be worth it."

Ben rubbed his unshaven chin, allowing the silence to become even more pronounced. "Three hundred grand is my standard rate for saving the world," he said at last.

"You son of a bitch,"

"That's three hundred…a piece," said Ben, stepping further into the room, flanked by Steph.

Elijah did his best to bury the rising fury within him. Ben and Steph were unprincipled, and at times, ruthless but they were the best at what they did. He would have given the shirt off his back and shares in the company if they could get Justine out.

"I also want a twenty percent share in your off the book projects, and I want it in writing, signed and witnessed before we leave this room," added Ben.

Be careful what you wish for, Elijah told himself. "You sure know how to kick a friend when he's down."

"A friend? You're having a laugh, right? This is compensation," said Ben. "Maybe you've forgotten how you sold us out, but we have very long and expensive memories."

Elijah promised himself he would find a way to repay Ben's ruthlessness one day. For now, he would let the thief have his moment in the spotlight.

"I'll draw up the papers and arrange the money transfer myself, the usual account?"

Ben turned to Steph, who was already nodding her agreement.

"Looks like we're going to be the richest corpses in this room," said Ben, rubbing his hands together. "Now I'm assuming our mysterious friend, Mr. Grey, has a plan to find this kid and your mum's partner that won't get us killed too…shit."

Everyone looked at the spinning, empty chair where Joshua had been sitting.

"At least someone here has the brains to get out while they still can," said Steph. "Now what are we supposed to do?"

"We stop the Book of Cademus before it's too late," stated Luther.

"We stop the Book of Cademus before it's too late?" said Ben. "Man, you've been doing this secret agent stuff for too long, you know that, right?"

Elijah took a deep breath and held it for a second. As he breathed out, he snatched up the phone and dialled the number of the one man who might know the whereabouts of the secret UN meeting. There was very little that went on in the world that he did not know of or influence in some way. The problem, as always, would be the price for the information.

"Miss Sheeva speaking, may I help you, Mr. Barrington," said a voice from the phone.

Elijah guessed his name was being displayed on a caller ID system. This was it; no more to do now except finish the call.

"Can you put me through to Mr. Alexander, please?"

Steph could not believe she had run out of cigars. There was an offer of one from Vincent, but she refused. She saw the brand of cigarette and would rather set light to her own tongue. Trying to distract her growing craving for nicotine, she looked at the strange collection of individuals and pondered over the circumstances that had bought them together. Elijah was back in his office consulting with a highly-placed source who he believed might know the location of the secret UN meeting, that had been forty-five minutes ago. At the time, Elijah explained his need to speak to his source in private. The others were reluctant to let him go, fearing he might try to run. Elijah defended himself by saying there was no way he was leaving his building in the hands of fanatics and thieves. Steph had stayed quiet during the exchange. She saw through the bravado. Elijah would not run because he believed those same fanatics and thieves were the best chance of ever seeing Justine again. He had promised to put the extensive resources of the company at their disposal; weapons, transportation, anything they needed Elijah was confident he could provide.

During the following three quarters of an hour, Steph watched the atmosphere shift from open hostility, though this was confined to Ben and Luther, to mistrust. These highly charged emotions began to wane whilst waiting for Elijah's return, finally giving way to a kind of finality as they all came to realise the only way out of this was to start working together. They all came from different backgrounds, possessed different skills, but the one trait they did seem to share was their professionalism, their desire to get the job done, whatever the personal cost. Steph was grateful that the situation was becoming more bearable, as it would help to lessen the chances of a fatality occurring. She glanced at the Reverend, who was relating their encounter with the Erogian to Napoleon. He was intent on gaining as much information as possible on the creature. Although Napoleon had been evasive at first in response to the Reverend's questions, some less than gentle prompting from his young assistant pushed him into being more forthcoming in his answers.

Steph then came to Ben, who was propped against the window, sipping his fourth cup of coffee, which in itself was important, as he hated the stuff. He appeared disinterested in what was happening around him, but Steph was not buying the act. She could only guess at what the sudden appearance of his brother was doing to him. In the years she had known him, Ben had only spoken fondly of his brother once, during one of the few times he had too much to drink. In his drunken state, he recalled a time where his brother came to his aid against five of the local bullies when they were kids. The result was the two of them laughing as the running footsteps of Ben's would-be attackers echoed into the distance, with threats of retribution being hurled back at them. Luther had draped an arm around his younger half-brother and promised him that he would always be there to look out for him, no matter what.

The promises of youth, mused Steph, too bad Luther had not been able to keep the same promise as an adult. After that night, Ben had never mentioned his brother again.

Today, everything had changed for Ben. Both brothers were heading towards a confrontation. All Steph could do was hope it did not end up with one of them in a body bag.

"Finally," said Luther. "So what's the word, Barrington, do we have a location?"

Steph turned and saw Elijah entering the conference room.

"We do," said Elijah, pouring himself a cup of coffee. "Does the Ulysses' station mean anything to you?"

"It's a small TORCH outpost that carries out meteorological studies," said Luther. "It's a low key set up, and it's in Antarctica, a pretty good choice for a meeting like this one."

"So how come you know about it?" asked Vincent.

"An agent I trained was stationed there at one time."

"Typical," muttered Steph. "Bloody Antarctica."

Ben looked at Steph and smiled. It was a smile edged with mischief. "Might be able to get some snowboarding done while we're there."

"It's always the hard way with you," said Steph, then she turned to Luther. "I don't suppose you know anything about the security."

"Whatever security measures they do have will be less sophisticated than those you encountered in Tokyo," said Luther. "If I was guessing, I'd say probably cameras and enhanced radar, the usual, all controlled from a central bunker. That's a standard setup for this kind of installation. And more than likely, an electrified fence will enclose the entire compound."

"You seem to know a lot about a place you have never been to," pointed out the Reverend.

"Most TORCH facilities use the same security measures depending on the threat level," explained Luther. "The Ulysses station's would be relatively low."

"But not only will the Secretary General have her own security staff, I would expect them to beef up the entire security set up." Steph looked at Ben. "This is risky as hell, going into a situation like this unplanned."

"I hear you," said Ben.

Steph mentally went over the variables of the mission along with what Luther had told them.

"We'll need transport, cold weather gear, live satellite imagery of the base, and the surrounding area. We'll also need equipment to track Ben when he's on the ground, and everything else on the list I gave you earlier."

Elijah nodded, but there was no hiding the fact from Steph that he was far from happy at the position he was being placed in.

"Everything will be waiting when you get to the plane. I can get you some satellite photos of the area maybe, but live footage? Come on, Steph, I haven't got the time to pull that off."

"Then it's no deal," cut in Ben. "There's no way either of us are going into this blind. I don't care how light the security is supposed to be, either we get that live feed, or we walk."

"I can get you the feed," said Luther.

"I'm sure TORCH has a policy against fugitives using one of their satellites," Napoleon pointed out.

"I wasn't planning on asking for permission. Now, I can get you what you need, but there's a condition."

"No way," said Ben.

"What is it?" asked Steph.

Ben pointed at Luther. "TORCH boy wants to come with us."

"I'm not leaving the safety of the Secretary General of the United Nations in the hands of criminals, even if one of them is my brother."

"We work alone," said Steph.

"I'm sorry; in what world was I was giving you a choice? You need that imagery and I can supply it, so either we have a deal or…"

"Whatever, man," said Ben, fuming. "But this is our show; you do what we say, when we say and how we say, got it?"

"Agreed."

"What about you, Reverend?" asked Steph.

"I feel I will be of more use accompanying Napoleon and Vincent."

"That's too bad, Rev," said Ben, trying to wipe the relief from his face.

"I don't know where you'd be accompanying us to, Reverend," said Vincent. "No one knows where the Cabal is, and even if we did find them, going up against them when they're at their most powerful is not one of our better plans."

"I think I may know someone who can help find the Cabal," said Napoleon.

"And he is?" asked Steph.

"None of your concern," said Napoleon firmly. "There are some truths I'm not about to divulge, certainly not to a room of people I've just met."

"So we're just supposed to accept that?" asked Elijah.

"You will if you want any chance of seeing your boss again."

"Is that some kind of threat? If it is, then I'm far from impressed."

"You should be," murmured Vincent. "You really should be."

"It's this simple, Barrington," began Napoleon. "We don't need or want your help. We have our own resources to call into play, and believe me, we will. Now, I can get the location of the Book of Cademus' stronghold, but if we're to have any chance of getting Jason and your mother's partner, if she's there, out in one piece, then we have to do it our way."

"Fine, all I'm saying is I want to be kept informed, that's all."

"So you can do something stupid like arrange some half assed pre-emptive strike on the Cabal before we get there," said Napoleon. "All you'll succeed in doing is getting Justine and Jason killed."

"Fine, I'll play it your way, Stone." He stepped in closer. "But if anything happens to Justine, there won't be a place on this Earth you'll be able to hide from me."

"Just so we know where we stand, my goal is to find the Cabal and stop them from resurrecting Sir Oliver. Jason and Justine's safety are a secondary concern."

Ben looked back to where the Reverend was now standing, alongside Vincent, who was looking far from happy with Napoleon's speech.

"Reverend," said Napoleon. "There's only room for one leader in this, if you have a problem with that, you're no good to me."

"I will follow your lead."

"Good, secondly, this is not a suicide mission. I have every intention of walking away from this. The world already has its share of martyrs, you want to join them, do it somewhere else."

The Reverend nodded but stayed silent. Napoleon walked over to Luther.

"Try not to get yourself killed, Agent Washington," he said, extending his hand.

Luther hesitated at first, as if caught off guard, then smiled and took the offered hand. "Likewise, Professor Stone."

Napoleon gave a final look back at Elijah. "I know Justine Hillman is important to you and this company, but if anything does happen to her, don't come looking for me. You won't like what you find."

Chapter Twenty-Nine

Jason faced the five individuals known only as the Cabal, who were, it seemed, the architects behind all the terror and bloodshed of the past few days. They stared at him as if he were a prize museum exhibit.

"Forgive us, Jason," said an elderly man, whose grey hair was all but gone; he was seated to the left of Justine. "The realisation of this moment has forced our manners to take second place."

The man gestured to a chair several feet in front of Jason, while straightening the thick-rimmed spectacles he wore. Jason was too tired to put up any arguments, at least not for now. Shuffling forward, he slumped, relieved, into the chair.

"First, I must apologise for my colleague's actions, she was not supposed to speak to you before this meeting."

Seeing the sneer on Justine's face, Jason thought it was a good bet the others had chastised her, and she was furious about it. As she sat there scowling at him, Jason hoped he never found himself alone with her, unless he was holding a weapon.

"My name is Sirus Crane. I am the voice of the Cabal, and I alone will speak for us all."

There was an impatient sigh from a stout, stern-faced woman who sat to the far right of the table. Crane's position was obviously not an arrangement that everyone was entirely happy with, Jason guessed.

"Who are the other three, then? I know her name is Justine and yours is Sirus, but what...?"

Jason's body became wracked with pain. It took all his strength to remain in his chair until the pain eased, leaving a renewed tiredness in his limbs.

"Unless I give you leave to speak, you will remain silent. Do you understand?"

Jason managed to stop himself from saying yes, settling instead for a nod.

"Do you know why you are here, Jason?"

Jason shrugged his shoulders, but said nothing.

Sirus smiled. "It's a rare thing to meet someone who can follow the simplest of orders, you have no idea how difficult it can be for some."

Even though he was not looking at her, Jason got the impression the comments were being aimed at Justine.

"It is fine to answer my questions, Jason, but you will not speak until spoken to; now again, do you know why you are here?"

"The ritual of restoration," replied Jason.

The angry look on Crane's face quickly dissolved into a thin smile, containing no warmth whatsoever.

"Again, my colleague has overstepped her bounds."

Jason imagined what was going through Justine's mind and was relived she was prohibited from speaking.

"Like many before you, Jason, you have been brought here for us to see whether you have what our order has spent centuries searching for. Some came here willingly, others were promised money for their time, in your case, however, more extreme methods were employed to secure your co-operation, and for that we are sorry."

Murder and kidnapping were about as extreme as it got, thought Jason.

"I can see that you doubt our sincerity, so as a gesture of goodwill, it may interest you to know why your adoptive parents were killed."

"I know the reason!" said Jason, ignoring Crane's warning about staying silent. He pointed at Justine. "She had them killed to get to me."

Sirus rubbed his chin as if he were working up to something. "You are right, Jason, we did order the Carsons' deaths, but not for protecting you."

Crane's claim made no sense to Jason. What other reason could there be? The Carsons' only crime was that of adopting him, and they paid for it with their lives.

"John and Mary betrayed the Book of Cademus and because of this, they were sentenced by us to pay for their crimes." Sirus leaned forward, his face taking on a sombre expression. "Believe me, Jason, we took no pleasure in this. Contrary to what others may have led you to believe, we are not cold-blooded murderers, your parents were amongst our most valued initiates."

Jason was unable to meet Crane's gaze so he focused on a small spider he had noticed earlier, scurrying along the floor. Why were they telling him such barefaced lies? Did they really think he was that stupid? The Carsons, members of a secret cult? Sure. he laughed to himself. He knew them; lived with them for all those years, if there had been anything out of the ordinary, he would have seen it. No, the Carsons had their faults, but they had loved him in their own way. It was only now he was beginning to realise the depth of his feeling for them, and how much he missed them.

"I know this is difficult to hear, but it's important that you know the truth," said Crane.

As Crane finished speaking, Jason was on his feet, silencing his commonsense, which was urging him to sit down. Rationality had left

Jason's world, replaced by a rage that was being strengthened by accusations made against people no longer alive to defend themselves.

"The truth!" he screamed, his head pounding. "You want the truth? You bastards killed two of the few people who ever gave a shit about me!"

"Calm yourself," cautioned Sirus. "I have no wish to harm you, but…"

Jason's mirthless laugh echoed through the room.

"No wish to harm…you butchered them and you want me to be calm?"

Sirus raised a hand, but his face became contorted with concentration and pain.

"What's wrong, Crane?" said Jason, striding towards the table. "You look ill."

The guards that had been standing motionless at the far end of the room made a move forwards, but a look from Crane halted their advance.

Jason was now standing a few feet from the table, his eyes burning with hatred and fury. If he had noticed the small look of acknowledgement that passed between Justine and Crane, he might have calmed down.

"Listen to me, Jason,"

"No, you listen, Crane, you want to use me? Fine, but don't sit there trying to make me believe you're the good guys because I've seen first hand just how good you are."

A line of sweat creased Sirus' brow. His eyes widened. There was a kind of excited look on his face that worried Jason, but not enough to stop.

"The only reason the Carsons adopted you, Jason, was that they knew you were of potential value to us, even if we did not at the time. Their plan was to use you to enhance their own position within our order."

Jason began shaking his head furiously. "You're lying."

"It's your life that has been the lie, Jason, from the moment the Carsons adopted you."

"I don't believe you," Jason's hand came up to the side of head, the intense pounding had now moved to behind his eyes.

"Don't you?" said Sirus. "Did you ever ask your father why he kept a gun in the house, or why your mother sometimes looked at you in fear?"

"Shut up!" Blood began to trickle from Jason's left nostril.

"They knew what you were, Jason, and it scared them. Your parents were opportunists, they never cared about you. To them, you were the prize; nothing more," chuckled Crane. "Certainly not their son."

"THEY LOVED ME!"

If the desired response Sirus had been seeking was all hell breaking loose within the hall, then his wish was granted. As the words left Jason's mouth, the large oak desk the Cabal were seated behind cracked in two, the resulting sections hurled across the room in opposite directions. Sirus was thrown back against the wall, two huge tears appearing across his chest spattering blood across his torso and arms. Struggling for breath, Sirus laid his hands across his chest and closed his eyes, as did the other members of the Cabal. Slowly, his wounds began to heal before Jason's tired eyes.

Sirus stood up, pulling the torn pieces of his shirt together, covering the scarred tissue that was still healing. Jason was on his knees, fists clenched, blood streaming from his nose, and tears from his eyes.

"They loved me," he whispered.

Bolivia, South America.

Vincent's thoughts were of the people milling around on the street below his hotel window. What, he wondered, would their reaction be if they became aware of the silent war going on around them? Like an unseen shadow, it threatened their way of life, their very existence. Smiling to himself, he shrugged off the thought. To care was a trait found in the individual, but not so freely within the masses. They would continue on until events could no longer be ignored, of course by then, it would be too late. Ignorance and apathy would pave the way for the riots and mass hysteria, the perfect breeding ground for the Book of Cademus to go about its work. Vincent knew the dangers all too well; he and Napoleon had dedicated their lives to the preservation of that ignorance. Such an overlooked pleasure, ignorance, he mused whilst draining the last dregs of his coffee. He would give anything to rekindle the feeling within himself.

It had been nearly a day since the strange meeting in Barrington's office. Napoleon had made contact with the Icarus Foundation, explaining the events concerning the Book of Cademus, and Grey's theory as to what they planned for Jason. Vincent was surprised at the speed at which they responded. Napoleon had stressed there was no time for protocols and lengthy explanations; now was the time for action.

The Foundation saw to it that a plane was chartered and made available to them, on condition that Napoleon was to provide them with the Cabal's location once he had obtained it. This was a precaution should they fail in their attempt, which Napoleon agreed to without hesitation, although he had admitted to Vincent that if they failed, it would be too late for anyone to act. However, Napoleon had been less than forthcoming regarding their eventual destination. It was during the three-hour journey to the airfield that Vincent managed to coerce their final destination out of Napoleon, as well as the identity of his mysterious source. He was a man who lived at a small monastery located somewhere in Asia. The monastery was, in reality, a special facility built and financed by the Icarus Foundation decades ago, even Napoleon was unsure of the exact date of its creation, but he was sure of the monastery's true name: Haven. It had been built for one purpose; to house those former members of the Icarus Foundation whose years spent facing the horrors of the unknown had finally proven too much for their sanity. The men and women who lived within Haven's walls were cared for by a staff of specialist doctors and nurses. For the more unstable and potentially violent patients, a security detachment was always at hand. No one left Haven unless they were deemed fit to rejoin the Foundation.

Vincent had known when he had become an investigator that he would never be able to return to his life as it was. No one left the Icarus Foundation. Yes, you could lead as normal a life as possible, a family, a career outside of Icarus, but leaving was not an option. You were always on call, at a moment's notice, you would be expected to drop everything. The real strength of the Foundation came not only from the men and women who worked for it, or the near limitless resources at its disposal, but rather the anonymity of its real work. The board of Trustees had already expressed their displeasure at Napoleon and Vincent's decision to reveal their most closely guarded secret to outsiders. Whatever the reason, the trustees promised the matter would be raised again once they returned from their mission.

Even though Vincent owed the Foundation his life, Napoleon's revelation concerning Haven caused him to question, for the first time, his decision to become a part of it. No one had ever told him about Haven. Napoleon had told him that one of the patients was being released from Haven, under armed escort, and would rendezvous with them at the hotel. The reason for their journey was that Napoleon's previous investigation into the cult led him to believe the Cabal's stronghold was located somewhere in South America, he just did not know its exact location.

The patient in question; Nathan Ash, had apparently not spoken in fifteen years.

Even though he was from before Vincent's time, he knew Nathan Ash had been one of Icarus' best investigators. Known as a risk taker,

Ash followed his own code, and as such, often found himself at odds with the board of trustees.

Until today, Vincent believed Ash had died over fifteen years ago, along with ten other investigators, the details of which were a closely guarded secret. Vincent could not take it all in. Nathan Ash had dedicated himself to protecting others and was rewarded with a padded cell. Vincent wondered if that was the fate awaiting him.

"You should get some rest," said Napoleon, who had just walked in.

"Why didn't you tell me about Haven before?"

"You didn't need to know."

"Not good enough, not by a long way!"

Even as he threw the punch, Vincent knew it would not connect, Napoleon would see it coming a mile off. Not that it mattered, it was more about the attempt than the result. This made the shock even more intense when his fist cracked against Napoleon's chin, knocking him back against the door.

"Better now?" said Napoleon, using his thumb to wipe the blood from a small cut on the side of his mouth.

"You have no idea how long I've wanted to knock you on that righteous ass of yours," said Vincent. "This isn't just your war, we're a team; you should have...."

"I'm sorry."

The two words were enough to completely destroy Vincent's train of thought, and about ten other insults he was about to hurl at Napoleon. "What?"

"You're right, I should have told you."

"Either you're an Erogian, or I just heard Napoleon Stone apologise and admit he was wrong in the same sentence."

"I should have told you about Haven years ago, but it's not a place I want to remember, let alone talk about."

"Because of Ash?" said Vincent, realising that he was pushing a subject that was best left alone. "What happened? According to the records, he died years ago."

"Would have been better if he did."

"Were you friends?"

"He was one of the people who trained me when I was recruited into Icarus. I trusted Nathan Ash with my life," Napoleon sighed. "I still would."

"What happened?"

"Nathan claimed to have discovered the whereabouts of the Book of Cademus' stronghold."

"Go on."

"Nathan's research indicated the stronghold was a castle dating back to the time of Sir Oliver himself, and located somewhere in South America. His plan was to launch a pre-emptive strike against the cult before it could grow any more powerful."

"Hang on a second," said Vincent. "How could Sir Oliver have been in Peru at that time, if I remember my history, America hadn't been discovered yet, at least not officially?"

"Nathan had discovered artefacts in South America that were linked to the Book of Cademus," explained Napoleon. "Artefacts that carbon dating placed around the time of Sir Oliver. This supported Nathan's claim that Sir Oliver had the castle built in secret, and he fled there with the Cabal when things became too dangerous in England. Nathan believed this castle to be the key to the cult's plans, but when pressed about the reasons for that belief, he seemed to either not want to share the information, or simply just didn't know."

The enormity of Napoleon's words left Vincent speechless. Was it possible that a knight of the first crusade set foot in the Americas after Leif Ericson and his Vikings?

"The board of trustees rejected his plan. The policies governing the discovery of a new cult, even one that has existed for as long as the Book of Cademus, were clear."

"We watch, we learn, we listen and we only act if the cult takes human life, be it by normal methods or supernatural."

Learning the creed of the Icarus Foundation had been one of Vincent's first lessons upon joining. Although they were not an organisation to shy away from the use of force, and that usually meant deadly force, it was not a choice taken lightly.

"The board felt there wasn't enough information about this re-emergence of the Book of Cademus to deem them a threat, they argued the cult may have adopted more harmless practices over the centuries."

"Sounds to me like the board screwed up."

"Remember, we only intervene when there is no other way," said Napoleon. "It's not a crime for people to worship something we don't believe in, however strange or bizarre it may seem, even if the very thing they hold most sacred is that which may ultimately destroy them. The day we start doing that, we might as well change our name to the inquisition."

"Hey, you don't need to convince me, but I'm guessing Ash didn't take the sit back and wait approach?"

Napoleon cracked a half-smile. "Nathan told me he was putting together a team for a fact-finding mission, he said he was going to get proof that the Book of Cademus were a threat, proof the trustees could not ignore."

"He wanted you to go with him, didn't he?"

Napoleon nodded. "He said it was the only way, I thought differently."

Vincent sensed Napoleon's reluctance to continue, he had never seen him like this; so unsure of himself. The sight was both sobering and unnerving.

"Nathan was a charismatic and respected investigator, he had no trouble recruiting ten others to his cause. I sat by and did nothing as they left for where Ash believed Cademus Castle to be located."

"Go on," urged Vincent.

"Days later, I went to the trustees and made out as if I had only just learned of Ash's plan. I doubt they believed me, but it didn't matter anymore."

"Why?"

"They had just received word that two investigators had been found in South America, one was badly wounded; the other, who didn't have a scratch on him, was Nathan. Before he died, the other investigator said that Nathan led them to a castle deep in the rain forest, but they were captured as they entered. In a ritual overseen by the Cabal, nine of them were tortured and sacrificed, but before his turn came, he was rescued by Nathan, who had managed to free himself."

"What happened to Nathan?"

"He escaped from the hospital two days later."

"So how did he end up in Haven?"

"The Foundation sent someone to bring him in."

Vincent's eyes narrowed. Napoleon was holding something back and he had a pretty good idea what that something was. "You?"

"Ash trained me, I knew how he thought, I was the logical choice."

There it was, concluded Vincent; the reason he had always been kept at arm's length, never fully trusted. Napoleon was afraid history would repeat itself.

"When I brought him in, Nathan was barely coherent and blaming himself for what had happened. It was decided the best place for him was Haven."

"But you disagreed with the decision, didn't you?"

"It doesn't matter what I thought, I did my job."

Vincent said nothing, what could he say? Napoleon had been forced to bring in a man whom he trusted; it was a disturbing image. Vincent was not sure if he could demonstrate the same commitment and single-minded ruthlessness if placed in a similar position.

"I know what you're thinking, but believe me, one day you'll understand."

"Understand what? That when we mess up one time too many, we've got a nice padded cell waiting for us, is that it? Or is it that you don't fully trust me? That you expect me to turn on you one day?"

"No. You'll understand there are no medals waiting for us, no cheering crowds. Our victories are small, short-lived, and always come at too high a price. You, like everyone else who works for the Foundation realises that even though they may hate doing this job, there is no one better equipped to do it. So we bury our dead, harden our hearts and we stand for another day. That's what it means to be a part of Icarus."

"You don't really believe that."

"Get some sleep. I'll wake you when it's time."

Before Vincent could say another word, Napoleon was gone.

Chapter Thirty

Napoleon threw down the last of the maps he had been studying. He had tried several times since his discussion with Vincent to continue his work on discovering the castle's location, without success. Jumbled images of his past sought to undermine his concentration. He remembered the look on Vincent's face when he had learnt about Napoleon's part in Nathan's capture. There was an inevitability to the look, as if Vincent had wondered how he would feel if placed in a similar position.

Napoleon shook the images from his mind. He had to focus, there was enough recriminations and blame waiting to be attached if he lived through the next few days. He looked again at the map, trying to push the idea of failure from his mind, but it remained like an unwanted house guest.

Cademus Castle: how many times had he thought of taking the fight to the enemy, storming its walls and delivering a fatal blow to the Cabal? What scared him now was those same thoughts had driven his mentor insane. Napoleon was so engrossed in his thoughts that he did not realise he was no longer alone until a mug of hot tea was placed in front of him.

"Didn't hear you come in."

"Most people don't," answered the Reverend, sitting down across from Napoleon.

"Until it's too late?"

The Reverend took a sip of his tea. "Something like that."

Napoleon cradled the hot cup in both hands and sat down. He looked at the gaunt and intense young man sitting across from him.

"Something troubling you, Professor Stone?"

"A lot of things, but right now, just you."

"Your meaning?"

"If I'm going to have you standing behind me with a loaded weapon in your hand, then there are a few things I'd like to know."

The Reverend acknowledged Napoleon's request with a slight tilt of the head, but said nothing; Napoleon took that as an agreement and continued. "Let's start with your real name."

As he waiting for an answer, Napoleon saw something in the Reverend's eyes, perhaps the reflection of another life, then it was gone.

"What's in a name? I could tell you anything. How would you know I was telling the truth?"

Napoleon met the unflinching gaze of the Reverend and held it. "It's about trust, trust is in a name, and I'm betting you haven't had to earn that in a long time."

"You do not know the first thing about me."

"I know you used be a man of faith, a man of principles, and then something ripped that veneer of goodness and decency away and left you raw. So instead, you clothed yourself in hatred and violence. You sought to root out and punish all those who didn't fit in with your view of the world."

The Reverend took another sip of his tea. "You see a lot for a man with one eye."

Napoleon lifted his eyepatch slightly and rubbed the scarred skin beneath, which for some reason had started to irritate him.

"I suppose I do," he agreed at last.

"How did it happen?" asked the Reverend, pointing at the eyepatch.

"It's a long story," said Napoleon, finishing the last of his tea and placing the cup on the floor between his knees.

"It always is," replied the Reverend, no trace of humour in his voice.

"About fifteen years ago, I was teaching at a small college in Kent when I was approached by representatives of a government agency. They told me they had been following my work for some time and were impressed. They were especially interested in my research on the various cults and religious sects that I had been conducting." Napoleon pulled a gun from its holster and began checking it, the last thing he needed was a misfire or jam at the wrong moment. "They asked about my thoughts on the paranormal claims made by some of the ex-members of a few cults. I told them I didn't have any strong feelings one way or the other. In my academic life, I had been trained to look at everything with a rational and unbiased view."

Napoleon, convinced his gun was in perfect working order, replaced it in its holster, his eye already scanning the room in search of something else to do. "They told me I was exactly the man they were looking for. I was offered the chance, as they put it, to help myself and save lives. All I had to do was infiltrate a sect called The Brotherhood and report on its activities. My cover story was that I was writing a thesis on their practices, and wanted to make sure they were given the opportunity to show what life was like within their ranks."

"And you said yes?"

"By the end of the day, I had already set up a meeting with several of the Brotherhood's leaders. They were friendly, approachable and after weeks of negotiation, I was given permission to enter one of their communes."

The Reverend sat forward, now clearly riveted by the story.

"Well, I couldn't pass up a chance like this; first-hand experience of a sect supposed to have links to the supernatural," said Napoleon. "After I published my findings I could write my own ticket, so without thinking, I agreed. Maggie went through the roof when she found out. In all the years we'd been married, I'd never heard her swear like that before."

"You were married?"

Napoleon paused as he considered a response to the question. He stroked the empty space on his finger where his wedding ring would once have been. "I know, even I forget sometimes. She told me not to go, that she trust didn't them." Napoleon laughed, but it was laughter born from pain. "She always made a lot of sense, did Maggie."

"I can assume you did not listen?"

"I moved into their compound and spent five months living with others, who like me, were new to the sect. They were made up of the usual waste that the rest of us so-called decent members of society don't give a damn about. Drug pushers, users, pimps, prostitutes, the homeless, the abused, and the unwashed from all over; they were all there. What did surprise me was the number of people from privileged backgrounds; bankers, lawyers, and quite a high number of ex-military, all there hoping to find answers, and maybe a little peace."

"You sound as if you admired them," observed the Reverend.

"I did. It's not easy to admit to yourself that you've lost your way, and even harder to actually try to do something about it."

The Reverend nodded. Napoleon guessed he knew more about the quest for redemption than most.

"Once a week, I was allowed to leave the compound, it was then I would meet my contact, who would relay my reports back to the agency. I must admit that towards the end of the six months, I began to feel more guilty about my reasons for being there."

"Because you discovered something about the Brotherhood you could use against them?"

Napoleon shook his head. "That was just it, after six months, I hadn't found anything. So I decided to leave the compound and return to my life and marriage, if I still had one. I sent word to the agency that I was coming out whether they liked it or not. That same evening, a note was slipped under my door. There was an address scribbled on it and a time; eleven pm."

At that point, Napoleon went back to checking over the equipment that lay in front of him, whilst he continued with his story. "The address turned out to be a slum house at the far end of the main town. Just before eleven, I saw several members of the upper hierarchy of the Brotherhood take a young man into the house. I gave them a few minutes to get inside before I approached the house, even then I knew something didn't feel right," Napoleon explained. "There were two men who looked to be standing guard at the front of the house. I worked my way round to the back unnoticed. I could hear what sounded like someone reciting something like an incantation. I couldn't make out the dialect, it was in a language I had never heard before. I decided to take a chance and forced open one of the looser wooden panels that had been nailed over the window."

"Not the wisest course of action."

"One of the worst mistakes of my life," confessed Napoleon.

"What did you see?"

"Too much."

The Casa 212-400 transport plane threaded its way through the frozen peaks, the sounds of its engine lost in the maelstrom of snow and wind. The snow-capped mountains spread out before the aircraft, taunting those foolish enough to challenge Mother Nature at her most ferocious. Dwarfed by the sheer majesty of the mountain range, the plane's two pilots fought the controls at every turn, drawing upon their combined experience to prevent them and their passengers from becoming another casualty of the icy wasteland.

Again, Steph caught hold of the controls, as they nearly broke free from her grasp. She made sure she kept a careful watch on the instrument readings before her.

"We need to bring the nose down," she shouted across to the other pilot. "If this turbulence pushes us up too high, we could stall."

The pilot, a gruff-looking man in his early forties, winked at her. His dark blond hair was tied at the nape of his neck with a black rubber band. Steph wished she had been able to talk Elijah out of the arrangement, but he was having none of it. They needed a plane and Sam Buchanan came with the plane, end of story.

"This is nothing but a breeze to the lady. Now you just keep checking our height and speed, and let me worry about the hard stuff."

A loud crash shook the plane briefly, but what set off the warning bells inside Steph's head was not the disturbance itself, but rather the location of it. It had not been caused by the snowstorm outside, but was more localized than that, within the plane to be precise. Steph had a pretty good idea what was causing it, or rather who.

"Sounds like your two buddies are working through a few issues," remarked Buchanan. "It'll cost you double if they put a dent in my plane."

"Bloody hell," said Steph, beginning to unfasten her harness. "They're like kids."

Buchanan reached across and grabbed her arm before she could leave her seat. He paused to relight the butt of his cigar, which even now was so close to his mouth, Steph thought it would singe his beard at any moment.

She glared at the hand restraining her. "You've got five seconds before people start getting hurt in here."

"Got some mouth on you, princess, I'll give you that," grinned Buchanan, still managing to keep his cigar butt clamped in the corner of his mouth. "We'll make a co-pilot of you yet."

"I'm still waiting."

"Trust me, you go in there now, and they won't thank you for it, besides, we're in the middle of a snowstorm in case you hadn't noticed; now, I can fly with my eyes closed, but you were the one who wanted that." He gestured to the co-pilot's seat Steph was halfway out of. "So make your choice, you a babysitter or a co-pilot?"

Though she hated having to admit it, Buchanan was right. The 'conversation' Ben and Luther were having was ten years overdue. Buchanan released Steph and she retook her seat.

"You touch me again, and I'll punch your lights out," she promised.

Buchanan leaned into the mini fridge beside his chair and took out a bottle of beer. Using the edge of his seat as a makeshift bottle opener, he was soon downing the contents.

"You know that's the same thing my third wife said to me," he said. "Did I tell you about the time I was nearly executed in a little place called Primera?"

"Please kill me now," said Steph.

Luther dodged the packing crate hurled at him. It smashed against the side of the plane, just missing the cabin window. He did not, however, avoid the fierce right hook that the crate attack had masked. The blow caught him square on the chin, sending him sprawling against the cabin wall. As he watched Ben approaching, Luther tried to remember what caused the fight in the first place, and soon realised there was no point in laying blame.

At first, Luther had been able to defend himself against Ben's fists, but then the attacks became more focused, an obvious training in unarmed combat began to shine through, and Luther began to realise his little brother was kicking his ass.

That was enough for Luther. He came forward. Ben smiled and stepped to meet him, aiming a vicious side kick at his brother's midriff. Luther brushed aside the attack as if swatting an insect, and delivered a punishing right hook. Ben was lifted off his feet, over a table and into a stack of packing cases at the rear end of the cabin.

Ben got up and touched his nose, as if checking for damage, then began wiping away the blood.

"You hit like a girl," Ben said at last. "I could've taken you."

"In your dreams, Ben, your technique is sloppy and you've obviously not been putting in the training you need to hone it."

Luther saw the hostility return to his brother's eyes.

"Listen, we've got about another ten minutes before we're over the drop zone, so how about we try pretending you don't give a shit; it shouldn't be too much of a stretch for you."

"Look, Ben, I know this sounds lame, but I am sorry about what happened, what I did to you."

"Bet your career didn't do too badly out of it."

Luther scowled and took a step forward. Some insults were harder than others to ignore. "It had nothing to do with my career; people's lives were at risk."

"What about my life, what was that worth?"

Luther was backed into a corner, every way he turned, he was in the wrong and he knew it. He had acted without thinking about the consequences, gambling his enemies would back off once he threatened to expose them. He could not have been more wrong.

"They framed me, man!"

This time, Luther did not tense for another fight as Ben walked towards him; this would be a different kind of fight.

"Because you had to play the hero, you couldn't back off and drop it like they wanted."

"I thought..."

"Well, whatever you thought, it wasn't good enough, was it?" Ben pushed Luther back a few steps. "Was it?"

"No."

"You know, I remember you coming to see me after I was arrested. You told me everything was going to be ok, that you would fix everything; all I had to do was trust you."

Luther wanted to say something, try to explain what had happened and why, but looking into Ben's face, he knew those words would mean nothing. Whatever the reasons behind his actions, the end result was still the same; nothing would bring back Ben's lost years.

"But I gave up on you when they shut my cell door on the first night."

"I never gave up," said Luther, knowing he had no right to plead any kind of defence for his betrayal. "I never stopped trying to get you out of that place."

Ben's mocking laughter carried through the compartment. "Save it, the world's full of people who never gave up, they're called losers."

"I'm sorry, Ben, I don't know what to say."

"You know, playing the caring brother is not going to bring her back; Mum will still be dead, I wonder who we should blame for that little mishap."

Luther could not believe what Ben had said, or rather what he was implying. This conversation was going somewhere he never thought it would; it needed to stop one way or another.

"Mum's car crash was an accident, there was nothing anyone could do."

"What, like my ten-year conviction for armed robbery was an accident?"

"Don't do this."

"Do what? Mum was a great driver, her hitting into that truck always seemed a little too convenient, maybe your friends…"

Luther grabbed Ben and thrust him against the cabin wall.

"I said don't," he said through gritted teeth.

"Don't what?" screamed Ben, throwing Luther's hands off. "Blame you for destroying my life?"

Ben held out his arms and slowly turned around. "Take a good look at your handiwork, Luther. This is who I am: The Hand, a thief and a hustler. Do you think Mum would be happy about the way you let me turn out?"

"Spare me the hard done by speech, Ben, it doesn't suit you," laughed Luther.

Maybe it was the constant one-way blame being thrown his way, or the snide insinuations about their mother's death that pushed Luther too far. Maybe he had just had enough.

"I did something I'm not proud of, something I swore I would never do after Dad walked out. I let you down and nothing is going to change that fact, or bring back those years in prison. But you need to know, whether you want to hear it or not, that because of what I did, a lot of lives were saved."

Luther could see Ben's angry expression as he moved as if to say something, but Luther got there first.

"No, you've had your say, and now it's my turn. Yes, my career is on the up at TORCH, but that came after years of doing every paper pushing assignment MI6 could find for me to do, and that included a year spent in the bloody post room."

"I thought you were the big hero, what happened, you screw someone else over?"

"Turned out I wasn't everyone's hero. When I went to internal security and told them I had proof that high ranking MI6 agents were selling government secrets, well, let's just say scandal was too mild a word."

"So I got sold out for some assholes who were selling off a few documents?"

"One of the documents they were about to sell before they were stopped was a list of every undercover MI6 agent, their location and any contacts they had. Now, if that information fell into the hands of the wrong people, it would have been signing the death warrants of every man and woman on that list, and I was not about to let that happen, whatever the cost."

Luther knew Ben understood what he meant by the term, but he was choosing not to say anything.

"Some of those arrested, I had worked with for years," Luther paused as he remembered the scene as one of the suspects, Brice Gordon, was arrested right in front of him. A year earlier, Brice had saved his life. "Internal security and the home office were all over us. For the next few years, it was like living under a microscope, the unofficial policy being that no one in our section was to be fully trusted. We all bore the brunt of what I had done, so I was not the most popular person when it got out that I had been the one who had blown the whistle."

"Why didn't you quit?"

"Why would I? I hadn't done anything wrong except safeguard the interests of the country I had sworn to protect; though I admit it was difficult to remember that when most of my colleagues never said more than three words to me. So yes, I was a real hero."

Luther reached behind him and pulled forward one of the packing crates and sat back down. "Anyway, this went on for about three years until I was approached by a member of the UN Security Council and offered a job at TORCH. I saw a chance to get back to doing what I was trained to do, which wasn't three post runs a day, and I took it."

Luther could not read Ben's face, but was pretty sure his story had had little or no effect on his brother. "I had to live with the consequences of my actions, the question is, can you?"

"What the hell are you on about now?"

"I'm talking about you blaming me for everything you've become, that's one line I won't cross with you."

"So it wasn't you that put me inside?"

"No, that was me, but what you did when you came out, the choices you made, you did on your own. I never made you what you are today, you did that yourself. If you're looking for someone to blame for that, then take a look in the mirror. You were twenty when you went in that place, you knew right from wrong when you went in there, and you chose wrong. I won't take the fall to ease your conscience because you might not like the man you've become."

"Then it's a good job that I do."

Steph was now standing in the doorway glaring at Luther. "Let me tell you something about your brother, shall I?"

"Steph, leave it," Ben said.

"No, I won't leave it! I've listened to his sermon for long enough. Do you know the amount of jobs we didn't take on because Ben said it wasn't right, that he didn't agree with what they stood for: can you believe that? Do you know how much money we could have made if he had bent those bloody principles of his and looked the other way once in a while?"

"He broke into a TORCH research centre and blew it up, and he's only here now for the cash Barrington is paying him. I would hardly call that principled, would you?" Luther threw back.

"We were framed for that, and the reason we ended up here in the first place was because Ben wanted to find the real people who destroyed the centre. As for Barrington, in case you hadn't been keeping score, he tried to kill us twice, so we got some payback," argued Steph. "Did he tell you that some of the money we make goes to help a lot of people, kids mainly who didn't have the same luck he did with the people who looked out for him in prison. He wanted to stop them from ending up there in the first place."

Luther raised an eyebrow. "I suppose he gives the rest of the cash to the poor."

"Look, he's no saint, we're thieves, plain and simple, so yes, a lot of the money we make goes in our own pockets, which, by the way is what I'm in it for; so it really does my head in when I have to work with someone whose conscience stops us from making some real cash," explained Steph. "But now that I've met you, I can see who's to blame. You need to get used to the fact that Ben hates you, and chances are he's always going to. Deal with it." She turned to Ben.

"I don't know what you're smiling about, Ben, you see this?" Steph held up a thumb and index finger, which were nearly touching each other. "That's how close I am to kicking your ass. You promised me you could keep it together, focus on the mission," Steph sighed. "So tell me, Ben, is this what you call keeping it together?"

"He had it coming," muttered Ben.

"He had it coming," repeated Steph, rolling her eyes in disbelief. "What are you - five? I swear, Ben, you or TORCH boy over there pull one more stunt and I'm out. I don't care how much we're being paid, there's no good having money if you're too dead to spend it."

Luther looked around at the chaos he and Ben had unleashed in the compartment, and knew Steph was right. This was not the time or the place to settle any old scores, not with what was at stake.

"I hear you," said Ben.

"Good," Steph replied, seemingly satisfied. "Now, we're about twenty minutes from the target zone. Time to put your game faces on, gentlemen, it's time to earn our pay."

Luther gave her a disapproving look and almost wished he had kept his thoughts to himself.

"What, did you think I was doing this out of the goodness of my heart? Wake up, TORCH boy, this isn't the A-Team; I work for cash, so the sooner you realise that, the better you'll feel."

With the message successfully relayed, the door was slammed shut, leaving the two brothers alone once again.

"Is she always…?"

"That cold, calculating, and ruthlessly efficient?" cut in Ben.

"I was going to say such a bitch."

"Yeah," said Ben, giving his older brother a strained half-smile. "She's that too."

"I heard that, Ashodi," came a muffled voice from the other side of the door.

Chapter Thirty-One

The Reverend was not sure why Napoleon had decided to be so open. His initial assessment of Napoleon was that he kept his enemies close, and his friends at a distance, if he had anyone he could truly call a friend. That was something the Reverend knew all too well.

"So what was it?" he asked. "What did you see?"

"There wasn't a great deal I could make out at first, just shadows. There were candles on the floor marking out a large symbol I had never seen before. There were a dozen or so naked men and women surrounding the symbol. They were chanting the same phrase over and over again, but I couldn't understand what it was. In the centre of the circle, I saw Paul, one of the Brotherhood's leaders. Beside him was a boy who couldn't have been any older than thirteen. I didn't need to see his face to know he was terrified."

Napoleon looked away, his eyes focusing on a neon sign on the other side of the road. The Reverend stayed quiet and waited for him to speak again.

"I should have done something to help him. Instead, I just stood there, my fear of being caught overrode any thoughts of intervention. But my fear was not brought on by the figures in the room, but by the creature that stood beside Paul. At first, I thought it was a dog, a huge one granted, but a dog none the less."

"I take it that was not the case," said the Reverend.

"Not unless there's a breed of dog that has scales for skin, a horn in its forehead and scarlet eyes."

"I see your point."

"Paul whispered something to the boy before walking out of the centre. I was too far away to hear what he said, but for some reason, the boy started to laugh. I'll never forget the sound, it was as if he no longer cared what happened to him; of course, that changed when the creature tore into him and the screaming started. Finally, I couldn't take it anymore, I cried out and all eyes turned to me. I tried to run, but I felt arms around me, then pain as I was struck from behind, then nothing."

"What happened next?"

"I was imprisoned at the compound for six months. They did just enough to keep me alive. They wanted to know how I found them that night, who I was working for. The fact I didn't know myself was a concept they weren't willing to explore."

"You could have given them the name of your contact in the agency," suggested the Reverend. "You owed them nothing, they obviously knew of the hidden agenda of the cult or at the very least, suspected it and yet chose to send you anyway, completely unprepared."

"Oh, the warning signs were there all right," said Napoleon, "but I was too wrapped up in making a name for myself to see them. Loyalty to the people that sent me was not why I stayed quiet. I was haunted by the face of the boy, the boy I should have helped. I promised myself I wouldn't give those bastards anything they could use even if it cost me my life."

"A costly penance."

"Very." Napoleon pointed to his eye patch and smiled sadly. "After they took my eye, I told them everything, even the name of my contact. I realised I wasn't willing to die for an ideal, no matter how noble and good it may have seemed at the time."

"Every man has their breaking point," pointed out the Reverend. "You should not blame yourself for what happened. You paid a heavy price for the silence you kept, most men would have broken at the very mention of torture."

Napoleon continued as if he had not heard the Reverend's words.

"Several nights later, I was broken out of the compound. I told the man who freed me about my betrayal of my contact's identity, but my warning came too late. My contact was already dead, along with his wife and two daughters."

"I am sorry, Napoleon, guilt is a terrible burden to carry."

"Yes it is," said Napoleon, as he began scooping up his equipment and loading it into a large black satchel. "I later discovered that it was not the government who had authorised my rescue. They had already deemed the situation too sensitive to risk an extraction."

"So who was the man that freed you?"

"Nathan Ash."

"The only man who knows the location of the Cabal?"

"I know what you're thinking, but the only reason I've had Nathan brought here is to help me find Cademus Castle."

"I don't doubt your motives, Professor Stone, even if you deny that part of the reason for arranging this meeting is to help your friend, but tell me what happened to Paul?"

"He had an accident."

"Accident?"

"The kind where someone ends up dead."

"And your wife?" asked the Reverend.

Napoleon stiffened at the question. "I came back to her a different man, weighed down with too much emotional baggage. I'm surprised she stayed with me as long as she did."

The Reverend stared up at Napoleon, unsure where the conversation would lead next. "Why have you told me all this?"

Napoleon smiled. "You know, I don't really know, I've never told anyone that, not even Vincent. I guess I needed to say it as much as you needed to hear it."

The Reverend stood at the comment, one of his guns already in his hand. "Why?"

Napoleon left what he was doing and moved over to the Reverend, ignoring the gun trained on him. "This act of yours may fool everyone else, but not me, I've been where you are."

"This is no act, I am…"

"A man who has suffered a loss and the only way he can come to terms with that loss is to become someone else, someone not held back by his own emotions," Napoleon told him. "You're just hiding behind this self-imposed mask of insanity. Well, my friend, I'm here to tell you that your mask is slipping."

Napoleon knocked the gun out of the Reverend's hand. "I've walked the road you're on. There's nothing at its end except more guilt and a trail of corpses. The more you look for vengeance, the more you'll drive away the peace you're looking for."

"You don't know anything about me," said the Reverend, turning his back on Napoleon to head for the door.

"I know you used to be a priest and you watched as someone you loved was killed before your eyes, and you were left for dead. I know that you have a darkness within you that you fought against all your life," Napoleon called after him. "That's probably why you became a priest in the first place. When Maria died, you gave that darkness full reign."

"You pried into my life," stated the Reverend, turning back. "For that I should kill you."

Napoleon smiled. "Wouldn't be the first time someone's tried. As for your past, for about a year, you were under investigation by the Icarus Foundation, though I never expected to meet the infamous Reverend face-to-face, let alone work with him."

"Why?"

"Your reputation for ruthlessness and talent for survival against overwhelming odds were almost inhuman, the board of trustees wanted to make sure you were not something other than human. All we found was a bitter man with a tenuous grip on reality."

"My grip on reality is fine."

234

"Really? Try explaining that to the innocent people you murdered in that crack den you burned to the ground."

"They were scum and needed punishment."

"They were addicts and needed help."

"As long as I fight on your side, what does it matter? You have taken lives. You expect me to believe you take no pleasure from punishing them as I do?"

"Damn you!" screamed Napoleon. "When I fight, it's because I must. I kill to protect those who cannot protect themselves. For you, it's an addiction; it's what gets you up in the morning, gets you through the day. You've crossed the line so often you can't see that most of time you're standing on the wrong side."

"Why do you care?"

"I care because we'll need a miracle to get inside Cademus Castle, let alone reach Jason in time."

"So there is no hope?"

"Oh, there's hope, but there's also a good chance none of us will survive this."

Napoleon retrieved the Reverend's gun and handed it back to him. "So ask yourself whether you want to face your fate like a member of the human race, or like the psychopath everyone believes you to be?"

The Reverend looked at the gun in his hand. "This is what I know, this is who I am."

"Then I pity you," said Napoleon, walking to the door.

"What do you believe?"

Napoleon stopped. "You sure you want to know?"

"No, but I am curious."

"I believe anyone can change, it just depends how badly they want it."

"What if a man doesn't know how to change? What then?"

"I guess that's where faith comes in."

The Reverend fell silent taking in Napoleon's words, seeing the sincerity in the man's face.

"Jonathan," he said at last, holding out his right hand. "My name is Jonathan Bishop."

"Secretary General Morton?"

Jane Morton walked towards Dale Beddings, head of her security team. His boyish good looks, despite his advancing years could lead someone to mistake him for a less experienced man, and they would be wrong. Dale was someone Jane trusted unreservedly.

"What is it, Dale?"

"We've just received word that the helicopter is less than an hour away."

"Let's get back inside then," she told him, trying her best to block out the icy blast of wind clawing at the hood of her parka. "I want to make sure everything is ready when they arrive."

She led the way back towards the large research building. The steel doors opened as they approached it, and two armed guards waited on the other side. Dale nodded to the guards as they passed by. Jane felt safe knowing Dale had hand-picked each member of the security detail for this assignment.

Jane hoped the research staff, who had been flown off the base several hours before her arrival, would understand one day how a few hours of minor inconvenience helped to save lives.

She walked through the compound, heading to the auditorium where the meeting was to be held. Her troubled thoughts continued to feed the seed of doubt within her mind.

"It is not too late to change your mind, Secretary General," advised Dale, whose penchant for outspoken honesty was a trait Jane had come to admire. "There's a dozen reasons you could give for calling off this meeting."

"There's a cancer within our organization, Dale and unless something is done, it will bring down everything the UN stands for. I'm not going to let that happen on my watch."

"If it gets out that you met, in secret, with members of the Security Council, members that you have close relations with," said Dale. "Well, at the very least we're talking about professional suicide."

"Professional suicide? What about doing what's right, isn't that worth risking my career for?"

By this time they had reached an elevator, Dale entered first and waited for Morton to join him, before pressing the button to send the elevator to the first floor of the facility. Jane knew Dale hated her stubbornness but it was his job to protect her, both from those who would do her harm, and occasionally even from herself.

"I'm not saying you should do nothing, but there are proper channels, safe channels open to you," said Dale, who clearly was not prepared to let the matter drop.

"Safe!" shouted Jane. She respected Dale's opinion in all matters of her job. There were times, however, when his rigid approach to protocols really got on her nerves. "Tell that to Pemrose and his team."

The lift came to rest and they stepped out into a corridor. "Don't go there, Secretary General," warned Dale. "Their deaths, while unfortunate, were not your fault."

"If not me, then who?" demanded Jane. "I was the one who authorised the creation of Pemrose's team. I will take full responsibility for my involvement in those deaths, and I will be held accountable for those decisions when all of this becomes public knowledge."

Jane held Dale's right arm, forcing him to stop and face her. "What I will not do, Dale, is allow their deaths to either go unpunished or be forgotten. Once the Security Council is behind me, I will find every person acting against this organisation's mandate, and they will face the full force of the law."

"At least postpone the meeting until we can secure a different location," advised Dale. "I don't like being in a place with such an obvious lack of security other than the presence of TORCH security personnel."

Jane found her herself laughing at the comment. "Well, Dale it would be difficult not to have TORCH personnel around at a TORCH-run facility, don't you think?"

Jane's attempt at humour was met with a stern look.

"Trust me, Dale," she said, her tone returning to serious. "My TORCH contact, a contact Pemrose personally vouched for in his reports, assured me this facility was secure and that the men under his command will not interfere or monitor our activities within this building. Their job will be to guard the perimeter of the centre and that's all."

"Are you sure he can be trusted?"

"He was as shocked as I was when I first learned of this rogue agency and its involvement with a cult. He has pledged to do everything in his power to implement any measures approved by the Security Council."

"And that is why I am here today, to ensure the final preparations for this meeting take place without incident," said a voice.

There in the doorway leading to the auditorium where the meeting was to take place stood a smiling Philippe Chardon.

Chapter Thirty-Two

Jason stood in awe of the panoramic view his position on the battlements of Castle Cademus afforded him. The first rays of sunlight cast themselves over the jungle, heralding the dawn and the promise of a new day. It was the most beautiful sight Jason had ever seen, and yet it was tainted with the knowledge that it was possibly the last dawn he would ever see. The thought brought back the tears, but a sudden calmness settled over his mind, pushing back the oncoming grief. At the moment, his emotions were the only thing in his life that were in his power to control. His life, what a parody those two words had become. If the Cabal were to be believed, then his course had been set from birth, his existence a means to an end. His mind was nothing more than a mystical hard drive, storing the last mental fragment of a man who died centuries before he was born. Any doubts as to the validity of the fantastic story were swept aside with his display of power during the meeting with the Cabal. Elemental Science, that was what Crane called it, a term penned by Sir Oliver himself. Whatever its given name, the power terrified Jason.

Crane had apologised profusely for any pain he had caused by his words, but the Cabal needed to be sure that Jason was indeed the one they were seeking. Crane went on to explain that within the untrained mind, these abilities lay dormant, sometimes never surfacing, but the portion of Cademus' mind had awakened and enhanced these abilities. At certain times, however, usually those where the emotions were heightened, these abilities could manifest themselves with devastating effect. It went some way to explain Jason's 'episode' at the university. Crane had told him that somehow, he had been able to tap into the mind of the creature they had sent to kill his parents, to feel what it felt, something thought impossible for someone with his lack of experience.

But for Jason, it was his real parents who now held his fascination. For the first time in years, he found himself thinking about them. Once he was old enough to understand the term 'abandoned', he wasted no more time wondering about strangers whose only common link was the genes they shared. He despised them for the life they had condemned him to, a life where everything he ever wanted was always just out of reach, despite the happy years spent with the Chens before their death. The meeting with the Cabal was forcing him to re-evaluate that position, and he did not like it. There was now the possibility that his parents had not abandoned him willingly, but were forced to do so to protect him.

According to Crane, the knights of Cademus, the same death squad that had kidnapped him from the university, had discovered the location of Jason's parents two months after he had been abandoned as a baby. The knights entered the house they were hiding in, their intent being to learn Jason's current whereabouts by any means necessary. Their moment of triumph was short-lived when they discovered both parents dead from a self-administered poison. Beside the bodies, they found a note that read; He is safe now.

Jason did not know whether to be grateful to Crane for telling him the truth about his real parents and their fate, or to hate him even more. How dare he corrupt the safe images of the malicious and cruel individuals he had spent years cultivating. Now, along with everything else, he would have to deal with the idea that his real parents had loved him so much, they had given their lives to protect him. He tried to blot out Crane's words; after all, he, like Justine and the other members of the Cabal, were already guilty of murder. Lying to Jason would mean little to such people, but the seed was now implanted in his mind and had begun to take hold. Years of hatred towards his biological parents were being forced to co-exist with the grief he was beginning to feel for their passing. They were never given the chance to raise their son, instead they had been forced to push Jason into a life they did not choose or want for him.

Jason's thoughts were interrupted by the sound of footsteps mounting the steps to the battlements. Crane had promised him full reign of the castle, but obviously there were limits to that promise. The ritual would be performed as soon as the preparations were completed. He was running out of time. As the guards neared to return him to his room, Jason promised himself if he saw a chance to repay the Cabal for all the harm done to him and those around him, he would take it with both hands.

Napoleon scratched his chin. The usually well-trimmed beard was starting to itch and was long overdue for a shave. Once more, he ran his eye over the copies of ancient texts faxed to him by the Icarus Foundation. He searched for any reference to the Ritual of Restoration, any scrap of knowledge that could be used against the Cabal.

"Not enough time," he mumbled. "Not enough time."

The Book of Cademus had proven time and time again, over the years, to be a powerful enemy. The effect Oliver Cademus' return would have on his followers was immeasurable. What damage would it inflict upon the fragile balance between good and evil that Napoleon and so few others fought and died to keep in check? The truth was, Oliver Cademus brought with him the keys to hell.

Napoleon's thoughts turned to Grey. There were many things about what was going on that were still a mystery to him, but one thing was abundantly clear, Joshua Grey, like his surname implied, stood in the middle, playing his own game, a game he had no intention of losing. Napoleon had his own theories regarding Grey, but for now there were far weightier issues to deal with, like the end of the world. Even if they stopped the Cabal, there was still the impending assassination of a large contingent of the UN Security Council. Their murders could incite enough unrest to throw the world into chaos, perhaps even another world war as the nations struggled to find someone to blame. He could not dwell on that now, all he could do was trust that the others in their strange group would be able to stop that from happening. The Reverend had assured him that the two thieves were not to be underestimated.

"Now here's someone who doesn't know how to relax," said Vincent, strolling into the room, looking fresh-faced. "You've studied those texts a hundred times now. What makes you think you're going to get anything useful out of them this time? If there were something there, you would have seen it by now."

Napoleon rubbed his tired eye and yawned. "You may be right."

Napoleon thought Vincent's grin could light up a small room. "You know I could really get to like this whole Vincent-is-right attitude of yours."

"I have the feeling it's going to be a day of firsts," confessed Napoleon.

"What did you say to the Reverend? I went to check in with him and he seems even weirder than he did before."

Napoleon smiled grimly. "I guess it's a day for strange behaviour as well."

"Talk to me, Napoleon," he said. "Something's got you worried, what is it?"

"If we can't stop the Cabal from raising Cademus, a lot more people are going to die."

"Which is why we're going to stop them before that happens."

"Even if we can convince Nathan to go with us, and somehow we make it past the supernatural defences that will no doubt be in place, and we are able to get inside Cademus Castle, we may still have to get past whatever it was I fought at the university, and that's not a prospect I'm looking forward to... and then there's Cademus himself."

"I'm not going to like this, am I?"

Napoleon pointed to one of the photocopied manuscripts. "I've been able to decipher this portion of text taken from a manuscript recovered by Nathan on his escape from Cademus Castle. This text was taken from a first-hand account of Cademus' supposed superhuman attributes. It speaks of his ability to control the elements."

"Control them?"

"If the text is to be believed, and my translation is correct, he was able to channel them through his body like some kind of human superconductor."

"I guess this is the part where I say we need a bigger boat?" said Vincent. "I mean, how are we supposed to fight someone that powerful?"

"With the only weapon you have left…faith."

Both men turned to see the Reverend enter the room carrying his two mini Uzi's. "Or alternatively, a little firepower never hurt."

"Rev," laughed Vincent. "I like your thinking."

Ben stirred his soup again. He still harboured the fruitless hope that the constant stirring would magically transform the brown, dishwater-like substance before him, into a four-course gourmet dinner. No such luck, the only change to the soup was the cracking of the thin layer of skin just starting to form over it.

"Staring at it isn't going to make it taste any better," said Luther, who was greedily devouring his portion of soup. "Trust me; it does get better the more you have."

"Sure it does," scowled Ben, unconvinced.

The howling wind outside served to remind Ben where he was, and how much he wished he was anywhere but stuck in a hastily erected shelter in the middle of Antarctica. His only company was a brother he hated, and the promise of capture and probable death in front of him.

The wall of the shelter flapped furiously against Ben's back, threatening chaos, should the ropes holding the shelter in place succumb to the will of the snowstorm.

Ben was well aware of the dangers of trying to travel while the storm was this strong, even in the snowmobiles they were using. Despite this knowledge, he would have risked frozen death rather than eat another mouthful of the soup he was now forcing his bowels not to jettison from his system by any means necessary.

"Same old Ben," said Luther, who had finished his soup and was pouring himself a mug of coffee. "Still the same fussy eater you were when you were a kid."

"Bullshit," Ben threw back, force-feeding himself more of the soup.

"Admit it, Ben, you know as well as I do how spoiled you were when it came to food," said Luther. "What was it you ate that time and then accused Mum of trying to poison you?"

Ben said nothing. The memory had come to him the minute Luther had mentioned the incident. It was just that right now, there were far more important things to consider than…

"Beans!" said Luther with a triumphant grin. "Baked beans and sausages in tomato sauce, you were sick everywhere."

"I was allergic to them," argued Ben. "Still am."

"Mum always said you were the difficult one," stated Luther.

"Funny, she used to say the same about you."

As the two brothers stared at each other, a silence pervaded the shelter. It was a silence that even managed to drown out the snowstorm outside.

"How long has it been?"

"Four years and three months," said Ben, eating more soup and finding its foul taste more palatable than the conversation.

"Have you been to see her since you got out of prison?"

"Why should I do that?" said Ben, surprised at the question. "She's dead, visiting her grave isn't going to change that."

Ben knew the words and the tone of them were harsh, almost to the point of uncaring. That assumption was far from the truth. He was terrified of going to his mum's grave. Doing so might allow him to begin to heal a wound he did not want healing, at least not yet. He saw the look of disappointment on Luther's face, and for a small moment, he felt a degree of shame. Then it was gone.

"I never realised until now just how much you've changed, Ben."

"Prison can do that to you, you should try it sometime."

"The storm's still got a lot of life in it," said Luther. "Could be hours before we can travel again."

Ben took the hint that Luther was not going to be drawn into another punch up, and in some way he was relieved.

"Maybe we should get a few hours sleep before we move on," suggested Ben. "We're ahead of schedule. We should reach the complex long before the UN members do. Besides, Steph's got us on a satellite feed back at the plane; we'll know if a penguin comes within fifty feet. Come on, I'll take first watch, I'll wake you in two hours."

"Good idea," agreed Luther, already unfolding the sleeping bag beside him. "For some reason, I can't keep my eyes open, must be more tired than I thought," he said yawning. "Besides, we have no idea what we'll be facing once we reach the facility, the assassins may already be there, waiting for the UN members to arrive."

"Well, if we're lucky, we can get them out before they can make their move," said Ben.

"And if not?"

"We move to plan B, now get some sleep," said Ben, taking out the satellite photos of the facility from his backpack. He knew the photos would not have changed in the last few hours since he had studied them, but he always liked to be sure. At least the intelligence provided courtesy of Will's hacking skills before they left for Antarctica seemed to back up what Luther had already told him. The Ulysses research centre was just three buildings; a security station, on top of which was housed a satellite dish that provided the base with its communication with the outside world. The second building contained bedrooms, a kitchen, a dining area and a recreation room for the security and research centre staff. The third building, which at four floors was the largest and most secure was where the research took place. In reality, it was actually the third and fourth floors where the main body of work was carried out. The first floor was where all the administration and entertaining of visitors was done. It contained an auditorium that held twice-yearly research conferences that the research staff hosted for the metrological community, as well as any impromptu events that cropped up. The ground floor housed a garage containing snowmobiles, snow ploughs and several other pieces of larger research equipment, there were also a few storage rooms. On the roof of the building was a large helipad for the ferrying of people and equipment to and from the centre. Ben was so engrossed in the plans that he failed to notice Luther staring intently at him.

"Ben," said Luther at last. "Whatever happens and whatever you think of me, it's been good seeing you again."

Ben did not acknowledge Luther's statement, he merely continued staring at the plans he was holding. He listened to Luther's breathing for some time, until it became shallower, indicating he had drifted off to sleep. Then quietly, subtly, the emotion crept through his subconscious seeking freedom. The emotion was not alone; it was accompanied by a thought that Ben had tried his best to keep hidden.

It's been good to see you too.

Ben gritted his teeth and then hurled the plans across the shelter. Luther stirred but did not wake. Ben did not know who he hated more right now, Luther, or himself for letting him begin to miss his only family, a conduit to a past that no longer existed. There would be no reconciliation, no happy families for the two of them, not now, not ever.

Chapter Thirty-Three

Napoleon stared at Nathan Ash. A man who, the last time they met, he had almost killed. No matter how hard he tried to purge the thoughts of betrayal from his mind, they still remained as strong as they did all those years ago.

Nathan was flanked by two men. It seemed that despite being in his sixties his former mentor's reputation was still something to be feared.

"Wait outside," said Napoleon.

"Sorry, Professor Stone, but our orders are to…"

"Don't make me ask a second time," said Napoleon making eye contact with the man.

"We'll be right outside if you need us."

Napoleon nodded his thanks to the men as they left.

"Hello, Nathan," he said, not thinking of anything more intelligent to say.

"You know, this is the first time I've seen the sunrise in over ten years," replied Nathan, absent-mindedly. "Like most things in life…overrated."

Nathan stretched out his arm and touched the window in front of him, sliding his hand down the length of it. "It's Cademus, isn't it? The Cabal are trying to raise him?"

"Yes," said Napoleon. "But how…"

"Send me back."

Napoleon ignored Nathan and instead explained everything that had happened to date. Nathan said nothing and Napoleon wondered if he was even listening.

"So if you don't help us, an innocent man will die and God knows how many will follow."

"It would not be the first time I had to wash the blood of the innocent off my hands," Nathan reminded him. "Have you ever wondered just how many people have already died in our noble little crusade, and how many more will die? So what's a few more matter?"

"What happened to you, Nathan, you used to be someone I could trust."

Nathan turned round and smiled. "Do you remember the others who trusted me? Do you remember what happened to them? I won't let you make the same mistake, Nathan Ash is dead, he died fifteen years ago. Now send me back!"

Nathan pulled a small device from his pocket; it was no bigger than the palm of his hand and looked like a silver pocket watch. He placed it on the table.

"Activate," he said quietly.

Instantly, a low hum enveloped the room. Napoleon moved to say something, but was silenced by Nathan's shaking head. He watched as Nathan moved over to the door, placed his ear against it for a few second before walking back over to Napoleon. He grabbed him by both arms and shook him.

"It's good to see you, old friend," he smiled. "You should ditch the beard, it puts years on you."

Napoleon did not know what concerned him more, the fact that Nathan seemed suddenly so, so normal, or the humming that was still coming from the strange object.

He stepped away from Nathan, unsure what was coming next.

"It's a sound dampening device, part science, part something else; it will block out anyone trying to eavesdrop on the conversation we're about to have." Nathan gestured to a chair. "You better sit down for this."

Puzzled, Napoleon took Nathan's advice and sat down.

"It all started sixteen years ago. Icarus received a report from an undercover investigator working within the Book of Cademus."

"This is ancient history," cut in Napoleon. "It was based on her findings, or rather the lack of them, that led the board of trustees to dismiss your claims about them."

Nathan nodded in agreement. "That's what everyone was meant to believe, including the Book of Cademus. It was that undercover investigator who first warned us just how dangerous and widespread the Book of Cademus had become. Under orders from the trustees, she remained undercover and continued to pass out information."

"A brave woman," said Napoleon.

"She should be," replied Nathan. "I trained her."

Napoleon was not surprised by the answer, he still remembered his own experiences of Nathan's training methods.

"She was unable to learn the identities of the Cabal," continued Nathan. "But she did uncover their plan to raise Cademus. Before she was discovered, she got word to me that the Cabal had in their possession a series of journals written by Cademus himself. One of the journals supposedly contained a passage describing the steps needed to perform the ritual of restoration. The journal also contained a section that no one had yet been able to translate, she theorized that once translated, this section might give us a way to disrupt the ritual."

"How did she manage to discover all this?"

"From one of the Cabal's personal bodyguards: according to him, the Cabal member charged with leading the ritual kept a replica of the journal in his study, along with the original, he had seen it there many times," explained Nathan. "The lovesick idiot was probably trying to impress her."

"You said she was discovered," said Napoleon, fearing the worst. "What happened to her?"

Nathan smiled. "Like I said, I trained her."

"She escaped?"

"Of course, and her testimony to the board of trustees was most compelling. She urged them to act before the Cabal could put its plan into action."

"So your sudden disillusionment at the board's decisions, your obsession regarding the danger posed by the Book of Cademus was nothing but…"

"Smoke and mirrors. It was too dangerous to let anyone else in on what had been discovered before we were ready to act."

"In case the Book of Cademus had infiltrated Icarus?"

"Exactly, so we decided to make it appear to everyone I had gone rogue."

"You did a good job," commented Napoleon, remembering what Nathan had been like back then. "I assume then that the story about you taking the fight to Cademus Castle was a half-truth."

"Yes, the real reason we went in was to find the journal," explained Nathan.

"Why not just destroy the copy and the original?" asked Napoleon. "No journal, no Cademus."

"The Cabal aren't stupid, they would not just have one copy, for all we knew they could have made hundreds," Nathan explained. "It was imperative the Book of Cademus never realised the replica had been tampered with, which was why it had to be left behind. While the others fought off the knights of Cademus, I slipped away, located the study the investigator had detailed in her report, and made a copy of the replica journal using a hand-held scanner."

"This is the part where I come in," said Napoleon.

"We needed time to decipher it and plan our next move, but we couldn't risk the Cabal discovering what we were up to, so the board of trustees put out the fake story that I had become unstable and, against orders, had taken a team into the castle. Those that came with me did not know what the real reason behind the attack was, we could not risk any of them being captured with that knowledge." Nathan cast his eyes downward. "Only two of us made it out, but the mission was a success."

"And they sent me to bring you in knowing that I would follow orders."

"No, I told them to send you because we needed to make my capture look convincing."

"I nearly killed you," Napoleon pointed out. "Did you figure that into your plans?"

"As I said, my capture needed to be as real as possible. I gambled that you would be good enough to stop me without killing me, luckily for both of us, it paid off."

"You mean lucky for you?"

"No, if I thought that night you had come to kill me, the outcome would have been different," stated Nathan. "There was too much at risk."

A grim smile formed on Napoleon's lips. That was the arrogant Nathan Ash he remembered. "So the last fifteen years in Haven not speaking was an act as well?"

"I deciphered the journal within my first year at Haven, but the trustees thought it best not to reveal my discoveries until the Cabal made its move. So I stayed and continued to research them as well as hundreds of other cults, passing on what I leant directly to the trustees," explained Nathan. "There were a few trusted people at Haven that knew I was there under false pretences, they just did not know why."

"I hope this is leading up to you saying there is a way to stop the ritual."

"There is a way," repeated Nathan. "I'm just not sure you'll like the method."

"If you're going to say we kill Jason before they can complete the ritual," Napoleon told him, "I've already considered that option, so I hope you have another suggestion that is less obvious."

Although he tried not to convey any emotion, the thought of having to kill Jason sickened Napoleon. What was worse was that when the time came, if there was no other choice, he would not hesitate in taking the shot.

"As I said, the journal is basically an instruction manual for the ritual," explained Nathan. "I found a passage that details a way to disrupt the procedure by using Cademus' power against him to create a kind of prison existing outside of our perceived reality."

"Meaning?"

Nathan leaned back in his chair and took up a miniature bottle of whisky that had been sitting atop the mini bar. He set the bottle down on the table between himself and Napoleon.

"Imagine this is Cademus," said Nathan, pointing at the bottle. "Using the ritual, we harness his power and turn it against him, forming a barrier around him."

Picking up a glass tumbler, Nathan placed it over the bottle. "He'll be trapped inside; a prisoner of his own power. It will tear him apart until he is nothing more than a whirlwind of energy, unable to become solid matter, and because it will take place outside of our perceived reality," Nathan dropped a cloth over the glass. "He will cease to exist as far as we're concerned."

"Maybe I'm being paranoid, but why would Cademus leave the means to destroy him in the same place as the means to revive him?"

"That's the question I've been asking myself for over a decade," admitted Nathan. "It could be a trap; it could backfire and kill us all, but it's a chance we can't afford not to take."

Napoleon was not convinced, but so far Nathan had been the only person to offer any kind of plan for combating Cademus. "How long will that hold him for?"

"Probably forever, give or take a thousand years," smiled Nathan, looking pleased with himself. His smugness quickly faded as the worried look grew on Napoleon's face.

"What?"

"Where's the part you're not telling me?" asked Napoleon. "The highly dangerous part."

"First, we need someone to read off the relevant passage within the journal to activate the energy traps, which are symbols drawn within a chalk circle; if Cademus steps into one, he'd be held for a few moments allowing the second part of the process to take place."

"Which is?"

"The person must then read the same passage backwards to complete the incantation and seal the energy vortex. All of this will only work if the person reciting the incantation has possessed a portion of Cademus' mind, as for a while, they will be able to tap into his mind and use the power there."

"And?"

"And for the procedure to work, the Cabal must complete the ritual of restoration, then we will have a timeframe of about twenty minutes before the energy residue from the ritual dissipates."

"So if we fail to stop the Cabal from using Jason, we have to let them raise Cademus. We're then supposed to, somehow get Jason away from the Cabal and Cademus, to use in a plan we're not even sure will work, all of which hinges on Cademus not killing us the moment he opens his eyes?"

"Be just like old times," said Nathan smiling.

Removing the glass, Nathan opened the miniature bottle of whisky and poured himself a glass.

"Ok, I admit as plans go, it needs work, but there is a good chance that once Jason reads the first part of the spell, it will begin draining Cademus' power, which might slow him down. Remember, he's been dormant for centuries; it will take time for him to realise the extent of his powers and how to use them, that might give us an edge, and it's the only plan we have."

"Besides killing them all before the ritual is completed, which is plan A as far as I'm concerned," said Napoleon, standing up.

"But the boy?"

"Don't you think I know that!" shouted Napoleon. "But our first goal must be to prevent the ritual from being completed, if that fails, at least now we have a backup plan."

"What now?" asked Nathan.

"I'll let the others know that we're leaving. I take it you know where the castle is and how to get in?"

"During my time at the Haven, I discovered another way into the castle, other than the one I used fifteen years ago, that would be our best bet."

"Ok then," said Napoleon, standing up. "I'll let your friends outside know that you're working with me now, I've got the authority from the board of trustees so it shouldn't be a problem."

Nathan stood up and stuck his chin out.

"What are you doing?"

"I know you were used by the board and me so you get one free shot then put it out of your mind, and we get back to the job, agreed?"

Napoleon walked past Nathan, knocking his arm aside as he did so. "You did what you had to do, forget it, I already have," said Napoleon. "Now, let's go, there's something else I need to talk to you about on the way."

"Best I ever trained," said Nathan, holding his glass of whisky aloft for a second before downing its contents and following Napoleon.

Chapter Thirty-Four

Wake up idiot! Luther's subconscious screamed at him.

His eyes snapped open and he reached out for his gun. A shot rang out, piercing the duffel bag he had been using as a makeshift pillow. Crouched by the entrance, he saw a man in white military fatigues, which were no doubt padded as insulation against the extreme cold. The man was aiming a M16 levelled at Luther's head. Luther both saw and shared the shock that his captor now had.

"Reardon?" said Luther. "Dave Reardon?"

"Jesus, sir I nearly killed you," replied Dave. "Do you know how much shit you're in?"

"I have a fair idea you're about to spell it out for me."

"Every TORCH agent is out looking for you. You're public enemy number one as far as Chardon's concerned, and where do I find you? Bloody two hours away at a secret meeting that I didn't even know was going on until yesterday."

Reardon nodded to a man who was just outside of the shelter, keeping Luther covered. Reardon placed his weapon on the ground and moved further into the tent. Sensing what was about to happen, Luther held out his wrists.

"For what it's worth, sir, I think this is all bullshit," admitted Reardon as he fastened the handcuffs around Luther's wrists. "But I have to take you in."

"I understand," said Luther.

"Good, because if you try anything, I will shoot you, nothing personal."

"Nothing personal."

Stepping outside, Luther could see that the snowstorm had subsided and the day was once more bathed in sunlight. The sun's glare reflected off the arctic floor, threatening to blind whoever saw it. It was then Luther saw Ben. He was handcuffed and on his knees facing him. Behind Ben, stood in a semi-circle were four more soldiers, one of them had a gun held against the side of Ben's head.

"Where's Corman?" demanded Reardon.

"He was round the back when we got here."

Just then, Corman appeared from behind the tent, like the others, he wore goggles and his hood was thrown over his head.

"Good job on finding them, Corman," said Reardon. "You take point; we're heading back."

250

Ben looked up at Luther and shrugged his shoulders. "I guess it's time for plan B."

Somewhere in South America.

From her hiding place beneath an old pickup truck, Isabelle tried not to look at the small chapel. Abandoned and unused by the people from her village for as long as she could remember, it was a place she hated being near.

On her right, she spotted a mass of curly black hair poking out over the top of a barrel. The hair belonged to her brother, Miguel, who was too busy coughing to notice anyone. Miguel was great at lots of things, but hide and seek was not one of them. Isabelle thought about shouting at him to find somewhere else to hide. She shook off the idea, after all, he never listened to her anyway, he was the oldest, and therefore knew everything, well, at least he thought he did.

"Not this time, Miguel," she giggled gleefully to herself.

Her laughter was short-lived as she realised she had lost count. She desperately tried to remember where she had got to; thirty-five or fifty-three, she could not be sure; counting was not one of the things she was good at. She needed to be sure, it could make the difference between another twenty seconds and...

"Ready or not here I come!"

The voice calling from the end of the small alley leading past the chapel told Isabelle the game had started. Any second now, Alonzo would be looking for them. Alonzo looked after them while their mother was out working. He was as funny as he was handsome. She was going to marry him one day, Alonzo did not know that yet, but he would. It did not matter that he was years older than her, after all, her father was years and years older than her mother, and they were very happy.

Sunset was fast approaching, causing the chapel to cast its shadow across the street, where it threatened to reach Isabelle. Instinctively, she shrunk further back under the truck, closed her eyes and prayed Alonzo would find her soon. There was something about the chapel she did not like, something that scared her. She wished she didn't have to see it every day, but as it was on her way to school, there was little choice. She could not convince Alonzo to take her and Miguel a different way without admitting her fears, and so she said nothing. Her mother had been understanding when Isabelle had confessed her fears about the chapel. She had said there was nothing to fear from the house of God. If that were true, thought Isabelle, why was it such a scary place and why had she never seen anyone go inside?

"Izzy! Izzy!"

Isabelle sighed. Only Miguel called her Izzy, he knew she hated the name, but that never stopped him.

Isabelle looked over at him and then to the spot he was pointing at. Her eyes widened when she saw the jeep coming towards the chapel, she had been so caught up in her own thoughts she had not even seen it. Their village was some distance from the main towns and that was the way they liked it, her father always said. Too many people there who do not know how to mind their own business, he would always respond whenever her mother raised the subject of moving there.

The jeep stopped in front of the chapel and four men got out. All Isabelle could do was lie there, frozen by the fear of discovery, praying she would not be seen. She watched as one of the men took off his grey felt hat and wiped his forehead with the back of his hand. The man was old, thought Isabelle, older than even her father, and yet he did not seem weak or helpless like Father was. Father could not climb the stairs anymore without his legs hurting, and so had taken to sleeping in his chair a lot. Isabelle thought the old man looked as if he had never slept a day in his life. The old man then, as if he knew he was being watched, turned and stared in her direction.

Isabelle was sure he could not see her in the twilight, after all, she had never lost a game of hide and seek.

Until now.

Isabelle did not know what to do as the man crouched down in front of her. He started speaking in her own language, telling her not to be afraid. Not many outsiders bothered to learn their language, which was the reason her father was paying a lot of money for her and Miguel to be taught English once a week.

Isabelle thought about crawling out and running for help, but as she looked at the man who was now smiling at her, she began to think that maybe he was not going to hurt the others.

"Don't move you two! I'm coming!"

Alonzo came running towards the men, carrying the machete that her father always made him carry for protection.

Another man, a man with one eye, stepped in front of Alonzo. Isabelle could not see what he did, but it must have been magic because there was no other way anyone could have taken the machete away from Alonzo.

Alonzo tried to fight, but the one-eyed man was too fast for him. He pushed Alonzo to the ground, where he stayed. Isabelle watched the man kneel down beside Alonzo and whisper something to him. More magic, concluded Isabelle, because the next thing Alonzo did was get up, without saying a word, and pick up his machete. He then went over to the barrel and dragged out a screaming Miguel, floods of tears streaming down his face. Isabelle watched the two of them approach. Alonzo was half carrying, half-dragging her terrified brother until they stopped by the pickup truck.

Alonzo's smiling face appeared under the truck, he held out his hand towards her. He did not look scared at all, thought Isabelle, but then why should he be? Alonzo was scared of nothing, she knew that.

"Come on out, Isabelle," he said, still smiling. "Time to go home."

Isabelle moved forward then stopped, catching a glimpse of the four men out of the corner of her eye.

"Trust me, no one will hurt you as long as I am here."

Those words gave Isabelle the jolt of courage she needed and, taking his hand, she allowed Alonzo to pull her out from under the truck. Miguel apparently had also overcome his fears and was now standing beside Alonzo, singing to himself. Without a word or a backward glance, Alonzo began leading them on the twenty minute walk to their parents' house. As they walked, Isabelle kept looking over her shoulder at the men, who were now moving towards the chapel entrance.

"Don't worry, they are not here to hurt us," said Alonzo. "They have come to visit the chapel."

"Why?" asked Isabelle, at the mention of the chapel. "It's a bad place, are those men bad too?"

Alonzo stopped and this time, he too looked back at the men. "I have no answer for you, Isabelle, let's hope they find theirs. Now come on, it's getting dark and your mother will have my hide if we're not back soon."

Isabelle took one last look at the men. The friendly old man waved to Isabelle. She smiled and waved back, suddenly feeling no longer afraid, before leaving with Alonzo and her brother.

"What did you say to the boy?" asked the Reverend.

"I told him I wasn't going to kill him and that we weren't here to hurt anyone," said Napoleon.

"That wasn't all he told him," threw in Vincent.

"I also told him that the next time he came at me with a machete, I wouldn't be quite so accommodating."

Vincent shook his head and sighed. "Always charming the locals, I wouldn't be surprised if he's gone off to arrange the usual reception for outsiders we always end up getting, you know, the one with burning torches, pickaxes and shotguns."

"Why don't you give that mouth of yours a rest?" advised Nathan. "Unless you have something useful to offer."

"How about my boot in your ass," Vincent muttered to himself, walking away to the jeep, leaning against the nearest door. Despite

Napoleon's trust in the man, there was something about Ash that did not sit well with Vincent, he could not put his finger on it but until he did, he was not about to turn his back on Ash anytime soon.

Nathan stood by the door and was studying it whilst referring to a tattered old notebook bound in brown leather. The Reverend was leaning over his shoulder, trying to get a glimpse of what was in the precious notebook.

"Wouldn't bother," said Nathan, without turning. "It took me over a year to decipher most of this, and I'm not about to waste time explaining it to you."

"Is there no one in this world you trust?" asked the Reverend.

"You're looking at him."

"You sure about this?" asked Vincent.

"I'm sure, this is the place."

"It's nearly sunset," said Napoleon. "They'll be able to start the ritual anytime after that so whatever we're going to do, it needs to be now."

"Don't rush me."

Nathan knelt by the entrance to the chapel, running his hand over the frail, wooden door. "Just need to make sure there aren't any…"

As Nathan carefully turned the handle there was a loud click. "Surprise!"

A second later, several thudding sounds were heard from the other end of the door.

"What the…?"

Vincent's words were cut short as a crossbow bolt smashed through the door, just missing Nathan's head. The bolt punched into the side of the jeep, four inches below Vincent's groin.

Letting out the breath that had been caught in his throat, Vincent stared at the bolt and then up at Nathan, all the while saying nothing, allowing his clenched fists to broadcast his anger to anyone who was interested.

"Shall we?" said Nathan. He switched on his flashlight and stepped inside.

The Reverend felt nothing but contempt and revulsion at what he saw. It saddened him that a place of worship, a house of God should feel so unwelcome, so alien to him. All the seats had long since been destroyed by decay and the ravages of time. At the far end of the chapel was a single small window, the last rays of sunlight spilling through it. In front of the window was a stone pulpit, the Reverend was reminded of days spent rehearsing sermons. He realised it was one of the few times he had thought about his life before Maria's death.

"Come on, Rev," said Vincent. "The world won't save itself."

Leaving his thoughts for another day, the Reverend walked over to Nathan, Napoleon, and Vincent, who was leaning against the pulpit. Napoleon was crouched beside Nathan, holding his flashlight over a section of stone floor tiles. The tiles were patterned, and to the Reverend they resembled the faded image of a winged bird holding a flaming sword.

"What is it?" he asked.

"The mark of Cademus," said Nathan.

The Reverend watched Nathan take out a small spray bottle from his bag, containing what looked like water. He moved around the upraised area, remaining crouched, spraying it with a covering of the liquid. After a few moments, there was a hissing sound, then small wisps of smoke began floating up from the stone tiles. Through the smoke, large cracks were forming in the tiles. As the smoke cleared, the Reverend saw that a section of floor had been eaten away, revealing a flight of steps leading down.

Nathan patted the bottle as if it were a friend of old. "Never fails."

"Holy water?" guessed the Reverend.

"Acid," said Nathan. "I thought it might come in handy."

"Did you?" threw in Vincent. "That's convenient."

"If there's a problem, Marconi, now's the time."

Vincent pushed himself off the wall. "My problem is that the last time you did this, everyone died except you, how am I doing so far?"

"Vincent," cut in Napoleon. "This isn't the time."

"Of course it's the time. This dinosaur's gonna get us all killed."

Nathan laughed. "Get you killed? You don't need me for that, boy, to be honest, I'm surprised an amateur like you has lasted this long. I wonder how many times Napoleon's covered for your mistakes."

Vincent's face flushed red. To the Reverend, Nathan did not appear the slightest bit concerned by Vincent's building anger; if anything, he seemed to find the whole situation comical.

"Judging by the look on your face," smiled Nathan, "it's quite a few times."

Before anyone could stop him, Vincent was going for his gun. Nathan threw himself across the hole and into Vincent, slamming him against the stone pulpit, the blow forcing him to drop the gun. He jammed his forearm up against Vincent's throat.

"Like I said, I'm surprised you've lasted this long," said Nathan. "You should drop this 'holier than thou' attitude you've been cultivating, you'll live longer."

Vincent stood there for a second as if taking in Nathan's words, before picking up his gun and shoving past him. "Screw you, old man."

ing his flashlight down into the hole, Vincent descended into the darkness.

Chapter Thirty-Five

"Where are they now?"

"Locked in one of the storage rooms in the east wing, Sir," said Reardon.

Dale sighed; if there was a worse case scenario than the one being played out, he was having trouble finding it.

"You said you know one of the men?"

"Yes, sir, his name is Luther Washington. He was one of my instructors," clarified Reardon. "I think you should listen to what he has to say."

"I have a meeting of the highest importance taking place within the hour, do you really think I have the time to talk to a man whose presence here is questionable to say the least?"

"Sir, do I have your permission to speak freely?"

Dale nodded.

"I've known Agent Washington for years and if he says that the Secretary General and the UN members she's meeting with are in danger, then I would believe him."

The worst case scenario was rapidly moving from bad to nuclear. No one was supposed to know Jane was here, let alone who she was meeting, save a few trusted people; certainly not some rogue TORCH agent

"Did he tell you how he knew about this meeting?"

"I would have thought, Monsieur Beddings, that it was obvious."

Philippe Chardon appeared at the entrance to the auditorium to Dale's left; Secretary General Morton was two steps behind him. Dale bit back a hasty reply which could have cost him his position, Chardon held a lot of sway. Jane trusted him, sometimes a little too much for Dale's liking.

"As soon as I heard the report of Washington's capture, I began briefing Jane on my own investigations into his recent behaviour."

Dale stiffened at Chardon's less than professional way of addressing the Secretary General of the United Nations.

"Washington is a traitor," stated Philippe. "A traitor of the highest calibre."

"Bullshit!" yelled Reardon.

"You would do well to curb that kind of outburst," suggested Philippe. "That is not the response I expect from people under my command, are we clear, Monsieur?"

"Sir, I request permission to…"

"No, you may not speak freely," said Philippe, raising his voice. "Now, I suggest you take your men and return to your patrol, Washington and his friend may have accomplices, find them."

"Sir, my men and I have just come off duty."

"Then the sooner you complete this patrol, the sooner you can return to being off duty, now get out of my sight before you don't even have a job to come back to!"

Dale could see Reardon was boiling with rage, and for a moment wondered, or rather hoped Chardon's tantrum would be answered with a right hook. He was both relieved and disappointed to see good sense win out. Reardon's face took on a kind of distanced look and he curtly nodded to Chardon.

"I'll go and wake the men, sir," he said, turning and striding swiftly down the corridor, Dale guessed before his temper could get the better of him.

"Forgive me," said Philippe. "My people are usually not so discourteous."

Jane smiled, squeezing his arm. "That's fine, Philippe, but did you have to be so hard on him?"

"Discipline among the subordinates is crucial, otherwise anarchy is allowed a free hand, do you not agree, Monsieur Beddings?"

"Save the debate on ethics for another time, Chardon," said Dale. "For now, I'll settle for an explanation of how you can accuse one of your own men of treason?"

"I did not intend sharing this information until I was sure of its authenticity, but recent events have changed that stance," he began. "I still hope my investigations will be proved inaccurate, as I have no wish to see a good man's career in ruins and his freedom stripped from him."

"We understand, Philippe," said Jane "Please go on."

Dale folded his arms; Chardon's opening salvo of emotion had fallen on deaf ears.

"I have proof that for some years now, Washington has been in league with the rogue agency you have come here to discuss," said Philippe. "Yes, Monsieur Beddings, Jane had told me everything and it sickens me to think such a thing has being going on under my nose, and it seems, under the noses of several of my predecessors. I have accepted full responsibility and have offered my resignation."

"Which has, of course, been refused," pointed out Jane.

"For which you have my thanks," said Philippe. "I also believe that Washington masterminded the destruction of the research centre in which Pemrose was killed."

"I've seen the report on that explosion. I thought your main suspect was a professional thief?" said Dale, trying to find a chink in Chardon's armour he could exploit.

"Yes," agreed Philippe. "And I still believe it was this thief, who calls himself The Hand, who is responsible, but the evidence suggests Washington paid him to carry out the attack."

"These are some serious accusations, Chardon, I hope you can back them up," warned Dale.

"Oh, I think I can," said Chardon. "The man Washington was caught with heading towards this location is The Hand himself."

Before Dale could be allowed to let Chardon's bombshell sink in, he was hit with a second blow. "I also have proof that he is Washington's half-brother."

"Jesus," was all Dale found to say.

"These men pose a significant threat to your meeting," stressed Philippe. "Which is why I have left instructions that no one is to have contact with the prisoners. Once your meeting is concluded, they will be transferred to our most secure holding facility for interrogation and eventually to stand trial for their crimes."

At that moment, Dale paused and pressed a finger against the small transmitter lodged in his right ear. "Ok, I'll let her know."

"What is it, Dale?"

"The members are ten minutes from touching down on the roof."

"Excellent," said Jane. "Philippe, it's time."

"Of course, Jane, I understand," replied Philippe, turning to leave.

Dale took hold of Chardon's upper arm, before he knew what he was doing. "You just drop this time bomb in our laps and you're leaving us to deal with it?"

Dale felt Jane's hand on his shoulder. "It's ok, Dale, Philippe is returning to TORCH Headquarters on my say so."

Dale released Chardon, without a word of apology.

"Dale, I need to convince a room full of people that TORCH has been infiltrated and has been used to fund unspeakable crimes for decades," explained Jane. "I'm going to have a difficult enough time as it is, without having the head of TORCH there beside me."

Although Dale hated the idea of being left with a mess not of his choosing or making, he was forced to see the sense in Jane's argument.

"I demand the right to interview the prisoners before the other members of the Security Council arrive."

"I am afraid I cannot allow that, you may be willing to risk the lives of Jane and her colleagues for your own curiosity, but I am not."

"I guess you're right," Dale relented.

"I understand your frustrations, my friend," admitted Philippe, patting his arm. "And although it goes against protocol, once both men have been placed within a more secure facility, I will allow you to interview both of them at your leisure."

For once, Dale was taken aback by Chardon's offer.

"Thank you, I appreciate that, Chardon," said Dale, before realising what he was saying.

Philippe offered his hand to Beddings, who shook it, more out of shock than anything else. "Please, my friend, it's Philippe, and now I really must go, my transport is waiting."

Philippe then shook Jane's hand and smiled. "Jane, I wish you every success in your meeting. I hope the other Security Council members open their eyes to this disturbing truth, as mine have been."

"I hope so too, Philippe," confessed Jane. "When I return from this meeting, we will have a lot to discuss, you and I."

Philippe wished he could have captured the look on Beddings' face as he branded Washington a traitor. The shocked expression would look exquisite framed and hung on his office wall. It would be a fitting tribute to those who sought to outmanoeuvre him. He had left Jane to her fantasy of fighting the good fight. She was soon about to get a lesson in power, delivered with such force that the whole world would hear it. Generations of the Cabal had planned and manoeuvred for this day, did she really think she could oppose that? The Cabal's almost inexhaustible fountain of knowledge terrified Philippe.

It had been them who had arranged for Elijah Barrington to employ The Hand to recover the disk from Pemrose. Philippe had believed at the time this decision was made because The Hand alone possessed the skills to enter the research centre undetected. He later discovered that this assumption was wrong and that it had to be The Hand, and no one else that entered the research centre. Aside from the damning family ties to The Hand, a paper trail had been laid linking Luther not only to the explosion, but also the murder of two agents that he had sent to Tokyo, the unexpected icing on the cake. Of course, it had been the Cabal who ordered their deaths. Everyone would believe Luther arranged their murder to cover up his involvement in the destruction of the research centre.

After the upcoming events of today, one third of the UN Security Council would be wiped out. Unlike other attacks of this magnitude, there would be no terrorist group to claim responsibility. It would then be up to members of the Book of Cademus, who were highly placed in governments around the world. They would become agents of chaos, sowing the seeds of distrust amongst their chosen governments. The process would take years, but eventually, the world would be plunged into a second cold war. With the promise of mutually assured destruction hanging over their heads, the people of the world would cry out for the voice of reason; that voice would belong to Oliver Cademus.

"I'm telling you for the last time, it's real!"

"You continue to say that, Bill," said George. "I continue to disagree, especially as the facts behind the basis of your argument are flimsy at best."

"Flimsy?" laughed Bill, cradling his mug containing one last mouthful of coffee. "Sometimes, I really do worry about you, George."

Bill and George were sat in the self-contained section within the security building. It was a simple enough arrangement: three members of the security staff were locked inside the bunker for twelve hours at a time, provided with all the essential facilities, but were not allowed to leave the bunker and no one was allowed entry until their shift was over. The main door was made from reinforced steel, and could only be opened by entering a six digit code, which changed with each new shift.

To have such a section was usual amongst many of the TORCH installations, but out here in the middle of Antarctica, it was overkill, in Bill's opinion. The only threat out here was the occasional penguin straying too close to the security fence, which then had to be rescued before it got fried.

"What's that?" said George, pointing at the screen in front of him. The footage from one of the cameras showed several figures moving just outside the security fence.

"Could be a patrol," offered Bill.

"Patrols don't usually come in through one of the side fences."

Bill looked closer. The men were all crouched along the length of one section of the security fence; they were also carrying automatic weapons.

"Jesus!" said a shocked Bill, moving for the phone.

"They're just sitting there, what are they waiting for?"

"For me."

Instead of carrying a tray of two coffees and George's hot chocolate as promised earlier, the third member of the security team stood in the doorway holding a Beretta fitted with a silencer. Two headshots later, and both men were dead, the winner of the argument they were having would forever now remain a mystery. The third member of the team shoved George's corpse out of his seat, and after taking his position at the console, he began to deactivate the security systems. He glanced at his watch and smiled to himself, they were ahead of schedule.

Dave Reardon led his team out to where their snowmobiles were parked. He was angry about being sent back out on duty, but he was even angrier for bringing the same fate down on the heads of his team. He knew they did not blame him, but it went without saying that Chardon had not made any friends today. He almost wished he had kept quiet about Luther's theory: almost. Once his patrol was over, he had decided to try talking to Beddings again. If what Luther was saying was true, then something very big was about to go down, and they were far from equipped to deal with the situation.

"Sir, Look!"

One of his men was pointing at the area in front of him. Following the man's hand, Reardon counted at least ten armed men moving in single file, silently through a hole in the security fence. Reardon threw off the shock at what he saw and was already pulling the rifle from his shoulder.

"This is what we're going to do," he began.

Too late, he noticed the man at the head of the intruders, who, seeing Reardon and his men, made two hand signals to those following him. At once, the men ran into pre-arranged attack positions, all dropping to one knee and taking aim.

"Oh shit," were Reardon's last words as the first salvo of suppressed gunfire tore through his uniform.

Luther paced back and forth in the small storage room. Here he was, the supposed rescuer of the UN, taken out like a first-year trainee. He had tried reasoning with Reardon during the journey to the centre, but his attempts came to nothing. He should have known better than to try, Reardon was just following orders, after all, that was what Luther had trained him to do. The worst of it was that he did not know how much time he had, or what was happening while he was stuck here. For all he knew, the Secretary General and the council members could already be dead. He still didn't understand how they had been found. Steph should have spotted the patrol and been able to warn them with more than enough time to spare. The more Luther thought about it, the less sense it made.

Ben, unlike him, seemed unfazed by his capture. He had joked and laughed all the way into the compound, in spite of the restraints and the weapons trained on him. At first, Luther thought he was trying to keep the soldiers off balance, waiting for their guard to drop. However, watching Ben stretched out on the floor, his coat drawn over him like a blanket, his snores filling the room, Luther came to the conclusion that there was no plan.

He kicked Ben's thigh hard. "You awake?"

Ben yawned and sat up rubbing his leg. "I am now. I should have you done for police brutality."

"I'm not in the police."

"I know, but TORCH brutality doesn't sound as catchy."

"No more games, Ben, not now. A lot of people are going to die unless we can get out of here."

"Don't worry, I've got a plan."

"Another plan?" laughed Luther. "Take a good look around you, this is where your last plan got us."

Ben looked at his watch, ignoring Luther. "Not another plan, you muppet, the same one."

"Oh, because that one worked out so well," said Luther, sweeping his hand around the storage room.

"That was part A and…" Ben pointed at the door handle, which had started to turn. "Here comes part B."

The door swung open and in the doorway stood one of the patrol members. Luther looked at the label on the uniform. It read Corman, the scout who had discovered their shelter. Corman came into the room and threw down a large duffel bag. He removed his hood, revealing long blond hair, which was tied into a bunch.

"We don't have a lot of time, on my way over here, I saw a chopper coming in to land on the roof."

"The Security Council members?" asked Ben.

"That would be my guess, whatever's going to happen, it's going to happen soon."

"Stephanie?" asked Luther, recognising the voice. "Is that you?"

Steph nodded. "Yes, it's me. Now we have to move we don't have long before they get here."

"But, but you're…"

"Yes I am. Now if you're finished, we need to leave right now."

"What the hell's going on?" demanded Luther as Steph led the way out of the cell and into the corridor, stepping over the two unconscious guards who lay on either side of the storage door.

"Listen, we don't have the time to…"

"You let them catch us."

"Nothing gets past you, Sherlock," said Ben with a smirk.

"And you didn't tell me because you wanted my reaction to the capture to be normal, right?"

Steph and Ben exchanged glances. "No," they said in unison.

"One, we don't trust you," said Ben. "And two, you would have thrown out a hundred useless reasons why an obvious plan like this wouldn't work."

"Fair point," conceded Luther. "But that still doesn't explain why Steph is..."

"Part C," cut in Steph, patting the duffel bag she was carrying.

Chapter Thirty-Six

Dale waited for the helicopter containing the seven Security Council members to land. He had left Jane in the auditorium along with four of his men. She had made it clear that she was far from happy about the arrangement. She had been the one who had asked them to come here in secret, without any explanation, the least she could do was to be there to greet them in person when they arrived. After much persuading from Dale, she relented and allowed him to take over the initial meet and greet duties.

The helicopter touched down on the roof. Dale shielded his eyes as he walked through the barrage of ice and snow being thrown up by the rotor blades. The helicopter door opened and Dale readied his best smile. He spotted the British Ambassador, waiting for him just inside the door. One look at the man's pale face and terror-filled eyes left Dale in no doubt something was wrong. He held back on taking any direct action, deciding to gain more information first.

"Hello again, Ambassador Fredrick," he said, shaking Fredrick's gloved hand. "Dale Beddings, sir, we met a few months ago at a charity banquet for UNICEF."

The Ambassador barely registered the greeting. Dale directed a casual glance over the ambassador's shoulder and counted six armed men behind the other members. It would take some serious marksmanship to get any of the attackers without hitting at least one innocent person.

"You can see your position Mr. Beddings," said one of the men, "I hope you won't give us any trouble."

"What do you want?"

"Secretary General Morton, where is she?"

Dale thought through his next words, he needed to buy time. "You know I can't tell you that, but if you..."

"Too bad," replied the man, firing a silencer round into Dale's forehead.

Dale's head snapped back, his body following, he was dead before he hit the ground.

Sirus traced his index finger under the last paragraph of words, and took a sharp intake of breath at what they represented.

"That which was sundered shall become whole once more, so as it was, so shall it be. The sleeper shall awake."

A heaviness settled on him, the likes of which he had never known. It was as if he felt the burden of generations of the Cabal, all their planning and hopes now rested with him.

Sirus closed and locked the container in which sat one of Sir Oliver's journals. The castle library held the other writings of their legendary founder, but at the moment, this particular volume was the most important. The journal detailed the steps needed to perform the ritual of restoration, though Sir Oliver had saw fit not to divulge where he had obtained such arcane knowledge.

Sirus knew if they were successful in their endeavours tonight, it would change the very nature of mortality. The greatest experiment any human had ever dared attempt, save in the realm of fiction, was about to come to fruition. Sir Oliver's dream was to grasp the hand of God; to pull himself so far up the evolutionary ladder as to stand beside the Almighty himself. If everything his predecessors sought to put into place was successful tonight, then Sirus would be able to talk to the man himself. The thought was intoxicating, like touching living history. There were so many questions to ask: would Sir Oliver have been aware of the passage of time? What extraordinary abilities had been developed as he lay dormant, storing the Earth's energy? At least they now had Jacob Covenant's descendant in their possession. Sirus had promised himself, on seeing Jason in that first shared mind link at his university, that once Sir Oliver was awakened, he would slit the boy's throat as a gift to Sir Oliver, and finally ending Jacob Covenant's traitorous line.

"We have a problem," said Justine, coming up behind Sirus.

"The entrance to the catacombs has been comprised."

"I've only just received the call myself, how did you know?"

Sirus chuckled inwardly. Justine was young in terms of her time as a member of the Cabal, and as such, she still relied on more traditional information gathering methods, whereas he and the others had more powerful tools at their command, which, in time, she would come to discover.

"Tell me, how did you find out?" asked Sirus, ignoring the earlier question.

"Some of the people of the village near the chapel are loyal to us. One of them reported that his eldest son saw four strangers enter the church, he said one of the men…"

"Had one eye," finished Sirus. "So the Icarus Foundation plans to interfere with the ritual; an annoyance, but an expected one. Go and rest, Justine, you will need it for tonight."

Justine stood her ground. "Are you mad, Crane? Did you hear what I just said? We have intruders, very capable intruders; we need to take steps."

"And what do you suggest, Justine?"

"We should gather the others and summon the mind creature," replied Justine.

"You convinced me to use the creature against John and Mary, I will not be swayed a second time."

The mere mention of the creature born from Sir Oliver himself was enough to darken Sirus' mood. He had always been against the misuse of Sir Oliver's mind in this way, but the others had convinced him time and again it was the only way. He did not think Sir Oliver would see it that way upon his return, if he remembered anything from before his awakening. Sirus hoped for the sake of himself and the other members of the Cabal that he did not.

"I will not risk a summoning when we are this close. We will need all our strength for the ritual. If our power or resolve lessen by a fraction, we will fail, and everything that we hope to achieve will be lost."

"In my experience, men like Napoleon Stone should never be left to their own devices," argued Justine.

"If they are using the catacombs, they will not be alone for long."

"That's enough!" shouted Greiger.

But the order came too late, unlike the blow delivered by Sanderson, his second in command. The backhand caught Jane full in the face, causing her to sink back into the arms of the two men that held her. They hoisted her upright, she was dazed but conscious. Greiger could see Sanderson considered it far from enough as he wiped the blood from a deep cut over his left eye.

Greiger shoved Sanderson out of the way. "You know our orders; she is not to be harmed, for now."

Greiger, together with four of his men, had forced his way into the conference room. He ordered the men to herd the UN members taken from the helicopter into the room. Morton had managed to get a punch off before being restrained.

Greiger saw the murderous gleam in Sanderson's eyes as he stood staring at Morton, who returned the look with a smile. Greiger glared at her, looking for some sign of weakness in the woman, to his surprise he found none. He was impressed, but orders were orders and he was being paid a great deal of money to follow his.

The operation was simple enough and the men he was supplied with were at the top of their game. Everything so far had gone according to plan. They had seized control of the helicopter without incident; the cost, two dead pilots and the security team guarding it, nothing they had not anticipated.

By now, his second team would have entered on foot and neutralised any resistance. Their next objective would be the placing of explosive charges throughout the three buildings. When complete, they would all be linked to the detonator he carried. Greiger could not wait to see the fireworks. There was just one loose end left to tie up.

"Sir, do you read?" a voice crackled through his earpiece.

"Yes I'm here. Have you found Washington and Ashodi?"

"No, sir," came the reply Greiger did not want to hear. "They've escaped."

"Take three men and find them," ordered Greiger. "Let the others finish planting the explosives, nothing must interfere with that."

Typical, thought Greiger, he knew everything was going too well. Their employers had contacted them during their flight with the captured UN members, to tell them about the thief and the TORCH agent caught trying to break into the base. Greiger had been offered a bonus if he killed the two men. It seemed now that the bonus was going to be a little harder to earn than he first thought.

"Problem?" smiled Jane.

"You would do well to worry about yourself, Secretary General."

"I would if I knew what was about to happen to us," she replied, apparently unimpressed by Greiger's threatening words.

"A fair question, which should be answered in kind," responded Greiger. "As you are no doubt aware, we are in control of this installation. Explosive charges are being planted throughout this base, and when complete, we will lift off and allow the explosives to do our work for us."

"Why the grand death-trap? Seems a little over dramatic to me, why not shoot us right now?"

"Believe me, I like this even less than you do, but my employers were very specific," explained Greiger.

"So really, you're nothing but a hired thug?"

Greiger pushed his gun up under Jane's chin, his eyes reflecting the anger behind them.

"Be thankful I'm a thug who does what he's paid to do."

"Be thankful I won't live long enough to tell everyone what a bad taste in aftershave you have."

It was one thing to be defiant in the face of one's enemy, but Morton's behaviour bordered on suicidal. The Jane Morton that Greiger had studied before leading this mission was self-assured and confident, but this was more than that. He became even more concerned when he stared into her eyes.

"Tell me, Secretary General, when did you start wearing contacts?"

A smile, brimming with malice played across Jane's lips.

"Well spotted."

Suddenly, Greiger realised what was happening, but unluckily for him, so had Jane. She threw her head back as Greiger squeezed the trigger. The bullet meant for her brain sailed upwards, punching into the ceiling. Despite the suddenness of the movement, Geiger reacted with equal speed. He aimed his gun at Jane's forehead, who swatted his gun arm aside as he fired, the shot whistling past her ear. Seizing his wrist, Jane twisted it in a clockwise motion. She winked as she applied a final burst of pressure, gratefully receiving the sound of Greiger's wrist breaking. The sound was muffled by the three uppercuts she drove up into his side. Greiger felt one of his ribs give way under the combined force of the blows. Dazed more by the shock of what was happening than the pain, he toppled sideways, allowing his head to fall into Jane's waiting hands. Without any apparent emotion or, it seemed, effort, Jane shot her left hand forward whilst pulling her right hand back, taking Greiger's head, but not his body, with her. The inevitable sound of a neck being broken was not only new to the ears of the UN Ambassadors, it would also be a sound most of them would take to their graves, along with the look of astonishment forever etched on Greiger's face as he slumped to the floor.

Sanderson was struck dumb. Greiger was one of the toughest mercenaries he knew. He had been killed, with ease, by an unarmed civilian, who moments earlier, Sanderson had taken great pleasure in striking and threatening with death. The hand of fear settled on the back of his neck, caressing the hairs it found there and he froze. His men, however, had no such concern for their own lives, and were already bringing their weapons to bear on the woman.

"I wouldn't…"

Sanderson was reduced to the role of spectator, forced to look on as his remaining men were bought down by shots coming from the darkened balcony behind Jane. One man, taking a bullet through the forehead, which made its bloody exit through the base of his skull, died before his brain had time to register the event. The second man had been slightly less fortunate than his colleague, as a bullet creased a path along the side of his neck. He was now on his knees, hurling curses into thin air as he tried to stop the blood spilling through his hands, which now pressed against the wound. Another round slammed into the man's forehead, putting aside any thoughts of anyone dispensing medical assistance.

"…do that," finished Jane.

Sanderson made no attempt to move, allowing his eyes to search the auditorium; it was not long before his search was rewarded. Up in the balcony facing him, he saw a man whose features were partially obscured by the gun sight he was looking through. Sanderson did not need to see a laser sight to know who the sniper's next target would be. He pulled his gun slowly from its holster and let it drop to the floor.

Jane looked at the gun then back at Sanderson. "That's no way for a solider to go out."

She craned her head back towards the balcony behind her.

"Stand down, I'll take care of this."

Sanderson watched the sniper place the gun by his side and place both hands on the balcony rail where he could see them.

"Just you and me now," Jane pointed out.

Sanderson threw a quick look in the direction of his gun before turning back to her.

"You want that, don't you?" she asked, pointing at the gun.

Sanderson remained silent, his eyes once more scanning the auditorium. Morton would not throw away her only advantage unless there was another trap waiting to be sprung.

Jane's words cut through his thoughts. "I know what you're thinking, why would she throw away her only advantage, unless she had something else lined up?"

Sanderson scowled, but did not voice his agreement with her theory, refusing to give her that satisfaction.

"The thing is, I've met men like you, and I know I can beat you."

Again, Sanderson's eyes were drawn to his gun. *Just keeping talking, bitch*, he said to himself.

"The question is whether you believe you're better than me enough to bet your life on it?"

Sanderson was moving for his gun as the last words left Morton's mouth. He realised this was his only window of opportunity. Morton was already moving, but he could not worry about that now, he was committed. His hand snaked around the gun handle and he pictured the bullet ripping the smug grin from Morton's face. As his finger closed around the trigger, he felt like his chest had been hit by a sledge hammer. He fell backwards, his head smacking against the polished floor. He pressed his hand against his chest, lifted it up and stared at the blood covering it. In between the fingers of his bloodied hand, he saw Morton standing over him, gun still in her hand. Even as the blood flowed from his body, he managed a look of shock as she threw off the blond wig she was wearing. She then tugged at her cheek, tearing off huge strips of what looked like latex, until a completely different woman stood over him.

"Who are you?"

"Someone better than you," said Steph, squeezing the trigger.

Chapter Thirty-Seven

Jason awoke refreshed from his first uninterrupted sleep in a long time: no nightmares, no night terrors, just good old-fashioned sleep, even if it had been during the day. He was back in the bedroom chamber where he had been taken upon entering the castle. Hours earlier, he had journeyed through the castle. As prisons go, it was one cloaked in history and grandeur. Jason knew Professor Stone would give anything to spend time here; his fascination, like Jason's, could not help but be held captive by the need to discover the secrets of times long past. It was as if secrets were lodged in every wooden beam, every piece of stone. As he wandered around the library, Crane had found him, after the guards had moved him on from the battlements, and told him the news he was dreading. The ritual of restoration was to take place tonight. Jason was told to go back to his room and wait until called for. With men standing guard outside, Jason searched every inch of the room, trying to find a means of escape. Finally, he collapsed onto his bed in defeat. It was then a wave of exhaustion struck him, and despite every effort to stay awake he eventually succumbed; the thoughts of what was to happen to him that night still uppermost in his mind.

Jason had been woken by the sound of footsteps echoing up the stone staircase that led to his room. He felt his stomach lurch; he had slept far longer than he had intended. The room was now shrouded in darkness, save for the flicker of torchlight carried across from the rooms facing his. So this was it, the moment he had supposedly been born for. Although he still did not entirely believe the Cabal's claims, it was difficult to ignore their conviction.

Jason heard the door being unlocked and moved back against the wall. He began taking deep breaths in an attempt to control his erratic breathing, whilst trying to keep his knees from buckling, taking with them his last shreds of courage. The thought of escape once more flew through his mind and out the other side. This was not some movie or work of escapist fiction, this was reality, and the reality was that there was no escape.

The door opened and Justine walked into the room followed by three men. No longer wearing her trouser suit, she was now adorned in a white satin dress, which flowed to the floor, allowing no part of her to be visible, save her slender neck, courtesy of a plunging neckline. She looked stunning, even if Jason reckoned she was old enough to be his mother. The three men with her were hooded and wearing red robes.

Their heads were bowed, obscuring their faces, a strange sound emanating from them, like a low hum. Men in robes, chanting, were not a good sign of things to come, Jason concluded.

"I take it you like the dress?" smiled Justine.

Jason turned away. He felt ashamed at allowing himself to see her in that way, after everything she had done.

"I never usually go in for them," Justine continued, seeing his discomfort. "I find them far too restrictive and cumbersome, but as one of the Cabal, I must be seen to hold with tradition, a small price to pay, especially on a night like tonight."

Two of the robed figures grabbed Jason as Sirus Crane came into the room. He was robed liked the others, but wore no hood, unlike the other members of the Cabal, who stood silent behind him.

Jason struggled against the two men who held him. Deciding he would not being taken to his death without a fight, he lashed out at one of the men, kicking him as hard as he could in the groin. To his surprise, the man did not flinch.

"It takes a lot for a Knight of Cademus to feel pain," Justine told him. "So either accept your fate with character, or be dragged to it with two broken legs; the choice is yours."

"There is no need for threats," said Sirus. "I'm sure he will be cooperative, isn't that right, Jason?"

"You can't threaten me," protested Jason, sensing some bargaining power. "You kill me and you have no ritual."

Sirus smiled and Jason knew he had made a mistake. A second later, the pain shot through his back as someone punched him in the base of his spine.

Sirus clicked his fingers and looked on as a screaming Jason was dragged past him.

Ben kept watch on the two men guarding the transport helicopter. He was hiding behind the door leading out onto the helipad. The images were being fed to him via a miniature camera attached to a fibre-optic cable, which he had slid under the bottom of the closed door. The men's manner screamed mercenary to Ben, they engaged in very little idle conversation, their minds, no doubt, focused on the task at hand.

The idea of rescuing diplomats and averting an international incident on a global scale was not in their usual repertoire, well not on his, anyway.

He tried not to worry about Steph, but it was difficult. She was unarmed and disguised as Morton. She also faced an unknown number of would-be assassins, whose main target was the person whose likeness she had chosen to emulate.

Ben knew failure here meant no payment, and they could kiss goodbye to any chance of clearing their names. There was, however, a more personal reason for Ben. The destruction of the research centre still played on his mind, he still felt responsible for what had happened. He had nearly walked out on a chance to get some kind of payback for those deaths, mainly, now he thought about it, to spite Luther. He would not do so a second time.

With the aid of the hidden tracking device Ben was wearing, Steph had been able to track them at a distance. In the meantime, Ben had taken great pleasure in watching Luther pass out from the drugged coffee he had given him. He had then sent out a random signal, knowing it would be intercepted by a patrol, before sending Steph a pre-arranged signal. They both hoped that the patrol would follow the procedure as outlined by Luther, and send a scout in first to make sure the patrol was not being led into an ambush. Ben had remained in the shelter pretending to be asleep, Steph lay hidden in the snow some distance away. Now came the tricky part, they had to allow the scout to put in his radio report before making their move as it was imperative that the patrol suspected nothing. Fortunately, the scout followed orders and made his report, one tranquilliser dart later, fired from Steph's sniper rifle and he was down. They then both placed the guard in a hole Ben had dug inside the shelter. The hole was then covered by the ground sheet and Ben's sleeping bag. The unconscious scout had been fitted with a breathing mask to keep him alive. Steph had suggested killing the guard as it was too risky to leave him alive, but Ben had convinced her otherwise. Thanks to Luther, they knew what clothes would have been issued to the security team, so that was easy enough to replicate. Fortunately, luck was with them as the man was around Steph's height and was of average build. It was a simple matter to allow the patrol to lead her into the base and to slip away. She had waited until Reardon had gone to report in before she began her search for Ben and Luther. After finding and freeing them, they all headed for the auditorium, where Steph had earlier located Morton. Not bothering with the niceties of trying to bluff their way through the four security agents guarding her, they made short work of them before handcuffing and hiding their unconscious bodies in a nearby storage room, drugging them to ensure their continued silence. They then tried to convince the Secretary General that they were here to help her. It was a difficult concept for her to grasp, especially when the first act of her supposed saviours was to remove those charged with her protection. Only when Ben mentioned his connection to Pemrose did Morton begin to take any notice. To her credit, Morton had taken it all in her stride, and to Ben's continued surprise, actually believed their story, though they refrained from lingering on the supernatural elements of the story.

All Ben could do now was wait and hope they had not underestimated the size or commitment of their enemy. Steph was one of the few friends Ben had in his life. She was his family and if anything…

"It's me."

Steph's voice came through his earpiece as clear as if she were crouched beside him. Ben took a moment to let the relief wash over him. He would never let on how concerned he was, Steph did not handle the touchy feely stuff well, and she would never let him live it down.

"You there?" Steph called again.

"I'm here. Is everyone ok?"

"Well, if you call three men dead ok, I guess everything's fine."

Ben felt a nudge in his ribs.

"What part of stay back and stay out of sight didn't you understand?" Ben asked.

Secretary General Morton was crouched just behind Ben, who was angry at himself for not hearing her come up the stairs. He knew he had to bring her along, two Jane Mortons would have been difficult to explain, but her constant questioning found Ben wishing he had left her behind. However, he was impressed with the way she dealt with the body of her head of security being discovered dumped at the bottom of the stairs behind some equipment. She merely told Ben who the man was and suggested they moved on. Ben could tell the death had hit her hard, and the tears and grief would come later.

"I understood you just fine," said Jane. "Now, if that's your colleague, I want an appraisal of the situation."

Ben blew the air out of his cheeks, culminating in a loud sigh; it was a good job they were getting well paid for this. "The other UN members are fine, Jane."

Ben caught the look. "Sorry, Secretary General," he blurted out quickly, at the same time wondering if she was related to Steph in some way.

"Excellent, then the next course of action is to secure the transport helicopter."

"Actually, I thought we'd just sit here for the fun of it," said Ben. "You political types. You really know how to state the bloody obvious."

Jane's lips curled into a vicious snarl. "And you really have no manners."

"Never had the time for them, love."

"When you're ready," Steph's voice shouted angrily through the earpiece.

"Sorry, you'd better start hauling them up here. I'll sort the transport out. Watch yourself, we don't know if there's anyone else left in the building."

"Same to you."

Ben turned to Jane, holding both hands in front of him. "Stay here." He spoke the words as if he were talking to an infant; the added hand gestures to emphasize his point did little to endear him to Jane, who he could tell was moments away from smacking him.

"Fine," she managed, to force through her gritted teeth.

Ben moved back to the door and once more checked the image provided by his miniature camera. Both men were now stood directly in front of the helicopter, a few feet apart. Ben picked up the tranquilliser gun that had been placed on the ground next to his camera, and backed up to the foot of the stairs. He pressed his thumb down on the detonator, triggering the tiny explosives placed against the door lock and the hinges. Given the time, Ben would have tried a more subtle approach, but as he shoulder barged the door, he knew there was a time for subtlety and a time for complete stupidity. The door hit the ice-covered roof and was sent sailing across it with Ben laying face down on it. The two mercenaries turned and fired on the unexpected threat. Gunfire tore the ice from around Ben as he slid towards the helicopter. Ben's aim, despite his disgust at having to use a firearm was perfect and both men were hit with several small darts. The toxin contained within the darts was instantaneous, causing both men to sink to the floor unconscious.

The door came to a stop. Ben rolled onto his back and let out a proud sigh of contentment. "Damn, I'm good."

Napoleon's torch sliced a thin beam through the dust and cobwebs of the darkened passage. Even with its horrific past, this castle, these catacombs were a window on history, a place where legends were formed; a place of awe. Ever the academic, Napoleon wished there was time to study the catacombs and the castle beyond more thoroughly. He placed a hand on one of the stone gargoyles that adorned the walls. A research team from the Foundation could spend years down here and still not fully take in everything this place had to offer.

They had been moving north through the tunnels for some time before entering the catacombs themselves, and so far, the journey had been without incident. Napoleon could not only feel tenseness within himself, but he also saw it in the others. They all kept their weapons to hand, expecting danger at every corner turned, or sound heard. There was something about the catacombs which disturbed them all, something unseen, it was a feeling that could not easily be put into words.

"How much further?" asked Vincent.

Napoleon watched Nathan look down at the copy of a map he had managed to obtain during his time at Haven. According to Nathan, the map was around nine hundred years old. It had supposedly been drawn by someone who had escaped the castle; it showed the interior of catacombs they were travelling through as well as the upper levels of the castle. The logical conclusion was that the map had once belonged to Jacob Covenant himself.

"Not much further," said Nathan, pointing ahead. "This passage breaks into a large chamber, from there, we'll need to climb up into another passageway that should lead us into one of Cademus' private chambers."

"You sure you can lead us to where this ritual will be carried out?" called out the Reverend, who was at the rear, and constantly looking back to ensure nothing was following them.

"No, I'm not sure, now stay close and be ready."

"Ready for what?" said Napoleon.

"Covenant wrote a name under the chamber we're about to go into. He called it the Mirror of The Damned."

"What's in it?" asked Vincent.

"I have no idea."

"No idea," repeated Vincent, his voice an angry whisper. "I thought you were an expert on this place."

"You thought wrong." Without another word, Nathan started forward again.

"You sure we should be doing this, boss?" asked Vincent.

"Unless you have a better suggestion, we stick to the plan," said Napoleon.

"Could be the last plan we ever stick to."

Napoleon did not answer. He had been so busy talking to Vincent and not looking at his surroundings that he had failed to notice the huge cavern they were now entering.

"Turn off your lights," ordered Nathan, staring at the cavern walls. "You won't need them."

They all complied, though Vincent hesitated at first. For a few moments, nothing, then slowly, the room began to grow brighter; at first Napoleon thought it was his vision becoming accustomed to the darkness, but then he realised what was happening. The walls themselves were glowing, or to be more accurate, the fissures in the rock were giving off a luminous orange hue, which in turn bathed the whole chamber in light.

"Welcome to the Mirror of The Damned," announced Nathan.

Chapter Thirty-Eight

Vincent followed the others into the chamber. He felt the gentle breeze that had been blowing against his back suddenly stop. He turned to see a solid wall where the entrance to the chamber had been. He walked over to the wall and touched it to make sure what he was seeing was real.

"Hey, you should see…"

Vincent turned again, this time to find he was alone. Looking around, the only exit from the cavern he could see was up. There was no way the others could have climbed that high in a matter of seconds.

"Napoleon! Rev!" he called out, only to find the names echoed back to him unanswered.

This was impossible; three men could not disappear from a sealed room. Vincent knew he could not stand here waiting for them to reappear, though he was unsure what he could achieve alone. He crossed the chamber to the wall facing him. After picking out a few natural handholds, he was confident he could scale the cavern wall without breaking his neck. He took hold of the first handhold and readied himself for the climb ahead.

"Vincent, where are you going?"

Vincent froze, his eyes fixed on the wall in front of him, his emotions tearing at him, willing him to turn around, but he fought the impulse because the voice he was hearing could not exist.

"Vincent, I'm talking to you, at least have the decency to look at me when I'm talking to you, young man."

Vincent took his hand away from the rock, swung around and drew his guns. What he saw opened up a well of grief within him and he dropped his weapons, tears filling his eyes.

"Mum?"

The Reverend backed up against the wall, the rational part of his mind was already closing in on itself. The thing had appeared soon after the others had vanished. It had stepped out from one of the fissures of light. At first, he was nearly blinded by the light enveloping the creature, but slowly the light faded and he was left gazing upon the one thing he desired above everything else.

"You're not Maria," he said at last.

"You should never have left us, Napoleon, you had such potential."

"You're not here, Paul, you don't exist," said Napoleon, unconvinced by the man who had appeared before him seconds earlier. "You're a figment of my imagination."

"Like the eye patch, by the way," said Paul, taking a step towards Napoleon. "It's a nice touch, adds to the whole package, but then, that was your dream wasn't it, Napoleon, to save people? The question is, why couldn't you save yourself?"

"When did you stop cutting your hair?" asked Vincent's mother. "You know I liked it when you kept it short and tidy. This," she ran her fingers through Vincent's hair. "This, makes you look like you should be in a rock band or something."

Vincent opened his mouth, but there were no words to convey his emotions. Whatever was standing in front of him making scathing remarks about his appearance, it was not his mother. Sophia Marconi had died when he was nineteen, killed in a road accident. It had been that event which had sent his life spiralling out of control. In the years following, he had tried to blot out the memory, but now the sight of his mother brought all those painful memories back. He tried to force his mind to accept the fact that this was not his mother. He shut his eyes and pictured her gravestone in his mind, attempting to use the image as an anchor to reality. When he opened his eyes, his mother was holding her arms out to him.

"I know you don't believe it, Vincent," said Sophia. "But it is me. I would never lie to you, son. You know that. You have to believe me."

"You're not my mother," Vincent's voice was shaky, filled with self doubt.

"You know I would never hurt you," said Maria. "But it is me. I would never lie to you, Jonathan. You know that. You have to believe me."

"Don't call me that," said the Reverend.

"Why? It's who you are?"

Maria reached out to touch his face.

"No!" the Reverend stepped back, out of Maria's reach. "I'm not that man anymore."

"Because of me?" asked Maria, tears welling in her eyes.

"Because of you."

"But I'm here now, Jonathan," she said, walking towards him. "I don't care who you are or what you've become. I still love you and I know you still love me."

"I still love Maria," admitted the Reverend. "But you are not her, you cannot be."

Maria held out her arms. "Can't I be, Jonathan?" she asked. "Are you really that content with your life? Would you throw away what we had and can have again because you lack faith in the unbelievable? That's not the Jonathan I remember."

The Reverend stared at every facet of Maria's face and body, looking for some telltale sign she was not who she claimed to be. He looked at her standing there, arms opened to him and before he could rationalize what he was doing, he was sinking into her embrace.

"You're dead," he said, the tears flowing unrestrained for the first time in years. "You're dead."

"Ask yourself, Napoleon, if I'm dead and you're talking to me, what does that say about your state of mind?"

"There's nothing wrong with my state of mind," said Napoleon. "It's this place that's affected my mind, creating false images."

"Do you still feel it?" Paul was pointing to the eye patch. "I always used to wonder what it would be like to lose an eye, I suppose that's why I had yours removed, I was a little disappointed to be honest, but I guess imagination is so much better than reality." Paul leaned in until he was inches from Napoleon's ear. "But then you know all about that, don't you, Napoleon."

"They believed in you, Paul, they trusted you," Napoleon threw back. "And you took that belief and twisted it."

The words spilled out of Napoleon's mouth before he could stop himself. He was beginning to feel his resolve weakening; he was sliding deeper into the illusion facing him, coming to regard it more and more as a living entity.

"Ever the romantic scholar, eh, Napoleon?" chuckled Paul. "You always used to see things so clearly, I wonder if you still do with only one eye. I offered them a family, a place where they could feel loved, where they could believe in something far greater than they knew and be made stronger by that belief."

"What you did to that boy didn't look like faith to me, more like cold blooded murder."

"Everything we do has consequences, Napoleon,"

"Consequences you've had to live with all this time, Vincent, on your own," said Sophia. "Not any more, not now I'm here."

Vincent stepped away from his mother. "Consequences, what consequences? What are you talking about, Mum?"

Sophia smiled and gave that look Vincent remembered so well. She always used to do it when she thought he was lying.

Vincent tried to hold back the images, the red light he did not see, the taxi that came out of nowhere, seeing his short life flash before his eyes, and then the realisation he was still alive. The tears came as he remembered, in his still slightly drunken state, joking with his mum about how his dad would go through the roof when he found out, and wondering why she was not answering.

"I shouldn't have left you," said Vincent, his face wet with tears. "I should have stayed with you."

"I was dead, Vincent," said Sophia hugging her son once more. "They would have arrested you, you had no choice."

"It was you that gave those people no choice, Paul. You allowed them to rely on you for everything, and you betrayed them."

"Don't be so modest, Napoleon, what you really mean is I betrayed you," said Paul. "And tell me, how did you repay my so-called betrayal?"

"This isn't real!"

"Oh, so, when the conversation gets too close to the mark, we're back to the 'I'm not real' argument, how convenient," said Paul. "Maybe I'm not real, maybe I'm that tiny splinter of guilt wedged in your mind as a reminder of what you did."

"I never meant to."

"What? Kill me? Murder me in cold blood?" laughed Paul. "Spare me the false platitudes, those words may allow you to sleep at night, but not here, not with me."

"I was in shock, being treated for depression after what happened, after what you did to me, I was…."

"You're a murderer, Napoleon."

"I'm a murderer, how can you love me now?"

"The Reverend is a murderer, Jonathan," said Maria, stroking his cheek. "But you don't have to be that person anymore."

"The Reverend is all I know," said Jonathan, gazing up at the face of the woman he loved. He could hardly breathe, he was so happy to see her face, to feel the warmth of her breath on his skin, soothing away all his worries. All those years living in the persona of the Reverend, submerged in a world of terror and violence, he had forgotten the face of true beauty. The sight of Maria smiling both uplifted and humbled him. How could he be deserving of the happiness he felt? But as happy as he was, he knew it could not last.

"He has brought me this far," said Jonathan. "I will not abandon the Reverend's work, not even for you, Maria, if you really are Maria."

Fallen Heroes

"What has he made you, Jonathan? A murderer? Is that what you wanted for your life? The man who saved me did not need guns; he did not believe in violence, he was a man who believed in peace."

"That man no longer exists, he died the same night you did."

"Oh, that man still exists, in there," said Paul, extending a finger towards Napoleon's chest. "You just hide him, under a veneer of fighting what you class as evil."

Napoleon fought for control of his mind. This was not real, something was drawing on his memories, his guilt, and turning them against him. The problem was, every time he looked at Paul, all he saw was the man who had destroyed his life.

"Do you remember what you did to me that night?" Paul smiled. "Of course you do, how stupid of me, you planned the whole thing from your hospital bed."

Napoleon tried to hide the regret he was feeling, but it was already too late.

"You came at night. I remember being woken by the sound of footsteps. I went to investigate and there you were."

This isn't real. Napoleon repeated the same phrase over and over again in his mind.

"You tortured me for hours, and you enjoyed every minute of it, even when you took my eye."

"You had to pay for what you did."

"Did my wife and child have to pay as well?" screamed Paul. "Because of them, you're going to stay here and beg for forgiveness for what you put them through."

The smallest of smiles appeared on Napoleon's face, and for the first time since he had seen him, he met Paul's eyes with his own unwavering gaze.

"You can't leave me, Jonathan, not again," pleaded Maria, throwing her arms round his neck. "You have to stay here with me."

The Reverend gently pushed her arms away. "I loved Maria, I would give anything to have her back, but not like this. I don't know what you are, but you are not the woman I loved."

"I'm your mother, Vincent; you can't turn away from me now. I've come here to forgive you."

"I like to think wherever she is, Mum's forgiven me and is proud of what I've chosen to do with my life," said Vincent. "The thing is, I can't forgive myself for what happened."

281

Vincent did not know how, but he was certain this thing was not his mother, something had changed in the last few minutes. It was as if he had been looking at her through a veil, wanting to believe she was, who she claimed to be but now that veil was gone.

"Do you remember what happened that night? What you did?" pleaded Sophia. "Don't make that mistake now, don't leave me."

"You see," said Vincent, fighting back the tears, "the more I listen to you..."

"The more I know you are not the Paul I remember," said Napoleon.

"Oh, so what am I, Napoleon? Still a figment of your imagination?"

"My guess would be the physical manifestation of the power that inhabits this place. You used images from my memories to create the person I'm talking to. Somehow, you were able to make me begin to accept a scenario I knew to be false, and if it were not for the mistake you just made, it might have worked." Napoleon took a step towards Paul, who backed away. "You were created to either keep us here until we're emotional vegetables, or we're driven insane by our own guilt, that ends now."

Another step forward. "You are only as powerful as the power our own guilt gives you, and our belief in the manifestation of that guilt. I know what I did was wrong, and one day I'll have to answer for that crime, but it won't be today, and it won't be to you."

A number of small, spider-like cracks began threading their way across Paul's face, allowing tiny shafts of light to seep out through them.

"You're still lying to yourself, Napoleon, you're a murderer," accused Paul, his voice now tinged with desperation.

"Paul never had a family. I placed the image of his family inside my mind and you took the bait," stated Napoleon. "That fact was indisputable. Any true incarnation of Paul, dead or otherwise, would have known that."

"That's impossible. You're too weak to create a memory powerful enough to fool me," said Paul, though this time, the voice was not his, and it was not human.

"It's amazing what you can do when you set your mind to it."

Napoleon smashed the butt of his shotgun across Paul's face, causing an explosion of light as part of his face shattered. Paul screamed as he covered the wound with his hand.

"What are you?"

"It is still me, Jonathan," screamed Maria, covering the wound that had appeared on her face.

Several more fissures began to open along the length of her body. She held out her hand. "Please help me, Jonathan."

The Reverend backed away from her. "Goodbye."

"Mum."

Vincent shielded his eyes as the thing he called his mother erupted, filling the cavern with a blinding light and showering him with shards of crystal. The light faded, and Vincent was left looking at a dazed Napoleon and Reverend.

"Is everyone ok?" asked Napoleon, brushing shards of crystal off his shoulders.

"You saw her too?" asked Vincent, wiping away his tears before anyone noticed. "Saw my mum?"

"No," said the Reverend. "I saw...I saw..."

The Reverend's voice faltered and he lapsed into silence.

"It's ok," Napoleon told him. "I think I've got a pretty good idea who you saw. We all saw someone different. Mine was a man I kil...murdered years ago."

Vincent heard the word murder, but made no comment; if there was one thing he knew now, it was that they all carried their own demons.

Napoleon saw Nathan standing over to one side, simply staring out into space, saying nothing. He walked over to him and placed a hand on his shoulder and gently shook him.

"Nathan, you still with us?"

For a moment, Nathan continued to stare as if in some kind of trance, then he blinked several times and nearly sank to the floor. Only with Napoleon's help was he able to keep his footing.

"Thanks," he said, regaining his balance. "Please tell me that thing is dead."

Napoleon shrugged. "I'm not sure, but I think it's finished with us."

Vincent saw the haunted look on Nathan's face. "Who did you see?"

"Terror, I saw terror."

Vincent was forced to lean against the cavern wall for support. "Why do I feel like I've just gone ten rounds with an Erogian and he won?"

"I'm guessing," began Nathan, nodding his thanks to Napoleon as he stepped away, "it was feeding on our life essence."

"You mean our souls," corrected the Reverend.

"If you like," conceded Nathan. "If we'd stayed here much longer, none of us would have had the strength to leave."

"Please tell me we're not coming out this way?" asked Vincent, who was beginning to feel more like his old self, though the image of his

mother was still fresh in his mind and would be there, he felt, for some time to come.

"No promises," said Nathan, pointing upwards. "We need to get moving, who knows how much time's been wasted."

Inserting his hand into one of the small fissures in the chamber wall, Nathan pulled himself up and began to climb. Napoleon and Vincent were right behind him. The Reverend, now alone in the chamber, carefully unclasped the small silver crucifix from around his neck. He crouched down on one knee and placed the crucifix on the floor. Closing his eyes, he laid his hand over the crucifix and mouthed a short prayer.

"Goodbye."

"Hey, Rev, you coming or what!" Vincent shouted.

The Reverend stood, took one look at the crucifix, now wet with tears, turned and without another word, began to climb.

Chapter Thirty-Nine

Steph appeared at the doorway to the roof. In her arms, she cradled her M16 as if it were her only friend in the world. Her face appeared calm, but Ben knew exactly what was running through her mind.

Steph would always remind him that this was the time when people got complacent, thinking they were home and dry. This was when mistakes got made and people ended up dead. Ben smiled at her. All he got in return was a curt nod, the scary thing was, with Steph in her full on professional mode, he was lucky to get that.

"Looks like the Calvary's here," he announced.

Steph came forwards, her eyes darting back and forth looking for any sign of trouble.

"Is she always so cautious?" said Jane, watching Steph's controlled and precise movements towards them.

"You have no idea," said Ben wearily.

"Are we clear?" were the first words out of Steph's mouth when she reached Ben. She cast a cautious look over the two guards, almost daring them to wake up.

"You know, sometimes a hello wouldn't go amiss."

The look Ben received in reply told him Steph was in no mood for humour.

"We're clear," he answered in a deflated tone.

He jerked a thumb over his shoulder at the transport helicopter behind him. "Now, you can fly that thing, right?"

Another look.

Obviously, sarcasm was off the list of acceptable behaviour as well.

"I'll fire her up," said Steph, offering the M16 to Ben.

Ben held up his hands and stepped back. "Whoa, what you doing? You know I don't do guns."

"Someone needs to cover the UN members, unless you want to fly the helicopter?"

"Point taken," conceded Ben, taking charge of the offered weapon.

Steph signalled to Luther, who immediately began ushering the UN members onto the roof, pointing them in the direction of the helicopter. Before anyone could stop her, Jane was sprinting over to help calm some of her colleagues, who were starting to panic. Both Ben and Steph stared at Jane as she began talking and pleading for calm.

"Stupid cow," sighed Ben.

"No arguments here," said Steph, as she headed for the helicopter.

She opened the doors to allow people to start getting in before making her way round to the pilot's side.

"Tell your brother I said thanks," she called, climbing in and shutting the door behind her.

"For what?"

But there was no answer. Ben watched her begin to flip switches, and listened as the engine came to life, along with the whine of the rotor blades as they began to turn, picking up momentum with every revolution, until they were a blur.

Ben took on the role of temporary bodyguard as the UN members filed past him to the chopper. He accepted their thanks with a nod, a smile or a one liner if he was quick enough. It was not often people were praising him for something he had done; the experience was unnerving, but not in an unpleasant way.

Luther came running over wearing the look of a man who had just regained his sight and had seen the sunrise for the first time. "I still can't believe you two actually pulled this off."

"Thanks for the vote of confidence," said Ben. "Besides, do you really think I would pass up all that cash by doing something stupid like getting killed?"

"Well, whatever your motives," said Luther, placing a hand on Ben's shoulder, "you did good here today, Mum would have been proud of you."

"Spare me the hearts and flowers speech," snapped back Ben, shrugging off Luther's arm. "Where's Morton?"

"She went to help one of the other Ambassadors; he shouted up to her when she was talking to the others, he twisted his ankle coming up the stairs."

"And you let her go! You bloody idiot!"

"Look, we've neutralised the assassins and Steph swept the building before we moved out," argued Luther. "Besides, Morton gave me an order to go on, and I followed that order, it's called the chain of command, something someone like you wouldn't know anything about!"

"Let me tell you what I do know, shall I, genius? There were seven UN Ambassadors attending this meeting, how about you guess how many I counted getting onto the helicopter."

"Jesus!"

Luther was already turning on his heels, but it was too late.

"Oh, come on, you've got to be having a laugh," sighed Ben.

In the open doorway, a gun in one hand pressed against Morton's temple, the other wrapped around her neck, was the last person Ben expected to see out here, though for some reason, he was not entirely surprised.

"Time to settle your debts, boy," smiled Clancy.

Jason walked up the spiral stone staircase, unsure of where it led or what would happen once he reached its end. His thoughts were on the ritual he was about to take part in. Jason was no authority on black magic or the occult, but he had learnt enough to know that when someone in robes says you're the star attraction at anything with the word ritual in front of it, then it usually ends badly for the star. The idea of a last-minute escape attempt was squashed by the two men who marched on either side of him. They kept in step with him, watching his every move. He looked behind and counted at least another ten men who trailed behind the Cabal, each one clothed in red like his two chaperones.

Jason remained silent, instead choosing to pass the time by counting the steps of the staircase. The procession came to a halt at step four hundred and eighty-five. Before them was an immense oak door. Jason, by this time, was breathing heavily, fitness was never one of his strong points and he hoped the door was not going to lead to another five hundred steps, otherwise his two watchdogs were going to have to carry him the final leg. He watched Sirus walk up to the door, which seemed to have no lock or handle.

"I seek entry into the sanctum of Cademus," Sirus called out.

The moment Sirus had finished speaking, a small inscription began to carve itself into the wood before their eyes.

Sirus drew a knife from his robes and closed his eyes as if tensing for something unpleasant. Jason watched, horrified, as Sirus slowly sliced a diagonal path across his right hand. Sirus' face displayed the pain he was feeling, but he did not cry out. Once finished, he turned again to the door, this time laying his bloodied palm over the inscription. Jason caught Sirus' momentary hesitation before he pushed his hand against it. This time, Sirus' screams swept through the darkened castle.

Napoleon heard the scream from the main hall. They had made good time since leaving the catacombs. After passing through Cademus' private chamber and out into the main hall, they had walked into a small detachment of men who had been left to guard the hall. The fight that followed was brutal and short-lived.

"What was that?" asked the Reverend.

He stepped over the three men he had just killed, to stand beside Napoleon.

"We're running out of time," replied Napoleon, blasting another man who suddenly appeared at the top of the stairs. Nathan was already vaulting over the tumbling corpse as he sprinted up the stairs. Another two men appeared in front of Nathan, surprising him. The first was taken down by a shot from the Reverend, the second toppled screaming over the staircase rail, Vincent's throwing knife jutting from his chest.

"So much for the element of surprise," said Vincent as he tore after the others.

Justine watched as the towering door evaporated before her eyes. In that moment, she became a believer. She dared to dream of the possibilities for herself and the Book of Cademus if the rest of the ritual turned out to be as successful.

Sirus stepped through the doorway, the first time in centuries anyone had done so. Justine and the other members of the Cabal held their ground.

Justine was neither a student nor a fan of history, she preferred to concentrate on her present or future enterprises, but in this place, even her jaded view of the past was rendered useless.

The entire ceiling of the room had been removed, providing her with a magnificent view of the night sky. Carved on the floor were arcane symbols and inscriptions she could not make out, but she felt sure they were the stuff of any historian's dreams. Lining the edge of the chamber were immense, scarlet coloured suits of armour. She walked up to one of them, marvelling at the intricate design of the Cademus family crest emblazoned on its chest. Each one looked about seven or maybe eight feet tall, she could scarcely imagine how heavy the armour would be to lift, let alone wear. What kind of men, if they were indeed men, filled this armor all those years ago, she pondered. Finally, she thought, the coup de grace, a stone altar in the centre of the chamber. Behind the altar, forming a semi-circle around it, were six mirrors, which seemed to be embedded in the floor. On top of the altar lay a glass coffin. Staring into the coffin, she saw a blond-haired man, dressed in a white, mid-thigh-length, collarless tunic, and a pair of black loose fitting trousers bound with fabric and laced up to his calves. The man looked as if were asleep, and not the corpse of someone who had supposedly died hundreds of years ago. Justine could hardly believe she was staring at the body of Sir Oliver Cademus.

"Astounding," she whispered. "Truly astounding."

Ben had to give credit to Clancy's determination and his desire for vengeance. He always believed he had a talent for getting under people's skin, but he never dreamed anyone would chase him halfway around the world to get their own back on him.

Clancy pointed at Ben's gun. "Slide it over here." As he spoke, Clancy pressed the gun against Morton's head, the implication was clear. "Don't make me ask you a second time."

Ben knew his best chance was to play along and hope Steph could come up with something. He slid the gun along the ice towards Clancy, who stopped it with his foot before kicking it back through the doorway behind him.

"Hands on head," ordered Clancy. "Both of you."

Ben complied, as did Luther.

"Well, well it must be my lucky day," said Clancy, grinning. "I'd come here to send a message to my former employers by screwing up the little assassination party they had set up. I was on my way here with some of my guys to secure the hostages, when we pick up a transmission between the two of you." Clancy shook his head. "Using names on an unsecured channel: sloppy, guys, very sloppy."

"You're not here to kill the Secretary General?" said Ben.

"Now you're getting the idea."

"You know this guy?" asked Luther.

"And you must be the half-brother," guessed Clancy. "You're a lucky man, Washington."

"How so?"

"If you had been my brother, I'd have gutted you first chance I got."

Luther scowled. "How do you know Ben?"

"Because of your brother, I've no team anymore, they were killed by my employers for failing to kill him," explained Clancy. "The men I've got with me are bargain basement stock, with less brain cells between them than an amoeba, Blacklight were the best there was, and between your brother and those bastards I used to work for, I'm all that's left, and once they find out I'm still alive, they're come after me with everything they've got."

"Do you have any idea who I am or how much trouble you're in right now?" said Jane. "If you surrender now, then the authorities may be more lenient with you."

Clancy smiled, despite himself. "Open your mouth again and I'll put a bullet in it."

Ben noticed the small device Clancy was holding. He had been around enough to know a detonator when he saw one.

"Last time we met, I underestimated you. My mistake, one I'm not about to repeat," said Clancy. "This detonator is tied into the charges that the team sent by my ex-employers placed all around this installation. It's fitted with a dead man's switch, which..." Clancy paused to press his thumb against a switch on the side of the detonator "…is now activated. If my thumb leaves this button, we all die."

"He's bluffing," called Steph, who was now in front of the helicopter, a pistol by her side.

"Am I now?" smiled Clancy. "Why don't you tell her what you think, Ben?"

"Steph, whatever you're planning back there, leave it, he's not bluffing."

Steph stood her ground. "I don't care if he has a nuclear warhead strapped to his ass, he's not leaving."

"Steph, is it? I hoped I'd run into you," he called. "So you're the one who took out Hammond." Clancy gave her an appreciative whistle. "Impressive, didn't think you navy lot were that hard, guess I was wrong."

"Say the word," said Steph, ignoring Clancy completely, "and he's gone."

Ben moved to say something, but was beaten to it by Clancy. "You know what, Steph? I understand a soldier never relinquishes their weapon, I respect that, so you can keep your sidearm. I know you won't fire, you're not that stupid."

Ben hoped Steph's anger and frustration did not override her good sense.

"Don't worry, when I leave and I'm sure no one is coming after me, I'll deactivate the detonator and make sure my men disarm the explosives before we leave," said Clancy.

"Why?" asked Ben, trying to drag out the conversation for as long as possible.

"Because I know how much this is going to piss off my former employers, that should go some way to getting even."

"Some way?"

"When I find out who they are, and kill every last one of them, then I'll call it quits."

"Glad I asked."

"No you're not, you're trying to buy time, but I'll put your mind at rest. I'm not here to kill you, Ben," said Clancy.

The shots were fired from Clancy's gun at the same time as Ben realised his plan.

"Steph!" It was too late, the bullets found their target, who slumped to the floor, breathing already erratic.

"I'm here to make you suffer," said Clancy, smiling. He shoved Jane towards Ben and sprinted for the door. Two men appeared at the entrance and began laying down covering fire. Ben tackled Jane to the floor as the noise of the gunfire deafened him. It was at least thirty seconds before it subsided. Clancy was nowhere to be seen, and his men were already backing away down the stairs until they too were gone.

Laying just to Ben's right was Luther's unmoving body. He had guessed Clancy's intent, but not his target. Throwing Jane off him, Ben scrambled across to where his brother had fallen, surprisingly finding himself hoping more than anything he was not already dead. He could not be dead, not like this, Luther was too tough to be put down by two bullets. The blood was already seeping through Luther's back onto the ice when he reached him.

"Luther! Luther!"

The faint wheezing sound as Luther forced air through lungs filling with blood was the only indication of life.

Luther's eyes flickered open and Ben saw the same overwhelming feeling of helplessness and inevitability he was feeling reflected back at him. Luther tried raising a hand, but was barely able to lift it. Ben took the hand and looked down at him. Even as he watched him, Ben knew he could not wipe away all those years in prison, but he was still his brother. He smiled and squeezed Luther's hand, and hoped it would be enough.

Luther smiled back.

Ben did not know how much time had passed before feeling a hand on his shoulder. "He's gone, Ben," said Steph softly.

Ben stared at his brother's sightless eyes. "He's still smiling."

"I'm sorry," said Jane. "If I hadn't been so pigheaded, none of this would have happened."

Ben got to his feet. "Get on the helicopter," he said, staring past Jane at the empty doorway.

For once, Jane did not argue.

Kneeling back down, Ben lifted Luther up. Steph followed him as he carried Luther to the helicopter, and laid him as gently as he could on the floor inside.

"Surely you don't expect us to fly all the way back to the airfield with a corpse?" complained one of the UN officials.

"I've never killed a man," admitted Ben, without looking in the direction the complaint had come from. "Don't make me start today."

With that, he slammed the helicopter door shut.

"You're going after him, aren't you?" asked Steph.

Ben looked down again at his brother's body through the helicopter door window. "No, Clancy will come after me again, and when he does, I'll kill him."

Chapter Forty

Was this really the body of Oliver Cademus he was looking at? Surely it was impossible, thought Jason. He did not struggle as he was taken to where Sirus, Justine and the other members of the Cabal were now standing at the foot of the coffin. He guessed by the shocked look on Justine's face that this was as big a shock to the system for her as it was for him. The realisation gave little comfort and only served to heighten his own fears.

"Look at him, Jason," said Sirus, pointing proudly at the coffin. "Sir Oliver himself, no sign of aging or decay, amazing."

Jason gazed upwards. The clear sky allowed the full moon to transform the entire plateau, immersing it in a silvery hue.

"There is nothing to be afraid of, Jason; you will take your place with us as the last member of the Cabal." Again, Sirus pointed at the coffin. "You're about to become a part of history, my young friend."

Sirus faced the two men who stood near Jason. "Release him."

The men released Jason and joined with the other knights of Cademus, who were taking their places on a dozen raised plinths, each one placed in front of a suit of armour.

"It is time," announced Sirus.

All the members of the Cabal formed a line a few feet in front of the coffin. Jason thought he saw Sirus shivering, and his forehead shone with sweat. Jason realised he was not the only one tonight to feel the touch of fear. Sirus held out both hands and closed his eyes. The other Cabal members came closer, each one taking the other's hand. Justine took Jason's hand, and at once, he felt as if his thoughts were not his own.

If you want to live through this, say nothing and do not move, came Justine's voice inside his head.

Jason could hear Sirus reciting something, his voice seemed distant, growing fainter with each phrase. Though he heard every word, Sirus spoke it in a language Jason did not understand. He became disorientated and nauseous. He tried to focus on a single spot on the floor in an effort to find his bearings, but it was no good. He fell forward and everything went black.

"Nathan?"

Nathan was busy trying to stop the knife, which was inches from his right eye.

"Don't wait for me!" he yelled, straining to keep his attacker at bay.

Vincent turned and took a step down towards Nathan. A hand seized his jacket, pulling him back.

"There's no time, come on!" said Napoleon.

Vincent hesitated.

"Come on!" called Napoleon again, who had already released Vincent and was continuing on up the staircase after the Reverend.

Burying his guilt, Vincent turned and sprinted up the steps.

With a cry of rage, Nathan rolled with his attacker down the staircase, ploughing into the path of five other knights, scattering them. His attacker, taking the brunt of the fall, lay with his neck twisted at an unnatural angle. Nathan got to his feet as the remaining knights came at him.

I'm too old for this, he thought as he leapt to meet the first man.

A minute later found Nathan looking down on the five knights, who lay unmoving before him.

"Then again," he mused before continuing up the stairs.

Jason was still on the plateau in front of the glass coffin, but everything felt different. He looked up and was horrified by what he saw. A swirling maelstrom of colours poured out across the night sky, as if the heavens had given birth to a new life form. Its tendrils stretched out in all directions, destroying any sense of normality or order. There was no moon, no stars, nothing save a deity, seemingly devoid of reason, who had transformed the sky into a canvas for its terrifying masterpiece. In his hand, Jason held the dagger that Sirus had earlier used to cut his hand.

"It's called the left hand of Cademus," said Justine.

She was the only other person on the plateau. Her arms were outstretched and her eyes were closed. "That fool Alvarez let Stone steal the other one, but don't worry, we'll get it back."

Terror was now being joined by confusion; where had everyone else gone? Nothing was making any sense.

"What's wrong, Jason? Isn't this what you wanted?"

Justine pointed at the dagger. "There is your one and only chance to save yourself, all you have to do is kill me. I wonder, do you have that kind of darkness within you?"

Jason hesitated. He did not know what he was supposed to do, this was all wrong. He was brought here to die, so why was he now being allowed to sit in judgment over his enemy. This had to be some kind of sick game, devised by the Cabal; somehow, this was all part of the ritual.

Jason pointed the knife toward Justine. "You destroyed everything I have ever cared about; you have to pay."

Although he had said the words, the voice he spoke them with was Sirus'.

"I know," said Justine.

The urge for vengeance swelled within him, growing more powerful by the second. He walked towards Justine, holding the knife before him. She would pay for stealing the life that should have been his.

Napoleon burst into the chamber, followed by the others. One of the knights moved to step off their plinth.

"Stay where you are!" shouted Sirus. "You'll disrupt the ceremony."

Snatching his hand out of the grasp of the Cabal member next to him, Sirus slammed it onto the coffin. A white stream of energy snaked up his arm from the coffin as centuries of stored energy was given an outlet.

"Napoleon Stone," Sirus hissed, raising his hand.

Napoleon and the others threw themselves in all directions as streaks of lightning flew from Sirus' fingertips, decimating a large portion of the wall behind them. No words passed between the four men. There was no going back now, they all knew what had to be done. The cruel irony was not lost on Napoleon. They had fought their way here to save Jason, only to become his executioners.

"I'm sorry," said Napoleon as he pulled the trigger.

The bullets tore through Jason's flesh, and he screamed, but to Napoleon it sounded more like a scream of euphoria than pain. He looked down at Jason's body, expecting to see the bloody entry wound, but instead saw nothing, the wounds were gone. It was as if they were firing blanks. Napoleon just stood there at a loss as to what to do next. They were no match for the Cabal's power, a power made stronger by the infused essence of Cademus.

Do it now Jason, make her pay.

Jason heard the thought and knew it was Sirus', but it did not matter, he needed no further urging. With all the hate, all the pain focused onto the blade, Jason, unaware he was dreaming, plunged the blade into Justine, driving the weapon forward until it was completely buried within her. He felt drained of all the anger and pain amassed throughout his life. He did not care about anything anymore. The knife was his world now, its blade nestled deep inside the woman he had come to despise.

Justine formed a tight-lipped smile as the blood spilled from her mouth.

"I have it," she said.

Jason's eyes shot open to find he was still in the chamber, but now the sky had returned to normal. Everyone else had returned, including someone he recognised at once.

"Professor Stone!" he shrieked, seeing the blood on his hands.

In front of him was the mortally wounded Sirus, blood pouring from a knife wound to the stomach.

"We needed you to release the portion of Cademus' mind you held of your own free will," explained Justine, who stood beside Jason unmarked, and still holding his hand. "You've just done that, thank you."

"Finally," said Sirus, turning toward the coffin.

"Bring him down! Don't let him finish the ritual!" shouted Nathan.

Vincent was up and running as the words left Nathan's mouth. Drawing a knife, he threw himself at Sirus. Sirus seized Vincent by the throat in mid-air with his free hand, and hurled him back across the plateau. Vincent sailed past the others, crashing into the wall where he lay stunned. Before anyone else could make a move towards him, Sirus slammed his hand down beside the other and screamed out the final incantation.

"The sleeper shall awake," translated Nathan. "We're too late."

Nothing happened.

Napoleon ran over to Jason, shoving past the other members of the Cabal, who were in no fit state to stop him and were struggling to remain standing.

Jason stared at the dagger he was holding for a moment, before letting it fall. "I'm sorry, Professor, but...I had to, I thought it was her...I thought..."

Tears filled Jason's eyes. Napoleon placed his arms around Jason as he continued to sob.

"I know what you thought, Jason, but it's all right, the ritual didn't work, you're safe."

"Am I?"

Napoleon was nearly thrown from his feet by a tremor that shook the castle to its foundations. He stared past Jason at the coffin and saw a small glow emanating from within it. As he watched, the light grew brighter and more intense; soon he was forced to look away. Whatever the Cabal had done, it had started a chain reaction. Napoleon looked at the other members of the Cabal. They were huddled together and looked as if they had become very aware of their own mortality. The twelve knights of Cademus who, until now, had been silent were now screaming and writhing in agony as if something was clawing at them, tearing the flesh from their bodies.

"What's happening?" said the Reverend, who was helping Vincent. The light now filled the entire coffin, and was spilling outwards into the chamber.

"He's coming," said Nathan. "He's coming."

"We need to go now," Justine told the other Cabal members; she had no intention of being buried under tons of stone. "Before this whole castle comes down on us."

"We must stay and protect Sir Oliver," said one of the Cabal.

"We have done all we can," said Justine. "We cannot serve him if we're dead, if he is as powerful as we hope, he will survive, and if not, he would want us to live, to continue what he started." Justine hoped her words were as convincing as Sirus'.

"What about Sirus?" asked one of the others. "We can't just leave him."

Justine looked at the unmoving body of Sirus. It was difficult to tell whether he was alive or dead. This was her chance, her chance to seize everything. If the ritual was a success, she would serve Sir Oliver faithfully as the new voice of the Cabal, if not, she would remake the Book of Cademus in her own image. The choice was easy.

"Leave him, he's dead."

Justine had not allowed herself to become dependant on the power being a member of the Cabal had brought with it. The power was a tool, nothing more. For the others, the years of having such powers at their command had made them feel invulnerable, with that power gone, or at the very least severely depleted, they were little more than frightened children, waiting to be led. It was a role Justine was happy to play. Snatching up the dagger Jason had dropped, she sprinted to a second door behind the coffin in the corner of the chamber, slashing the dagger across her palm as she ran. She placed her bloodied palm against the door, hoping it would respond to another member of the Cabal.

"I am Justine Hillman, I am Cabal."

She was relieved when the pain in her hand lessened and the door before her dissolved. She took one last look at the coffin and prayed she was not making the hugest mistake of her life, before she and the other members of the Cabal fled from the chamber, the entrance collapsing in upon itself, making any pursuit impossible.

"Damn it !" shouted Napoleon.

Moments earlier, he had seen a woman lead the other members of the Cabal out, through another door. He had given chase only to be beaten back by the entrance's sudden collapse. He could not believe he had been within striking distance of the Cabal and they had escaped.

296

By now, the tremors were getting worse, large sections of wall which had stood firm for hundreds of years were now displaying giant fractures all over their surface, threatening to give way at any moment.

"He says we're too late," said Jason suddenly. "He says Cademus is coming…we have to leave, we have to leave now."

A wide-eyed Jason ran for the door, where he was grabbed by Nathan. "Whoa boy, who told you this?"

"I did."

Standing just in front of the glass coffin was Joshua Grey. Napoleon levelled his shotgun at Grey. "No more games, Grey, no more riddles: what's going on?"

At that point, tendrils of energy poured out from the coffin and across the chamber, each one enveloping the now dying and disfigured knights of Cademus. Their screams became louder, if that were possible.

"Their pain will be short-lived." Joshua told them "It will be nothing compared to what he will do to those who have stood in his way."

"There is still a chance," said Nathan, pulling out the small journal. "The spell, Napoleon, it's now or never."

"It's too late for that," said Joshua. "You have to get Jason away from here."

Napoleon looked at Grey for some sign of treachery; he found none. Shielding his eyes, he looked in the direction of the coffin. It was now nothing more than a column of light stretching up into the heavens, threatening to tear the night sky asunder. In his years working for the Icarus Foundation, Napoleon had never seen a display of power on this scale, or felt so helpless against it.

"Nathan," he said quietly, without turning. "You and the Reverend take Jason to the main hall, do the spell there."

"I'll need at least ten minutes to prepare."

"You'll have them."

Napoleon knelt down and retrieved Vincent's guns. He walked over to Vincent and held the guns out towards him.

"Can you fight?" he asked, taking no notice of the pain on Vincent's face.

"I…I don't…"

"Can you fight?"

Vincent looked at his guns then up at Napoleon. "I can fight," he replied, taking the guns.

Nathan clamped a hand onto Jason's shoulder, dragging him forward. "Time to go."

"But I…"

"Listen, Jason, I need you to do this, we all do, but you put one foot wrong or try to engage me in some kind of debate about staying to help, then God help me, I'll kill you myself. Now move!"

With that, he shoved Jason towards the entrance.

"Don't be a hero, Stone; ten minutes, just give me ten minutes."

Napoleon nodded.

The Reverend made no effort to move as Nathan and Jason left. He walked over and stood beside Napoleon, saying nothing.

"Are you insane?" shouted Joshua, whose usual demeanour was showing signs of strain. "You cannot win against this man. If you stay, you will die."

Napoleon looked at Vincent, then across at the Reverend. Finally, his eyes turned to Joshua; a single look passed between the two men.

Joshua began to fade from sight. "Fools, you blind fools."

As he finished the words, Joshua was gone.

Chapter Forty-One

Jason sprinted down the staircase, his lungs struggling under the exertion. Behind him, he heard the voice of the old man Napoleon had called Nathan, urging him on and then being forced to look on in shame as the supposedly old man tore past him.

Jason increased his speed, his every step now threatening to send him sprawling down the staircase, as all around him the castle continued to be caught in the grip of increasingly more violent tremors.

He followed Nathan into the main hall, where he gaped in revulsion at the bodies of the fallen knights of Cademus that littered the floor. The main castle doors were opened and Jason saw the members of the Cabal fleeing through it and out into the courtyard, beyond which lay the jungle.

"What about them?" he said, pointing as he tried to purge the image of the dead knights from his mind.

Nathan was on his knees with a small piece of chalk. He was busy sketching something on the ground in front of him, whilst constantly referring to the book he held. "No time to worry about them now."

Jason caught sight of Justine amongst the others, and once more felt the rage within him.

"Don't even think about it," warned Nathan. "Now stand here."

Nathan was pointing at the large chalk circle he had just drawn. There were several hastily scribbled symbols in the circle's centre. As Jason stepped into the circle, Nathan was already moving away to sketch out more circles around the hall, ensuring each one matched the relevant image within the journal. Once he had finished, Jason counted at least ten of the chalk drawings scattered around the hall. Nathan quickly inspected his handiwork and made a few alterations to some of the drawings before returning to stand in front of Jason inside the circle. Jason watched fascinated as the other chalk circles vanished.

"Don't worry, it's part of the spell," explained Nathan.

Nathan carefully laid the open journal on the floor, between himself and Jason.

"What now?" Jason asked.

Nathan held out his hands, palms facing upwards, towards Jason. "Place your hands over mine."

Jason did as he was told without hesitation. He stared at Nathan, waiting for his next instruction.

"Before we start, you need to know that..."

"This is dangerous, I may not survive," said Jason. "Just tell me what I need to do."

Nathan smiled. "You're still linked to Cademus, at least for the moment," he said. "We're going to use that against him. Now, do you see the book on the floor?" Jason nodded. "I want you to focus on it, picture it in your mind."

Jason stared intently at the journal.

"Got it."

"Good, now I want you to imagine it lifting in front of you, can you do that?"

"I'll try."

Jason was aware that he was being asked to do something similar to what had taken place during his first meeting with the Cabal, so it had to be possible. He shut his eyes and tried to imagine the journal rising up from the floor, but it remained where it was.

"Focus, Jason," whispered Nathan. "Focus."

Jason was no longer listening to Nathan. The image of the book rising upwards was the only thing he concentrated on. He heard a faint rustle, opened his eyes and saw the journal, hovering, level with his chest. He buried the need to celebrate for fear of breaking his concentration.

"Excellent, Jason, now imagine yourself reading the journal,"

"I can't."

The journal began to dip towards the floor.

"You can't, but Cademus can, you have his power within you now, believe you can read it and you will."

Jason took a deep breath and closed his eyes once more. This time, he imagined himself in a windowless room filled with locked doors.

He·imagined mouthing the word open, and watched as all the doors were flung open, flooding the room with light.

Jason opened his eyes. "I understand."

"Can you read the incantation?"

"I always could," said Jason, unsure where the words had come from.

"Excellent, time to get to work."

Jason began to feel steadier on his feet. "The tremors have stopped."

"Calm before the storm," said Nathan grimly.

Napoleon watched in awe as Cademus' body momentarily became translucent, allowing it to pass through the coffin before becoming solid once more. The body continued its ascent into the sky, all the while waves of energy rippled across it. Now suspended at least twenty feet in the air, the body came to a halt and was thrown into a series of convulsions, each one more powerful than the last, each one threatening to tear Cademus apart, such was their ferocity. Napoleon and the others again fought to stay on their feet as the chamber continued to shake. The energy surrounding Cademus and the knights suddenly dissipated and the body was dropped hard onto the chamber floor, where there it lay, steam rising from every pore.

Napoleon stood in silence, trying to comprehend what it was he had just witnessed.

After a single intake of breath, the centuries-old corpse lifted his head. Through a mass of long, tangled and dirty blond hair, a pair of the clearest, most fiercely blue eyes Napoleon had ever seen studied them intently. For several moments, the man tried to speak, but to no avail. He quickly gave up on attempting speech and instead focused his efforts on pushing himself onto his knees. He remained there for a second or two, taking some more breaths before finally he was able to force himself into standing upright. The man gazed up at the night sky and smiled. Napoleon guessed it was probably the first time he had seen the sky in centuries.

"If either of you have a plan," whispered the Reverend, "now would be a good time to share it."

"They were right...it worked," the man said at last, his English perfect. "The doubt was always there, but it actually worked."

"Cademus?" said Napoleon. "Sir Oliver Cademus?"

"For my sins," replied Cademus, bowing. "And you would be Napoleon Stone."

Vincent fumbled, but just managed to catch one of his guns as the shock caused him to release his grip on it momentarily.

Cademus pointed to Vincent. "And this somewhat unsure young man is your assistant Vincent, and next to him, God's instrument of vengeance no less."

"Do not mock me."

"You are mistaken, Reverend," frowned Cademus. "I would never mock a holy man, even if the path he follows is different from my own."

"I see you have some residual memories from the former hosts of your mind?" deduced Napoleon.

"I remember everything and yet nothing," said Cademus, cryptically. "I do know that you came here to prevent my awakening."

"I suppose there's no point trying to convince you to climb back into that coffin of yours?"

Cademus smiled.

"I am afraid I cannot oblige," he replied. "But the fact you stand your ground shows you are men of character, men I could use."

"If this is the part where you try and get us to join you," said Vincent, "don't waste your time."

"I have had little else to waste for the last nine centuries," remarked Cademus, running his hand along the glass coffin. "You seek to destroy me because you believe me to be evil, and yet none of you have ever set eyes on me before this night, have I no chance for defence?"

Napoleon did not know why they were still talking, but for now was happy to do so; he was already gathering his strength for the inevitable conclusion to the conversation.

"Your evil is legend, we do not need to prove or disprove it," said the Reverend.

"And how have you come by this knowledge?" said Cademus, looking at Napoleon and Vincent. "Evil wears many faces, my religious friend, and some are worn with the intention to do good. You, better than most, should understand that."

"Do you deny that your cult slaughtered hundreds in your rituals?" accused Napoleon. "That you allowed your followers, your own family, to sacrifice themselves so you could escape?"

"Do you deny that you have killed in your quest to preserve what you believe is right, Napoleon?" shot back Cademus, turning to the Reverend before Napoleon could form a reply. "Where is your denial for the death and destruction you have visited upon your fellow man, Reverend?"

Cademus smiled when the only reply received was the cacophony of sound being carried from the jungle surrounding them.

"As I thought," he said at last. "Do not think to lecture me with your antiquated notions of good and evil. You have all gorged upon the darkness within your hearts, and now, cloaked in your own hypocrisy, you come before me parading yourselves as pillars of virtue. Be careful, heroes, perhaps one day you will find yourselves standing where I am, facing men such as yourselves who seek your destruction."

Napoleon began to understand how Cademus had managed to rally so many to his cause;, the power of his words was difficult to ignore.

"All I offer is the chance to live, without guilt or revulsion for what you do, to embrace the chaos that exists within all our souls; where is the crime in that?"

"Free to kill and destroy without any thought of consequence, chaos for all eternity under your leadership," spat the Reverend. "Is this the new world you have returned to bring us?"

"I come to offer freedom, a freedom not built on the moral ramblings of a society too fearful to embrace its potential. Yes, for a time chaos and destruction will rule, perhaps forever, but it is our right to make that choice. The Book of Cademus will merely light the way for that change."

"No," said Vincent, stepping forward, "That's not the world I fight to see realised."

The look was shared by Napoleon and the Reverend.

"So be it," said Cademus.

The ground beneath Napoleon trembled and a low hum filled the air around them. The sky above Cademus' head, which had been a clear, moonlit summer's night, was now beginning to change dramatically. Thick black clouds, tinged with the same purplish hue now found in Cademus' eyes were forming from thin air, spiralling outwards, obscuring the moon from sight, and soon after came the first rumblings of thunder. To Napoleon, it was as if he had been plunged into the midst of winter as freezing winds buffeted him and the others.

Cademus lifted his right arm and stretched out his hand, as if trying to snatch something from the air above him. "You made a mistake journeying here this night."

A bolt of lightning streaked down from the sky. Napoleon dived forward, the others hurled themselves to either side. The lightning struck the ground, tearing huge chunks of stone from the chamber floor and launching them into the sky.

The Reverend flew backwards, propelled by the shockwave bought on by the lightning strike. He brought his mini Uzis to bear, firing off a steady stream of bullets before being slammed against the chamber wall. Cademus raised a hand and smiled as the bullets flew to his palm, as if it were a magnet.

"Impossible," said the Reverend.

"Interesting," said Cademus, closing his hand around the bullets.

Cademus opened his hand to reveal a solid metal sphere, formed from the bullets. As the sphere levitated over Cademus' hand, spikes sprung out of its surface.

"Very interesting."

The sphere shot towards the Reverend, who caught off guard watched as death raced toward him. Vincent hurled a fist-sized chunk of masonry, which knocked the sphere off balance and straight through a wall. Hefting his blade, Vincent dropped to one knee and threw it at Cademus, who sidestepped the weapon easily. He moved in and taking Vincent by the throat, lifted him into the air.

"Not again," said Vincent.

"Is this the best your century has to offer?"

He hurled Vincent against the wall as if he were a paperweight. Vincent hit the wall hard and, winded, he sank to the floor. The Reverend rushed towards Cademus, firing as he ran. To his amazement,

Cademus' entire body became water, his facial features, which were still visible, took on what looked to be a smile, as the bullets passed through him with no effect.

"Pathetic," laughed Cademus, reverting back to solid form.

The laughter vibrated across the chamber, hitting the Reverend like a sonic boom; he crumpled to the floor without a sound.

All the while, Napoleon had done nothing, he had been conserving energy, building it up within him. He waited for his chance, his one chance. He watched Cademus standing over Vincent, then his gaze turned from Cademus and Napoleon knew this was it. His breathing became deeper, more controlled as the energy within him fought for release. He controlled it, tempered its full fury, he knew to unleash the power would probably kill him. That did not matter, Nathan had asked for ten minutes, and that was what they were going to give him. Cademus, as if sensing something, turned from Vincent and looked across at Napoleon.

Lifting his shotgun, Napoleon whispered the word of power, releasing a bolt of energy. Cademus brought his hands together, trapping the energy between them. He began rotating his hands around the energy, reforming it into a ball of swirling light and flame.

"I expected more from you, Napoleon, my Cabal hold you in high regard: a pity."

Cademus hurled the trapped energy back at the now weakened Napoleon, who managed to drop to his knees. The energy ball swept over his head, obliterating most of the wall behind him. Napoleon started to feel the same pain building up within his chest as he had felt back at the university. Desperately, he tried to catch his breath but he was finding it more and more difficult to breathe.

Looking through eyes that were already growing dim, he saw Cademus coming towards him, each step brimming with confidence.

The pain in his chest was now unbearable. "Not now," Napoleon whispered, fighting to stay conscious. His vision swam as the pain increased and then everything went blank.

"Napoleon, Napoleon Stone."

Napoleon opened his eyes and found himself unable to see anything, just darkness. He remembered what had just happened to him and the most obvious thought flew to his mind. He was dead.

"Not dead, but rather a single breath away from death."

The voice belonged to the woman now walking towards him. She was young and possessed a kind of innocent beauty Napoleon instantly warmed to. She was wearing a t-shirt and jeans, her dark brown shoulder-length hair was tied into a ponytail.

Hardly the dress code for an angel, he thought, and there was something about the woman, something familiar.

"I'm not an angel, but thank you for the compliment."

"Who are you?"

"Someone who is about to give you a second chance at life," she extended her hand. "All you need to do is take my hand."

Napoleon hesitated. "There's a price, isn't there?"

"Does it matter?"

Napoleon imagined what was going on in the chamber while he was here. "No."

"The price is to keep him safe, Napoleon; he deserves to have a chance at the kind of happiness I would have given him if I had lived."

"Your Jason's…"

"Goodbye and thank you."

The woman touched Napoleon's palm, and at once he could feel himself slipping away.

"Save my son."

Napoleon opened his eyes, to see Cademus bearing down on him.

"Did you think I would be so easily defeated, Demon Stalker?"

He backhanded Napoleon, who was taken off his feet and sent sprawling back towards the rear of the chamber. Napoleon landed badly and felt his ankle give, although not broken, it was badly twisted. Again, Cademus came to stand over him. With a speed that defied the eye, Cademus' hand shot towards Napoleon's chest, or rather the heart that lay beneath it. Displaying reflexes born from years of living with the spectre of death hanging over everything he did, Napoleon caught hold of Cademus' wrist a hairbreadth from its target. Napoleon sensed a power filling his veins, the like of which he had never known. The woman had given him more than his life back, she had given him a chance.

"Did you think I would be?"

Even as he held Cademus' wrist, Napoleon could sense his newfound strength lessen. Cademus' hand moved towards his chest. Napoleon could see out of the corner of his eye that both the Reverend and Vincent were still down: he was alone.

You are not alone, though by rights, you should be dead by now.

It was Grey. For the first time since they had met, Napoleon was glad to hear the disembodied voice inside his head.

His power will wane; your friend has begun the spell as we speak. You must keep him at bay a little while longer.

305

Then, as abruptly as it had come, Grey's voice was gone, but something remained, something that fuelled Napoleon's aching limbs ...hope.

Forcing the last reserves of power into his mind, Napoleon pulled back his right fist and smashed it into Cademus' face with everything he had. Sparks of energy flew from the blow as it broke through whatever the barrier was protecting Cademus from harm; such was the force of the blow as it connected, Napoleon was thrown several feet backwards.

Stunned, Cademus stumbled up, blood streaming from his broken nose.

By now, Napoleon was on his feet, shotgun in hand. He fired off two rounds. Cademus, although still dazed by the first pain he had felt in centuries, was able to deflect the first shot, but staggered under its force. He was not so fortunate with the second shotgun blast. It caught him in the chest and he was propelled back through the glass coffin, landing in the midst of the broken glass. Cademus touched his face, looked at the blood on his hand and smiled.

Several shards of glass that had lain around Cademus rose up from the floor, held there by nothing more than Cademus' will. The glass fragments slowly began to turn, as if searching for something or someone. Finally seeing their target, they sped towards Napoleon. Running forwards, the Reverend threw down his guns and produced his crossbow. Throwing himself into Napoleon, he pushed them both out of the path of the flying glass, firing his crossbow as he hit the floor beside Napoleon, who was still firing from his shotgun. The bullets were little more than an annoyance to Cademus, but the steel bolt plunged into his chest, again driving him backwards. He glanced down at the bolt embedded in his chest, with a kind of morbid detachment. Taking hold of the bolt in one hand, he wrenched it clear, hurling it in disgust back at the Reverend's feet.

"You think to blind me from the real threat," said Cademus. "You think an old man and a boy can harm me!"

Cademus turned and looked at the remains of the ten knights of Cademus, each one lying at the feet of a suit of armour.

He began mouthing the same phrase over and over again. Each time he said the words, his face grew paler, more drawn, as if he were somehow aging before Napoleon's eyes.

"What's he saying?" asked the Reverend.

Napoleon was already getting to his feet. "Get ready."

"He's weakening," said Vincent, who had regained consciousness and was pointing at Cademus, who was now bent double, but still repeating the same phrase. "We've got him..."

It was then each of the ten suits of armour split down the centre. Hands burst out of each suit as ten men pulled themselves out. Each man stood at around seven foot tall, their pupils white, blood trickling from their eyes. They all wore crimson robes similar to the corpses in front of them, which they were already stepping over. Between them, they carried an assortment of weapons; some carried short swords, some daggers, two carried broadswords, and the last carried a large battle axe.

"…On the ropes," finished Vincent.

Cademus fell back behind the men. He slammed his fist down into the chamber floor, sending cracks out in all directions. The floor in front of him gave way and tumbled into the depths of the castle. He smiled at the three men as he stood ready to drop through the hole.

"You fight with honour and courage, and that is always worthy of respect." He gestured to his men, who began to advance on Napoleon and the others. "But my part in this battle is at an end, I have wasted far too much time indulging you as it is."

Cademus shouted out something to his men before dropping through the hole and out of sight.

"He's going after Nathan and the boy," said Napoleon echoing what he believed the others were already thinking.

He looked at the Reverend, whose reply was a slight nod before he stepped into the path of the approaching knights.

Napoleon turned to Vincent. "Once the fighting starts, make for the stairs."

"No way, Napoleon, not this time."

"Listen, Vincent," said Napoleon, keeping one eye on the men, who for the moment had halted their advance and seemed to be content so long as no sudden moves were made. "Nathan can't protect Jason alone. This is what we do, this is who we are." He pointed to the door. "Go, go now."

"Napoleon….I…"

Vincent's words were caught in his throat as the newly-created knights of Cademus, no doubt growing tired of waiting, ran headlong towards them. Not risking a backward glance Vincent made for the doorway. Seeing him move for the door, one of the knights leapt across the room. He landed in front of the doorway and was already swinging his broadsword at Vincent's head. Unable to stop in time, Vincent threw himself down, avoiding the swinging blade as he slid between the knight's legs. He fired his guns at point blank range as he slid under the knight, the bullets piecing the robes and the knight's groin. The result was not pretty, but was fatal. With the sounds of battle behind him, Vincent raced down the steps.

Chapter Forty-Two

Cademus strode into the main hall enraged. Everything he had planned and hoped for was being jeopardised by a handful of fools, with no concept of how much larger the game they were playing actually was. He wondered, could his order have diminished so much? He had seen the bodies of his followers on the stairs and here in the hall. So many dead, defeated by so few. His respect for his enemy grew.

His greatest disappointment was in the Cabal. In his time, the Cabal was something to aspire to; fierce friends and allies who represented everything the Book of Cademus sought to teach those strong enough to listen. It sickened him to see the descendants of those who would have given their lives for him and he for them, now little more than fawning sycophants. They were a shadow of what the Cabal once was: only one had stayed by his side, he would be rewarded, the others would pay a heavy penance for their betrayal.

Across the room, he saw the descendant of the traitor whose treachery had led to centuries of imprisonment. He would take great pleasure in seeing the flesh torn from the boy's body.

"Jesus," said Jason, staring past Nathan. "He's alive, he's really alive."

"Read, boy!" yelled Nathan.

Jason tried to cast out the grief he was feeling. Cademus' appearance meant Napoleon and the others were probably dead; there would be no more help coming now.

Jason forced himself to look away from Cademus. Even though the fear and sadness remained, his focus was now back where it needed to be, on the journal. He shouted the next line of the incantation.

"You think yourself strong enough to stand against me?" Cademus scoffed. "This is my hour, boy."

Cademus held out his hand. The journal appeared to respond to Cademus at first, it moved an inch before stopping and holding its ground.

"This circle protects itself by drawing on Cademus' power, he can't hurt you whilst you stand within it," said Nathan.

Cademus lifted his hand again, only this time, white streaks of energy were coiled around it.

"Last chance, boy," said Cademus. "Give me the journal and live. I will not be bested by your family a second time."

Jason, drawing on his fading courage, began the last line of the incantation as Cademus hurled two blasts of energy from each hand. Jason finished the second the blasts hit. The energy smashed against an invisible barrier and dissipated into thin air, leaving only a putrid burning odour to give any indication of its presence.

"Nicely done, Jason," said Nathan. "Nicely done."

Jason looked on as Cademus staggered back, as if disorientated.

"Out!" shouted Cademus, grabbing his head in his hands. "Get out of my head."

His eyes turned to Jason and narrowed.

"Why is he still here?" said Jason. "I thought you said it would make him disappear?"

"Stay calm. Do nothing until I say, do you understand?"

Jason was about to push Nathan for more information when he heard a grinding sound coming from above his head. He and Nathan looked up at the ceiling. Cracks were beginning to appear, a shower of dust and small stone fragments started to fall on them. The mini rock fall alerted both of them to the possibility that the incantation might not protect them from whatever Cademus was planning.

"Let us see how well you fare buried alive," announced Cademus, still looking shaken. "And when you have drawn your last breath, I shall take what is mine."

"Nathan?" said Jason, already regretting his earlier defiant stand.

Nathan was staring at the spot where he had drawn one of the chalk circles. Jason looked, Cademus was tantalizingly close to one Nathan had drawn. Nathan finally returned Jason's questioning stare, but said nothing, there was nothing left to say.

The ceiling above their heads finally gave way and came tumbling towards them.

Napoleon turned as the knight of Cademus that was lunging towards him slumped at his feet as a crossbow bolt sliced cleanly through his chest and out the other side. It buried itself in the right arm of the knight behind. The Reverend came at the knights, ducking under the blows aimed at him, his crossbow now discarded, he fought on with two daggers. He moved like a whirlwind of destruction through his attackers; by the time Napoleon joined the fight, three knights already lay dead. Both men fought as if possessed in their efforts to prevent anyone from following Vincent. They had backed up nearly all the way to the door, leaving their opponents with no choice but to go through them if they wanted access to the staircase. At the height of the battle, the knights, who were now down to more than half their number, backed away to regroup. The Reverend and Napoleon looked on as the knights they had

309

killed slowly began to get to their feet and rejoin their comrades, cuts and gashes were healed before their eyes, dismembered parts re-grown.

"Regenerating undead knights," Napoleon sighed, battling the exhaustion within him. "Why am I not surprised."

Napoleon slid his shotgun back into its holster and considered his next move. The Reverend was gripping the edges of his coat, wearing an expression Napoleon had never seen him use before. He was grinning. The Reverend opened his coat enough for Napoleon to see several tiny pouches fitted into the lining. Napoleon knew a bomb when he saw one.

"God go with you," said the Reverend.

"And you."

Napoleon turned and half ran, half limped through the doorway.

Jason shut his eyes and braced himself for the crushing impact. It took less than five seconds for him to realise his bones were still intact. He opened his eyes to find the entire ceiling section hovering a few feet above his head. After a second or two, the ceiling rose upwards and repaired itself as if nothing had happened.

"Hello, Oliver."

Cademus' face went pale when he heard the voice. After nine hundred years, it was clear to Jason that Cademus could still be surprised.

"You!" was the only word Cademus could find to say as Joshua Grey descended the main stairs into the hall.

Joshua said nothing to Jason or Nathan as he walked past them. He stopped when he was stood halfway between Cademus and the others.

"You were the last person I expected to see this day."

"Where else would I be?"

"You should have stayed hidden," said Cademus, his hands once more pulsating with energy.

Joshua folded his arms, apparently unimpressed by the threat.

Cademus turned his palms outward, allowing the power within to pour out at Joshua, who stood motionless. Joshua lifted his hands, keeping them apart. The energy slammed into the space between his hands, pushing him backwards as the power flowed into his veins, seeking his destruction. Inch by inch, Joshua was forced backwards, his feet driven into the floor itself. He came to a halt, the energy still buffeting him like a hurricane, his body shaking under the strain being placed on it. Joshua fell onto one knee and Jason wondered whether he was witnessing his final moments.

"Enough!" Joshua screamed, pushing himself up.

The streams of energy attacking his body exploded outwards, filling the hall with light before they vanished, allowing a long overdue silence to settle within the hall.

"Still overconfident I see, Oliver," scolded Joshua, breathing hard as he stepped out of the crater in the floor and moved back to his earlier position. "You must know by now that your power has its limits."

"I had not expected to wake to battle, but it is of no matter, I will still prevail."

"Oh, the power is within you, but you are like a child learning to walk, you are unfocused, undisciplined," said Joshua. "Every time you use it, you bring yourself closer to the abyss."

"The abyss! Where do you think I have been for the last nine centuries?"

Cademus took a step forward and Jason braced himself, but once more was disappointed as Cademus fell just short again, his foot now skirting the edge of the invisible circle. Jason wondered how much more tension his heart could stand.

"It was your choice to submit yourself to the ritual, Oliver," said Joshua.

"I sought to ensure my message, my purpose lived on to serve mankind, my role was that of prophet, not conqueror," argued Cademus. "But then the desire for power and conquest was never mine, was it?"

"What's he talking about?" said Jason, suddenly not caring just how much out of his depth he was.

Cademus smiled malevolently. "The boy does not know, does he? Were you too fearful to tell him the truth?"

Cademus stared at Jason. "See, Jason, see the truth."

"Don't listen to him, Jason," said Joshua.

"How?" asked Jason, flatly ignoring the warning.

"You possess a keen mind, boy, but the world you live in dulls your senses. The waking nightmare that has haunted you was in truth a memory, my last one before I was entombed within the coffin. Think back to it now, boy, picture the memory in your mind and you will be there."

"Don't do this, Jason," pleaded Grey.

But Jason was no longer listening, not to Joshua, not to Cademus. He pictured the images of the nightmare from which so much had been triggered. He was surprised how quickly the images came, unfortunately so did the terror that had come with it, which he fought to overcome. But this time was different, now he was there by choice and he knew what he was seeing, and it held no terror for him. He stood within the chamber once more with the hooded figures, who he now knew were the original members of the Cabal, as they attempted to pervert the laws of nature.

Go closer, Jason, see.

311

As Jason moved closer, he noticed one of the figures turning to leave, the others too engrossed in the ritual to see what has happening. Unlike the last time he had experienced the nightmare, Jason did not give in to his fear and flee. A lot had changed since he last stood here. He was now here willingly, seeking answers, and he would not be swayed from that quest. He lunged forwards, grabbing the fleeing figure's hood with both hands, pulling it back as he did so. The shock of what he saw there sent him spinning out of the memory and back to where he stood.

"Are you ok?" asked Nathan. "I thought I'd lost you there for a moment. What did you see?"

"Him," whispered Jason, pointing at Grey. "I saw him."

"Are you sure? Maybe…"

"No, it was him, I saw him. He was leaving the ritual."

"Well that would mean…"

"That I was Jacob Covenant," said Joshua. "I should have told you earlier, Jason. You should have not learned the truth this way."

"The truth!" said Jason. "Do you even know what the word means, Joshua, Jacob or whatever your name is."

"I know you may find it difficult to understand."

"That my only living relative is the one that caused all of this in the first place, no, I understand that perfectly."

"It was the fact that you are my only descendant, Jason, which brought me here tonight, to protect you," explained Joshua.

"And what? I'm supposed to thank you?" said Jason, who, like when he faced the Cabal, felt something beginning to stir within him.

"Jason," said Nathan. "Jason, you need to listen to me."

Jason was shaking with rage, and then a trickle of blood flowed from his nostril, followed by blood from his eyes and ears.

Nathan reached out to touch his forearm, but as his fingers brushed Jason's arm, Nathan screamed in agony. He was thrown from the circle and sent hurtling across the hall. With his eyes still locked on Joshua, Jason either did not see what happened to Nathan, or was past caring. He was also oblivious to the fact he had now stepped out of the chalk circle. All Jason knew was what was surging within him made him powerful; his fears and doubts had fled in the wake of that power. No more, he thought, no more being used, no more being lied to.

"So, Grandfather," he began. "Can I call you that? I can't be bothered to add all those greats before it. Tell me why I should thank you?"

"Cademus is using you, Jason," said Joshua. "It's what he does, what he's always done, using others to achieve his ends. That power within you now, you're drawing it from him, and he's letting you do it."

"You mean like you used me, Grandfather?"

Jason casually backhanded Joshua, who was rocketed up into the ceiling, his shoulders and back taking the full brunt of the impact, before he crashed to the floor, face first. Joshua lay there, unmarked, but clearly shocked at the power of the blow. Joshua was then lifted from the floor, his arms and legs outstretched as if they were about to be torn from their sockets.

"Like you used Napoleon and the others?"

Joshua's upper clothing was torn from him, exposing his chest and arms.

"My adoptive parents were murdered while you did nothing!"

Three flaming claw marks, appearing from thin air, raked across Joshua chest, he winced, but did not cry out.

"What about Mr. Hunter, do you even know who he was? Someone else who tried to help me, dead now because of you."

Jason leaned his head to the right slightly, as if directing something and a single gash tore open along Joshua's right arm.

"What about my real parents? Should I thank you for their deaths, Grandfather? Should I, you bastard?" said Jason.

Joshua's skin erupted into flames and he slowly began to turn on the spot as if he were being roasted alive.

"Do you know what hell's like, Joshua, my hell?" shouted Jason. "Well now you're getting a taste of it, hope you like it!"

The flames grew brighter, more intense, and finally, Joshua screamed; the force of the cry propelled Jason backwards and he crashed through the wall. The flames now gone and with no wounds to show what he had endured, Joshua collapsed onto the floor barely conscious.

Chapter Forty-Three

All his life, the Reverend had longed to create a better world, somewhere people could feel loved and at peace. It was one of the reasons he had become a priest. He knew now, the kind of peace he desired for himself could only be found on the other side of death.

The ten undead knights approached. The Reverend bowed his head.

"The time for prayer is over, little man," said one of the Knights. "Time to learn what it means to defy the will of Cademus."

The Reverend opened his eyes and looked up. The same knight who had mocked him stepped forward, and died instantly.

"You will not be allowed to win this day," promised the Reverend.

The knights advanced.

Yea though I walk through the valley of the shadow of death.

One of the knights hurled a dagger. The Reverend clapped his hands together, trapping the blade in mid-air. He flicked his wrists forward, sending the blade spinning back to its owner. Too late to see the danger, the knight's body arched backwards as the dagger buried itself in his forehead.

I will fear no evil.

Two more knights came towards him. Sheathing his daggers, the Reverend tensed both forearms, and two small objects no bigger than a matchbox slid from the sleeves of his coat and into his hands.

For thou art with me.

Instead of retreating, the Reverend ran headlong towards them. Thinking their foe had resigned himself to a quick death, both decided to oblige. One stepped confidently forward, bringing his sword round in a wide arc in an effort to deliver a decapitating blow. At the same time, the second knight went down onto one knee, swinging his blade at the Reverend's knees. Both attacks were delivered in unison, with near perfect accuracy, save one minor flaw; the Reverend. He threw himself through the opening left by the swinging blades. and diving past the bewildered knights, he hurled the devices he held at each man.

"Detonate," said the Reverend, falling into a forward roll and into the path of another three knights. Already bracing himself for their attack, he barely registered the two explosions behind him, or saw the devastation wreaked upon his two victims.

Thy rod and thy staff they comfort me.

Using his momentum, the Reverend sprang up and forwards, arms outstretched, the two knives now returned to each hand. The three knights tried to bring their weapons to bear, but it was already too late. The Reverend loomed into view, his face twisted with rage. He cannoned into them, plunging his twin blades into the throats of two of the knights, the third being carried to the floor, along with the others by the force of the attack.

Thou dost prepare a table before me in the presence of my enemies.

Seeing a new threat out of the corner of his eye, the Reverend dispatched the third knight and rolled to his left, hurling one of his blades in the same motion. The space where a second earlier his head had been was now occupied by a huge battle axe and a rush of wind as it whistled past. Unlike the axe wielder, the Reverend's aim was true, his knife slamming into his attacker's temple.

Thou hast anointed my head with oil, my cup overflows.

Scooping up a discarded sword as he rolled, the Reverend came to his feet, barely managing to deflect an attack. Stepping inside, he thrust his blade through his opponent's chest. Pain flared from the Reverend's side, he span, sword now clutched in both hands, allowing it to bite deep into his enemy's neck and through to the other side. Deprived of its head, the lifeless body swayed for a second and then toppled to the floor. Sensing movement behind him, the Reverend reversed his blade, allowing the incoming attacker to run onto it. The move, however, came too late, for even as he ran onto the blade, the knight plunged his own sword deep into the Reverend's back. The Reverend stumbled forward a few steps then fell onto his hands, blood spilling from his mouth. Hoping he had given Napoleon enough time to get clear, he reached into his jacket pocket and took out the detonator.

The remaining knights, seeing the danger, paused even as the others the Reverend had already killed were beginning to re-form.

The knight closest looked down at the bloodied and dying Reverend.

"What manner of man are you?" he asked quietly, his voice almost respectful.

The Reverend met the knight's eyes, his finger poised over the detonator switch.

"I am wrath."

Sirus opened his eyes, but remained still. The pain in his wound was finally starting to grow fainter; his plan to reserve a tiny portion of his own power to heal his wound before channelling the rest into completing the ritual had worked beautifully. Before passing out, he remembered seeing Sir Oliver awaken from his glass coffin. They had achieved the impossible, they had conquered death. Now, with their leader back amongst the living once more, the world would soon be a very different place. He wished the other generations of the Cabal could have shared in his moment of glory. It was the last thing that went through Sirus' mind as the fireball created by the Reverend's bomb engulfed him, his dreams of power incinerated along with his flesh.

Joshua stared at the gaping hole in the wall and the darkness beyond. He buried his face in his hands.

"Forgive me, Jason."

"Nice try, Grandfather," laughed Jason, stepping back through the ruined wall into the hall. Something seized Joshua's throat and begin to apply pressure. "Let's see you try that without a head."

"Kill me if you wish," said Joshua, fighting for each breath. "It's no more than I wished upon myself a thousand times."

Jason hesitated.

"Kill him!" screamed Cademus. "Be free of his lies and treachery!"

"Yes, kill me!" said Joshua. "But let that choice be yours; not mine, not his. All your life, you've wanted the power to choose your destiny. Well, now you have that choice, Jason, make it and then live with the consequences."

Jason stared at the seemingly beaten Joshua and wondered if his grandfather was not as injured as he was leading him to believe. Cademus, who had come forward, was screaming at Jason to end Joshua's life.

Jason could feel himself becoming calmer, more rational. Although the words came from a man he now hated, there was truth in them. Taking another look at Joshua, he began to walk towards the chalk circle. At that moment, three knights of Cademus were hurled, unconscious, into the room followed by Vincent. He ran over to Nathan and helped him to stand.

"Get me to Jason," ordered Nathan.

Taking an arm, Vincent hoisted Nathan to his feet and began helping him across the room.

"You fool!" Cademus bellowed across the room. "What are you doing?"

"Making a choice," said Jason, stepping back into the circle.

The chalk circle and its symbols faded back into sight. Cademus cursed as he stood rigid, unable to move as the trap was now revealed. At once, Jason felt drained and weak; he fought to keep himself upright. By this time, Vincent and Nathan had joined him within the circle.

"Keep me standing," Nathan told Vincent, who nodded and held onto the old man.

"My arm, lift my arm."

Gently, Vincent lifted Nathan's broken arm until it was level with his other, already outstretched arm. Jason was already copying Nathan's movements and within seconds, the journal was once more floating between them. It flew open at the page containing the incantation.

Jason was drawn to the ugly gash that was steadily seeping blood into Nathan's right eye, as well as other assorted injuries, injuries he knew somehow he had caused. He opened his mouth to say something, but Nathan got there first.

"Apology accepted," said Nathan coughing, his mouth now stained with blood. "Now read, the incantation must be read backwards to complete it."

Needing no further encouragement, Jason once more turned to the journal. This time, the words flew into his mind, there was no hesitation. As he read the text in reverse, everything - the pitch, the tone, the pronunciation, was all perfect.

The symbols drawn within the circle were now glowing, and had begun to travel around the inside edge of the circle, gathering speed. They were then lifted from the floor, continuing to spin, faster and faster around Cademus.

Jason continued to recite the incantation. This time, it was infinitely slower as he took care with each word, ensuring there would be no mistake. Every so often, he risked a glance at Cademus, who was struggling to little avail against the spinning symbols that held him.

"Don't look at him!" warned Nathan.

"No! No! I won't go back," screamed Cademus from inside the maelstrom of energy building up around him. "Remember our bargain and help me now, give me the strength I need…"

The swirling energy around Cademus seemed to grow dimmer and he was able to push one of his hands through the energy barrier.

"You see?" he said, pushing his hand even further outwards. "The Altus Imperium protects their own, you are nothing to them, nothing!"

"He's breaking free!" shouted Nathan. "Read, boy, read!"

Jason sped up his reading, his focus beginning to waver, giving way to panic. He shouted out each phrase in the hope of granting more strength to the prison that Cademus was gaining more power over with each second. He saw Cademus force his other hand through the barrier.

"We're not going to make it!" yelled Vincent.

At that moment, Napoleon Stone came into the hall. Seeing the situation, he turned and limped towards Cademus.

Nathan made a move as if to leave the circle, but was restrained by Vincent. "We need you here."

"Napoleon!" called Nathan. "Napoleon! What's he doing?"

"What you trained him to do," said Vincent.

Napoleon grabbed hold of Cademus' wrist, and was thrown backwards.

Cademus laughed. "You cannot win, Demon Stalker, you have no power here."

Ignoring the taunts, Napoleon got up and approached the maelstrom of energy. This time, when he grabbed Cademus' wrist, he held on. The energy from the maelstrom lashed at his skin, but he held his grip. His clothes were torn and blood seeped from gashes on his upper arms and torso, but still he held his ground.

Seeing the danger, Cademus seized Napoleon by the throat, but Napoleon's own grip held firm. He stepped forward, pushing Cademus and himself back into the vortex. Both men screamed as the full power of the maelstrom hit them.

"Release me, or you will destroy us both!" warned Cademus.

"Finish the incantation, Jason! I can't hold him for long!" urged Napoleon.

Jason shook his head, tears in his eyes.

"If you don't, all the death, all the suffering you've seen will have been for nothing. Finish it!"

Memorising the final phrase, Jason shut his eyes and mouthed the last words of the incantation. The power surged out of Jason and into the maelstrom. It struck both Nathan and Vincent, instantly robbing them of consciousness.

Jason opened his eyes. There, ahead of him, was a sight that would haunt his dreams for years to come. Two mortal enemies still locked in a life and death struggle even as they faded from sight into nothingness.

Vincent's eye's flickered open and he sat up.

"Did we win?" he asked weakly.

Jason looked around and saw Joshua had once again vanished.

"No," said Jason, hurling the journal across the room.

Epilogue

There were giants in the earth in those days; and also after that, when the sons of God came in unto the daughters of men, and they bare children to them, the same became mighty men which were of old, men of renown.

Genesis Chapter 6, Verse 4

Jason removed the two lilies from their wrapping and laid each one on a headstone. He paused as he laid the last flower on Napoleon's. It was more of a memorial than an actual grave because there was no body to bury. He pushed his hand into the soft earth, closed his eyes and imagined Napoleon, still alive, still teaching. It was a pleasant thought, but it did not stop the tears from falling.

The streetlights had just come on and night was fast approaching. Jason had waited for the others to leave before coming back his own. He was still struggling to come to terms with everything that had happened, and it would be a long time before he would be able to fully understand and accept it all, despite the varied and numerous explanations from Vincent, with whom he was now living.

Sharing a house with Vincent had turned out to be a lot better than Jason could hope for. Funny, smart and laid back, Vincent was like the big brother he never had. The one trait he admired most in Vincent was his openness. After their return from Cademus Castle, which was now under the control of the Icarus Foundation, Vincent had explained everything to him, including the attempted assassination of UN Security Council members. The sheer scale of what they had managed to avert blew Jason's mind, but he did his best not to dwell on it too much. However, the one thing he did obsess on, or rather the one person, was Justine Hillman. She had escaped, along with the other members of the Cabal, all except for Sirus Crane, whose body was found within the wreckage of the chamber, along with a man called Jonathan Bishop. Vincent did not really say much about him except he had died to save others.

Vincent had taken Jason to see someone called Elijah, in an attempt to convince him of Justine's deceit. Five minutes into the explanation, Elijah had them thrown out of the building, hurling accusations at Vincent for allowing the kidnappers to kill his mother's partner. Jason almost felt sorry for him; he could understand what it was like to desperately cling to a truth you know deep down to be a lie. He was sorry

Elijah had Justine for a boss, especially as Jason promised himself the next time he saw her, he would make sure he had a weapon in his hand.

The Icarus Foundation had offered Jason a place within the organisation if he wanted it. Vincent would not give his opinion on the matter, but Jason got the impression that he did not want him to say yes. For the moment, Jason had not given them an answer; everything was still too fresh in his mind, too raw. His days were filled with going over how he could have changed things, done something differently so that so many people would not have died because of him. His nights, when he could sleep, were filled with nightmares, although the medication was helping with that. Vincent suggested he undergo counselling, but he refused; after what happened with Mr. Hunter, he just could not face it. No amount of counselling could explain why anyone would give their lives to save his. The thought was a humbling one.

"Yes, that is quite a paradox, isn't it?"

The voice came from behind Jason and he recognised it at once.

"Covenant," he said, without turning. "Figured you'd show up sooner or later."

"Grey," corrected Joshua. "My name is Joshua Grey now, Jacob Covenant and his lust for power died centuries ago."

"If you say so," said Jason, stuffing his hand into his coat pocket. "So what are you doing here? Come to check up on your handiwork?"

"I came to honour the fallen," said Joshua, staring at the graves. "They gave their lives, with no thought of reward or praise. Such a thing is far too rare."

"And no one will ever know what they did," added Jason. "They deserved better than that."

"Has everything that's happened taught you nothing? Do you think these men would want statues erected in their names, or cities named in their honour? They did what they did because they believed it to be the right thing to do. If you wish to honour them, then remember their sacrifice."

Joshua fell silent as he watched Jason's shoulders sag, heard the sobs and saw the tears. He reached out to touch him, but stopped himself. Instead, he settled for standing behind Jason, making no sound, allowing the young man to face his grief alone. After a minute, Jason drew his forearm across his eyes, leaving them bloodshot, but dry. As Jason turned to go, he found Joshua blocking his path.

"You still here, what are you after now?" said Jason angrily, feeling embarrassed that Joshua had seen everything.

"Forgiveness," said Joshua. "Whether you like it or not, I'm your only family, Jason."

"That's where you're wrong: I have no family. The only reason I didn't kill you was because you wanted me to, and I was not about to give you the peace you want. The last time we spoke, I asked you if you wanted to see my hell." Jason moved closer. "Well, this is it, it's called life and you get to spend yours paying for what you did."

"There are many things you still do not understand, Jason. I cannot explain it now but you have to…"

Jason held up his hand. "What? Trust you? Sorry, I'm fresh out of trust, especially where you're concerned."

"I understand. I hope one day you will understand what I did was what was needed to be done, every time I speak with you, there is more at risk than you know."

Jason pointed at the graves. "You think they thought about the risk?"

This time, Joshua did not answer.

"You want me to start trusting you, Grandfather, then why don't you start by telling me how you've managed to stay alive for all these years, and why you gave up your piece of Cademus' mind, when you went to all that trouble to get it? And most important of all, who are the Altus Imperium?"

Grey went pale as if someone had just walked over his grave. "Where did you hear that name?"

"Don't you remember? Oh yeah, you were nearly unconscious, weren't you?" Jason was enjoying the fact he knew something the almighty Joshua Grey did not. "It was the last thing Cademus said before I sent him back to hell with one of the few people I've ever trusted."

Joshua stepped in closer. "If you listen to nothing else I say, Jason, listen to this piece of advice and take it back to the others that still live. Forget you ever heard about the Altus Imperium."

"Like I really care what you think," said Jason glaring at Grey.

"Listen to me, boy," said Joshua, taking Jason's arm. "You have no idea what you are getting yourself into!"

"No, you listen," said Jason, his voice calm. "I don't need anyone else thinking for me, certainly not someone who spent the last nine centuries running. So unless you're going to give me some answers, get out of my way."

The two of them stared at one another for a few seconds before Joshua released his arm and stepped to one side. Jason strode past him, saying nothing. Joshua watched him leave; he waited until he was some distance away and then he smiled.

Philippe Chardon rolled into the middle of his bed, his companion stirred, but returned to sleep. A few minutes ago, he had been contemplating waking her; after all, at the prices her brand of special service came at, he intended to make her earn every penny. This kind of diversion was just what he needed.

Philippe had spent the day attending the last of the debriefing sessions surrounding the assassination attempt on the Security Council members. Satisfied that he had played no part in the affair, the investigation had cleared him of any wrongdoing. Luther Washington was dead and although unofficially pardoned by Secretary General Morton, and praised for his actions, she would not risk knowledge of the secret meeting getting out. As a result, Washington was still being blamed for the research centre explosion and the deaths of the two agents. Upon her return, Morton had seen to it that Luther was given a proper burial with full honours, despite the charges against him, charges he could no longer defend himself against.

Despite all this, Philippe was far from happy; maybe this was due to the state of the art security system that had been circumvented, or the six unconscious bodyguards who were sprawled in various parts of his house. His discomfort could be attributed to the urine staining his pyjama trousers. None of those reasons were as disturbing as the figure clad head to foot in black, who was perched at the foot of his bed pointing a silenced pistol between his legs.

"What do you want?" said Philippe.

The man did not respond.

"Money, power, anything you want, I can give you."

Silence.

"Please answer me," pleaded Philippe.

"Too late for begging, Mr. Chardon," said the man, as he stood and moved to the open window. "I just wanted to show you how easy it would be to do it. You won't know when it's coming or where, maybe in your office, or that massage parlour you sometimes like to visit on a Friday afternoon, because you like the extras they do there. Maybe you should check the toilet next time you have to go. I might have left you a gift, the exploding kind."

"Just tell me what you want? Whatever they're paying you, I'll triple it."

The man removed his hood, and for a moment, Philippe thought he was staring at Washington's vengeful spirit. He quickly realised that what he was seeing was not supernatural but merely a family resemblance.

"The Hand," he whispered.

"I know you didn't pull the trigger that killed Luther, but I do know you were the one who hired Blacklight, and had Luther framed. That makes you number two on my list."

"I have no idea what you're taking about."

"Elijah told me, even showed me a video of your meeting. You shouldn't really have dealt with him face-to-face you know, he isn't a very trustworthy man, but then you'd know all about that."

"I can give you whatever you want," Philippe was on the verge of hysteria. "Just tell me what you want?"

"My brother," said Ben quietly. "Can you give me that, Mr. Chardon?"

With that, Ben fell backwards out of the window. Philippe snatched the gun from under his pillow and ran to the window ledge. Looking out, he saw nothing but the quiet street below.